BENJAMIN FORREST AND THE CURSE OF THE MISCREANTS

CHRIS WARD

"Benjamin Forrest and the Curse of the Miscreants (Endinfinium #4)"
Copyright © Chris Ward 2019

The right of Chris Ward to be identified as the Author of this Work has been asserted by him in accordance with the Copyright, Designs and Patents Act 1988.

All rights reserved. No part of this publication may be reproduced, stored in a retrieval system, or transmitted, in any form or by any means without the prior written permission of the Author.

This story is a work of fiction and is a product of the Author's imagination. All resemblances to actual locations or to persons living or dead are entirely coincidental.

ABOUT THE AUTHOR

A proud and noble Cornishman (and to a lesser extent British), Chris Ward ran off to live and work in Japan back in 2004. There he got married, got a decent job, and got a cat. He remains pure to his Cornish/British roots while enjoying the inspiration of living in a foreign country.

www.amillionmilesfromanywhere.net

ALSO BY CHRIS WARD

Head of Words
The Man Who Built the World
Saving the Day

The Fire Planets Saga
Fire Fight
Fire Storm
Fire Rage

The Endinfinium series
Benjamin Forrest and the School at the End of the World
Benjamin Forrest and the Bay of Paper Dragons
Benjamin Forrest and the Lost City of the Ghouls
Benjamin Forrest and the Curse of the Miscreants

The Tube Riders series
Underground
Exile
Revenge
In the Shadow of London

The Tales of Crow series
The Eyes in the Dark
The Castle of Nightmares
The Puppeteer King

The Circus of Machinations

The Dark Master of Dogs

The Tokyo Lost Mystery Series

Broken

Stolen

Frozen

Also Available

The Tube Riders Complete Series 1-4 Boxed Set

The Tales of Crow 1-5 Complete Series Boxed Set

The Tokyo Lost Complete Series 1-3 Boxed Set

Endinfinium Books 1-3 Boxed Set

For Jenny Avery

THE CURSE OF THE MISCREANTS

*Just because the voices tell you to do something,
it doesn't mean you should
but if in doubt, consult the nearest teacher.*

> Extract from *The Pupil's Handbook, Revised Ed.*
> Endinfinium High School
> (Author unknown)

1

BENJAMIN

It appeared that the sky was falling. Lying on his back, Benjamin Forrest stared up at the grey popcorn puffs of the clouds as they raced past, becoming increasingly dizzy as the light surrounding everything flicked on and flicked off. Eventually, unable to take any more, he squeezed his eyes closed, rolled onto his side, and retched into the grass beneath him.

When he opened his eyes again, he was lying on a patch of grass beside a flowerbed, with a warm sun beaming overhead.

The sky wasn't moving. The world wasn't flickering between day and night. In fact, it appeared to be a pleasant mid-summer's day.

He sat up. Blades of recently cut grass had stuck to his clothes, so he brushed them off as he looked around. He appeared to be in some sort of museum park. A little way behind him stood an old biplane, the scuff marks in the ground by its wheels giving it the appearance of recently having landed. Further away, other old planes stood a respectful distance apart, each with signboards giving information about them, some with ladders leading up to the cockpits so visitors could look inside.

Benjamin stood up. His legs felt stiff, as though he'd been sleeping for a long time. Days or weeks, perhaps. He shivered, feeling a deep internal cold as though his body were as lifeless as the metal-and-wood hulks around him.

Something seemed strange about the park. He closed his eyes, trying to remember how he had gotten here, where he had been yesterday, or during whatever period in time now counted as yesterday. Perhaps nowhere. Perhaps it didn't matter.

Then he realised the problem.

No visitors.

If this was a museum park—and it certainly appeared to be, with paths snaking between the displayed aeroplanes, picnic areas, signboards directing people to different areas of the park—shouldn't there be people?

Perhaps it was closed.

Or perhaps something else.

He closed his eyes again. A humming sound was coming from all around, but he couldn't tell if it was in his head or not. It felt like it was coming from the inanimate objects around him, especially from the planes.

He reached up and touched the side of the nearest plane, an old fighter jet. Despite being in the shade, the metal was warm. Benjamin closed his eyes once more, concentrating, and felt a sight vibration under his fingers.

Nearby rose a wooden viewing platform. Benjamin climbed the steps to the top, some fifteen metres off the ground. From here he could see the whole park. To his left stood a two-storey museum building which probably housed indoor exhibits, while the outer area stretched in a wagon wheel around it, taking in all kind of vehicles, from tanks to old cars and even recreations of ancient wooden sailboats. It was the kind of place Benjamin would have loved to visit with his family—

Family?

Where were they?

In fact, where was anyone he knew?

His heart thundered with the onset of a sudden panic. He searched his memory for a name, any name that felt familiar. At first it was like swimming in a black void. Then, with a cough and a gasp the word "Wilhelm" fell out.

'Wilhelm,' he said again.

My friend. You're here, aren't you? I know you are.

He didn't know how he knew, but he somehow did. Wilhelm, his friend—no further details yet forthcoming—was somewhere in this park with him.

Benjamin began to turn in a slow circle, eyes narrowed as he searched the field of old vehicles, squinting into narrow spaces, cubbyholes and alcoves, shadows. As he turned to the south, what he had at first thought was part of the humming sound, he now realised was a separate, immense creaking noise which became even louder, causing him to look up.

Some miles distant, far beyond a railing fence that marked the park's boundary and beyond even a leafy area of suburbs surrounding it, something incredible moved across the countryside.

It looked like a gigantic rolling ball of rubbish.

Benjamin blinked and gave himself a light slap on the cheek, but it was still there.

It towered over the surrounding countryside, perhaps a hundred metres high. It wasn't an exact ball, but more an irregular, nobbly one, like a giant piece of crumpled newspaper. What it was made out of he couldn't be sure, but bits stuck out that had obvious shape—a car here, the remains of a house there—and as it moved, objects seemed to fly up from the ground and attach to it like metal filings to a giant magnet.

The sound he had heard was it crushing a house. As he watched, it did the same with another, inching forward over the structure and then slumping down with a sudden thump. Then, unceasing, it continued its slow onwards motion, squashing flat everything in its path.

Benjamin was still staring at it when a loud crack came from behind him. He turned in time to see a door flap back against the wall of the main museum building and a diminutive figure rush out. Another cry came, but it was more of a frightened, desperate yelp than one with any real expectation of aid. The figure, stumbling as it ran, darted off the path and in among the exhibits as three taller figures barreled out the door and raced in pursuit.

Two carried silver metal poles which sparked at one end. The other had a net slung over his shoulder.

'Come back here!' the foremost shouted, waving at the others to spread out into the exhibits. From his vantage point, Benjamin could still see the fleeing figure running around the park's perimeter, trying to find a way out. It was a boy, fair-haired, perhaps a couple of years older than him. Even though his memory was still jumbled, he felt certain this wasn't Wilhelm.

As the three pursuers spread out, the figure darted back and forth through the exhibits. Benjamin saw him reach out to touch a motorboat on a stand, only for an explosion of sparks to burst from where his fingers had brushed. The boy jumped back, clutching his face in surprise as the boat slid off its stand and bumped a few feet forward before falling still once more.

'Stop, Miscreant!' shouted the nearest pursuer,

zigzagging between the exhibits to corner the boy outside a toilet block. The boy backed up, hands raised into the air.

'Stay back!' he shouted as the pursuer lowered his staff, pointing it at the boy's midriff.

'Come quietly,' the pursuer said. 'Don't make this more difficult than it needs to be.'

'I'm warning you!' the boy shouted, feinting forward, but the pursuer had the air of a professional, stepping back out of range, keeping the staff lowered, its flickering tip between them.

The other two pursuers had quietly surrounded the boy from behind. One was leaning up against a side wall, ready on the widest side if the boy made an attempt to escape, while the one with the net had climbed up onto the toilet block's roof and was creeping forward, spreading out his net as he went.

The boy was moments from capture. Benjamin, feeling an uncanny sense of connection with the boy as though an invisible thread joined them, opened his mouth to shout out, only to have a hand clamp over it and wiry arms drag him to the floor. He struggled, breaking out of the grip holding him, but as he turned, expecting to see one of the other strange men, he saw a short, young boy with tight curls of brown hair pressing a finger to his lips, desperate eyes imploring quiet.

Wilhelm; it had to be.

'We can't help him,' Wilhelm whispered. 'Not yet. Not here, at any rate.'

From the ground below came a sharp hiss. Benjamin got to his knees and peered over the platform's safety fence. The boy lay still on the ground outside the toilet block while the three men spread out the net. Benjamin watched as they rolled him onto it. Two lifted it between them, and with the third holding the metal staffs, they carried him away, back across the park and through the door into the main building.

Benjamin's heart was pounding so hard it was a few moments before he could speak. When he did, he turned to Wilhelm and said, 'Where were you?' as though that would answer all the questions he had, as though he had any idea where he himself had been.

'Woke up in there,' Wilhelm said, pointing to the building. 'Thought I'd travelled back in time until I realised it was some kind of museum. Was just getting the layout of the place when that kid came running through with those guys on his tail.'

'Did you see what he did?'

'You mean, making that boat move? That, and the rest. He touched a pair of plastic horses inside and they started kicking until one of those men jabbed them with his prod thing.' Wilhelm shrugged. 'Kid would have got along with you pretty well, which is another reason why we have to keep out of sight of those men.'

'What do you mean?'

Wilhelm frowned. 'Did you just wake up?'

Benjamin nodded, pointing to the old biplane sitting on the grass. 'Over there. I'm still not quite sure what's going on.'

'Yeah, me neither, but I think it's best we keep our heads down in case those guys come back.'

2

MIRANDA

Who am I?

The girl looked around her, hoping to establish some kind of landmark which would give her an idea of who she was, or where she had come from, but there were only the hills, the trees, and the rocks spreading out around her until they faded into distant fog like the edges of a giant map. She felt groggy as though she had just woken up, and had an odd sensation of having briefly woken up before passing out again, although her mouth felt colder than the rest of her. Nearby, she saw a stream gurgling down the hillside, and saw other scuff marks in the mud alongside. She must have woken long enough to take a drink, and then passed out again.

Around her, though, the landscape looked normal, except ... it didn't.

She frowned. Nearby, a cluster of flowers appeared to be plastic straws with lumps of cotton wool on the top. Behind them were bushes made out of shreds of old clothing hung over rusty knives and forks. At first it looked like some bizarre art display, but when she tried to pluck off a pink ribbon she found it fused neatly to the spoon beneath it as though it had simply grown there, and indeed little pink buds suggested the growth of more ragged clothing was about to get underway.

Not far from where she sat on a patch of warm grass was a small, rocky crater. Scuffs in the grass led from it, so she could only assume that from the grass stains on her bare feet that she had crawled out of it while still in some kind of unconscious state. The hollow looked recently gouged, suggesting she herself had caused the impact, despite the impossibility of the situation. Besides feeling a little stiff, she was unhurt, making a fall from the sky impossible, unless something encasing her had broken apart on impact. Besides the rocks and bare earth, however, there was nothing.

Who am I?

The question continued to bug her as she climbed to her feet and began to follow a rough gravel path up a hill towards a stand of trees. Other questions were beginning to arise, such as where she would find food, or shelter, or help, but she felt a growing stoicism that she could overcome all of these in time. She might not remember her name, but she remembered a resourcefulness, an ability to deal with difficult situations, and she now leaned on it like a warm, comforting cushion.

The hill crested at a little copse. She looked behind her, seeing only more hills, some topped with trees, others bare. One hill dipped sharply into a wooded valley.

She followed the path through the trees until it emerged on the other side. Below her was a long, grassy slope leading down into another valley and another line of hills beyond, but it was beyond those that the girl found herself staring, her mouth falling open in surprise.

The fog had drawn back, revealing jagged,

snowcapped mountains rising in the background like the teeth of some giant sleeping beast. Above them, great thunderclouds swirled, bolts of lightning cutting through the air to crack into the mountainsides.

The girl shivered, pulling tight what she realised was the remains of a grey boiler suit. It was a couple of sizes too big and smelt musty and old, bits of the fabric flaking off in her fingers. A hood that hung back over her shoulders was frayed to uselessness, and if she had been wearing shoes, they were nowhere to be seen. As she stared at the view in front of her, every instinct told her to turn and run away from the mountains, to chance her luck with whatever might be behind her rather than to approach, but she found her feet moving forward, following the path, wanting to know what was in the valley beyond the next line of hills, the valley that would surely rise again at the foot of the mountains themselves.

She was halfway down the hill to the next stand of trees when the ground abruptly fell out beneath her. After a moment of terrifying weightlessness, she landed with a bump on a bed of soft earth, finding herself in a narrow pit no more than three feet wide. The top was a couple of feet above her head, the walls smooth as though dug with a giant bore. She ran her hands over the earth, looking for handholds, picking what she thought were a few small rocks out of the surface, only to find that they were tiny plastic animals. She stared at one small, grey rhinoceros as it nestled in the palm of her hand, only for it to suddenly rear its head and butt her wrist.

With a scream, she dropped it onto the ground, where it began to run around in circles, occasionally butting her feet, until finally it began to tire and sat down on its haunches by the wall. A couple of seconds later it keeled over on its side and went still, returned to its original shape.

The girl reached down and tentatively prodded it with a finger, only to find it cold and still.

She didn't have time to dwell on what kind of magic infiltrated this place, because the sound of voices came from above, slowly approaching the pit. There was nowhere she could hide and no way to get out in time, so she waited until a shadow appeared overhead and then gave her best show of anger, growling like a wildcat to show she wouldn't come lightly.

The shadow gasped, hands coming up in surprise. Then, slowly, it peered down into the hole. As the girl's eyes adjusted to the light framing the figure's face, she realised it was an old man, thick-bearded, his head covered with a garishly coloured fur cap, dressed in a kaleidoscope of colours which looked like a thousand different garments all sewn together. In one hand he held a spear, in the other a collar and leash.

'If you're planning to eat me, just be warned that I'll fight you every step of the way. I have teeth and claws sharper than any animal.'

The man, his initial surprise replaced by a look of amusement, chuckled. 'Angry, like your hair,' he said.

The girl frowned then drew up a handful of the hair that hung nearly to her waist and studied it. He was right. Crimson red, the colour of fresh blood. A tingle of recognition flickered through her, but it was gone before she could grasp it and hold on.

'Who are you?' the girl snapped.

'I'd like to ask you the same question,' the old man said. 'I'm just an old trapper and fur trader, a wild man living in these wild parts. I was hoping to find something for my dinner, but it looks instead as though I've found a dinner companion.'

The girl glared at him. 'I don't know who I am,' she

said, holding her glare as though her predicament were specifically his fault. 'I woke up just over that hill. I don't know where I came from or who I am, and I'm not likely to find out while sitting in this hole, am I?'

The little rhino had got up and begun to butt her again. Feeling a certain affinity with the futility of its actions, she leaned down and picked it up, balancing it in her palms as it thundered back and forth across her fingers, occasionally turning to butt the insides of her thumbs.

'As a general rule, nothing comes out of that pit alive,' the stranger said. 'However, since you already appear to have made a friend, I suppose on this occasion I could make an exception. If I throw you down a rope, would you promise not to either chew it up or later use it to strangle me?'

The girl glared at him again, maintaining an air of defiance. 'I'll try not to,' she said.

'I suppose that's a fair compromise.'

The man unhooked a coil of rope and tossed it down. The girl put the little rhino into her pocket then wrapped the rope around her forearms.

'Ready? Heave-o.'

By using the pit walls to brace herself, and the rope to give her lift, the girl was able to scramble out. As she sat down on the soft grass, the stranger, straining on the rope, fell backwards, also landing on the grass. A bag tied to his waist came loose, spilling out little metal objects. He let out a frustrated groan and began scrabbling for them.

The girl saw her moment to escape. She leapt to her feet and bolted off down the hillside. She had gone no further than fifteen steps, however, when something caught on her foot and sent her sprawling across the grass.

She sat up, rubbing at her right ankle, which had twisted beneath her. A line of knotted cord had wrapped around it, a slipknot sliding tight. She felt for it, finding it to be durable plastic. She slipped one finger beneath and pulled it loose, only for it to snap tight again.

'Hey!'

Again she pulled it loose, this time slipping her foot out and shuffling back. The cord, tied to a protruding tree root, darted at her like a snake, missing her foot only by a couple of inches.

A shadow fell over her, and she looked up. The stranger stood above her, a grin on his face. He waved a hand at the energetic cord and it went still.

'I'm afraid you've stumbled across my hunting field,' he said. 'Now, if you wish, you could make a break for it, or you could let me lead you to a safer area from where to start. Passing, of course, my humble forest abode, where, should you wish to rest, I can no doubt find you a warm bed and something hot to eat.'

'I'll think about it,' the girl said, but climbed to her feet and stood waiting for further instruction.

'I'll begin walking,' the stranger said. 'Feel free to follow.'

He turned and headed off down the hillside. The girl watched him for a few seconds before stumbling in pursuit, her ankle aching with each step. As he disappeared into the forest, she called out, 'Hey! Wait a minute!'

The man's face appeared between the trees. He frowned at her. 'Did you hurt yourself?'

'Yes, thanks to your stupid snare. Can't you wait a minute?'

She squatted down, removed her shoe, and began to massage her ankle. The cap of bone was ringed by a dark bruise. She glared at it, wishing for it to heal itself as quickly as possible.

'No!'

A hand fell on her shoulder, pushing back. Her hands came free from her ankle and she rolled across the grass, sitting up and glaring at the old man.

'Not here!' he hissed. 'Not this close! It's not safe!'

'What isn't?'

'What you were doing. Come on, get up. I'll do it. I know how to keep it hidden.'

He waved a hand at her ankle and it went numb, as though encased in a block of solid air. She couldn't move it, but when she lowered her leg to the ground she felt no pain.

'It's not far,' the old man said. 'This way.'

He took her arm and led her into the trees. The girl stumbled over roots and fallen branches, some of which resembled regular trees, others which were rusty protrusions of metal or plastic or even glass, sometimes appearing to be rubbish, other times seemingly fused with the trees themselves as though they had grown out of the trash around them.

'Here,' the old man said. He pointed at what looked like a wardrobe set into a tree. As the girl approached, she realised that was indeed what it was. The tree however, was growing out of a large earthen mound, and as the old man pulled open the right-side door, she saw a little cavern inside, lit only by a candle on a shelf by the far wall.

The man waved her inside, and the girl entered, finding herself in a small cave. The man shut the door then waved a hand and the room filled with light. The girl stared as a little kitchen and living room appeared, a connecting passage at the rear leading to a study and a bedroom. Everything seemed hollowed out of the earth, with the furniture salvaged and repaired. The light came not just from the candles but also from lamps standing in the corners, bathing everything in a warm glow.

Nowhere, however, did she see any kind of wiring or power source.

'What is this place?' she said, turning around, trying to take it all in.

The stranger threw his bag down onto a chair which shifted to catch it neatly like a dog moving for a ball. 'I had assumed you were simply lost,' he said, 'but having seen your crater, it is perhaps safer to assume that you are in fact a newcomer. In which case, I'd better give you a crash course on where you are, and what's going on, at least to the best of my somewhat limited knowledge.' He waved a hand at the door. 'The rather hostile and at times inhospitable place outside is known by a word you probably won't have heard anywhere else.'

'Which is?'

The man smiled. 'Endinfinium.'

3
BENJAMIN

'Over there,' Wilhelm said. 'There's another one of those vans. And there's tape outside that building, too.' With a frown, he added, 'Come on, sort yourself out.'

'Hang on a minute.'

Benjamin's new shirt had come untucked, so he frantically stuffed it back into the trousers which were a little too small. Both of them had decided to jettison the ragged clothing they had woken in, poaching some from a display inside the museum. In dusty shirts, sweaters, trousers and shoes taken from a display titled "The '90s Family", they both looked a little unusual, but both agreed it was an improvement on a ragged grey boiler suit and a filthy school uniform.

Benjamin pulled the strip of bright blue tape he had untied from the museum's door an hour before and looked at the words printed on it.

NO ENTRY. SUSPECTED MISCREANT ZONE.

'Does that mean there's another kid in there?'

'Could be. Or perhaps they just think there is.'

'If we could find him, we could figure out what's going on.'

'And get ourselves caught as well?'

Benjamin sighed. He lifted a hand, remembering the warmth he'd felt when he had touched the door and seen it spring open. 'Well, you'd be all right.'

'Guilty by association. I doubt they'd stop to ask questions.'

Wilhelm pushed Benjamin down behind the row of wheelie bins across the street from the van sitting outside the taped-off building.

'I have an idea,' he said. 'It's a bit old-school, so best to let me handle it. You can go in there and blow stuff up after I'm done, but let's try to keep this simple.'

Benjamin gave a shrug as agreement and peered out as Wilhelm crossed the street, then assumed an innocent pose as he strolled towards the van. His friend seemed to be coming to terms with everything a lot quicker than he was. Whether Wilhelm remembered more than he said, Benjamin didn't know, but so far their collective memory stretched back only as far as some big explosion, then a patch of darkness, and then waking up in the museum.

There was a word, *Endinfinium*, which Wilhelm had found scratched in the dirt of the World War II exhibit he had woken up in, as though he had written it there before passing out, but neither of them was quite sure what it meant.

Outside the museum, it would be easy to assume they were in a regular town. A car park gave way to a tree-lined street, which led past a sports ground to a town centre filled with shops. Benjamin, despite a distrust of his memory, held an idea of what a town should look like, and this, while ticking most of the boxes, left a few unchecked, leaving him with a lingering suspicion that something was not quite right.

It had taken a while to put his finger on it.

There was no litter. Nothing, not a single gum wrapper. There was no junk: no TVs dumped in alleyways or on unused patches of ground, overcome by grass. No cars that looked abandoned, no shopping trolleys hidden among the undergrowth alongside the road.

They had passed a couple of abandoned houses, but these too were bizarre: stripped bare of anything except their stone walls; no doors, windows, light fittings, wires, pipes … all gone, leaving behind only a ghostly stone frame.

Even the wheelie bins behind which he now crouched were unusual. They were bolted to the ground and fitted into rails which ran along the road to a corner where presumably they would be collected. Three of the four were currently empty, but the fourth had a lid secured by a padlock. Inside, a rustling trash bag bounced around as though trying to fight its way out. Benjamin had thought it was a person trapped inside, but after a few minutes of whispering questions through the plastic they had guessed otherwise. Wilhelm had then performed a little experiment which left Benjamin with a cold feeling inside.

He had torn a strip off his shirt and held it up. 'I don't need this bit anymore,' he said, then let it go.

There was no wind, yet the strip of material had flown away as though caught in a gale, rising high up over the houses and disappearing to the south.

Benjamin remembered what he had seen in that direction: the giant, moving ball of litter.

Wilhelm came running back, sliding down beside him, breathing hard. He looked up with a grin. 'I let their tyres down,' he said. 'Now it's your turn.'

'My turn?'

'Yeah. I could hear them inside. They've almost got him. You've got to go over there and stop them.'

'Me?'

Wilhelm patted him on the shoulder. 'Yes, you.'

'How?'

'I don't know, but one thing I do know is that you're one of them. One of these Miscreants. And while things are only coming back bit by bit, I'm pretty sure that among them … you should be king.'

Before Benjamin could reply, the house's door banged open and two men emerged, dragging a large net. The figure it contained was still, perhaps a result of the sparking metal staff in the hands of a third man coming behind.

'Now,' Wilhelm hissed, pushing Benjamin from behind.

The men carried their captive around the back of the van, opened the doors and tossed him inside. Benjamin, standing exposed on the street after Wilhelm's prod, hurried across as they went back around the front and climbed in.

The van started up, bumping a few feet along the street before coming to a stop. Benjamin ran around the back as the front doors opened and someone got out. He peered around the corner and saw a man lean down to inspect the flat front tyre, then theatrically slap his forehead before opening the door again and leaning back inside.

Benjamin lifted his hands, staring at them, wondering what he should do. He remembered feeling the warmth in the wood under his palm, so grabbed the door handle and squeezed it tight.

'Open,' he commanded.

The lock exploded with a shower of sparks, throwing him backwards. As he climbed up from the ground and brushed himself off, the figure inside the net began to struggle.

'Help me!'

Benjamin ran to the back of the van and pulled open the drawstrings at the mouth of the net. It tingled under his fingers, but as soon as he had made a space, a boy's face appeared. Dirty, with unkempt hair and a couple of scrapes on his face—one fresh, the other old—the boy smiled.

'Are you one of them?' he asked. 'Thanks.'

'Let's go,' Benjamin said, not sure to what the boy was referring, but nevertheless determined not to get caught by the men with the electrified metal prongs.

He helped the boy down then pointed to where Wilhelm was hiding. 'Go,' he said, then turned and put his hands on the back of the van, closed his eyes and tried to make something happen.

'Buzz off,' he said.

Another explosion threw him backwards. Benjamin sat up and opened his eyes as the dust cleared to reveal the van sailing through the air, two large side flaps working like the stumpy wings of some awkward bug. Leaving a smoke trail behind it, the van made it over the first line of houses then went plummeting down, landing with a muffled crash.

'How on earth did you do that?' the boy said, and Benjamin turned, surprised to find both the boy and Wilhelm standing at his shoulder.

He shrugged. 'No idea.'

'I've never seen anything like that before,' the boy said.

'Benjamin's a bit special,' Wilhelm said, patting Benjamin on the shoulder and smiling, even though the look on his face suggested he was just as surprised. 'What happened over there?' he asked, turning to the boy.

The boy shook his head, then, as though suddenly

losing whatever adrenaline rush had helped him escape, he slumped, hands on his knees, breathing hard.

'I got noticed at school a few weeks back. I'd kept it hidden for more than a year, but some kid started pushing me around and I lost it. I heard there were gangs of us in the big cities, helping each other out, so when the dog-catchers showed up at my school the next day, I bailed. Headed for Bristol, but there were way too many dog-catchers around, so moved on. You guys are from one of the gangs, aren't you?'

'Um, yeah,' Wilhelm said. 'That we are.'

The boy smiled. 'That's great. I'm Ray. Ray Summers. I'm from Torquay, but I suppose now I'm a Basingstoke boy.'

'Wilhelm,' Wilhelm said. 'And this is—'

Ray lifted a hand, cutting him off. He frowned, then looked back over his shoulder. 'Did you hear that? Was that a siren? With power like yours I imagine you're like a bulb glowing in the dark.' He glanced nervously from one to the other. 'If I could give you boys some advice, it would be to keep out of the open during daylight. Sorry, I'd better go. Someone's waiting for me. They'll be wondering where I've got to.'

'Hang on a minute!' Benjamin called as Ray started jogging away.

'See you boys around,' Ray called. 'If you're here long enough, maybe we'll bump into each other again.'

Wilhelm made a half-hearted attempt to follow, but gave up as Ray darted into a side street. He walked back to where Benjamin was still standing, shaking his head.

'Odd chap,' he said.

Benjamin stared at his hands, as though they were somehow responsible. 'What happened there?'

'Your guess is as good as mine. He was pretty jittery. I don't think he wanted to risk getting caught again.'

Benjamin frowned. Something the boy had said was jogging another memory.

'Wait … Basingstoke. He said this was Basingstoke. I'm from Basingstoke!'

'How do you know that?'

'It just popped into my mind when he said it.'

Wilhelm shook his head. 'No, we're from Endinfinium, wherever that is. Whatever it is. I knew it the moment I woke up and saw that word.'

'Before Endinfinium.' Benjamin squatted down, squeezing his eyes shut, trying to remember. Pictures, words, images … they circled in his mind, slowly forming themselves into some sort of reality.

Wilhelm was staring at him. 'You might be right. Not about Basingstoke, but in general. When you said it, I felt something stir.'

'Me too!'

'Like we got given a good shake or something and its going to take a while for it all to fit back together.'

'Exactly!'

Wilhelm put a hand on Benjamin's shoulder. 'But while we're waiting, I think we should do it somewhere safe. That kid was right. I can hear another one of those vans coming. They have a certain irritating whine about them, don't you think?'

Benjamin, still lost in concentration, stood up. Wilhelm was right, something was approaching. Wilhelm was staring at him, as though expecting him to lead, so he pointed to the nearest alleyway. 'That looks as good a way to go as any.'

With Benjamin leading, they jogged until they reached a leafy park a few streets away. On a man-made knoll they sat down on a bench behind a screen of trees, keeping a lookout across the park for any signs of the dog-catchers.

'Miscreants,' Wilhelm said. 'That's an interesting term. I've heard it somewhere before ... but I can't think where.'

'Endinfinium,' Benjamin said. 'It's what they called errant magic users, ones who wouldn't follow the rules.'

'Magic users? Rules? What are you talking about?'

Benjamin looked at him and frowned. The flow of memories cut off like a silenced alarm. 'I don't know,' he said. 'Or at least I did, when I was saying it, but it's gone now.'

'We're not from this world, are we?' Wilhelm said suddenly, before blushing as though it was the most ridiculous thing in the world to say. 'I mean, I thought at first Endinfinium was just another country, but it's not. It's a whole other world, and we've been there and come back.'

Benjamin gave a thoughtful nod. 'I think you're right.' He rubbed his chin for a moment, trying to gather his thoughts. 'However, I think that in light of those scary guys with the electric sticks and the nets, and the kids they call Miscreants running around—not to mention the weird things that I seem to be able to do and those giant rolling balls of rubbish—it might be better to focus on our survival *here*, rather than spending our time figuring out about *there*.'

'You mean, look forward instead of back?'

Benjamin nodded. 'That's right.'

'Sounds like a plan.'

'Yeah, it does.'

'So what's the next thing? Where do we go from here?'

Benjamin shrugged. 'Since when have I been the leader?'

'Since today. Since you woke up with the power to make vans fly through the air and I didn't.'

'I suppose that's a fair point. Doesn't mean I have better survival skills. You seem to have a flair for it.'

Wilhelm grinned. 'Thanks. How about we tag team it?'

'Sounds good.'

'So first, let's work on what we have. You said this was your hometown, right? How about finding someone you know who might help us?'

Benjamin stared at the park through the trees. Across a wide playing field was a line of detached houses, hidden behind tall privet hedges. He stared at their tile roofs, their chimneys, the TV dishes, trying to attach himself to a sense of familiarity. Across to the left, his gaze drifted over a children's woodchip play area, a tall tree—

'That tree,' he said. 'I used to climb it.'

Wilhelm patted him on the shoulder. 'That's good. More. Which way did you walk when you came down here?'

Benjamin pointed. 'That road. And I didn't used to walk, I used to ride my bike.'

'Great! What colour was it.'

'Blue and black, and—ow!'

'What?'

Benjamin rubbed his head. 'Wow, that hurt. I felt like someone was punching the inside of my skull.'

As Wilhelm stared at him, he rubbed his head again. The pain was still there, but it was quickly subsiding. For a moment he had felt like someone had pulled his brain out and put it back in upside down.

'There,' he said, pointing to a dirt track that led through the trees to the left. 'If you go down there, you get into a wood. There's an old quarry area which kids turned into a bike park. I was down there one day with my brother, David, and something … happened.'

'What?'

Benjamin squeezed his eyes shut, grasping at the memories.

'We were coming back, and there was a truck coming around the corner, and something came out of the woods looking for David, and—' The memories cut off again. Benjamin sighed. 'It's gone.'

'So, that's where you played. Where did you live?'

'Up that way.'

'Sure?'

'Sure.'

'Then let's go.'

Wilhelm jumped down from the bench and set off across the park in the direction Benjamin had pointed. As he reached the other side of the playing field, he paused, waited for Benjamin to catch up, and then pointed at a wooden sign post stuck in the ground near a gate preventing cars coming onto the grass.

BEWARE MISCREANTS
IF YOU HAVE ANY SUSPICIONS AT ALL, REPORT THEM TO YOUR LOCAL PROCESSING CENTRE TODAY
CALL THE BELOW NUMBER TO SPEAK TO AN ADVISOR

'Shall we call it?' Wilhelm said. 'See what happens?'

A glass BT phone box stood on the other side of a small car park. Benjamin and Wilhelm memorised half the number each, then made for it. As he opened the door, Benjamin said, 'Wait. I don't have any coins.'

'Don't worry, that code is a free phone number.'

'How do you know that?'

Wilhelm frowned. 'I don't know … I just do.'

Benjamin dialed the number and held up the receiver. He pressed a volume switch to increase the volume so they could both hear, then held it out between them.

'Miscreants Reporting Hotline, how may I assist you today?' came a woman's voice.

Wilhelm waved at Benjamin to hand him the phone. 'I'd like some further information,' he said, smirking at Benjamin. 'There's this kid at school who acts like a real dick. I was wondering if he's a Miscreant?'

'Does he display any kind of unusual power?'

'Like what?'

'Like the ability to move objects, or set fire to things using his hands?'

'He set fire to my school bag.'

'With his hands?'

'No, with a lighter he pinched out of a corner shop. But you know, he used his hands to light it.'

'Well, that's just bullying. Anything else? Anything that suggested a … paranormal ability?'

'He always seems to know where I'm going after school. He's always waiting for me, wanting my shoes or my homework or something.'

'But nothing more than that?'

'That's pretty bad, don't you think?'

'It's not really our definition of an official Miscreant.'

'Well, you see, I looked it up in the dictionary and it kind of is.'

As Wilhelm smirked, Benjamin hissed, 'Don't prank her. Just ask her what one is.'

'Is this a serious call?'

'Yeah, of course. Look, what should I be looking for?'

The woman on the other end sighed. 'Our systems tell

us that you're on the corner of Meadow Park in Basingstoke East. We have three units in the immediate area. I'll arrange for one to come down and have a direct talk with you. You can ask them any questions you might have.'

'Hang up!' Benjamin hissed.

Wilhelm slammed the phone down. 'Well, that wasn't much help.'

'No thanks to you!'

'Well, I suppose I kind of lost my chain of thought there, but I was getting around to it.'

In the near distance, an engine revved.

'They're coming,' Benjamin said. 'Let's get out of here.'

4

MIRANDA

'Good morning, Miranda. Are you feeling better?'

Miranda. She frowned as she sat up, pushing back a pile of blankets, some of which felt warm even though they had been nowhere near her body. One moved on its own and she flicked it away, horrified, before realising it was no different from the little plastic rhino which was lying on the pillow beside her. As she stared, the rhino rolled over, stretched out its legs, and then appeared to settle back to sleep.

'Miranda. That's my name, isn't it? It just feels right somehow. But how could you possibly know?'

The stranger was sitting in a chair on the other side of the room. He smiled. 'You were talking in your sleep,' he said. 'Well, more like shouting. '"My name is Miranda Butterworth!"' It woke me with quite a start.'

'It definitely sounds right,' she said. 'Did I say anything else?'

'You said something about a school. I'm guessing you meant Endinfinium High, as I don't know of any other. I did wonder if that might be where you were from. It's been a while since I encountered anyone from those parts all the way over here in these parts.'

Miranda frowned. 'I don't remember anything, although now I hear the name, I've started getting images of towers and classrooms and things.'

'Your memory was jolted by some kind of trauma. It's my guess that it'll come back in time, especially now you have a couple of yardsticks to go on.'

'Where am I?'

'A long, long way from Endinfinium High. About as far as it's possible to go, in this direction at least. Although, distance, like everything else about this place, is a relative term. It depends on how you're travelling.'

'How do you think I got here?'

'Well, having seen that crater I presume you made upon arrival, I would guess via some kind of aerial door.'

'A what?'

'A door in the sky. A door that came from somewhere else, that allowed you to escape from something else. A door that, perhaps, you opened yourself, mostly likely without any idea how, or any idea how you could ever do it again.'

'I don't get it.'

'Well, it's not something I could practically demonstrate, because I don't know how to do it either. It's more of a concept.'

'It sounds like a load of rubbish. How could I create a door in the sky?'

The stranger shrugged. 'Well, that's a question, isn't it?'

'And why didn't the fall kill me? If I made that crater, it should have blown me into little pieces.'

'I'm guessing it wasn't strictly you who created that crater, but more what you did to protect yourself.'

'And what was that?'

'You used the same power that you used to open that door to create a cushion for yourself. Quite likely the impact was a little bit of a shock to your system, hence your waking up with a little confusion.'

'What power?'

'Well, you tell me. I saw what you did before. I'd guess you have some control of reanimation magic.'

'Of what?'

'It's the binding force in all of Endinfinium. Reanimation magic is what creates, and dark reanimate is what destroys.'

Miranda rubbed her eyes and pulled the blankets off of her knees. Woken by a gust of air, the little plastic rhino jumped up from the bed and buried itself into a pocket of Miranda's shirt.

'Perhaps we should talk more after you've gotten cleaned up and had something to eat,' the man said. 'I've got some fritters cooking.'

'Who are you?' Miranda asked, remembering she knew even less about this strange man than she did about herself.

'My name is Olin Brin,' he said, standing up. 'I'm a simple botanist. I study Endinfinium's flora, mostly so I can figure out what I can and cannot eat. Come on, now. I've got a little washroom at the back and I've assembled some clothes that might fit you. We'll talk again over breakfast.'

Miranda studied him for a moment. He was tall but stocky, almost bearish, with a thick ginger beard that was disguised by the selection of garish colours he wore, the remnants of dozens of old items of clothing. Even inside, he wore around his belt an array of items useful for forestry work. She spotted a penknife, a fold-up saw, a tape-measure, a length of rope, a thermometer, a small net, a compass, and a few other items the use of which she couldn't guess. It was clear Olin Brin was prepared for every eventuality.

'Thanks,' she said, standing up and following him down a narrow corridor to a door at the end. Olin pressed against the wall for Miranda to squeeze past.

'You'll find everything you need in there, but if you need anything else, just holler.'

Miranda went inside and closed the door. It had once been the door of a house but its corners had been rounded to make it fit into the tunnel. Hinges were set into a lump of protruding rock, and an added bolt lock slid into a metal tube embedded in the earth on the other side.

The bathroom, lit by a small log fire in one corner with a pipe above it to take the smoke, looked entirely salvaged. A metal bath had been sanded free of rust, and an old rug covered most of the dirt floor. The taps were fed by pipes that led up into the dirt roof, but when she turned them, Miranda was surprised to find that one ran properly hot, the other properly cold.

The bath felt amazing. Miranda lay in it until she felt shriveled to half her original size, then climbed out and dried herself with a towel Olin had hung over a wooden chair. It felt far softer than those she remembered from the school—another memory trickling back—as though he had taken an old one and infused it with animal fur.

A sink also ran with hot and cold water, and a mirror fixed to a wooden plank behind it revealed her face in a series of flickering shadows. Despite seeing herself for the first time since waking, the flowing crimson hair, the hard eyes, and the thin lips felt familiar. She stared at herself for a long time, letting little snippets of memory drift back, both of the school and the time before, when she had lived with other girls who looked just like her, and Miranda

Butterworth had been a name not yet chosen by a girl known only by a numerical code.

Olin had left a pile of clothes on another chair. Miranda selected from three pairs of durable combat trousers, five T-shirts, and two sweaters. A pair of thick woolen socks made her feet tickle, but when she emerged from the bathroom and walked back down the hall, she felt ready to take on the world, whatever it might be.

'You look much better,' Olin said. 'How's your ankle?'

Miranda frowned. She had forgotten all about it. 'Fine,' she said, looking down suspiciously, half expecting to see a wooden stump in its place.

'That's good. You're ready for your next adventure.'

Miranda smiled. 'Thanks for helping me.'

'You're welcome.' Olin held out a plate. 'Breakfast. Vegetable fritters. A mixture of good and bad, as always, but when you mix it up and add a little sauce, it's passable as real food.'

Miranda took the plate and sat down. The fritters were pancakes filled with lumps of vegetable. She spotted some carrot and some sweet potato, but most she didn't recognise. She took a tentative nibble and found it better than she had expected.

'Wow. Not bad.'

Olin grinned. 'It's okay, isn't it? This far west the food is a little … spicier than what they serve over in that school. Personally I blame the groundwater.'

'Where exactly are we?'

'We're in the foothills of the High Mountains, a few miles west of where all the bad stuff happens.'

'The bad stuff?'

'I don't know how much you remember, but we're in the Dark Man's territory. The Shifting Castle is barely ten miles, as the litter-crow flies.'

Miranda frowned. 'The what? Now that you say it, I remember seeing something.'

'You might have. You were close enough. We call it the Shifting Castle. It's where the Dark Man lives, and, as many believe, is trapped.'

'Who's the Dark Man? The name ... it rings a bell, but I don't quite remember.'

'The Dark Man is the lord of dark reanimate, and some say the creator of Endinfinium. No one knows for sure, but he's dangerous. Very.'

'But if he's trapped...?'

'Only his body is trapped. His mind, and his influence, and his power, are as free as the ghouls and the wraith-hounds which haunt these forests at night.'

Miranda shivered. Even though she didn't understand the meaning of Olin's words, something about them made her afraid. She was about to say something more when Olin abruptly stood up.

'Good, you've finished. Come on, now. Let's go and get a little fresh air. I need to check over my fields.'

Without another word, he headed for the front door and threw it open. Miranda squinted into the sudden brightness as a fresh breeze tickled her face. Olin marched outside, stretching his huge arms over his head.

'A fine day,' he said. 'The suns are shining. I have a good feeling about today.'

Miranda hastened to follow as Olin took a trail through the woods, emerging in a wide clearing. Vegetable plots had been laid out across an area as large as a playing field. Rows of multi-coloured plants as garish as Olin's clothes spread out before her with militaristic organisation.

'These are regular carrots,' Olin said, pointing to some green shoots poking out of the ground. 'They came from a packet of seeds I found inside an old garden shed buried in the earth. I was surprised they sprouted, but they're on their fourth generation now and still going strong. I also managed to grow cauliflower from the same source. Unfortunately, a packet of Brussels sprouts from the same collection failed to germinate. I was heartbroken.'

Miranda looked up at him. 'Are you sure about that? Even I hate sprouts.'

'You hate sprouts?' Olin laughed. 'You're missing out. Nature's gift to mankind are Brussels sprouts.'

He led her a little distance further on. Here, the vegetables looked unfamiliar. One bulbous thing had purple leaves but a bright red root. Another type looked like dark brown sticks poking out of the ground, topped with plumes of yellow leaves. They gave off a smell which Miranda found familiar.

'Are they what I think they are?'

'In part. Mars Bar long potato. Don't ask me how that came about, but once I'd managed to breed out the remains of the wrapper, they became safe to eat. At least, I'm still going strong. They taste bad with practically everything, but if you grate a little into hot water … it's pretty divine.' He shrugged. 'Well, compared to drinking hot water on its own.'

'And what's that?'

'That red thing? It's still a work in progress. Its origin was a tomato plant fused with a beach ball. I took two cuttings and cross-pollinated them for a few generations, slowly weeding out anything that looked like plastic. I couldn't quite do it, but I managed to get it so that the plastic only grows around the outer skin. Peel it off, and you have something that tastes like tomato crossed with potato. Again, I'm still working on the best complements for it in cooking.'

Miranda turned on her heels, taking in the

smorgasbord of bizarre vegetables. 'Is it really safe to eat all this stuff?'

Olin smiled. 'It's my mission in life to find out. I've been eating variations of these vegetables, plus whatever I catch in those traps—except yourself, of course—for nearly forty years. And, well, it might not be turning me into a princess, but I'm still here, aren't I?'

'Looks like it. But why?'

'Somebody has to do it.'

'What do you do with them? Do you give them to other people?'

'No. I work alone. No one else lives this close to the Shifting Castle without being one of the Dark Man's minions. On the plus side, it makes for a nice place to work without distractions.'

'What about the Dark Man?'

'Oh, he has no interest in me.'

As if on cue, a howl rose from the forest behind them. Olin immediately dropped into a crouch, spreading his cloak out around him like tent.

'Wraith-hounds. Quickly, under here.' He lifted a flap and waved for her to crouch down beside him. He draped it over her and put a finger to his lips. 'Stay quiet now.'

Something moved in the trees beyond the vegetable garden. Miranda felt a sudden hot flush, sweat breaking out on her brow. As the creature stepped into view, she realised her suspicions were confirmed: she had encountered one of these before.

It stood waist-high, a mixture of metal and flesh in the shape of a dog, metallic jaws snarling beneath canine eyes. Dog ears twitched, and a segmented broom handle of a tail flicked back and forth.

'Reanimated corpses or souls of dogs fused with

inanimate objects,' Olin whispered. 'I've seen other wraith animals, but dogs are easily controlled.'

Three others stepped out of the grass behind the first. One of them lifted its head into the air and sniffed.

'What are they doing?' Miranda whispered.

'They smell us, but they're confused. They're not intelligent creatures, but they have instinct.'

The first wraith-hound began to move forward. It walked among the vegetables, its nose to the ground, ignoring the plants entirely. Beside Miranda, Olin gave an uncomfortable shift, his hand reaching out of his cloak, lifting in the direction of the creature.

It abruptly stopped, lifted its head, and gave a low whine, then turned and ran back to its companions. Together, they disappeared back into the woods.

'Quickly now,' Olin said. 'We must return to my house at once.'

Miranda felt the urgency in his tone and didn't dispute it. She stayed close as he hurried back across the vegetable garden and into the trees, intersecting with the path a little way down the hillside.

Movement in among the trees now set her heart racing. What else was out there? What might be pursuing them?

A dark shadow shifted up ahead. Olin gasped, lifted a hand, and the creature vanished among the trees. Olin was breathing hard, limping a little. Miranda glanced behind them and saw creatures slinking out onto the path as they followed, sniffing at their tracks.

'What was that thing?' she whispered as at last the knoll where Olin's house was hidden came into view.

'I'll tell you when we're safely inside,' Olin said.

Another howl rang out behind them. This time it was answered by several others. Deep in the trees, movement came again, vegetation shifting as something huge began to move.

'Quickly, inside,' Olin said, waving Miranda ahead of him. She wasn't quick enough and found Olin shoving her from behind, sending her sprawling into the main room. Angry, she sat up and turned around to berate him, but Olin wasn't looking at her. He was peering out through the door at the eyes of something massive moving through the trees. A high-pitched, fluttery sound came from near the door, and Miranda realised it was Olin whimpering in fear. She clambered up and went to stand beside him as something black and massive pushed through the undergrowth. Orange eyes gleamed above glistening jagged metal teeth as long as her arm. Its mouth opened wide and it let out a deafening roar just as Olin slammed the door shut. Instead of locking it, however, he ran his hands over the fittings, muttering something under his breath. The roar came again, but this time it was quieter than before. Olin, face streaming with sweat, opened the door again and peered out.

The creature was gone, a trail smashed through the undergrowth revealing its path. Olin stared out into the forest for a moment, then slammed the door again and stumbled back inside.

He slumped down into a chair and leaned his head back.

'Close,' he muttered, sounding out of breath.

'What was that thing?'

'A tar-bear,' he said. 'A reanimate made out of crude oil waste and old car parts. There are a few around. They emerge from the tar pits down in the valley in front of the Shifting Castle. Deadly. Very, very deadly.'

'How did you get rid of it?'

Olin lifted his head and fixed Miranda with a stare.

'That's the easy part. I used a little reanimation magic. The question I have is: why did it come up this far in the first place?'

All the mirth and joviality Miranda had come to expect of Olin was gone, and the way he stared at her suggested he was looking at the answer.

5

BENJAMIN

'No, not this one. I thought it was because that shop's the same, but I don't ever remember there being an HSBC bank on my street.'

'Perhaps you've been gone longer than you think and they built one?'

'There wasn't a Superdrug either.'

'Well, same reason.'

Benjamin shook his head. 'No, this isn't it. Let's keep walking.'

As they made their way through Basingstoke's town centre, searching for landmarks which would jog Benjamin's memory, he began to feel more and more spooked. While the town had elements he remembered—the greengrocer opposite a war memorial was definitely the one his mum had once taken him to, because he clearly remembered the time David had pulled a box of apples onto the floor—but other things were completely new. There were shops he didn't recognise, even chain stores that looked unfamiliar. And one of the biggest changes was that most of the charity shops were gone. He had seen two larger ones, but most of the small ones were now empty shop-fronts with "tenant wanted" signs in the windows, as though someone had gotten really keen on old stuff and bought up all of their junk.

Then there were other changes. There were far less people about than he might have expected for what they had discovered, from an electronic calendar in the town square, was a Saturday. And those who were about walked in a hunched, suspicious way, eyes darting around, wary of everyone and everything. There was almost no conversation, no chance meetings, no jolly conversations between old friends. At one point, Benjamin had seen two people recognise each other, look up, mutter 'All right?' then duck their heads and go on their way.

'No rubbish bins,' Wilhelm had said as they came to the square, and he was right. Not one. Benjamin looked around, spotting a man exiting a chip shop. The man dropped a chip, but the moment it struck the ground it bounced up again as though caught by a sudden wind. The man gave it a distrustful glare then turned his back as the chip bounced across the road, bouncing higher and higher until it flew out of sight over a line of houses.

'Sorcery,' someone nearby to Benjamin said, but when he turned around to see who had said it, all he saw were lowered faces and turned backs.

He wasn't sad when they left the shops and the reluctant shoppers behind. Finally, on the northeast corner of a crossroads, he spotted something he recognised.

A small Methodist church sat behind a set of railings. Across the street was a boarded-up corner shop which may or may not have been where his mother took David and him to buy sweets, but Benjamin remembered walking past the church on the way to town.

'This is definitely the way,' Benjamin said. 'I'm sure.'

'Sure?'

'Sure.'

Wilhelm nodded. 'Right, let's go.'

No sooner had they turned the corner than they saw a dog-catcher van speeding towards them. Wilhelm grabbed Benjamin's arm and they ducked into the churchyard as the van rushed by.

'Close one,' Benjamin said. 'Do you think it was looking for us?'

Wilhelm shrugged. 'I think it's safest just to assume that all of those vans are after us. I certainly won't be stopping one to ask for directions, at any rate.'

After passing a couple more out-of-town specialist businesses, the street transformed into bland suburbia, row upon row of nearly identical estate houses. Benjamin began to feel a strange mixture of nostalgia and unease, partly because he remembered living in such a house, and also because it was clear from the changes to the town centre that walking back into his old life would never happen.

When he reached the sign at the end of his road, he stopped so suddenly that Wilhelm bumped into him.

'What is it?' Wilhelm said, rubbing his hip.

'This is it. Victoria Road. I'm a hundred percent sure. I didn't know it until I saw it, but I live down here.'

'Live or lived?'

Benjamin took a deep breath. 'We're about to find out.'

Wilhelm patted Benjamin on the shoulder. 'Then let's get this over with.'

The street curved around to the right. They were walking on that side, so it was impossible to see more than a couple of houses ahead, but with each step Benjamin got more of a sinking feeling in his stomach. He looked at the numbers, counting them off: 2 … 4 … 6 … 8….

And then he stopped.

'Oh,' was all he could say.

'What? Come on, Benjamin. What? That one, right? Number 14?'

'Next to it.' Benjamin could barely find the strength to lift his arm and point.

'That's not a house. It's a playground.'

'I know.' He stared at the pretty set of swings, roundabouts, and slides set into a small, leafy area among a few young trees. The playground apparatus all looked newly painted. The grass glistened in the sun, the leaves of the trees shook in a light breeze. Not a single piece of plastic wrapper fluttered anywhere.

As they stood and watched, a couple of little kids ran out of the door of the adjacent house, skipped along the pavement and rushed into the playground. In seconds, the swings were creaking, the children's laughter echoing over the wind.

'That was my house,' Benjamin said, throat feeling tight as though he might cry. 'I lived at Number 16. See, Number 14 here, and over there is Number 18. My house used to be here. I know it was.'

'Where's it gone?'

'How should I know?' Benjamin walked forward a few steps and kicked out at a clump of grass. 'I'm absolutely sure it was here. I even recognise the colour of next door's front door, and they've still got the taped up crack in the bathroom window that my dad always joked they were too poor to replace.'

Wilhelm turned to look. 'So they have. That suggests it's the same people that live there. Let's go and ask.'

'Ask them what?'

'We're getting nowhere moping around, are we? Let's go and see if they know where your house went.'

Benjamin's feet felt frozen to the spot. 'I'm not sure.'

'Well, I'll go and ask, then. You stay here if you want.'

Benjamin spurred himself into action as Wilhelm marched up the neighbour's path. He caught up just as Wilhelm lifted a hand and rang the doorbell. From inside they heard the ringer stuttering—Benjamin's dad had always joked about that too: that they were too poor to change the batteries.

A shape appeared behind frosted glass. 'Who is it?' came a woman's voice.

Benjamin opened his mouth to say something lame about having used to live next door, but Wilhelm spoke first.

'It's Ben and Will, two scouts from the local group. We're taking orders for boxes of charity biscuits for next week's fete.'

Benjamin was still frowning at Wilhelm as the door opened. An old lady in a blue apron with dolphin patterns on it appeared. Her hair—white with silvery streaks—was tied back.

Benjamin stared. Mrs. Taylor. The old crone who had once shooed him out of her back garden after climbing over the fence to collect a tennis ball. She had been old then, but now she was properly old, not just the child's old he remembered. She had to be pushing seventy, if not more.

If she recognised him, she showed no sign. She cocked her head at Wilhelm, who gave a wide smile.

'How many would you like? It's for charity, you know. We'll bring them round next Tuesday. A pound each.'

'I didn't hear anything about that, but since they're so cheap, I'll have five. Do I need to sign anything?'

'No, a verbal agreement is all that's required, plus payment up front.'

'Um, what?'

'Otherwise we'll over order. Doesn't make good business sense, does it?' Wilhelm grinned again.

'Well, wait a moment, I'll get my purse. Since it is only a fiver. Can't buy much at all for that these days.'

Mrs. Taylor returned, brandishing a note, which Wilhelm pocketed almost as soon as it touched his hand. Mrs. Taylor looked down at them, but fearing Wilhelm had thrown them off topic like he had before, Benjamin stepped forward.

'Um, I don't know if you remember, but didn't there used to be a family living next door?'

'At number twenty? Yes, the Timpsons. Horrible lot. Kids used to steal anything that wasn't bolted down. Feral little things.'

'No, the other side.'

'Oh.' Mrs. Taylor frowned. 'Yes, but that was years back. How would you know about that?'

Benjamin swallowed down the terrifying confirmation that he wasn't back in the time he remembered, but somehow in the future. He had suspected it, but now Mrs. Taylor nailed it home.

'Um, they were friends of my dad's.'

'Oh, that would be Benjamin's family. There were two brothers, weren't there? I never really knew the younger brother. David, wasn't it? But Benjamin, he was a lovely boy. Looked a bit like you, actually, although my memory isn't what it was. Shorter hair, a bit younger perhaps, when he disappeared.'

'When he … ?'

'Yes, he went out to play and never came home. Isn't that the way it usually happens? Vanished without a trace. Gosh, looking back on it now, it was like a TV movie, but at the time … horrible. I'm afraid it's not something I like thinking about. Perhaps you should ask your dad about it.'

'Well….'

'His dad's dead,' Wilhelm said. 'Train crash.'

Benjamin baulked, but Mrs. Taylor put a hand on her head as though the worst thing in the world had just happened.

'Oh, I'm so sorry to hear about that.'

'Years ago,' Wilhelm said. 'He's over it now.'

'I was just wondering what happened to them,' Benjamin said. 'My, um, dad said they were … really nice.'

Mrs. Taylor shrugged. 'Well, they were all right. Terrible series of events, though. The boy disappeared, and the other boy—the ah, special one—ended up in a coma. Went on for months. He finally woke up, but he was never the same. Had to go to a special school and all that. Everyone said he was weird; he kept saying he saw ghosts, and no one liked that. Jennifer—Mrs. Forrest—just withdrew. You never saw her anymore.' Mrs. Taylor sighed. 'And they say things happen in threes, well I suppose then there was the third.'

'The third?'

'Yes, after Benjamin's disappearance, and David's coma, there was the bin lorry.'

'I'm sorry, the what?'

'The bin lorry. Overturned on their car. Killed them all.'

Benjamin sagged, Wilhelm catching his arms and keeping him from falling. Benjamin tried to find the strength to stand on his own, but his legs were jelly, his mind a fuzz of images that wouldn't stay still. He heard Mrs. Taylor ask if he wanted a drink of water, and Wilhelm replying that his friend was prone to "sudden turns." Then Wilhelm was helping him back down the driveway.

'Hang in there,' Wilhelm said, helping Benjamin down the street and into an alley that put them out of sight. Benjamin, his strength slowly returning, limped along beside him as far as a bus shelter at the far end where they sat down on a plastic seat.

'You all right?'

Benjamin shook his head. 'I think so.'

Wilhelm put a hand around his shoulders. 'That must have been a shock. I mean, you must have figured something was up when you saw that playground, but hey, that was a bombshell and a half.'

'Mum and Dad … David … my family.' Benjamin shook his head. 'When she said they were killed, it was like being hit in the chest, but now … I don't know. Shouldn't I be crying or something? The thing is, I can barely remember them. They're like strangers who I feel I should care about, but I don't really feel sad, just shocked.'

'I get you,' Wilhelm said. 'I don't think anything about this place is quite how it's supposed to be. I mean, all those Miscreants and dog-catchers, and bits of rubbish flying through the air … those great big wheel things … I'm not sure this world is any more real than the one we came from.'

'Yet we're stuck here.'

Benjamin chipped a bit of paint off the seat and watched it launch up into the air, flying away on a wind of its own making.

'And we have to figure out what to do next.'

Wilhelm pulled the five pound note out of his pocket. 'Well, thanks to that old biddy, we're rich.'

'Rich? That's only a fiver.'

'Could buy a three-course meal where I'm from. Or should I say … *when.*'

Benjamin smiled. 'Well, *when* I'm from, you'd be lucky to get a bag of crisps and a couple of Cokes.'

'Which means that now it's probably barely worth a bus ticket.' Wilhelm sighed. 'No wonder that old bat's eyes lit up. She probably thought she was scamming us.'

'I suppose it's better than nothing. We might be able to feast on a bag of crisps between us.' Benjamin stood up, testing his feet, and then made to tuck in his shirt. His eyes scanned a map of the town on the bus shelter wall, set behind a sheet of clear plastic. Surrounding it were various advertisements for local businesses: chip shops, cafes, a couple of taxi companies, a yoga teacher, a care home, a gardener, and an antiques emporium.

Benjamin frowned. The name over the advertisement seemed familiar.

Sebastien Aren's Antiques Market: Buy and Sell.
Your rubbish is my gold

And below the text was a picture of an antique telephone Benjamin recognised; one he had seen before, a million miles away on a shelf in a room at the top of a castle, not far from a window through which two suns shone.

'Grand Lord Bastien,' he whispered.

'What?'

'Look at this. Sebastien Aren. Didn't you ever read your handbook for … Endinfinium?'

'My handbook?' Wilhelm's eyes widened. 'Oh … my *handbook.*' He shook his head. 'No.'

'Well, I did. The Grand Lord … he signed it Sebastien

Aren. He's here. He's right here in Basingstoke. Look. This telephone … I saw it in his room. It has to be him. Maybe he can help us.'

Wilhelm nodded. 'Well, there's only one way to find out.'

6

MIRANDA

OLIN, WHO HAD AT FIRST BEEN FRIENDLY AND OPEN WITH Miranda, had begun to change somewhat. Providing her with piles of old books he had salvaged over the years, he expected her to stay inside and out of sight while he went to tend his vegetables and scavenge for food. At first, with her memory still little more than a handful of confusing images, she was happy for some quiet time, passing it by reading ancient novels, history books on a world she didn't remember, and books describing animals she had never seen.

By far the most interesting were the cookery books, and with Olin's limited ingredients, she took it upon herself to adapt old recipes and provide Olin—who seemed happy to live off vegetable fritters—with something interesting to eat each night. Many of the listed items she could only guess at the taste at, with Olin offering only limited descriptions: 'Well, turmeric, it's kind of spicy but dry. Sage, that tastes like someone dropped an onion in a bowl of lettuce.' Sometimes she would pick through the drawers of his salvaged kitchen units, testing the contents of each bottle or jar with the tip of her finger, learning gradually the point of grating, mashing, dicing, slicing, and pulping, coupled with grilling, frying, boiling, baking, roasting, and steaming, until she felt like she could return to Endinfinium High and get a job as head of the kitchens.

As the time passed and her memories focused and solidified however, and despite Olin's increasing delight at a series of pies, curries, stews, roasts, and salads, many of which had him salivating and pontificating over food from his distant childhood which he remembered only by taste, Miranda became increasingly aware that she was out of place and soon needed to leave.

Olin, who for weeks had only allowed her outside to accompany him for short periods of time, citing the increasing danger of these badlands near to the Shifting Castle, was reluctant. It was only the reemergence of her magic which pushed him to agree.

Despite sensing she had some kind of power, it had felt out of reach, tucked away on a high shelf of her consciousness where, no matter how hard she stretched, she could not quite reach it. One day, though, while playing with the rhino that, despite its silence, had become almost as good a friend as Olin, she reached out to pick it up and found herself moving it with the air alone.

The words of an old teacher came drifting back: *Push and pull. That's all it is. You just have to learn different ways of doing it, and the kind of things you can do it to. You're not just pushing around objects, but the very fabric of the world.*

Edgar. She remembered him now, a secretive teacher who had taken her under his wing when she began to show signs of having a power over reanimation magic which was forbidden. He had labeled her a Miscreant, an errant magic user, one which the school's inner teaching circle would reject and cast out if her ability was discovered.

There were rules to be kept, of course, and one of them was to deny the very nature of what Endinfinium was about.

Three basic types of magic user. Summoner, the strongest, capable of wielding great power, but only for a short time and at a great cost to the wielder's physical strength. Channeller, capable of using small amounts of magic to perform mostly simple tasks. And Weaver, someone who had no power on their own, but when close to a Channeller could amplify their magic almost to Summoner levels.

Most children at Endinfinium High were Weavers, she remembered now, their latent power kept hidden by a series of school rules. A few—perhaps one in ten—were Channellers, and had to be carefully protected to prevent them detecting—and in the event of doing so using—their magic.

Then there were Summoners, of which during her time, there had only been two known among the pupils.

One had been her best friend.

It had taken a couple of days of striving to remember his name. Finally, the name of the author of one of Olin's books, Ben Collins, had jogged her memory.

Benjamin Forrest.

And once she remembered Benjamin, the name of her next closest friend, Wilhelm Jacobs, had popped into her head.

As had the last memory she had of them.

In grave danger.

'I have to go back,' she told Olin one night, after dinner. 'I know you think I'm in danger, but I can't stay here forever. And my friends, I have to find them.'

Olin took a deep breath. 'It won't be easy.' He rubbed his eyes. 'There's something I need to tell you.'

'What?'

'I know what you are. I know you're a Channeller, because I'm one too.'

Miranda lifted her hands, as though that would explain it. 'I've felt it coming back over the last few days,' she said. 'When I woke up I couldn't remember anything about who I was, or what I was, but now ... most of it's complete.'

'Which puts you in more danger than I had imagined. When I found you, I thought you were a newcomer. Most know nothing of themselves, and while many have latent power, they don't know how to access it or use it. We used to bring them in, lie to them, make them take the Oath—'

'We?'

Olin looked up suddenly, as though realising a terrible mistake. 'I meant—'

'You were part of the school once, weren't you?' Miranda stood up, gripping the edge of the table, before relaxing and sitting back down. 'I suspected it, you know. I found some clothes that looked like old school uniforms, some pens and pencils with school labels on them ... you were exiled, weren't you?'

Olin sighed. 'Eventually,' he said. 'But not as a pupil. I got through that all right, because I believed the lies like all the rest. It wasn't until I was grown up, when I was working as a caretaker, mostly dealing with cleaning or maintenance, that I discovered my power, and started to experiment.'

'What kind of experiment?'

'It started with the cleaners. Do you remember those nearly mindless people who work in the school? I figured out they were reanimated corpses. No one had ever really examined them before. I also surmised that the ghouls were creatures built of rubbish but infused with the tormented souls of the dead. With the cleaners and the ghouls, I had a body, and I had a soul, trapped in separate vessels. I thought I could bring peace to both by fusing the soul of a ghoul with the body of a cleaner.'

Miranda stared at him. 'Is that, um, ethical?'

Olin gave a bitter laugh. 'Oh, heavens, no. But was I some kind of mad scientist, a witch doctor? Nothing of the sort. I was trying to help, in the only way I knew. Of course, things didn't go according to plan, and eventually I was found out and exiled.'

'Your experiments didn't work?'

Olin looked up, and his gaze was so intense Miranda had to look away. 'It is a fool who underestimates the Dark Man,' he said. 'He is the creator, and all dark reanimate exists like a web he created, all threads connected to one another. We are just people, given a little sprinkling of something, a mere taste. I was naïve; I thought I had power.' He shook his head. 'I had nothing.'

'So you came here to pursue a more, um, leisurely lifestyle?'

Olin sighed. 'I felt like I had failed, but I still wanted to do some good. I spend my time now creating vegetables, purifying the strains to make them safe to eat. Whenever I succeed, I send a set of seeds to the school. What they do with them, I don't know.'

'But why so close to the Shifting Castle? Aren't you in constant danger?'

Olin looked down. 'I have my reasons. For one, the land is volatile here. Plants grow with a speed multiple times of that near the school. I can achieve in a few months what might take years to achieve elsewhere.'

'But there must be more danger with it.'

Olin stood up suddenly. 'I think we've talked enough for one night,' he said. 'We will talk more in the morning.'

Miranda had a thousand more questions, but it was

clear Olin no longer wanted to talk. She watched him stump down the hall, then went to the small bedroom he had allocated for her and acted as though she were getting ready for bed.

Hidden in a corner, though, she had already begun collecting supplies. A bag held some dry foodstuffs, as well as a few items she might find useful that Olin wouldn't miss—an old hunting knife, a length of rope, a net, a bag of firelighters in case she couldn't get her magic to make fire.

As soon as she heard snoring from behind his bedroom door, she pulled on her clothes, including an old jacket she had found, and hoisted the bag over her shoulder.

She felt some trepidation as she pulled open the heavy door and stepped outside, but the world wasn't as dark as trapped inside for so long, she had begun to imagine. Her memory of the two suns had returned, and she remembered that while the larger yellow sun had always set, the smaller red one had made a low circuit of the world, never dipping below the horizon, giving what otherwise might have been night a spectral orange glow. While it reminded her of the burned orange eyes of the ghouls, it made passage through the trees as she headed for the hilltop far easier.

A flicker of lightning flashed above her as she broke through the trees onto the hill's bare crest. Flame erupted from the earth no more than twenty paces distant. Miranda fell, rolling away into a basin-like hollow as another bolt of lightning flashed down, striking the ground close enough to shower her with clods of hot dirt.

Too close. Were they targeting her?

She had no time to stop and figure it out as a third blast cracked the sky. Miranda climbed to her feet and ran for the treeline, breaking through into the comforting undergrowth as a fourth bolt smashed down, this one striking the precise bowl where she had sheltered.

She headed on, moving downhill again, already unsure of her direction, wishing now that she'd waited until morning, until Olin had gone out to tend his vegetables or check his traps.

Downhill, she reminded herself. If she went downhill she would find a river, and if she found a river she could follow it, and rivers always led to the sea.

It wasn't much of a plan, and it felt even lighter as a howl rose from the forest up ahead, answered by another at her rear.

Something ominously big moved through the trees nearby. In the dim glow left by the red sun it was difficult to make out, but she saw a great blackness, like a giant, moving shadow.

A tar-bear.

More howls echoed out of the forest ahead of her. Miranda started to run, keeping her eyes on her feet to avoid tripping, also fearing more of Olin's traps. By now she had no idea of her direction, aware only that she had to keep moving, that if she stopped she was dead.

The trees abruptly parted, and she found herself on a wide shingle shore bordering a trickling river. Clogged with junk, some piled into heaps, smaller pieces moving in fits and starts, it was hard to even see the water, but the floodplain was a couple of hundred yards wide.

Clapping her hand over her mouth, she stifled a little gasp. Not this direction. She had gotten it so very wrong.

Through a crack in the mountains rising out of the foothills across the river, the snow glowed with an orange tint, and an angular building appeared, built into the slope of one of the inner mountains. Over such a distance she realised it had to be massive, hundreds of metres high, but its structure felt impossibly out of focus. Was the tallest tower on the right or the left, or wasn't there one at all?

The Shifting Castle, lair of the Dark Man, constantly moving, rearranging itself. Miranda's eyes hurt just to look at it, so she squeezed them shut.

When she opened them again, glowing orange eyes made a line along the opposite shore a hundred paces away.

She turned, but found the same thing back the way she had come. Some were low to the ground, others twice her height—tar bears.

And in the sky, thunder clouds were rolling out from their permanent position above the Shifting Castle, like an approaching tidal wave set to wash her away.

'Push and pull,' Miranda muttered, her voice trembling.

Something moved in her pocket, startling her, but it was only the little rhino, running back and forth. She remembered something Olin had said, about the land being volatile here. Perhaps whatever power she had would be amplified. There was only one way to find out.

A shrieking howl made her slap hands over her ears. A hush fell over the lines of ghouls, and for a moment, even the rustling of their bodies fell still. Then, with a single grating wail, they came rushing forward.

'Back!' Miranda screamed, and a wall of shingle rose up, curved, and crashed down on the nearest ghouls. Some fell, others lay twitching beneath larger boulders, but the others came on, knocking the rocks aside, feeling nothing. Miranda tried again, but this time her magic felt sluggish, the rocks barely lifting knee-high. A couple of ghouls tripped, but most rushed through the distraction, undeterred.

As the twin lines of ghouls converged on her, Miranda

ran for the trees. She saw other eyes there too, and as she broke through the tree line, claws came swinging out of the gloom. She dodged one, knocked one aside with her magic, and took another on her shoulder, a blunt strike like a broom handle which knocked the wind out of her. She stumbled but forced her legs to move, aware that the large thing crashing through the undergrowth to her left could cut her in half with one strike.

More ghouls came at her out of the trees. Some had the bodies of animals—cats, pigs, dogs, even one as tall as a horse, but their similarity came from the human skulls where their faces should have been, burnt orange glowing from empty eye sockets, their hollow jaws clacking lifelessly. Miranda quickly lost the energy to scream, using all her efforts to raise little bursts of magic to push their blows aside, unhook their cold, bony hands from her ankles and wrists.

Her strength, though, was fading. The woods were full of them, every shadow holding something monstrous. The rhino in her pocket was panicking, mirroring her thundering heart. Above her, lightning crashed down, and in its glow, she caught sight of something running towards her.

'Olin … ?'

'Miranda! Down!'

The ghouls fell away in a sudden burst of light, limbs exploding, skulls cracking apart. Sweat soaked Olin's face, and his beard was caked with blood. He snarled into the trees, then lifted his great cloak and swept it over her.

'Be still. Do not move or we both die here tonight.'

Miranda had no strength to speak. She curled into a ball on the spongy undergrowth, like a child returning to its mother's womb, cupping her head with her hands. She tried to cry but had no strength even for that.

7

SNOUT

SIMON PATTERSON—THE BOY KNOWN BY MANY AS Snout due to his slightly upturned nose—did as he was told and stood with his arms by his sides at the end of the Year Three's line as Professor Loane took the stage inside the Great Hall of Endinfinium High School.

For once, no one was tittering or poking each other secretly while the teachers fussed around at the stage side. Everyone was silent, watching, waiting, wondering what was about to happen.

Things hadn't been normal in some time, not really, ever since that big scary thing that had shown up outside the school had floated off again and dropped over the edge of the world.

Classes had been subdued, the teachers absentminded to the point of inability, and even old Gubbledon Longface, the pupil's dormitory housemaster, had slacked off on his constant reminders to set their shoes neatly and wash their hands in the sink by the way in.

'First,' Professor Loane began, speaking into a microphone connected to two reverberating speakers on either side of the stage which had reanimated to an extent that they had needed to be taped down, 'we'd like to welcome you back to the new school term here at Endinfinium High.'

Murmurs of dissent came from further down the line. Snout felt it too but said nothing; it might be the official start of the new term, but the only holiday since the last one had been a couple of weeks of mostly forced confinement to the dormitory while repairs were made to the school, so most kids were feeling a little salty about starting back again so soon. While Endinfinium High was essentially a boarding school, none of the pupils had an actual home to go back to, so the teachers believed long periods of inactivity provided too much opportunity for mischief.

'We have nine new pupils entering the school this term. Would you please give them a warm reaction.'

There were muted claps as nine confused-looking boys and girls were herded up onto the stage. Snout remembered this moment well: waking up in the middle of nowhere, with no idea how you'd gotten there, often with some monstrosity looming over you to tell you don't worry, you're safe now, even when you felt anything but. And to top it all, finding out that while you might be in some nightmarish version of Wonderland, you were still expected to go to school, learning all manner of banal subjects, while outside the window, two suns hung in the sky, the sea dropped off the edge of the world, and plastic bags flew around like giant butterflies.

He had never felt so confused in his life.

The kids—more than usual for a mid-year enrollment, perhaps due to the same recent events that had caused such upheaval around the school—had finished nervously introducing themselves and been herded back off the stage, into the wide-load safety of Captain Roche, the gym teacher who was wider than he was tall, this term assigned to be the new Year One form teacher. Snout felt sorry for them: Roche was a snarly, nerve-shredding teacher, intent on getting the physical best out of groups of apathetic kids who'd rather be wading through heaps of water-damaged comic books washed up on the shore every day, now dutifully collected by the three-member strong Comic Book Club, of which Snout was the newly elected president. It was a position he had accepted with great pride, even though there were rumours that Old Cleat down in the library was getting a little frustrated at the sudden competition.

'Now, for the benefit of the newcomers, plus those of you who might have forgotten, it's time to introduce the teaching staff.'

They were an odd bunch, Snout had to admit. Towering Mistress Xemian was at least twice as tall as Captain Roche, who resembled a bulldozer. Fearsome Ms. Ito had a permanent cast on her left leg which was almost as much of a distraction as her black-and-white checkerboard hair. Even Edgar Caspian, who might have looked like a normal man in down-to-earth clothing, had elevated himself to something unique with a purple wizard's hat and long, flowing cloak. Now that reanimation and its uses was officially on the syllabus, Snout was quite looking forward to earth science classes this term, particularly in light of his own unique ability.

Each teacher gave a speech. While Ms. Ito's was short and snappy, 'Shut up, belt up, and listen up,' the bland-to-the-point-of-invisibility Professor Rufus, the moral education teacher, prattled on for at least ten minutes about the importance of kindness to others.

'And now, to the committee appointments for term,'

Professor Loane said, recapturing the stage after a good half hour of exposition. Snout tried to ignore a growing urge to visit the toilet. 'First of all, after, uh, the expiration of Miranda Butterworth's term, we'd like to introduce the new head prefect.'

A few murmurs came from around Snout again, particularly along the line in front of his, the Year Twos, the classmates of the suspiciously absent trio of Benjamin Forrest, Wilhelm Jacobs, and Miranda Butterworth. All three had disappeared a couple of weeks ago, at the same time as the scary thing and the big scary battle on the beach. None had been seen since, but more alarmingly, their names had rarely been mentioned, as though someone had sprinkled fairy dust over the school to erase them from existence.

A figure stepped out of the shadows to the stage side. A hush came over the assembled pupils and even the lights appeared to darken.

Godfrey, curly mop of jet-black hair framing a sour face with almost cat-like green eyes, stepped out of the shadows. He had forgone the official school uniform for a black sweater and trousers and a black cloak that hung to the back of his knees. Two places down from Snout, Cherise White muttered something about pantomime season, but Godfrey's smile was triumphant as he walked to the centre of the stage.

The clapping was lacklustre except for Derek Bates, Godfrey's right-hand man, although Snout made sure to mimic large, gregarious claps just in case Godfrey looked in his direction.

'I know what you've been saying,' Godfrey said, leaning into the microphone as though he might eat it. Snout wouldn't put it past him to try. 'Too much study, not enough play. And I know what they've been saying,' he added, waving at the teachers. 'Too much play, not enough study. Well, friends, colleagues, comrades … it's time we satisfied both worlds. Work harder, play harder, that's our motto for this term. We get sharp: we snap to attention and we get our hands up in class, get our homework handed in on time. And we get those eyes off our back. We get time for ourselves, to learn, to explore, to enjoy … and we get our holidays. Who's with me?'

A few muted shouts were the only answer. Standing at Godfrey's shoulder, Professor Loane looked pained as he leaned forward to borrow the microphone. 'Well, thank you, Godfrey. I think we're in for some surprises this term.'

Godfrey shuffled off the stage, but instead of going back to stand with the other kids, he resumed his position among the teachers. Snout had heard the rumours and was pretty sure he would soon confirm they were true: Godfrey no longer lived in the dormitory with the other kids. He had a special suite in the teachers' tower. Snout had overheard Derek Bates boasting about it to some of the first years, even though he hadn't seen it himself—they had fallen out after Snout had taken Benjamin Forrest's side during the scary stuff that had happened.

Professor Loane tapped the microphone to still the shuffles and mutterings among the crowd. 'I'm afraid our headmaster, Grand Lord Bastien, is unable to come to our assembly today. He is feeling quite under the weather. However, he has prepared a speech I will now read out.'

Murmurs suggested mixed feelings among the pupils. Snout had seen the Grand Lord on previous occasions, and he wasn't like the other teachers, despite how unique they all were. Instead, what little of him you could see wasn't really there at all: you could see through him quite clearly. The teachers, when pushed, referred to him as a displaced spirit. The pupils considered him a ghost, and while some enjoyed the freak show of his appearance, others found it too scary, even in a place like Endinfinium, where night's most terrifying creature was a reanimated refuse sack which would rip you off the cliffs and throw you to your death on the beaches far below.

'It is with great pleasure,' Professor Loane read, 'that I welcome you to our fine school. You may be struggling with circumstances, or the new experiences that you are no doubt undertaking with each passing hour, but here you will find safety, security, and comfort. And here we will educate you to live and survive in our most unique environment. Many challenges await, but like countless previous generations, you will rise to them and overcome them.'

Behind him, Snout heard a couple of yawns. Professor Loane's rapid, deadpan oration made an already-dull speech positively sleep-inducing.

'And to the pupils who are still with us, you are making great strides in your progress, and we are proud of what you have achieved. You are a credit to the school and we wish you all the best for the coming year.'

With a satisfied grunt, Professor Loane folded the paper and put it back into his pocket. Snout glanced along the line and saw other kids looking equally surprised. It had been about as generic a speech as one could be. No mention of Benjamin, Wilhelm, or Miranda, no mention of the huge scary battle which had taken place just a few weeks before, no mention of any of the other strange events or changes that were clear to see. It was as though the speech had been written a couple of minutes before the assembly as an obligatory place-filler.

Snout frowned. Perhaps it had.

'Well, that's all,' Professor Loane said. 'You may all go

back to your new form rooms now and meet your form teachers for this term.'

This allocation of form teachers was new for this term. Previously, Mrs. Martin in the school office had typed up a timetable for each school year and pinned it up in the dormitory entrance. Gubbledon had covered the job as form teacher as well as it could have been expected, but it seemed there was a greater need for control.

The new form teacher for Year Three was Ms. Ito. Snout gulped. As they reached their newly allocated form room on the second floor of the science block, Snout found himself at the back of the line. Ahead, kids were trying to push through the doors, no doubt desperate to get the desks farthest from the front, but something was coming out, blocking the way. Snout stood back as one of the cleaners—those empty-faced, near-mindless humans who wandered around the school doing menial tasks—came backwards out of the door, dragging what looked like an overlarge bottle of weed killer with a spray shooter at the end of a pipe attached to the top.

Chamomile spray, a liquid that soothed the constantly reanimating sections of the school, allowing for their safe use. On a special day once a month, all pupils and staff got involved in a big spraying event, but the rest of the time it was one of the cleaners' tasks. However, since the big scary thing that happened, there had been far fewer cleaners around. Snout had seen a couple drop dead without warning, while others had suddenly woken up from their near-vegetative state, taken a look around, and run screaming through the corridors until the teachers and other staff had managed to corner them and calm them down. To the best of Snout's knowledge, most were now housed in a hastily erected boarding house in the school grounds, while processes took place to establish some kind of further education scheme. The kids, of course, had christened the place the "new nuthouse," and made jokes about it during outside gym classes and excursions whenever it came into sight.

The cleaner moved out into the corridor, clearing the entrance to allow the kids to resume their battle for superior seating. Snout, stuck at the back, had just reached the door when a loud crack sounded on the wooden floor behind him, and a terrifying voice boomed, 'You, boy! Stop right there!'

With sweat trickling down his cheeks, Snout turned around. He tried to stare at his shoes as Ms. Ito, cast, witch's cloak, long pointed nose, and crazy-black-hedgehog-writhing-in-white-candyfloss hair, came to a stop in front of him.

She was small, barely up to his shoulder, despite appearing a giant of epic proportions as she stalked the front of a classroom, but her eyes held an emptiness that made Snout long for the warmth and comfort of his bed.

'Why are you late for class?'

'I'm not—'

'Do not dare make an excuse, fool boy. Answer the question or I'll send you for a number of cleans that will make your eyes water.'

Snout gulped. With Ms. Ito, the threat was very real anyway, but in light of the loss of so many cleaners, the locker rooms downstairs, where smaller items were taken for regular deanimation, were worryingly understaffed. Traditionally used as a punishment, when once forgetting your math homework would have seen you sent for an arbitrary twenty-five cleans, now you might get two hundred and fifty. There were rumours going about that a dormitory room was in the process of being installed, so that really bad punishments could involve a multiple-night stopover.

'I wasn't quick enough to get to class the required five minutes before the bell,' Snout said, his voice taking on an annoying high-pitched tone he knew would see him mocked in alternative circumstances. 'I'm sorry. I was foolish. It won't happen again.'

Ms. Ito grinned, the first time Snout could ever remember seeing her smile. Her teeth, like her hair, were a chessboard of black-and-white. None, however, seemed natural; it was as though pegs of ivory lined up beside pegs of black obsidian.

'You're a good boy, Simon,' Ms. Ito said. 'I know you won't let it happen again. However, examples need to be set. What would the other kids think if they thought I was going soft? Two hundred cleans. And if it happens again, it'll be four hundred. Now, get yourself to a chair and … sit!'

'Yes, Ms. Ito!' Snout said, almost snapping to attention. He stepped back just as her casted leg came swinging around, scything through the spot he had been standing in a moment before. She grinned again, more sadistically this time, as he backpedalled towards the door.

'Front row,' she snapped. 'I like to keep an eye on troublemakers.'

'Yes, Ms. Ito!' Snout said again, bumbling into the classroom, aware that every eye was on him, every single pupil wanting to burst into laughter but holding it inside for fear of retribution. Once they were done with form time, the rest of the day would be a living hell, he knew. At least he was used to it.

He sighed. It was going to be a long term.

8

BENJAMIN

'The road layout's changed,' Benjamin said. 'On that map, I'm sure this one went straight on, but there's a warehouse there now.'

'Perhaps you're looking at it the wrong way round.'

Benjamin shook his head. 'No, I'm sure of it.'

'Let's just ask someone.'

'But what if they think we're Miscreants and call the dog-catchers?'

'Well, we'll run away again. We're getting good at it, aren't we? Look, I have an idea. We'll ask someone old. They'll probably think we're their long-lost children or something.'

'And they'll tell us the directions as they were fifty years ago.'

Wilhelm sighed. 'Let's at least try it. Better than standing around being lost. And you know, old people like antiques, don't they? That's because most of them *are* antiques.'

Benjamin shrugged. 'Okay, go on then. There's one.'

An old lady had appeared out of a house further up

the street and was slowly moving in their direction, leaning on a Zimmer frame which clacked as she shuffled along.

'Excuse me!' Wilhelm called, hurrying across the street. 'Can you tell us the way to Sebastien's Antiques Emporium?'

The woman stopped. She squinted through thick bifocals, then lifted a hand as a look of anger spread across her ancient face.

'Are you taking the mickey out of me, little boy? I won't stand for it. You little punks these days, you have no discipline—'

'We're trying to find the antiques shop where my gran sold my grandfather's war medals,' Wilhelm said. 'She needed money to pay for her heating, but we wanted to buy them back.'

The old woman frowned. 'What are you talking about?

'The, um, war?'

'Why would she need to pay for heating? It's government-funded, you lying fool. You wanted to rob me, didn't you?'

Benjamin caught up with Wilhelm just as the old woman pressed a button on the surprisingly high-tech Zimmer frame and a section of metal pole stuck out, already fitted with a handle to be used as bashing tool. She grabbed it and swiped at Wilhelm's head.

Swinging in from the right, it was close to Benjamin. 'No!' he shouted, sticking up a hand to block its trajectory. As it struck his palm he felt a little jerk as the magic did its work. The stick turned to jelly, then exploded, showering them all with silver gunk. As Benjamin started to wipe it away, it reverted to its former material and tinkled to the road below.

'Sorcery. You're Miscreants,' the old woman said. 'I should have known.' One old finger jabbed at another button on the Zimmer frame. With a cruel smile, she said, 'So, what is it you're looking for? Do you have a pen and paper? I'll draw you a map. It might take some minutes with my arthritis, you know.'

Wilhelm frowned. 'Um, let me check my pockets. I might have.'

Benjamin, however, had caught the look in her eye, and over the light breeze, he heard a distant siren, confirming his suspicions.

'She's trying to stall us!' he said. 'Quick! Run!'

He made for the other side of the street, but behind him, Wilhelm grunted. Benjamin stopped and turned back. Wilhelm was lying on the ground, the old lady having tripped him. His hands were up, trying towards off blows as she tried to poke him with the feet of her Zimmer frame.

Benjamin ran back and pulled Wilhelm out of range, muttering, 'Very sorry to have bothered you, ma'am.' Wilhelm muttered something a little less polite under his breath, but let Benjamin pull him away.

'Her walker had an alarm,' Benjamin gasped. 'She called the dog-catchers.'

From around the corner up ahead, a van skidded into view, accelerating hard, overhead light flashing, siren blaring.

'Look normal,' Benjamin said, slowing and walking with his head down. 'Don't look at them.'

'Too late!'

A skylight had opened in the van's roof and what looked like a cannon rose into view. Benjamin stared at it a moment before it emitted an airy *poof* and something silvery plumed in front of them.

A net. Benjamin dived for the grassy verge as it landed over them, but he was too slow. As if automated, it spread out across them, weighted down along the sides. Tiny electrodes in the knots buzzed, making it hard for Benjamin to concentrate. He gritted his teeth, trying to call his magic, to make it do something, but it felt shut off like a tap.

'Benjamin, take my hand!'

Wilhelm was reaching out as the net lowered down. Somewhere nearby, Benjamin heard a man's laughter. It made him angry to think they'd been trapped like a pair of strays. They were children, people, they had rights—

'Take my hand!' Wilhelm said again. 'Use me!'

Benjamin didn't understand. Then their fingers touched and the world filled with light and motion. They were flying through the air, tumbling over. Benjamin saw the green of a tree and reached for it, feeling a muff of sticky fir branches strike him in the face. He was still holding Wilhelm's hand and he gripped it tight, pulling Wilhelm with him.

The tree was cold, and a branch had scratched his back, but it felt real when so little else did. Benjamin opened his eyes and saw Wilhelm nearby, shaking with fright, clutching a branch hanging out over a metal frame below.

'Weaver,' Wilhelm said, looking up, his voice shaking. 'I didn't know I could still do it, until now. I suppose I can.'

Benjamin wasn't sure what he meant, but the shouts of the dog-catchers came from nearby. Benjamin tried to orientate himself and realised they'd flown right over a line of houses into a children's play park on the other side.

'Quick, lean on that branch and let me down,' Wilhelm said.

Benjamin put out a foot, pushing Wilhelm's branch until the smaller boy could safely reach the climbing frame below. With Wilhelm's position secured, he reached up and helped Benjamin down.

'Stop!'

Two men appeared through a gap in the hedge. One held a metal prong, the other a net.

'They always work in threes,' Wilhelm whispered. 'Where's the third?'

Benjamin turned at a rustle of sound behind him. A man leapt out of the shadows from an alley, metal prong thrusting forwards. The air tingled as it missed Benjamin by a piece of paper's width.

'Back!' he screamed, putting his hands on the metal climbing frame and willing it to help him. Beneath his fingers he felt a sudden bloom of heat, and when he pulled with his mind the whole frame rose out of the ground, coming as easily as though it were made of straws instead of metal frames.

He threw it at the first two men, watching with satisfaction as it spread out like a net, encircled them, then set hard, leaving them trapped. The third man, his nerve gone, rushed to help his colleagues.

'Come on,' Wilhelm said. 'It won't take them long to find a way out. How on earth did you do that?'

Benjamin shook his head. 'No idea,' he said, even though, as he had thrown the malleable climbing frame, he had used the magic in a different way from before. He had not been striving only for his own safety, but with anger in his heart, a desire to hurt.

He had done it with hate.

~

For the first half an hour, they simply got as much distance between themselves and the dog-catchers as they could. No doubt their pursuers had radios, backup, perhaps even helicopters they could send out if necessary.

'Right, here's another map,' Wilhelm said, standing under the protective cover of a different bus shelter. 'This one's a bit newer and the antiques place is marked. Do you recognise that street?'

'Trayden Hill,' Benjamin said. 'Yes, I used to walk up there to go to school. I don't remember ever seeing an antiques emporium, however.'

'Not the kind of thing a kid looks for though, is it?'

'I suppose not.'

'Can you find it from here?'

Benjamin shrugged. 'Maybe. I'm pretty sure it's that way.'

Wilhelm stared. Benjamin pointed out of town, towards a forested hill.

'Really?'

'No, I'm joking. It's behind us.'

'Oh.' Wilhelm clapped Benjamin on the shoulder. 'You're such a comedian. Thought I was going to die laughing.'

'I'm still working on my routine.'

'Well, best not to book that live tour just yet. Come on, let's hurry up. It's nearly lunchtime and I can't focus when I'm hungry. Perhaps we should break into that fiver on the way?'

～

With a large portion of chips split between them, they walked up Trayden Hill. It looked a little different, with many of the old shops closed down. One with a faded estate agent's sign over the window was even rattling on its foundations as though preparing to take off and join the great moving rubbish heap to the south. Benjamin noticed that parts of it had been bolted to the ground with heavy-duty metal joints screwed into concrete.

'There,' Wilhelm said, pointing across the street at a narrow two-storey building fitted neatly between an insurance company and a bank. 'That's it.'

Sebastien's Antiques Emporium was like something out of a Victorian postcard: a quaint red brick building with two protruding bay windows fitted with latticed bull's-eye glass panes. A heavyset mahogany door was in stark contrast to the modern automatic doors of the properties on either side. Glancing up, Benjamin saw similar windows on the upper floor, with a sloping tiled roof and a little chimney puffing smoke clouds.

'So, did we, like, just half time-travel?' Wilhelm said. 'I mean, if you cup your hands around your eyes and just look at that shop, we could be two hundred years ago.'

'I suppose it fits its purpose,' Benjamin said.

'Right. Well, how about we pretend that you're Pip and I'm that orphan kid who wants more soup.'

'Oliver Twist, and it was gruel,' Benjamin said. 'Kind of like they used to feed us at the school.'

Wilhelm's eyes lit up. 'I remember that now! When did you remember?'

'Just now. Popped into my head. Do you remember that time I reanimated Godfrey's lunch into a snake that bit his face?'

Wilhelm stared. 'Oh ... I do now. You got busted for it, didn't you?'

Benjamin nodded. 'Yeah. I got two thousand cleans for that, but it was totally worth it to hear his screaming. Godfrey ... I wonder what happened to him?'

'Nothing good, I expect. Come on, let's get off the street in case those dog-catchers show up again.'

They hurried across to the emporium, pausing outside. 'What do we say?' Benjamin said.

'We'll figure it out. Come on.'

Wilhelm went first, pushing through a heavy door Benjamin found was carpeted along the bottom, leaving it nearly impossible to open. Once inside, breathing hard from the simple exertion of getting in, he looked around, finding himself in the most eccentric bric-a-brac shop he could have imagined. Despite the shop's narrowness, it was deep, with no visible end to the displays of objects going back hundreds of years, so numerous that, in places, they were practically on top of each other.

Children's toys possibly older than the shop; ornaments made of iron, glass, wood or precious metals; gramophones; wireless radios and other old machines all neatly arranged on shelves five or six levels high and standing so close to each other that it was impossible to turn around. You had to keep going forward into a labyrinth of antiquity or risk knocking everything over on the way out.

'Look at all this stuff,' Wilhelm said, holding up an intricately carved wooden fire engine wagon which looked to have been restored with dabs of red paint slightly lighter than the surrounding colours. 'The ladder is clockwork. If you wind the mechanism here it extends up. Seriously, look at it. It's so smooth it doesn't touch the sides.'

Benjamin craned his neck to see. It was only a fire engine made of wood, about the length of his hand, but the craftsmanship was exquisite.

'Whoa….'

'It was handmade in the Scottish Outer Hebrides circa 1890,' a voice said, coming from everywhere and nowhere at once. Wilhelm jerked upright, bumping into Benjamin, who just managed to stop himself from crashing into the shelf stack behind him.

'That particular piece was designed and built by a family business run by Garth McRory, a well-respected toymaker across the United Kingdom at that time. Every piece was crafted by hand from driftwood found on the local beaches. Five generations of the family maintained the business, but alas, it died an unnatural death during the Great War, when the last two sons went off to fight and never came back. Sadly, I don't have the horses that it once came with, but I have a couple of other McRory pieces lying around … possibly the last in the country, more's the pity.'

Benjamin and Wilhelm both looked for the owner of the voice. Such was the layout of the place that it could have come from anywhere.

'Here,' the man said. 'Keep walking forward and you'll see me. Or you could look up at the mirror above your heads and give me a little wave.'

Both looked up. An ornate mirror hanging from the ceiling gave a tiny upside-down view of a man sitting behind a desk. Benjamin squeezed around Wilhelm and found the man sitting barely arms' length away, close enough to have stuck out a leg and kicked them.

'Welcome to my emporium,' he said, standing up.

Benjamin tried not to stare but it was impossible. Memories of Grand Lord Bastien and the time they had spent together in the headmaster's tiny tower chambers came rushing back. Bastien helping him to come to grips with his powers, teaching him to control a level of magic that few possessed, offering advice, words of comfort, stern warnings when necessary.

Grand Lord Bastien, a translucent spirit wrapped in human robes, felt like a shadow of the man towering before them. Sebastien Aren was way over six feet, the suit he wore neatly pressed, spectacles perched on the end of his nose perhaps for show rather than necessity. His hair was mousey brown, straight, flopped over a growing bald patch in the middle. Woody brown eyes, a kind smile. Every bit the school headmaster.

'Are you looking for anything in particular?' he asked, and Benjamin realised they had both been staring. 'It's rare that I receive two gentlemen of your age on my premises. It's rather a haunt of the middle-aged, those pining for an era long passed.'

'Um, Grand Lord—'

'What's that? The board games are over in the far corner.'

'I mean, sorry—'

'You're not after a board game?'

'No, I mean—'

Wilhelm shouldered Benjamin out of the way. 'What my friend is trying to say is that we need your help.'

'Well, I gathered that, otherwise you wouldn't be here. What are you? Card game collectors? Those are on the third row from the front. Or if its Matchbox cars, second box under the window. I have quite a few in mint condition, and I'll do you a good discount if you take the lot.'

'No, you don't understand.'

Sebastien frowned. He pushed his glasses up his nose and craned forward. 'Perhaps you'd better start from the beginning.'

Benjamin took a deep breath. 'Well—'

'Excuse me one moment,' Sebastien said, grabbing a spray can from the desktop. Benjamin and Wilhelm looked around. Something near the front of the store was rattling. As they watched, an old packet of playing cards plumed from the shelf like a flight of moths. In a V-formation they crashed into the window and began fluttering against the glass. Sebastien, with a frustrated grunt, lifted the spray can and doused them. As the spray hit each, they fell motionless to the window seat below.

'Label fell off,' Sebastien muttered, scooping them up in one hand, then picking the box and a price sticker off the shelf on his way back. 'Ah, they're damp now.' He spread the cards in his fingers, shaking them about, then picked out a couple of main offenders and wiped them with a handkerchief he took from his pocket. Satisfied, he slipped them back into the box and closed it, then fixed a white price label back onto the front. He started to turn back to the shelf, then paused. He glanced at Benjamin and Wilhelm, then held out the pack of cards.

'A gift,' he said. 'You pair look like the kind who might enjoy a game of trumps.'

'Thanks,' said Benjamin. Sebastien's hand was nearer to his so he reached out and pocketed the pack of playing cards. As he slid them into his pocket, he noticed they felt warm to the touch.

'Ownership,' Sebastien said, returning to his seat behind the desk. 'It's a wonderful thing. How lovely it is to feel owned by someone or something. I can assure you, those cards will behave from now on, now they've found someone to love.'

'What happened to them?' Wilhelm asked. His eyes were still wide as though he'd seen a ghost, despite everything that had happened to them.

'They animated,' Sebastien said. 'Aren't they teaching you at school about it yet?' His eyes narrowed. 'You're not runaways, are you? What is it some people call those poor kids? Miscreants?'

'No, we're just not from round here,' Wilhelm said with

a frantic shake of his head, as Benjamin nodded in agreement.

'Well, I—'

'—am a bit forgetful,' Wilhelm cut in. Benjamin threw his friend a sideways glare, but Wilhelm gave his ankle a nudge as though to say "keep quiet."

'Nothing's been the same since the Doctor's discovery,' Sebastien said. 'I mean, I know it's worked miracles in some places, but not everything that's thrown away is junk.' He spread his arms. 'Look at these things. You're surrounded by history. The Doctor can't just erase that because it might be in the way.'

As though to illustrate his point, Sebastien leaned over and lifted up something that had previously been out of sight. An old gramophone, the overlarge speaker pointing at them as Sebastien wound a handle on the device's back.

'This is the last of its kind,' he said. 'I bought it from a man who was going to throw it in the rubbish. He had no use for it, said it didn't even work. Well, I've managed to fix the spring mechanism, so it's just a case of fixing the needle and it'll work like new. How could anyone say this was worthless, that it should be destroyed for good, for no man to ever know of its existence? It's priceless. Don't you understand?' He frowned as he looked at them. Benjamin glanced at Wilhelm and wondered if he wore the same blank expression.

'Who are you boys?' Sebastien said again. 'You really aren't from round here, are you?'

Benjamin gave a tired smile. 'Not of late,' he said. 'Not until we woke up here a few days ago.'

'You woke up here?'

'In the old war museum,' Wilhelm added. 'I mean, it looked interesting and all, but we were a little preoccupied, not having any memories or any idea of what was going on. Things have changed a little since then and we've begun figuring things out.'

'And what exactly have you figured out?'

Benjamin reached out and lightly touched the gramophone with the tip of his forefinger. A light hum began to emit from the speaker and the machine's body began to shake. He removed his finger, letting the machine go still, and looked up into Sebastien Aren's disbelieving eyes.

'My friend is just trying to keep us out of trouble,' he said, 'but, the more time that passes, the more certain I am that we might be Miscreants after all.'

9

MIRANDA

Her whole body hurt. She opened her eyes and looked up, and found she was back in Olin's house, lying under a pile of blankets, but instead of the room he had allocated her, she was in his own bedroom near the back.

'What's going on?'

Olin appeared in the doorway. He pulled hands from his pockets and rubbed his chin. 'Well, you're alive. That's good. The wards are stronger here. It'll keep them from smelling you.'

'Smelling me?'

Olin's face darkened. He appeared about to shout, then creased his mouth and looked away. When he looked back, his face had softened a little.

'What you did was stupid beyond words. Yes, I've gathered that you're a strong-willed young lady who doesn't like being held captive, but I assure you that was never my intention. I was only trying to protect you, and after your ridiculous and nearly deadly escape attempt, I hope you understand why.'

'I'm sorry.'

'Right, and so you should be.'

'Why didn't you tell me what was going on?'

'Because I wasn't sure myself. Since I found you I've been sounding out the reaction to you among the creatures of the woods. I've been trying to figure out how safe you are outside, with or without my protection. I told you, I'm a scientist.'

Miranda felt her cheeks burning. She didn't need Olin to tell her what a fool she had been now that the memories had come flooding back, but as others—those of the school and her friends—continued to swamp her, she knew her decision was one that soon needed to be repeated.

'I have to leave,' she said. 'I thought I could just walk away, but I was wrong. But I still have to leave. My friends need me.'

Olin nodded. 'I understand. To the ghouls, wraith-hounds, and others, though, you are like a source of fresh food. You'd barely make it a mile, even during daylight. It was only that I found you so soon that you avoided them. You need to learn to hide your magic. We're too close here to be safe.'

Miranda narrowed her eyes. 'How do you hide it?'

Olin shrugged. 'Years of practice.'

It was an excuse, and Miranda sensed it. Olin, who had seemingly lived alone all this time, wasn't adept at social situations. A lie had shone out of his words like a beaming torch.

'Tell me the truth.'

Olin turned away, but Miranda climbed up from the bed and hurried after him, catching up as he leaned over a table and began pulling vegetables forward, muttering under his breath.

'I can feel it,' she said.

Olin's frenetic movements stopped. 'Feel what?'

'At first I wondered what it was. Like a kind of shadow over everything. I thought it was coming from the background, from the Shifting Castle or all those monsters in the woods, but it's not. It's coming from you. The magic you're using … it's dark reanimate, isn't it?'

Olin shook his head. 'No.' He turned to face her, his eyes down, misery etched across his features. 'It's a taint,' he said, sighing. 'I was experimenting on ghouls, and one of them attacked me. Not just with its claws, but with magic. I didn't want the other teachers to find out, so rather than repel its attack, which is a natural reaction, I drew on its magic, thinking I could just throw it aside. It became part of me.'

He sat down on a stool and pulled up his trouser leg. Miranda gasped at the sight of pieces of metal, glass, and paper fused with Olin's skin.

'You see, I'm part given over to this world. Not a ghoul, nor a walker, but something else. You, Miranda, are from another world. I am part of Endinfinium now and more affected by its rules than others.' He sighed again. 'The teachers never trusted me, and it was the excuse they needed to cast me out. I wandered for years, my existence meaningless, until I arrived here. I thought to throw myself at the Dark Man's feet, but when I realised the creatures here saw me as no threat, I gained a renewed purpose in my life.'

Miranda nodded. 'They think you're one of them. You've been alone out here ever since?'

Olin's eyes took on a faraway look. 'Not always, but….' He shrugged. 'Long ago I shared my life with someone, but she left to pursue her own adventures. Anyway, that's a story for another day. I'm safe enough here. The creatures ignore me, leave me alone, sometimes even help me on occasion. I can walk among them undetected, although recently I've noticed changes. More activity, the departure of great war hosts. It's made me afraid for my safety.'

'I have to leave,' Miranda said. 'Come with me.'

Olin shook his head. 'I can't go back. I can't face them again. In my way, I'm happy here. But … I can help you.' He smiled. 'You only had to ask.'

∽

After what had happened before, Miranda felt nervous about straying too far from Olin as they walked through the forest, even though he had told her that while close to him she was protected by his ward. Back in the trees she saw huge shadows moving, but none came close.

Soon, they emerged from the woods onto grassland, rolling hills stretching away. The mountains rose in the background, but Olin took a path leading north that kept them to the valleys, out of sight of the Shifting Castle to the west.

'Where are we going?' Miranda asked, when Olin called a break in a stony hollow sheltered on three of four sides. 'We've been walking for hours.'

'I'm taking you to meet your guide,' Olin said. 'I have friends here, of a kind. People—or others—who can help you get back to Endinfinium High, if that's what you really want.'

After a short break they continued on, the grasslands flattening out until they came to a wide river that seemed to be coming in from east to west.

'It takes a circuitous route down from the northern mountains,' Olin said, by way of explanation. 'Eventually it joins with the Great Junk River, but this is the safest place I know of to cross.' Before Miranda could reply, Olin walked to the shoreline, absently kicking a rusting can back into the water. He spread his arms and called, 'Jacob, where are you?'

At first nothing happened, then something began to shift in the water. The current backed up, and Miranda found herself stepping backwards up the shingle shoreline to avoid her feet being soaked.

Something huge and red the length of a swimming pool rose out of the water. She at first thought it was a submerged fire engine, something she'd only seen in picture books. Then she realised that it *was* in fact a submerged fire engine, but was also something else entirely.

Football-sized eyes blinked at her and a wide mouth where the fire engine's cab would have been opened to reveal lumpy steel incisors.

'Good morning, Olin-friend,' a deep voice boomed. 'What sees you wandering this far north?'

Olin smiled. He turned to Miranda. 'I call him a fire-hippo,' he said. 'He's a reanimate, like those you've no doubt met at the school. Not everything this far west is controlled by the Dark Man. However, perhaps because of the hostility of some of the locals, reanimates here tend to keep themselves to themselves.'

'Olin-friend?' Jacob said. 'Who is this you've brought with you? Your daughter? Has it been that long?'

'No, no,' Olin said, sounding a little flustered. 'A young lady who's lost her way. I'm helping her to find her way back to Endinfinium High.'

'My name's Miranda,' Miranda said. 'Miranda Butterworth.'

'How pleased I am to make your acquaintance,' Jacob said. 'I'd offer to shake your hand, but mine are somewhat wet.'

Aware that whatever Jacob considered a hand was

likely to dwarf her entire body, Miranda just smiled. 'That's completely fine.'

'We need to get across the river,' Olin said. 'We're heading for Rilston Mead.'

'Certainly,' Jacob said. 'And when you see that messy old fool, give him my regards.'

Without another word, Jacob began to sink back down into the water. Miranda turned to Olin. 'Where's he going? I thought he was going to help us across.'

'Wait for it,' Olin said. 'You're about so see where he gets his name from.'

Jacob was completely submerged, but a silvery square had protruded from roughly where the centre of his back would have been. As Miranda watched, it opened out, unfolded and then extended until a silver fire engine's ladder crossed the entire stretch of the river, touching down on the now-receded shoreline on either side.

'Jacob's ladder,' Olin said with a sheepish grin. 'A bit of an in-joke. It's quiet in these parts until the Dark Man gets riled up. Right, over we go. Just don't look down.'

Even though the sluggish, rubbish-choked river looked no more than waist deep in the few sections where she could see through the rubbish to the bottom, crossing the ladder was not dissimilar to the terrifying rope bridge not far from the school. It bounced up and down with each step, sometimes low enough to splash the water, with only the area near Jacob's central ladder fixture offering any stability. It didn't help that as she tried to cross, Jacob appeared to start laughing, causing the ladder to bounce up and down, nearly throwing her off.

'He's not quite in his right mind,' Olin said, as he jumped down onto dry land and helped a nervous Miranda down after him. 'Although, for the reanimates, I've never been quite sure what a right mind should be.'

'Are there many of them around here?' Miranda said. 'He's enormous. He'd be useful in a battle with the Dark Man.'

'Reanimates are everywhere, if you know how to find them,' Olin said. 'But, they stay out of everything unless directly threatened. Endinfinium is their world. We and all the taints and spoils that we bring are the outsiders. They've found peace among themselves. They let us fight our wars alone.'

'But isn't the Dark Man a threat to them, too? I remember, they stood with us when the school was threatened.'

'That's because the school is their world,' Olin said. 'A threat to the school is a threat to their existence. But a threat only against the people … that is not their business. They care nothing for life and death. They are what they are, and they remember what they were, but they feel none of the emotions that drive every action we take.'

They took another rest, although Jacob, his need for conversation apparently exhausted, didn't join them. Miranda watched the languid flow of the river, the junk choking it slowly floating past, bobbing up and down like a nightmarish rubber duck race with no end.

'Where does it all come from?' she wondered, idly munching on a vegetable fritter Olin had handed to her.

'Somewhere else, where it's served its use,' Olin said. 'And here it gets to begin again … eventually.' With a sigh, he stood up. 'Come on. We're nearly there.'

'Where are we going?'

'You'll see in about fifteen minutes. Let's keep going. I want you on your way by the time the yellow sun goes down. In these days, who knows what might emerge after nightfall.'

Olin picked up his pace with Miranda trailing behind.

She still had many questions, but while Olin had no more answers than the teachers at the school had had, he was a little more willing to share them.

'There,' Olin said, giving Miranda a relieved grin as they crested the hill. 'He's still here.'

'Who?'

Miranda's eyes searched the valley below, but she saw only a grey shed with a gravel trail leading into its back end, the surrounding flatland littered with smaller junk, as though a storm had whipped off the river and deposited half its contents here.

'Rilston Mead,' Olin said. 'Let's go.'

No more enlightened than she had been before, Miranda followed Olin down the hill towards the shed. As they got closer, she realised it was much larger than she had first thought, more of a warehouse a couple of storeys tall, long enough to house a couple of buses parked end to end.

From inside came the hum of machinery, and by the time the shed's two shadows had fallen over them, Miranda realised that the gravel trail wasn't a gravel trail at all, but a small stream running down the hillside, one so clogged with shredded paper that it was barely recognisable as a stream at all.

Olin stopped outside two double doors. Above them was a curved iron sign which read:

RILSTON MEAD
COMMUNITY RECYCLING PLANT

'Excuse me?' Olin said. 'Mr. Mead, are you there?'

What Miranda had thought were two dirty windows as big as she was tall set into the walls to either side of the door suddenly blinked, throwing up a cloud of dust. Miranda was so stunned she took a step back.

The doors scythed back to form a mouth. 'Olin Brin. Long time no see. What do you want?'

'I came to ask you for help, Mr. Mead,' Olin said.

'How kind of you. Do I look like a charity?'

Miranda covered her mouth to suppress a sudden urge to laugh. Rilston Mead sounded like a grumpy old man.

'No, you look like a fine, friendly recycling plant,' Olin said. 'One that it is an honour to live within visiting distance of.'

'So of course you only visit when you want something.' Rilston's eyes rolled upwards, then he suddenly coughed, emitting through his doors a gust of dusty wind powerful enough to knock Olin and Miranda off their feet. 'I do apologise,' he said, as they got back up, 'but as I'm sure you're aware, I don't get much opportunity for conversation.'

'I'm sorry,' Olin said. 'I've been busy.'

'Doing what?'

'You know, the usual things.'

'Bah,' Rilston said. 'You've been avoiding me.'

'If by avoiding you, you mean not taking day-long treks north, then I suppose the answer's yes.'

'I knew it. Consider your request denied.' Rilston's eyes closed, and his mouth went still. He once more looked for all the world like a normal, regular warehouse.

'Excuse me, Rilston?'

'Call him Mr. Mead,' Olin hissed.

'Sorry, Mr. Mead? My name is Miranda Butterworth. It's very nice to meet you. Olin might not have said, but he's told me so much about you. I couldn't wait to meet you, and I've been telling him to hurry up the whole way, but you know, he's such a slowcoach….'

Rilston's eyes snapped open. 'And what did he say?'

'Um ... that you tell great jokes?'

Rilston's eyes bowed then creaked downwards in a mechanical frown. 'Did he now? What's a recycling plant's favorite breakfast cereal?'

'Um ... no idea.'

'Shredded Wheat.'

Miranda, who had only heard of it from listening to Benjamin talk about his home life, forced a laugh. Beside her, Olin gave a pained snicker.

'What did the plastic bottle say to the recycling plant?'

'Don't know.'

'Twice to meet you.'

Miranda pretended to double over with laughter. 'Please stop,' she said. 'I'll be sick in a minute.'

Olin wiped a tear that might have been genuine out of his eye. 'Miranda here wants to return to Endinfinium High, but she doesn't know the way. If you help her, you could tell her jokes the whole way there.'

'How delighted I'd be,' Miranda said, forcing a smile while at the same time wondering how this old grey building could help her.

'I'll think about it,' Rilston said. 'Go away and come back later.' His eyes closed and his mouth-door slid back across, as though the matter were already final.

Olin took Miranda's hand and together they retreated a little way up the hillside. 'Just give him a little time,' Olin said. 'He's a cantankerous old thing, but a lot of the reanimates are. Something about having their use rejected, I think. And for Rilston, it must have been worse than for most. An entire recycling plant, no longer wanted. Thrown away like the rubbish he used to sort.'

'He just floated down the river like the rest?'

Olin shrugged. 'I can only assume so. The rivers tend

to ebb and flow. He was probably dumped there by a flash flood. Or he walked there. I have no idea whether he has legs or not.'

Miranda looked around her. What she had first assumed were piles of trash were actually intricate models made out of papier-mâché. Some of them seemed to have life of their own, quietly fluttering despite the absence of wind, some shaking back and forth as though planning to take off into the air.

Olin pulled out his bag of vegetable fritters and handed one to Miranda. 'We'll give him a few minutes to think about it,' he said. 'He'll probably call us back over soon.'

'How are you expecting him to help me?' Miranda asked.

Olin gestured at the models surrounding them. 'He can make anything in a matter of minutes. I'm hoping he'll make you some kind of vehicle to take you back to the school. It would take you weeks to walk.'

'Perhaps I could try doing something for him?' Miranda said, an idea springing to mind. Before Olin could respond, she stood up and skipped down the hillside, poking among the plants and strange models for something that might help.

'What are you looking for?' Olin said, coming up behind her.

'I'll know it when I see it,' Miranda said. 'I think we have to go back to the river.'

Olin told Rilston that they were going for a short walk, but the recycling plant didn't respond. Back by the river, Miranda walked upstream from the shallows where Jacob lay submerged, scanning the bank for what she might need.

'Ah, here,' she said, triumphant, spotting a rusty metal

can poking out of the weeds. Whatever label it might have had was long gone, but she could see around the rim a telltale line of blue. She reached down and gently rocked it back and forth until the ground released it.

'Paint?' Olin asked.

'I thought Rilston might like to brighten up a bit,' Miranda said. 'It doesn't look like he has the means to do it for himself.'

'He won't let you paint him!'

Miranda planted her hands on her hips and pouted. 'We'll see about that.'

They arrived back a few minutes later. Rilston was still apparently dormant, the rustling of a few of his models the only movement in the valley.

Miranda turned to Olin. 'I need a favour,' she said.

'Sure?'

'Put a ward over me for a couple of minutes. I want to use a little magic.'

Olin looked a little uncomfortable, but shrugged and told her they were probably far enough north to be out of the Dark Man's immediate range.

'When I give the word,' Miranda said. 'We have to be quick, because I want to get this done before he wakes up.'

'I hope you know what you're doing,' Olin said. 'If he refuses to help you, it's a long walk to Endinfinium High.'

'You'd have to come then,' Miranda said, elbowing him in the side. 'Keep me safe.'

Olin muttered something under his breath about having bad knees. 'Okay,' he said. 'Ready when you are.'

Miranda looked down at the paint pot and exerted a little influence on the rusted-shut lid. It popped with a sharp crack, splashing her with rust fragments. Inside, as she had expected, the paint had dried hard. Miranda glanced at Rilston, checking he still slept. The old recycling plant didn't move. Miranda picked up the paint pot and carried it around Rilston's side, where she had seen a trickle of water—cleared of the paper waste which clogged the stream going in—exiting and pouring into a pipe that perhaps emerged at a river further downslope.

Push and pull.

Simple.

She pulled at the temperature of the air, drawing the heat, pushing it into the dried paint, melting it. She then looked at the draining water and pulled, drawing it upwards in a channel, mixing it with the paint and then directing it in a spray across Rilston's walls and roof.

It took less than ten minutes to cover Rilston in a rather fetching sky blue wash, which, set against his former grey colour, transformed him from a bland, old-fashioned warehouse into something which looked more like an art museum. Satisfied, Miranda stood back, nodding with satisfaction.

'You can wake him up now,' she said.

Olin walked back around the front with Miranda following. 'Um, Mr. Mead, are you still there?'

Rilston's eyes snapped open. He frowned at Olin then his eyes began to revolve. Miranda stared as Rilston's front end rose off the ground and began to elongate, as though he were actually a giant caterpillar, until he could twist his head around to look back down his length.

'What have you done to me?'

Miranda beamed. 'I gave you a makeover,' she said. 'You look fantastic. You're the prettiest recycling plant I've ever seen.'

Rilston twisted back around, dropping back down to the ground. Wide eyes stared at her. 'You really think so?'

'It's fantastic,' she said. 'I doubt there's a prettier reanimate in the whole of Endinfinium.'

'Really?'

'I've seen loads, and none of them compare to you.'

Rilston grinned at her then abruptly scowled again in the direction of Olin.

'I like your friend,' he said. 'You should keep better company.'

Olin shrugged. 'I usually don't keep any company.'

'That's my point.' Rilston's head twisted again, this time to loom over Miranda. 'How would you like me to help you, little girl?'

'I'd love some way to get back to Endinfinium High as quickly as possible,' Miranda said. 'I'd be very grateful if you were able to help.'

'My pleasure,' Rilston said, throwing a pointed look at Olin as he settled back into position. 'Just give me a moment.'

Mechanical clunking sounds came from inside the recycling plant. A whistle blew and a puff of smoke emitted from a chimney in the roof. Rilston coughed a couple of times, then shooed Miranda and Olin back a few steps.

'How do you expect me to work when you cramp me for room?' he grumbled. Then, his doors stretching into a wide grin, he said, 'Are you ready? I really think this could be my finest achievement.'

He settled back into his original shape. Then, with one final puff of smoke from the chimney, the machinery went quiet, and the faint hoot of pipe music began from somewhere inside. Miranda glanced at Olin, who shrugged.

The doors slid open wide, and a wooden transportation cart slid out. Balanced on top was an enormous, beautiful swan made from thousands of sheets of intricately folded paper.

Miranda glanced at Olin again. 'Not quite what I had in mind,' Olin said.

With a brief squawk as though to establish that it was in fact real, the swan gave its feathers a dramatic rustle then spread its wings wide. An elegantly curved head turned to Miranda, and a mournful, dreamlike voice said, 'Ready when you are, dear.'

10

SNOUT

'And you're in charge of the stationery closet,' Ms. Ito said to Snout, Fat Adam, and Tommy Cale at his shoulder. 'The worst offenders have already been moved, but what's left is deemed safe. I will be doing a thorough check when you're finished, and if I find anything has been fudged over, the three of you will be spending a night making up for it in the locker room. Am I clear?'

'Clear!' Snout said, as two voices echoed his own. Ms. Ito glared at each in turn, then turned and stumped off.

'Right,' Snout said. 'Let's get suited up.'

Waterproof boiler suits had been provided in a big plastic bucket, but in the ensuing free-for-all, Snout's team had been left with one over-large one, one tiny one, and one that had begun to reanimate, meaning it was already soaking wet on the inside. Manfully, he took that one, leaving Fat Adam to wear one that was still too big and Tommy one that was still too small. With zips only partway done up, they shouldered their chamomile canisters and approached their assignment.

'You boys can rock-scissors-paper for who goes left and right,' Snout said. 'I'll take the middle.'

'That's the central aisle!' Tommy whined. 'That's the easy bit. All that stuff's been cleared away.'

'It's where the stove heaters and chopping machines are,' Snout said. 'If there's any danger in here, I'm taking it for you. All you'll have to deal with is a few rolls of tape and the odd stapler.'

Adam and Tommy continued to grumble, but both accepted that a path fraught with the dangers of reanimated felt-tip pens and piles of rulers was better than choppers and shredders. Some of the more complex items had actually reanimated beyond the effects of chamomile spray, and had to be asked politely to perform their required function.

The closet was less a closet and more of a cavernous hall, although like most rooms in Endinfinium High, it was likely a far different size to when it had been originally labeled. Within a few steps Snout had lost his team among the stacks, and found himself surrounded by towering metal shelves loaded with all manner of office supplies, most of which he'd never seen used in any classes. He knew whole teams of cleaners were charged with recovering goods from the beaches and the shore of the Great Junk River, breaking open discarded filing cabinets and storage chests, removing whatever might be inside and drying or repairing it if necessary. The school had a policy that everything recovered might be needed at some point, so the stores were packed to the rafters just on the off chance that the supply ever dried up.

He turned a corner, and found a shredding machine had switched itself on and was shifting from side to side, trying to break free of a rope which tied it, wild dog-like, to a steel post.

The machine appeared to be growling. Snout pointed the nozzle of his chamomile sprayer and gave it a solid dousing. With a final grunt emitting from its shredding orifice, the machine went still. Snout took a deep breath. It always felt like he was killing them, but within a few days it would begin to shudder and shake, then, if left unattended, it would first make a nuisance of itself, and then, eventually, obtain full sentience.

And that was a big bucket of worms which he was glad, as a mere pupil, he didn't have to consider.

He reached the back of the room. Somewhere off to his left he heard Tommy gasp in fright, while behind him to the right the sound of Adam spraying drifted over the gentle background hum of items not yet treated with the chamomile calming agent. Still, it sounded like they were nearly done.

Snout turned, giving the back of the room a final look over. As his eyes fell over a filing cabinet at the back, he froze.

The door was open, a shimmering figure standing inside.

Snout let out a croaking gasp, which sounded like the wheeze from an old set of bellows as the figure shifted.

It was most likely a girl, or perhaps a boy with scraggly long hair. The pale skin of arms and legs showed through ragged clothing.

Eyes opened, shining green.

One arm lifted.

'Come,' came a rasping voice which might or might not have been inside his head.

Snout gasped again and staggered back, bumping into the stack behind. A box of crayons fell from a top shelf, took a glancing blow off his forehead and scattered across the floor. His eyes involuntarily followed them, and when he looked up, the filing cabinet door was closed, the figure gone.

'Simon? Are you all right? What happened?' said a voice to his right, and Snout let out a whimpering cry. Fat Adam stepped out of the stacks, chamomile sprayer held over his shoulder like a spear. 'What's the matter? You look like you've seen a ghoul.'

Snout couldn't bring himself to speak. He pointed at the filing cabinet.

'What? In there? Let's have a look.'

Before Snout could stop him, Fat Adam marched up to the filing cabinet and flung open the door.

A pair of coats swung from a rail in front of a dusty mirror at the back. Adam gave one of the coats a tug so it slipped off its hangar, then turned to Snout and held it up.

'Woo!' he said.

'Shut up,' Snout croaked. 'That's not what I saw.'

'What did you see?'

'A girl. Or maybe a boy. She or he spoke.'

'What did she or he say?'

'"Come."'

'Is that all?'

'Then I got distracted. When I looked back, the door was shut.'

Fat Adam shrugged and stuffed the jacket back into filing cabinet, not bothering to put it back on the hangar. For a moment Snout stared at his reflection in the dusty mirror, then Adam shut the door.

'You're just spooked,' Fat Adam said. 'Come on, let's go find Tommy and get out of here. My side's done. What about you? You had the easy bit. All the big stuff.'

'Done.'

'All right?' came Tommy's reedy voice. 'Got a couple of pen racks doing a dance over here. Come take a look before I squirt them.'

Fat Adam shrugged and moved off. Snout stayed behind, staring at the filing cabinet for a long time.

∼

Snout thought about reporting what he had seen to Ms. Ito, but his irascible form teacher was about as approachable as an active volcano, so he waited a few days until his next earth sciences class with Professor Caspian. Snout, who always seemed to be the last pupil to leave every class, hung back a little longer than usual until the other kids had filed out, then made a point of meeting Professor Caspian's eye.

'Sir ... do you have a minute?'

'What's up, Simon?' Professor Caspian said, coming through the desks towards him. 'You looked a little preoccupied today. I expect it from most of this lot, but not so much from you.'

Snout grimaced. 'I, um, think I'm seeing things.'

Professor Caspian spread his hands. 'This is Endinfinium. You probably are.'

'Scary things.'

Professor Caspian frowned. 'Like what?'

'I saw a girl. Or it might have been a boy. She had green eyes. She was in a mirror, or she might have been a coat hanging in front of the mirror. She asked me to come.'

'Where?'

'In a filing cabinet in the stationery room. But when we opened it, there was nothing there. Just a couple of coats and the mirror. I think I'm going mad.'

'Have you seen her since?'

Snout shook his head. 'No.'

'I'll take a look in the stationery room. If you see her again, let me know. After what happened a few weeks ago, it's likely there's been some lingering effect left on the school. It's important that we root it out and remove it, for our own safety. You know you're supposed to report anything untoward to your form teacher, don't you?'

'My form teacher is Ms. Ito.'

Professor Caspian chuckled. 'Okay, I see your point. Come and tell me instead.'

'Okay, sir, I will.'

Professor Caspian gave Snout a pat on the shoulder, then wished him the best for his next class period. Snout hurried out, aware he was late for Captain Roche's P.E. class. Today's activity was sand running, something Snout neither enjoyed nor saw the point to. Neither could he see why it would ever be of much use to any of them, considering there was only one sandy beach within half a day's walk, and the effort it took to reach it—a perilous descent down a narrow and rocky cliff path—meant that few people would have the energy left to run across the sand once there.

The class, a mixture of first and second year pupils, had to meet outside the main school entrance at ten thirty. Snout had already used up five minutes of the fifteen minute break talking to Professor Caspian, and now had the vastness of the school to negotiate in only ten minutes, or risk being allocated yet another arbitrary trip to the locker room. His hands were still sore from completing Ms. Ito's opening punishment the evening before, and if he went down there again so soon, he might as well put his name over one of the locker room doors.

He was nearly there when he turned a corner and ran straight into Godfrey.

A puff of something that wasn't Godfrey's scrawny chest sent Snout sprawling to the ground. He looked up into Godfrey's green, snake-like eyes, and felt a momentary flutter of panic.

They had been mates once, but not anymore.

'Oh, didn't see you there,' Godfrey said. 'Where are you off to in such a hurry? Not late for class are you, pig-boy?'

'I just had to talk to a teacher for a moment,' Snout said, not risking trying to stand up, afraid Godfrey might just employ his magic again. It was a known secret that of the three common forms of magic use, only Benjamin Forrest and Godfrey were known to possess the strongest type. While the teachers now acknowledged it and taught some aspects of the nature of Endinfinium's power in class, they didn't openly teach its use nor encourage it, and using magic in any way within the school or for the harm of others was utterly and comprehensively prohibited. If the teachers found out what Godfrey had done, he'd be in the locker room for months, if not expelled. Unfortunately, it was his word against Snout's, and only one of them was the head prefect. The other was a boy who was facing his second punishment already, on only the second day of term.

'I'm afraid I need to get going,' Snout said, but still made no move to pick himself up. Godfrey stared down at him, green eyes narrowed, a sneer on his unpleasant face.

'My society is recruiting,' he said. 'I'm sure you'd make a good member.'

'What society is that?'

'The Dark Reanimation Society. It's getting popular, you know.'

Snout frowned. Once kept secret, Godfrey's appreciation society had now been accepted under the patronage of the sinister Professor James 'Dusty' Eaves. Officially, all they did was talk about ghouls and other creepy things that had been seen in the forests or described in school history books, drawing pictures or acting out stage plays, but Snout suspected otherwise. There were rumours that Godfrey wanted to learn the use of the darker side of the magic that permeated everything in Endinfinium, but no one was brave enough to openly accuse him.

'I'm busy,' he said, giving a shrug. 'I'm running the Board Game Club this term, and the Horticulture Society. I'm also president of the Comic Book Club and the Traffic Cone Appreciation Society, so I don't have much free time.'

Godfrey lifted an eyebrow. 'Isn't that because you spend half your time in the locker room? You know, pig-boy, I could have you sent there any time I like. I'm head prefect now. I have the teachers in my pocket.'

While Snout couldn't imagine Ms. Ito ever being in anyone's pocket, Godfrey was never to be underestimated. Making an enemy of the most powerful boy in the school —particularly now that his only rival, Benjamin Forrest, had disappeared—was foolhardy.

'I'll think about it,' he said.

Godfrey made a point of stepping over him, letting rip with a loud guff as he did so. Snout held his breath, hoping the smell of sour beans and rotten carrots wouldn't linger too long.

'I look forward to seeing you there,' Godfrey said. 'Bye-bye, pig-boy.'

Snout waited until Godfrey had disappeared around a corner, then frantically jumped to his feet, flapping a hand in front of his face, certain Godfrey had used a little more of his magic to keep the stench from dissipating. As he hurried for the school's main entrance, Snout wished he had the guts to stand up for himself. Without Benjamin around to keep him in check, and the teachers seemingly oblivious to his actions, Godfrey was getting out of control.

11

BENJAMIN

Sebastien Aren didn't look convinced. He looked from Benjamin to Wilhelm and back again, lowering his glasses, then lifting them back up.

'Are you sure I haven't seen you somewhere before?' he said.

'Not yet—' Benjamin began, but Wilhelm put a hand on his shoulder to cut him off.

'Probably on wanted posters,' he said. 'We're everywhere. We're the most daring Miscreants in the land.'

Sebastien chuckled. 'And the most fanciful, I dare say. Is there some reason you're telling me this without fear of my notifying the authorities? After all, we barely know each other.'

'We know you,' Wilhelm said. 'You're famous.'

Sebastien lifted an eyebrow. 'Along the length of this street, perhaps, but only for my eccentricity. So what is it exactly that you want me to do for you?'

'We need help.'

'What kind of help?'

Benjamin glanced at Wilhelm. 'This will probably

sound like we're making it up, but … we came here from another world.'

Sebastien began to laugh. 'You're right. It does sound like you're making it up. However, I was young once. I remember what it was like. And, it's true, the world has become so strange over the last fifteen or twenty years that I could almost believe such a thing existed.'

'We're not making it up,' Wilhelm said. 'It's true.'

Sebastien smiled. 'Well, despite seeing obvious signs that yes, indeed, you could be Miscreants, I remain unconvinced of the existence of this other world.'

'We blew up a refrigerator filled with trapped human souls, then flew over the edge of the world in a reanimated biplane, blacked out for a bit and woke up here in Basingstoke. Which is where Benjamin here came from in the first place, although at some point in the past.' Wilhelm gave a stern nod and then folded his arms, as though his summary was all that was needed.

Sebastien frowned. 'Okay, so let's assume that every word of what you just said is true. Trying to carry the burden of all of that must be a little confusing, don't you agree? You need to compartmentalise a little, manage your tasks. What is it exactly that you are trying to achieve at the current moment? In particular in relation to showing up and making a nuisance of yourselves in my shop?'

Benjamin sighed. 'I'm from Basingstoke,' he said. 'When I recognised where we had woken up, I went to find my family. However, my house is gone, replaced by a children's playground. My old neighbour said my family had died in an accident.'

'Well, I'm very sorry to hear that.' Sebastien gave him a grandfatherly pat on the shoulder. 'I don't suppose you could tell me your family's surname?'

'Forrest,' Benjamin said. 'My name is Benjamin

Forrest. My brother's name was David.' He frowned. 'My mother ... that lady said her name was Jennifer. But my dad ... I don't remember.'

Sebastien lifted one eyebrow, and then abruptly stood up.

'I'm just an old antiques dealer,' he said. 'If you want something, you really only have to ask. No need to create elaborate schemes and lies to steal from me.' He glanced up at the mirrors. 'Is there another of you, hiding out somewhere, filling his pockets with toys while you spin me this web of rubbish? Honestly, sometimes I think it would be a good thing if those rubbish collectors took people—'

'We're not lying!' Benjamin shouted, loud enough to make a cut-glass chandelier overhead tremble with a sound like water rushing over seashore shingle.

Sebastien glared at him. 'I find it very hard to believe that. You come in here, throw me some cock and bull story about another world, claim you're Benjamin Forrest ... I'm sorry, but it all sounds a bit too far-fetched for me to believe.'

Benjamin turned to Wilhelm. 'Come on, let's get out of here—' he began, just as the shop door banged. Wilhelm, not looking at him, ran to the window and peered out. After a moment he turned back, expectation in his eyes.

'Did you see him?' Wilhelm asked.

'See who?'

'That kid we saved from the dog-catchers. He was right there, peering through a crack in the door. He must have been following us.'

The two boys looked at each other. 'Do you think he'll call them?' Benjamin said.

'Don't be stupid. We saved him, didn't we? He's probably keeping close in case they come after him again. I think we're in real danger, Benjamin.'

Sebastien Aren was running a hand through the longer strands of hair crossing his scalp, his face pained. 'What's this about saving a boy from the dog-catchers?' he said, suppressing a sigh. 'Come on, enlighten me with some other fanciful story.'

'We saw a boy getting caught,' Benjamin said. 'We freed him.'

'Benjamin turned their van into a giant bug,' Wilhelm said, chest puffing with pride. 'Then later we trapped them under a climbing frame we turned into a net. I helped with that.'

'Wilhelm's a Weaver,' Benjamin explained, to Sebastien's stunned expression. 'He can't use magic on his own, but if he's close to a Summoner or a Channeller, he can amplify their power.'

'Right….'

'The kid we freed, he ran off, but I suppose he's been following us around the last few hours.'

Sebastien shook his head. 'I don't think I've ever heard so much rubbish in my life, but there's one way to find out.' He turned and headed into a back room behind the till. 'Come on,' he said. 'You might as well make yourselves at home. Let's see what the local news has to say.'

He waved them to an old leather sofa then switched on an old cathode rod TV, adjusting an aerial at the back to pick up a signal. 'Never trusted these modern ones,' he said, as way of explanation. 'They track everything you watch, don't you know? I had to make a few adjustments to be off the radar, but it seems to work.'

A picture appeared in grainy colour of a newscaster. Sebastien waited patiently through a report on a local dam restoration project before the local news headlines came back on again. First up was a dull feature on the town's new mayor, but as the picture changed to one of a crashed dog-catcher's van lying on its side, Wilhelm and Benjamin sat up.

'People are warned to be on the lookout for two boys seen in the local area who have exhibited tendencies of extreme vandalism,' said the announcer. 'Both are considered highly dangerous and should not be approached.'

'A bit late for that,' Sebastien muttered.

'One is described as being mop-haired and is approximately five feet seven inches tall. The other, slightly shorter, was described by witnesses as "mousy."'

'What kind of description is that?' Wilhelm said.

'At least you're not mop-haired,' Benjamin said. 'Not like we're in any position to get a haircut, are we?'

'Any sightings should be immediately reported and the boys should not be approached,' the announcer continued, as the view changed to one of a wrecked play area where a team with cutting saws was hacking its way through a distorted climbing frame. Two men sitting inside were wrapped in grey blankets as though recently rescued from a flooded cave.

The scene changed, a sports logo appearing on the screen. Sebastien switched off the TV and turned to the boys.

'Well, it does appear to be true that you're highly dangerous vandals, although on the surface you don't look it. However, I'm still a little confused here. Firstly, you can't be Benjamin Forrest.'

'But—'

'We made the names up!' Wilhelm said suddenly, cutting him off. 'Look, the truth is, we don't remember our real names, but when we woke up in the museum, we chose the first names we saw.'

'And one of them was Benjamin Forrest?'

Benjamin glanced at Wilhelm, whose flared eyes suggested it was a ploy to buy them some time.

'Um, yeah, I saw the name written on something. A local history display. Benjamin Forrest of Basingstoke. I don't remember why he was famous.'

Sebastien Aren rolled his eyes again, but appeared to relax at this new explanation. 'If you stick around long enough, you'll find out.' He turned to Wilhelm. 'What about you?'

'Same. Didn't like the surnames so picked Wilhelm and Jacob. Added an S because no one trusts a man with two first names, do they?'

'But that S makes you highly trustworthy?'

Wilhelm grinned. 'Don't I look it?'

Sebastien lifted an eyebrow. 'Absolutely. So, they're made-up names. I must say, while that raises more questions, it does make me a little relieved. So, I'm dealing with two nameless runaways.'

'We're not runaways,' Benjamin said.

'You came from another world, wasn't that it?' Sebastien appeared to be fighting down laughter. 'I mean, you boys have some tales, that's for sure. I live such a dull life, I should be enjoying every minute of this ridiculous charade.'

'So will you help us?'

Sebastien spread his arms. 'Help you to do what exactly? Isn't that what I've been trying to establish?'

'Not get caught.'

'You know, I'm just a simple antiques dealer.'

'And we're just kids. We didn't do anything wrong.'

Sebastien sighed. 'All right. You can stay here for a couple of days. I have a guest bedroom upstairs which you can share. We need to keep an eye out for your little follower, though. I don't think he's dangerous, but he might attract attention. In the meantime, I think it might be a good idea to get out of this stuffy old shop for a while. Do you boys fancy a little fresh air?'

'Where?'

Sebastien smiled. 'My favourite place. The town dump.'

12

MIRANDA

THE GIANT SWAN PREENED ITS FEATHERS LIKE A PLANE getting ready for flight. Miranda eyed it warily, wondering how she would cope with flying. Olin shrugged and smiled.

'Not quite what I had in mind,' he said.

The swan, apparently finished, tilted its perfectly moulded face in Miranda's direction. 'Ready when you are, dear,' it said. Beyond the rustling texture of its voice was a soothing, grandmotherly tone. 'I will take you wherever you wish to go.'

Miranda turned to Olin. 'Thank you for everything,' she said. 'And I'm sorry I was such a terrible house guest.'

Olin laughed. 'You're young. What can I say? One day you'll be an old relic like me. At least you will if you keep yourself out of trouble.' He wrapped her up in a mammoth, bearlike hug. 'And when you get back to the school, give my regards to a man called Cleat, if he's still there.'

'Cleat! He was the librarian. Quite a, um, character.'

Olin smiled. 'That's the one. Enjoyed many a game of chess down in the bowels of that grey old place. Let him know I'm doing well, and that I think about him from time to time.'

'Will do.'

'Now, my girl, you get out of here before it rains. I don't think that bird will last too well in a thunderstorm.'

'I'm a swan, dear,' the bird said. 'The queen of all birds.'

'I don't doubt it. Look after Miranda, won't you? I've grown quite fond of her.'

'She will be perfectly safe,' the swan said, turning up her nose as though to suggest otherwise was a terrible affront.

Miranda approached the bird. Only close up did she notice that the swan was fitted with a papier-mâché saddle and harness.

'You'll be fine, dear,' the swan said. 'In the unlikely event that you fall, my speed and agility mean I would safely be able to swoop and interrupt your downward trajectory before you struck the ground, unless you are low enough in any case that it would not hurt.'

Miranda gave a pained smile, wondering how much a bird that had only come into existence a few moments ago knew about the laws of aerodynamics.

'Do you have a name?' she asked.

The bird preened its feathers. 'I belong to you,' she said. 'It is up to you to choose an appropriate one. Be aware, however, that I possesses a certain level of pride, and something rather … ridiculous … might have a negative effect on our ongoing relationship.'

Miranda smiled. In her pocket the little plastic rhino was charging about as though to remind her that she already had a pet, but this … this was different.

'Enchantress,' she said. 'Your name is Enchantress.'

The swan's feathers ruffled with pleasure. 'You have chosen well. Now, we must be going.'

Olin came forward to help Miranda climb aboard. Safely in position, she thanked him one last time, then waved goodbye. Enchantress lifted her huge wings and they sprang up into the sky, Olin and Rilston Mead shrinking rapidly below her. A landscape that she had only ever seen in peaks and troughs spread itself out like a tapestry.

'How high would you like to go, dear?' Enchantress asked, craning her head to look at Miranda out of one eye. 'I'm quite sure I could fly as high as the suns, but that might worry you a little.'

Miranda had been so fascinated by the landscape below that she hadn't given a thought to being scared. She suddenly realised how high she was, with only a papier-mâché bird between her and a long, terrifying drop.

'I think we're probably high enough,' she gasped.

Enchantress made a little sound in her throat Miranda assumed was a chuckle. 'That's quite all right, dear. In which direction would you like me to fly?'

Careful not to let go of her harness, Miranda looked around her. Behind was a dark green carpet of forest lifting and falling with the undulation of the land until it vanished into a foggy haze. In front, hilly grassland stretched as far as she could see, empty and open, occasionally traversed by herds of moving creatures that could have been running horses or deer, or whatever version Endinfinium had created. To her left, in the far distance, rocky spires rose out of the fog, marking that direction as east. Olin had brought them someway north, so Miranda gave the reins on her right a little tug.

'We should go back that way, I think,' she said. 'Back the way we came, then west, to the coast.'

'You're in charge, dear,' Enchantress said, spreading

her wings and gliding in a graceful arc that spun the world around beneath them. 'Wherever you wish to go, it is my utmost pleasure to take you there.'

∽

It felt like they were moving a lot quicker than they were, with the wind whipping into her face, but below them the ground crept past as Enchantress made her languid way south. With Rilston Mead, Olin, and Jacob's river far behind them, the ground below was a tapestry of forest interspersed with occasional outcrops and cracked by rivers. Miranda had never seen so much world at one time in her entire life, and found herself entranced by the scene below, leaning over so much that on occasion Enchantress would nudge her back into her seat, offer a chuckle, and then say, 'Careful not to fall out, dear. Those trees look a lot softer than I expect they are.'

Miranda shifted back into her seat, but then noticed something below which made her grin with excitement.

'I think that's Olin's vegetable garden,' she said, pointing at a square cut out of the surrounding trees. While she couldn't see the plants themselves at this distance, lines of dug earth were clearly visible.

'I imagine the sight of vegetables must be making you hungry, dear,' Enchantress said. 'If you see an appropriate spot for lunch, please let me know and I'll set us down.'

Miranda hadn't thought about it, but now that she did, her stomach was beginning to ache. She hadn't eaten anything since Olin's vegetable fritters earlier in the day, and had neglected to bring anything with her. While the idea of setting down in Olin's vegetable garden filled her with nerves, she remembered an orchard of fruit trees he had once shown her a little further inland where the apples always seemed to be ripe. She instructed Enchantress to fly lower, until she caught sight of the orchard ahead of them.

'I'm sure he won't mind,' she said, half to herself, as Enchantress set them down.

It felt strange to be back on solid ground. Miranda's legs had turned to jelly and she had to lean on Enchantress's back for a couple of minutes until she felt capable of walking. The fruit trees were nearby, some apples and pears, and one of a strange hybrid halfway between an orange and a banana which Olin often used in his fritters. She picked a couple of each, careful only to choose smaller ones that Olin wouldn't miss, then tucked them into her shirt.

'Let's get going,' she said, climbing back on, eyeing the tree line beyond the orchard with suspicion, as though an army of tar-bears might come rushing out. As Enchantress rose gently into the air, her fear slowly dissolved, and soon they were circling high again, the forest reduced to a child's play mat.

'Where next, dear?' Enchantress asked.

'I suppose we should head for the coast,' Miranda said, but even as she said it, she felt an opportunity had presented itself, one that she might never have again. She glanced west at the mountains mostly covered in fog, only a few distant peaks poking up into the clear sky.

It was foolhardy, surely ... but when would she ever get another chance?

She remembered the lightning striking the hillside so close to her. But the sky was clear now, not a cloud to be seen. And the Dark Man wouldn't be looking for her in the sky. Enchantress was a reanimate, and as long as Miranda didn't use her magic, she wouldn't be noticed.

'Can you go a little higher?' she asked. 'Higher than those mountaintops?'

'Of course, dear, although you might want to brace yourself for the cold. Do you have anything thicker to wear? And we're likely to experience a little more crosswind than you're used to. Do you have a specific place in mind?'

'I'd like to have a look at the Shifting Castle,' Miranda said. 'It's to the west, in a crack in those mountains. We'd better not go too close, but I'd like to just see it clearly.'

'It sounds intriguing,' Enchantress said, reminding Miranda that the swan had only come into being a few hours before and was unaware of the potential danger.

'Just be careful,' Miranda said. 'It's where the Dark Man lives. It's dangerous. We mustn't go too close.'

'Certainly. You say the word and we'll turn tail to the east.' Enchantress's lilting voice sounded full of the spirit of adventure.

They headed for the fog bank, Enchantress slowly gaining height to fly over the top. Beneath them, the ground turned white, as though they flew over a frozen lake, punctuated only by the occasional island of outcrops. The air began to turn cold, the wind to increase in strength, whipping Miranda's hair so violently that she bunched it up behind her head and stuffed it down the back of her sweater.

Enchantress, seemingly unconcerned by the weather's increasing aggressiveness, implored Miranda to hold on tight while she spread her wings wide and plumed her tail feathers to balance their flight path. Foothills began to appear out of the fogbank below them. Then, in a sudden rush like a racehorse clearing a fence, they were past it, the wide expanse of a river valley spreading out below, banked on the far side by pyramidal foothills rapidly rising into at first forested, then bare rock mountains, their peaks hung with cones of snow. Miranda baulked at the sight of a bank of thunderclouds far back into the mountains, creating a grey, impassible wall. She looked at Enchantress's face, wondering whether to order the swan to turn back, but the bird appeared unconcerned.

'Oh, is that what you're looking for?'

Enchantress's head tilted as though to indicate where Miranda should look. At first she saw nothing in the shadows among the mountains. Then, what she had thought was an outcrop moved, and the Shifting Castle revealed itself.

Stood on a plateau cast in permanent shadow by the looming peak overhead, its dark grey blended into the rocky cliffs behind it with only a few of the highest towers catching any sunlight. It faced east, and even from this distance, Miranda could tell its sheer size dwarfed Endinfinium High.

Its size, however, was the only thing she could be sure about the Shifting Castle, because it was living up to its name. Every time she blinked, part of the castle changed places. Like an evolving steam engine, no tower, gallery, battlement or parapet was ever in the same place for more than a couple of minutes. Some rose up or down, or slid from side to side like pistons and gears, while others would deconstruct or build themselves right before her eyes, one lump of stone at a time.

'What a strange place that appears to be,' Enchantress said, glancing over her shoulder at Miranda. 'Would you like me to go a little closer?'

Miranda wanted to shake her head and tell Enchantress to turn back, but a funny feeling had come over her, a sense of ease, as though there was nothing to fear at all from the Shifting Castle, and that it was no different from any of the other oddities she had encountered.

'Yes, just a little closer,' she murmured, not really recognising the voice as her own. 'It won't hurt, will it?'

'As you wish,' Enchantress said, dropping them into a languid, swooping dive that arced around the mountainous wall in which the castle was situated. Miranda felt dizzyingly happy as they came closer, the immense, shifting blocks of stone, pallets of wood, walls of glass and towers made of materials she had never before seen all growing in her vision until the castle filled the sky.

'Should we attempt to land, dear?' Enchantress said.

'Yes ... land ... good idea....'

'Oh, that's not nice.'

Miranda shook her head, feeling the breaking of a trance at Enchantress's words. She summoned her magic and pushed outwards, feeling a tingle at the outer edges as though for a while something else had taken control of her.

'What happened?'

Enchantress was looking up at the sky. 'Rain,' she said. 'I'm afraid that somewhat disagrees with me.'

'Rain? But it's a clear sky—'

A huge black oval shape appeared over the castle's uppermost towers. The hum of engines filled the air, and a fine, mist-like spray fell across them. Miranda wiped a hand across her face and it came away with dirty water.

'What was that?'

'I believe we're under attack.'

Miranda gasped. The shape was almost above them now, as long as some of the beaches around Endinfinium high, as bloated as a whale. An airship. She had seen one in a picture book back at the school. Filled with gas and powered by a propeller, they had become popular before aeroplanes took over the skies.

As the airship moved in front of the yellow sun, Miranda felt a huge downward gust of air as it turned in their direction. Unlike conventional airships, this one had massive underside flippers beating at the air, keeping it airborne.

'Fly, Enchantress, fly!' she screamed, as another burst of spray peppered across them. In front of her, black spots on Enchantress's papier-mâché feathers began to swell up into small baubles. Miranda ran her fingers over them, feeling the dampness, seeing shreds of paper come away beneath her fingertips.

The great swan wheeled around, huge wings flapping. Behind them lumbered the monstrous airship, its outer hull black but with an orange tint as though a fire burned inside it. Its huge flippers flapped at the air, allowing it to bounce along in their wake, while cannons fitted into its underside cabin sprayed them with water.

'We have to go higher,' Miranda shouted. 'We have to get above it.'

Enchantress, still seemingly unconcerned, looked back at Miranda and nodded. 'I'll try, dear,' she said, her voice almost lost over the growling wind.

They went into a steep ascent. Miranda clung like a barnacle to the harness as it went taut around Enchantress's body. The wind was getting stronger, buffeting Miranda back and forth. Her hair came free from where she had pushed it, the wind whipping it around her face, but she didn't dare let go with one hand to stuff it back inside her sweater again.

As Enchantress leveled out enough for Miranda to slip safely back into the seat, she glanced behind her. The airship was some way back now. It still pursued them but without their maneuverability, it was struggling to keep them in range. Miranda patted Enchantress on the back, whooping with joy.

'You did it!'

'Maybe, dear. Don't get excited just yet.'

Miranda frowned. Enchantress was continuing to fly, but feathers were coming loose from the ends of her wings and fluttering away behind them.

'Enchantress, are your wings wet?'

'Only a little. Nothing to worry about, dear. Not just yet.'

'What does that mean?'

'Well, it might be wise to find somewhere to land and dry out a while.'

Miranda was about to reply, when they suddenly lurched. A great handful of feathers broke off Enchantress's left wing and nearly struck Miranda in the face as they broke apart.

'Head straight down,' Miranda said, heart beating fast. 'Head back into the fog. We can lose the airship there.'

'Them, dear. Lose *them*.'

Miranda looked back. Three other airships had appeared behind the first, spreading out to form a line in front of the mountains. To her dismay, two of them had rooftop cabins which bristled with water cannons, meaning they could now attack from both below and above.

'I'm sorry, Enchantress,' Miranda cried, angrily wiping away tears. 'I never should have suggested we go to look at the castle.'

'Quite all right, dear,' the swan said. 'I am at your beck and call, day and night.'

'Down!' Miranda said. 'As fast as you can. Into that fog, where we'll lose them.'

'As you wish, dear.'

Enchantress began a long, sweeping descent that made Miranda's stomach lurch and her face ache from the chilling wind. The airships kept coming on, propelled by their immense flippers that made them look like giant turtles with headless, oval bodies. Spreading out, they looked to cut off Enchantress's path to north and south, shepherding her away from the mountains.

As the mountains fell away behind them, the fog closing in, Miranda lost all track of direction and distance. Enchantress sailed on, huge wings still beating with peaceful ease as though enjoying a Sunday stroll, but now they were pocked with holes and baubles where the water had damaged them, and as they swooped through the fog, Miranda wiped condensation off her brow and realised she had made another mistake.

In front of her, paper began to peel away from Enchantress's neck, rolling up and dropping away into the whiteness below. Miranda, desperate, felt for her power, and then released it. What could she possibly do to help the giant bird?

Above came the drone of huge flippers, the downdraft swirling the mists around them. If they headed up, they would surely be caught. Miranda doubted her power would do much against the four giant reanimates.

'Oh, this fog, dear, it's so difficult to see. Perhaps you should take a nap until we find somewhere with a better view?'

Miranda leaned forward, an idea slowly forming. 'Enchantress, I'm going to make us a path. Fly into it as quick as you can, then as soon as we reach clear air, find somewhere on the ground to hide out of sight of the airships.'

'Certainly, dear, your wish is my command.'

Push and pull. Miranda concentrated, imagining herself reaching into the fog and pushing the very air itself. It swirled in front of them, then suddenly a misty tube appeared. At first it was indistinct. Then, at the far end, Miranda spied a patch of green.

'Go, Enchantress!'

The swan beat her wings, propelling them forward. They swooped through the fog tunnel, breaking out into bright sunshine. Miranda grimaced as they soared so close to the ground she could have reached out and touched it. She glanced back once and saw the shadow of a massive airship moving through the fog, and then she was hanging on for all she was worth as Enchantress swooped and dived through a patch of hilly grassland punctuated by towering rock stacks. As they approached a larger one, Miranda spotted a dark opening at its base.

'There!' she shouted. 'A cave! That's it, Enchantress! Go!'

The bird swooped low, hovering just a few feet above the grass. They were halfway there, when the bird suddenly jerked left, knocking Miranda sideways out of the saddle. As she hung on to the reins with one hand, she saw the end of Enchantress's left wing lying in the grass behind them.

'I beg your pardon, dear,' Enchantress said. 'That was rather unfortunate.'

Miranda opened her mouth to reply, but it was too late. The thickly twisted paper of the reins snapped beneath her fingers, and she tumbled to the ground. Thick grass cushioned her, but something hard struck her head and everything went black.

13

SNOUT

'Let me in!'

Inside the door, Derek Bates, Godfrey's chief cohort-in-crime, was laughing, face pressed against the glass. Snout shook the door handle then pounded on the door, but Derek just stuck out a tongue and began to laugh again.

'Don't worry, pig-boy, the Scatlocks will help you. Oh? Is that them coming now?'

Snout backed away from the door, peering over the edge of the precipice at the beach far below. There was certainly a rustle of movement from the cliffs, but whether the Scatlocks, those pesky reanimated plastic bags with the cumulative power to knock a boy off the narrow path that led over to the dormitories, would take to flight, he couldn't tell.

He glanced back across the path, wondering whether to just run back to the dormitory and give up on dinner. It was true he was late, but that was because he'd been organising his sock drawer by colour code and had gotten a little excited by the blend of colours he was creating. He hadn't even heard the dinner bell.

'Bye-bye,' Derek said, turning and running off down the corridor.

Snout glanced down at the cliff face below. It wasn't quite sheer, but it was close enough. While he had known no one personally who had fallen to their death, there were a dozen tales that went around the dorms of kids who had gotten locked out at night, kids who were never seen again, kids who showed up years later as mindless cleaners.

'Help!' he shouted, banging on the door again.

As a rustle like a thousand paper kites blowing in the wind came from below, Snout realised his mistake.

He had woken them up.

The Scatlocks broke away from the cliff face in a sudden wall of flapping white-and-silver. Snout dived for the path as he'd been taught in emergency drills, lying as flat as he could, covering his face with his hands. While the Scatlocks weren't antagonistic like the nocturnal Haulocks, their larger refuse sack cousins, their chief danger was their sheer number. Snout squeezed his eyes shut as the world became a chaos of rustling plastic.

Then, almost as soon as it had come, it had gone, and someone was tapping on the glass.

Snout lifted his head, expecting to see Derek's laughing face. Instead, Ms. Ito was glaring through the glass, her pointed nose bending against it, her breath covering it in steam.

The door opened and Ms. Ito's head peeked through, seemingly extending from her body as though she were part human, part witch, part giraffe.

'What on all Endinfinium do you think you were doing? Fool boy. Get inside at once. Much as it wouldn't bother me to see you fall off, I don't want my perfect dinner monitor duty blemished. Stop playing the idiot and get inside.'

'The door was locked, miss,' Snout mumbled.

'Cat got your tongue? Swallowed it and coughed it back up? Speak up!'

'The door was locked!' Snout shouted, his voice cracking into a girly high-pitched sound he'd found commonly happening of late. The school nurse said it was due to 'changes,' but none of the other boys seemed to be talking in a voice which switched between girl and cheese grater mid-sentence.

'Locked? Don't be ridiculous. Do I look like I'm holding a key? A little sticky, maybe, but not locked. I'll have a word with Roche about doing a bit more physical in physical education. Not gaining any muscle with all those star jumps, are you?'

'I'm sorry, miss.'

'Quite. Now get to lunch before five hundred cleans becomes a thousand.'

'Five hundred cleans...?'

When Snout looked up, he was sure he saw the hint of a smile on Ms. Ito's face, but it was gone in an instant, replaced by that familiar glass-cracking glare.

'Five hundred. You didn't think I was going soft, did you?'

∽

By the time Snout reached the dining hall, the last first years had gone in and he was left with only the scrapings from each metal bowl. In the time he had been in Endinfinium, the food had barely improved, but there had been signs of greater adventure in the menu of late. A week ago they'd actually had passable hamburgers—even though Snout couldn't be sure it was real meat—and yesterday had been bread rolls which actually tasted like bread, rather than chalk mixed with water. Today's delight had been pizza, but as Snout reached the tray, he found it empty, the handwritten cardboard sign lying on the floor. He dutifully picked it up and handed it one of the cleaners on lunch duty. The empty-eyed, reanimated corpse gave him a vacant grin then scooped some crusty, overcooked mash into his bowl.

Tommy Cale and Fat Adam were sitting on a corner table. Godfrey, Snout noted, was sitting at the end of the teachers' table, next to Professor Eaves and only two places along from Professor Loane, who looked as glassy-eyed as the cleaners. Godfrey was saying something about pupils' rights to a regular dress-down day while Professor Eaves and Professor Loane nodded along. Further down the table, Captain Roche, taking up three spaces on the bench, rolled his eyes and tucked into his mash.

'Where have you been?' Tommy whispered to Snout. 'The pizza was great. Or it would have been, but Derek nicked mine. I'd only had one bite.'

'Derek locked me outside on the precipice,' Snout said, then went on to explain what had happened. 'That door was locked, I know it. But what can I say? No one will believe me.'

'That explains why he was late,' Fat Adam said.

'And why he nicked my pizza,' Tommy Cale added. 'That technically means you owe me a piece.'

'You can have some mash,' Snout said.

Tommy shook his head. 'I'm good, but thanks for the offer.'

'Can I have some?' Fat Adam asked.

'No!'

They ate in silence for a couple of minutes. The Sixth and Seventh Years had already cleared away their dinner things, and the dining hall was rapidly emptying out.

'Seen any more people in cupboards or mirrors recently?' Fat Adam said, swallowing down the last of his mash and looking as though he needed to fill the void left by food's absence with conversation.

'Adam's been checking for you,' Tommy Cale said. 'Haven't you, Adam?'

'Shut up, no I haven't.'

'You checked your wardrobe twice last night.'

'No, I did not!'

Snout glanced over his shoulder and saw Derek Bates sitting with a couple of Godfrey's other cohorts on the next table from the teachers'. As though aware of eyes on him, Derek looked up and gave Snout a wink.

'You're in for it this term,' Tommy Cale said. 'Now that Benjamin and Wilhelm have disappeared, Godfrey and his mates have no one to pick on.'

'Ah, they'll find some first years,' Fat Adam said.

'It's stupid,' Tommy Cale said. 'Godfrey's supposed to be the prefect, yet him and Derek dunked Phil Boon last week and totally got away with it. Phil got busted for being in the third floor toilet block without permission. Dusty said he knocked a hundred cleans off Boon's punishment because he'd got his hair wet, but Godfrey and Derek just got a pat on the back. They said they found him there and were trying to stop him putting his head in the toilet.'

'Godfrey's starting to run this school,' Fat Adam said, his frown suddenly vanishing behind an inappropriately timed grin. 'Ah, look. They've just loaded up the dessert tray again.'

Before Snout could reply, both Tommy Cale and Fat Adam rushed off to join the line for an extra portion of custard. Snout, having lost his appetite, glanced over his shoulder. Godfrey had gone, but Derek was smiling as

Professor Loane commended him on a recent piece of homework.

Snout frowned into his mash and took a bite of the bland gunge. Fat Adam might have been half-joking, but he was right. Ever since all the bad stuff that had happened and Benjamin's disappearance along with Wilhelm Jacobs and Miranda Butterworth, the lines of authority had become blurred. Sometimes it really did feel like Godfrey was in charge.

'I got you some,' Tommy Cale said, returning to the table and immediately upending half a bowl of custard onto what remained of Snout's mash. 'No hard feelings, but I'll be asking next time we have pizza.'

Snout just smiled, and then wiped a chunk of custard off the back of his hand.

~

The locker rooms felt quieter than usual. Most punishments were after dinner, but with an afternoon set aside for self-study, Snout headed down straight after lunch. The brightness cast by the two combining suns outside was but a memory in the gloomy, dank school basements. Snout, jumping at every bump and creak, made his way down narrow stone staircases and along winding corridors. Some had shifted even since his last visit, with temporary signs taped to the walls to indicate the directions to other subterranean chambers containing archives, stores, or maintenance rooms.

The sin keeper, a reanimated suit of armour, stepped out of his regular booth by the door. Snout shuddered at the sight of the faceless hole behind the mask, and the curved katana hung at the sin keeper's waist.

'State your punishment,' came a hollow voice created by wind sucked up through the armour's empty cavities.

'Five hundred cleans,' Snout said. 'I didn't realise a door wasn't locked.'

It sounded ridiculous, but the sin keeper simply moved aside to let him go through a door behind. The only way to enter the lockers was to state your wrongdoing; even if you needed to visit someone in the middle of a long sentence you still had to admit to some minor misdemeanour.

The door opened onto a line of booths against the wall of a chamber. Set into the far wall was another door, through which cleaners came and went. The locker room was designed for the safe deanimation of all the smaller items from the school which had begun to take on a life of their own: crockery, stationery, clothing, and anything else that could fit into a small box.

Snout took a door at the far end, near to the other door. The conveyor entered at that end, meaning those seated closest had first dibs on all of the easy stuff. When the lockers were busy and you had to take one far away, you ended up with all the awkward, potentially dangerous stuff like knives and statues, or things you might have to take apart to clean properly, like photograph albums or clocks. On a good day, you could kill off fifty cleans by grabbing a bag of jumping rulers or a box of vibrating erasers.

As he sat down and shut the door behind him, a counter on the wall above flickered over to 500. Snout sighed and pulled open a sliding door to reveal the conveyor belt beyond.

Like on his previous recent visits, the conveyor was overloaded. He grabbed a stack of vibrating plastic bowls to get him started, but it was clear that the cleaner shortage was causing problems. Many larger items such as light fittings and chairs, which would usually have been deanimated on location by teams of cleaners working around the clock, had been shoehorned onto the conveyor. Now they were clogging things up, being too big to get inside a booth and causing a backlog behind them. As one awkwardly tilted teacher's desk jerked past the upper corner of Snout's booth, a pile of junk accumulated behind it cascaded down across his table and he wasted several valuable minutes grabbing the jumping, spinning, bouncing things and throwing them back onto the conveyor.

Finally settling down to work, Snout pulled a cloth and a bottle of chamomile spray off a shelf and began the usual procedure of spray-spray-wipe, stacking the quietened bowls up on one side, away from their more excitable friends. Snout had taken a long time to come to terms with cleaning, fearful that he was in some way taking away life. One day, after confessing his fears to Professor Loane, the teacher had taken him aside and explained that it wasn't actually possible to stop the reanimation process; all they were doing was calming it down. Too simple to ever gain a human-like sentience, the bowls would eventually reanimate to a point where they flew around like psychotic birds, a danger both to themselves and anyone nearby. The spray would restore them to a base level of motion invisible to the naked eye, but, left on their own, they would eventually begin to hum and vibrate all over again. That he wasn't murdering them was something hugely comforting to Snout, who, by his own admission, was perhaps too conscientious for his own good.

A bucket sat by his feet for him to fill with deanimated items. When it was full, he pressed a button on the wall. A few seconds later the door opened and the leering, expressionless face of a cleaner appeared, picked up the bucket, and took it away. A few moments afterwards, his counter ticked down by a couple of dozen numbers. Snout sighed. It was two less than the number he had counted, meaning he had failed to deanimate a couple of items properly. They would now be thrown back on to the conveyor for a second round.

He was about halfway through his quota when he decided to take a break. Another shelf held refreshments—bottles of cold chamomile tea, as though the pupils weren't sick of the smell already—so Snout opened one, leaned back on the chair and took a long drink.

When he looked back up, a cupboard lying on its side was moving past. One door slapped open, and a girl's face peered out. It was translucent, the outlines of the cupboard visible through it. Whether it had a body or not, Snout couldn't tell.

Hollow eyes flashed green. A hand lifted.

'Come,' a voice said. 'Help.'

Snout pushed himself away and fell off the chair. When he looked up, the cupboard had gone past, its door closed again. He scrambled backwards and barreled out of the cubicle into the entry chamber, pushing himself to his feet as he did so. Only as he broke into a run for the main entrance did he see the sin keeper stepping out of his booth to block the way.

A handless glove pulled the sword free. The other held a crossbow. Snout had never known them used but didn't want to take the chance on an emotionless reanimate.

He skidded to a halt as the sin keeper pushed through the door to stand before him.

'Do you have permission to leave before the completion of your allocated task?'

'There's something on the conveyor,' Snout said, voice cracking again. 'A girl. In a cupboard. I saw her.'

'Wait. Do not leave.'

The sin keeper pushed past. The sword waved, directing him where to stand. Disturbed by the commotion, a couple of other cubicle doors opened and faces peered out. Snout recognised one as Cherise, a tearaway third year girl. She scowled at him and slammed the door shut. The others ducked out of sight as the sin keeper swung around.

'The cupboard went back into the loading room,' Snout said, pointing at where the conveyor went back through a hole into the wall. 'I saw her. No one's allowed back there, are they?'

The sin keeper looked awkward as he ducked and leaned into Snout's cubicle. His large helmet swung back and forth, then he stepped back out.

'Nothing,' he said. 'Finish your quota. Punishment for time-wasting is an additional two hundred cleans.'

Snout groaned. Inside his locker, he heard the click of the ticker counter flicking over.

The sin keeper returned to his booth outside the main door. Feeling a hot flush on his neck to signal his reluctance, Snout squeezed back into his cubicle and sat down. A couple of minutes later, the cupboard slid past again, but this time both doors were open and the inside was clearly empty.

The girl was gone. But how long would she stay gone? And what did she want from him?

14

BENJAMIN

'Here, take these,' Sebastien said, handing a plastic pac-a-mac each to Benjamin and Wilhelm. 'It's pretty wet out there.'

The sky was a clear, cloudless blue. The trees on either side of the dirt trail leading past the sign that said BASINGSTOKE MUNICIPAL DUMP looked dry, as though they hadn't seen rain in several days. Noticing their confusion, Sebastien smiled as he added, 'You'll see in a few minutes.'

They climbed out. Wilhelm ran one hand appreciatively over the curves of Sebastien's beautifully restored vintage car. It hadn't made for the most comfortable of rides, but it certainly looked pretty.

'People never stop throwing things away,' Sebastien had said in answer to their questions. 'I wanted to appreciate something precious for just a little longer.'

Sebastien led the way up the dirt path from the car park. They came around a corner to a secondary car park where people unloading large items could stop, but Sebastien had baulked at the uneven, muddy lane that led to it. Behind this second car park, the dump began. Benjamin smelled chamomile in the air then noticed the huge sprayers angling over the dump from all sides.

'The only way to keep it all there,' Sebastien said. 'Without those sprayers, the whole lot would begin to move in a couple of days, flying off to join the nearest tumbleweed.'

Tumbleweeds.

The pet name for the giant moving balls of rubbish moving slowly across the countryside. Headed for London, Sebastien had explained, to a place he had never seen. They began in the farthest reaches of the country as handfuls of litter sticking together, gradually moving across the land, collecting more garbage on the way, until some of them were nearly a mile high.

'Don't they scare you?' Wilhelm asked, as they climbed up a set of steps to the main dumping area, from where a view of the countryside behind them was revealed. In the distance, an enormous tumbleweed was visible, slowly rolling across the fields.

Sebastien laughed. 'Sometimes I could really believe you two aren't from around here. Of course they scare me. But they move so slowly. It wouldn't be hard to get out of the way, wouldn't you think?'

'You'd hope so,' Benjamin said.

The tumbleweed made him uneasy, so he turned his attention to the dump. Unlike the image his mind had thrown up of such a place, this wasn't the stinking domain of leftover food, dirty nappies, and torn plastic bags. Gravel paths snaked between wooden barriers reaching to about waist height, behind which heaps of unwanted items were stacked, many of them in surprisingly ordered lines. In places it was clear people had been lazy—Benjamin noticed a fridge-freezer dumped on top of a ordered line of CD players, but in others he saw signs of organisation: a box of DVDs which had been alphabetically arranged; clothes hung on actual rails; TVs lined up so as not to touch each other, with clingfilm taped over their screens.

'The dump is for items someone else might want,' Sebastien said. 'It's a prime hunting ground for the poor, the pupil population, and for an antiques dealer like myself. I come up here as often as I can, to claim anything beautiful or artistic before the spray starts to ruin it.'

Most of the stacks were several layers deep. Beneath a line of pristine TVs, for example, were others less pristine, many of which now lay on their sides, screens and casings cracked, kept here only by the spray trickling down from those above.

'How do they fly off on their own?' Wilhelm asked. 'I mean, that's not normal, is it? Not here, at any rate.'

Sebastien gave a brief frown at Wilhelm's last statement, then shrugged. 'I'm not a scientist. I'm an antiques dealer. Things change. Life evolves. You either adapt—'

'—or you die,' Benjamin finished.

An uneasy silence fell among them. They walked on a little way, until Wilhelm asked, 'So, what are we looking for?'

'As you might have noticed, I specialize in old toys,' Sebastien said. 'The dump's toy section is near the back. Let's go.'

His eyes had lit up, Benjamin noticed. Wilhelm's, too, as though they were both children at the gates of a toy wonderland.

'Wow! Look at all these!'

Benjamin rolled his eyes as Wilhelm swooned over a box of heavily-muscled action figures. He had played with such as a kid, but had grown out of them. As Wilhelm lifted a couple and began a mock fight in mid-air, another fragment of memory returned.

'You've never seen those before, have you?'

Wilhelm shook his head. 'We didn't have anything like this back at the—' He looked up. 'The orphanage.' He frowned. 'Huh. I suppose that's why I have no memory of any family.'

As Wilhelm, seemingly unconcerned, returned to his battle, Benjamin caught Sebastien's eye. The man gave him a soft smile, as though unsure what words would make any difference.

Wilhelm was an orphan, and another thing had come to mind. Benjamin picked up a folding robot toy. 'Wilhelm? Ever seen one of these?'

Wilhelm turned, peered at it, then shook his head. 'Nope. Looks awesome, though.'

'They were huge when I was a kid. Everyone had them. What toys do you remember?'

Wilhelm frowned. He leaned over the nearest fence and plucked someone out of the pile. 'We had these,' he said, turning and holding up a rusty metal car. 'Oh, and these.'

A spaceship vehicle. Benjamin recognised the brand. It was something his father might have played with.

So, as he had expected, both Wilhelm and he were existing in their futures, although their pasts were from different times. He looked at Sebastien, wanting to explain this revelation, but the old man already thought they were lying. Until he could prove their identities, it was best to stay quiet.

They began to wander off along the paths in search of more treasures. Sebastien made a racket as he climbed over a fence in an attempt to reach something half-buried in the centre. Wilhelm had found a box of racing cars and was reliving a childhood he had never had by racing them in circles dug out of the gravel path.

Benjamin wandered further in, passing monuments to his childhood with every step. There was a broken-down brick castle a friend across the street had owned, the US-only version of a movie spaceship another friend had had but frustratingly always refused to play with when Benjamin visited because he had already played with it to the point of boredom. Long-forgotten childhood memories came rushing back like snakes out of the dark, and Benjamin reveled in them, daydreaming of hours whiled away waging toy-soldier wars on tribes of fierce dinosaurs, of exploration missions up the impossible ascent of stairs-mountain, of—

He looked up, shaking his head as though to throw off a dream. He had reached the very back of the dump, where only one badly maintained chain-link fence separated the gravel path from an invasion of lush forest. Caught up in the overflow of the chamomile sprays overhead, the nearest vegetation was waist-deep with ferns, nettles and other undergrowth. Benjamin glanced at it, started to turn back, then paused.

Something had moved out among the trees. Something small, metallic, curves and angles glinting in the sun through the canopy overhead.

DANGER KEEP OUT signs hung at awkward angles from the fence, in places pulled down by climbing weeds. The ground under Benjamin's feet felt strange: soft and squelchy, which, despite the constant falling spray, none of the other areas of path had. He glanced back and saw Sebastien hard at work among a pile of children's toys. Wilhelm was nowhere to be seen, but his voice drifted back, taking on multiple accents as his newly acquired toys waged a great battle.

Neither was watching him. Benjamin climbed over the nearest downed section of fence and waded out into the forest.

He had gone no more than a dozen steps when he saw more movement among the undergrowth. This time he got a clear look as something barely as high as his knee stepped out from behind a fallen tree and ran deeper into the forest.

Benjamin stared.

A teddy bear, its coat soggy and dirty, but unmistakably a toy from the bright blue of its fur and a pull cord trailing behind it that fed into its back.

Benjamin hesitated only a moment before giving chase.

The bear reached a cluster of trees, where it paused, leaning between two lower boughs. It looked back, and button eyes squeezed into a frown as it spotted Benjamin watching.

'What do you want?' it said in a squeaky voice, the sound coming from inside its chest. 'This is no place for you.'

Benjamin was too stunned to reply, but the interaction was pulling forth yet more memories, that once upon a time he had spent so much time in contact with reanimated creatures, that he even considered some of them friends. He felt no fear as he watched the bear, which gave him a quick wave and then bolted away into the forest.

He lost sight of it further in, but there were others here, too. A tiny train raced over fallen leaves like a snake, its wheels replaced by tiny feet. A kite flew through the air above him, pointed sides flapping like butterfly wings, while a yo-yo rolled past, following its only string, which went on ahead, catching on protruding twigs and then flinging its wooden body forward like a weirdly jumping caterpillar.

Everything he saw was heading in the same direction. Benjamin passed a KEEP OUT sign that was shaking on its stake as though wanting to break free, then stepped over another low fence which reverberated beneath him. Something was up ahead, just through the trees.

Round a thicket of hawthorn he caught sight of the bear again, skipping along beside a plastic doll holding its shredded dress against itself as though to protect its modesty. Steam was rising out of something in the earth up ahead, and as Benjamin watched, the bear held out its hand to the doll, which took it. Then, with an audible 'Three, two, one...!' they both jumped.

Benjamin stopped. They had vanished. The ground where they had jumped was just normal ground, stones and leaf litter and—

It was revolving like a whirlpool of greens and browns, a section no more than an arm's length across swirling around, stones bobbing up and down in the earth as though the soil were water. Benjamin stared. It—

'Whoa!' His feet slipped out from under him as the ground gave way. Stones and leaf litter rushed down a little slope and disappeared into a swirling eye of forest matter, drawing in the ground around it. He tried to scrabble back, but his foot got caught, his shoe flipping off, disappearing into the eye, the rocks falling with it. The ground beneath him began to move, pulling him closer like the arms of a hungry giant tilting him up to drop him into its mouth—

'Back! Idiot boy! Can't you read the signs?'

Hands reached under his armpits, hauling him out of range. In a moment the forest was still, the revolving eye gone, the patter of tiny feet quickly receding and then going still. Benjamin, one missing shoe revealing a hole in the end of a dirty sock, looked up into Sebastien Aren's livid face.

'I thought you were running me a lie,' the old man said, shaking his head back and forth, his cheeks cherry red with anger. 'But you two idiots really aren't from round here, are you?'

15

MIRANDA

She was lying in a bed, but it didn't feel like a regular bed. There were pokey bits and really soft bits, as though it was a bag which had been filled with whatever could be found and then stuffed underneath her. Her left shoulder ached, and she wondered if this was what dislocation felt like, or whether her shoulder was just badly bruised. The rest of her body felt pretty beat up; she was sore from scratches and bruises in a dozen places, but nothing felt seriously damaged.

As she rose, a figure which had been sitting in a chair at the end of her bed suddenly jumped up and scurried out of the room. Miranda stared through swinging beads hung over a doorway, her vision slowly backtracking to take in a small, gloomy bedroom, its walls made of bare stone, furnished with a few items that looked salvaged, and lit by a gas lamp standing on a rickety table in a corner. The floor was a threadbare rug over earth, her bed a cluster of handmade blankets with the mattress-bag on top of several empty bottle crates.

'Um, hello?' Miranda called. 'Is anyone there? Thank you for not killing me, but I was wondering—'

A shape appeared, pushing through the doorway. Miranda stared. The child that had run from the room now stood backed up against a young woman, glossy black hair hanging almost to her waist, a beautiful face wasted on the shreds of clothing she wore. The child, too, was angelic, despite the gloomy light leaving much of her face in shadow.

'Welcome,' the woman said. 'My name is Alamy, and this is my daughter, Rosa.'

Miranda muttered, 'Pleased to meet you,' while hiding her surprise that the woman was old enough to have a child. 'Where am I?'

'You're in a safe place. You had a fall, but you don't need to worry. You're safe now.'

'Where's Enchantress?'

'Enchantress?'

The little girl looked up. 'I think she means the swan, Mummy.'

Alamy's face darkened. 'That thing ... has been taken where it won't cause any more harm.'

'Enchantress is my friend. Please tell me she's safe.'

Alamy's expression didn't change. 'It ... she, if you call it that, has been contained.'

Miranda started to get out of bed. 'I need to see that she's all right.'

Alamy came forward, and Miranda felt herself pushed back beneath the covers by an invisible wall that could only be reanimation magic. She tried to call her own to repel it, but where it should have been, there was nothing. Just ... emptiness.

'Trobin said you might cause trouble,' Alamy said,

turning to the child. 'Rosa, run for him. Bring him here so he can talk some sense into her.'

'Will she be all right, Mummy? She's so pretty. Will she stay?'

'Of course she will,' Alamy said. 'Now run along. Trobin was up near the school the last time I saw him.'

The girl hurried off, leaving Miranda alone with Alamy. 'You can't keep me prisoner,' she said. 'I'm trying to get back to the Endinfinium High School. I need to find my friends.'

Alamy rolled her eyes. 'The school … so, you're from there after all. Trobin had hoped you were pure, but you're still young. There's time.'

'Is it far?'

'Not far enough.'

Miranda pushed herself up. 'Who are you people?'

Alamy looked taken aback. 'We're the people who saved your life. It's best that you remember that before you start giving anyone lip. And that's not to mention those accursed airships that have been circling overhead for the last few hours. We don't know why they're looking for you, but we'd certainly like them to go away.'

'I'm sorry.'

Alamy's mood abruptly changed. 'That's quite all right. You're only young, and you've had a terrible fright, after all.'

'Yes, I have.'

Alamy came over to the bed and gave Miranda a pat on the head like she would her own daughter. 'You just rest a little longer. When Trobin gets here, we'll all sit down for dinner and have a good long talk about what to do next.'

Trobin didn't take long to appear. Rosa came running back in with heavy footsteps following her. The beads spread and a lithe figure stepped into the room. Miranda almost choked. Trobin had the head of an overlarge dog, ears flapping down over his neck. Then she realised it wasn't his actual head but an elaborate headdress. A narrow, mousy face poked out from beneath the dog's chin. A hooked nose hung over thin lips. His eyes were so small she couldn't see them until he removed the dog's head to reveal a bald scalp beneath.

'You are the girl that fell from that reanimate bird,' he said, in a thin, nasally voice that sounded like someone was pinching his voice box. 'It captured you, didn't it?'

'Um, well—'

'Because that's how it appeared. You woke up somewhere nearby, and that creature captured you, planning to take you to the Dark Man. But then it changed its mind and decided instead to use you for its own devices. The Dark Man sent his forces to capture you, and you made a jump for freedom when you saw our caves.'

Miranda forced a smile. 'That's exactly how it happened.'

Trobin's eyes narrowed even further, until they disappeared into folds in his face. 'Because that's the story we will feed to the rest of the community, to prevent you being strung up as one of the Filthy, or sent back to the Dark Man as an offering to his mercy. Do you understand?'

Alamy glanced at Trobin, an easy smile on her face. Miranda gave a slow nod. 'I understand.'

'Good. I do not care for your truths. In truth lies danger, and I will not endanger the lives of our children.' He turned to Alamy. 'I must go. The council has called a meeting in the main chamber. I fear what might be decided.'

Alamy took his arm and gave it a squeeze. 'I'm sure you can charm them, swing them around.'

143

'I'll do what I can.' He looked back at Miranda. 'But our hospitality is worthless if it brings harm to our children. Those airships are still circling. There might be nothing I can do to protect her.'

'You've done enough as it is. Do you have no time for something to eat?'

Trobin shook his head. 'The meeting starts in one hour.'

He went out. Alamy came and fussed over Miranda, telling her to rest a while longer, checking her cuts and bruises. Rosa hung by her waist, staring up at Miranda as though she were an angel fallen from the sky.

'I'll prepare something to eat,' Alamy said at last. 'Please rest a little longer. Rosa, come with me. Don't bother Miranda.'

They went out, leaving Miranda alone. A sudden weariness came over her and she found her eyes closing. When she opened them again, little Rosa was standing beside her bed.

Miranda gasped with the girl's eyes so close to her own, but as she shrank back, Rosa smiled.

'Is it true you fell from the sky?'

Miranda laughed. 'Well, I suppose so. It wasn't intentional. I was supposed to be flying in it, but we had a little trouble.'

'Where did you come from?'

'Endinfinium High. It's a school on the coast. A long way from here. Did you go there?'

Rosa shook her head. 'No. We have another school here.'

'Another school? Really?'

Rosa shrugged. 'It's just Trobin and a few others who teach us. It's really boring.' She crouched down and leaned her head on the edge of Miranda's bed. 'My mother went to Endinfinium High, though. I heard her talking about it with Trobin once.' She smiled suddenly, eyes twinkling. 'I'm not supposed to know.'

'How old are you?'

'Six. And you?'

'Thirteen.' Miranda shrugged. 'I think.'

'Wow, you're so old.'

'Thanks. Sometimes I feel a lot older. How many of you are there here?'

'About fifty who live in the community. There are some others who come and go. Explorers, I think.'

'Are you all Weavers?'

Rosa frowned. 'What's a Weaver?'

'A non-magic user.'

Rosa laughed. 'Like in a storybook? Don't be silly, but that's an interesting name.'

Miranda frowned, remembering the force that had pushed her back into the bed. 'You have no magic here?'

'Look, I might be just a kid, but I'm not stupid. You don't have to talk to me like I'm four or something.'

'Where I come from, some people can use magic. Like to move things around.'

Rosa laughed. She hit the side of the bed as though she'd never heard something so ridiculous. 'You're funny. I thought you might be, with hair like that. Where on New World did you get that dye?'

'It's natural.'

'But it's like paint.'

Miranda felt a pang of her old impetuous anger returning, but reminded herself the girl was only young and didn't know better.

'Not everyone has the same colour hair,' she said, trying not to grit her teeth. 'I mean, you have brown hair, your mother has black hair, your dad has no hair—'

'He's not my dad,' Rosa snapped. 'He's Trobin. He hangs around my mother, but he's only protecting her until my real dad comes back.'

'Where did your real dad go?'

'He went to visit the Dark Man.'

Miranda wasn't sure what to say. 'Why did he do that?'

Rosa shrugged. 'I don't know. I don't remember.'

'When was this?'

'A few years ago. When I was little.'

Miranda felt a prickle of fear, and wished she could feel her magic, but where its protection lay was only a sense of emptiness.

'Do a lot of people go to see the Dark Man?'

Rosa shrugged. 'A few. I don't know.'

'Rosa!' Alamy's sharp cry came from the outside room. 'Come here, please. I hope you're not bothering Miranda.'

'No, Mummy. I'm coming.'

Rosa stood up, gave Miranda a brief smile, and then went out. A couple of minutes later, Alamy appeared though the beads again. She now wore a dirty apron around her waist.

'I've made some lunch,' she said. 'Can you walk, or would you like it in bed?'

Miranda swung her legs out onto the floor. While her shoulder still ached, her lower body felt fine. 'I'm okay,' she said.

Through the hanging beads was a small kitchen. The rooms were reminiscent of Olin's place with their salvaged furniture, although here there was no sign of magic use. Old cupboards and shelves were propped up on bricks or held together by string. The walls, floor, and ceiling too looked like natural caves rather than having been carved out of the soil like Olin's place.

Alamy leaned over a wood-fired stove, the smoke

dissipating through a hole in the ceiling. As the jingling beads signaled Miranda's entrance, she turned.

'Sit down,' she said. 'Soup is ready.'

Miranda took a chair at a rickety table with one leg propped up by a pile of children's toy blocks. Alamy brought her soup in a chipped porcelain bowl and handed her a wooden spoon.

The soup looked like a watery version of what she had once faced daily at the school, chunks of unidentifiable vegetables in a thick broth. She lifted some to her lips and took a sip. While it wasn't unpleasant, it had no memorable taste, but she forced a grateful smile for Alamy as the woman sat down across the table and watched her eat like a sensitive cook testing a new recipe.

'Is it okay? Would you like more salt?'

'It's delicious, thank you.'

'Soon you'll have your strength back.'

After Miranda finished the soup, Alamy took the bowl and spoon and washed them in a bucket standing in a corner. Unlike Olin's homemade system, it appeared these people had no running water.

'Trobin will be back soon,' Alamy said. 'Then we'll know what to do.'

'I'm thankful for your hospitality, but I'm afraid I must leave as soon as I can.'

Alamy gave a fierce shake of her head. 'No, I'm afraid that's not possible. The airships are still circling. It's too dangerous to go outside.'

Alamy looked up at the ceiling, and a realisation dawned on Miranda. 'We're underground, aren't we?'

'It's the only way to keep our children safe.'

Miranda pushed back her chair and stood up.

'Where are you going?'

Miranda didn't answer. She bolted for a connecting

door and found herself in a gloomy corridor hewn out of bare rock. Alamy shouted after her, but Miranda was quick on her feet, cutting into and out of several connecting passages until she had left the woman far behind.

Exhausted but certain she was out of range, she slowed to a brisk walk. The tunnels were silent all around her, but they reminded Miranda of the bowels of Endinfinium High. All she had to do to get out was to keep on heading up.

At each turn, she took the branch which seemed to angle upwards. The tunnels were all alike, lit by dim orange lights in the ceiling which reminded her uncomfortably of ghouls' eyes, but the higher she climbed, the more man-made they felt. The very lowest, where Alamy's rooms were, felt so deep they were carved from natural honeycombs in the rock, but here were signs of drills and chisels. Finally she stepped though an opening and found the walls covered with cracked and dusty tiles, the floor concrete.

The tunnel stretched away to either side, but in front of her was a sharp drop that ended in a flat space with two metal strips running its length, from a pile of downed rubble at one end, to a similar pile at the other.

Miranda stared.

An old railway station. Miranda turned around, looking for a way out. She had come up a set of stairs carved into the rock, through a tunnel which had perhaps been built by Alamy's people or their ancestors. The curve of the roof suggested an underground train, and there, on the wall, she saw the dusty remnants of a sign.

With one hand she wiped away the dust covering the letters.

LONDON UNDERGROUND: CHARING CROSS

Miranda had heard of London. It was in a lot of the books she had read in the dormitory: the capital of England, the country outside the lab where she had been created.

For a moment the sudden rush of memory knocked her off her feet. She found herself on her knees, head bowed, staring at her hands making prints in the dirt, wondering where her magic—that which she had spent so long trying to learn and perfect under the watchful eye of Edgar Caspian—had gone, why it had left her alone when she needed it so badly.

The smell. It was in the smell, and the drip-drip of water running down the walls around her.

Chamomile. She noticed a bucket beneath a crack in the ceiling which was nearly full, and she crawled over to take a look. It tasted fresh but with a hint of the flower that calmed everything, like cold chamomile tea. She recognised the smell from the soup Alamy had given her, and the scent from the bed's mattress. The dried stalks that hung with beads across the doorway.

The smell of chamomile had been so pervasive that she had blocked it out entirely, but its presence everywhere explained so much. These people were magic suppressors, the plant's presence so prevalent that it prevented reanimation, and blocked the use of any magic.

Miranda concentrated, feeling inside herself.

Yes.

It was still there, buried deep, its absence perhaps exacerbated by the trauma of her fall, her exhaustion. She felt for it, pushing lightly, and saw the dust plume away beneath her feet.

She stood up, and heard voices.

Walking further along the abandoned station, she found another opening in the wall. This led to an ancient, calcified escalator heading up. The voices grew louder as she reached the top exit. To the right, a bright light shone through an opening. Miranda crept along the wall and peered through an old doorway into a chamber large enough to hold a hundred people. As her eyes adjusted to the sudden light, Miranda gulped, shrinking back. She thought to flee again, then remembered the bizarre headdress Trobin had worn, and realised the crowd of animals with oversized, inanimate heads was actually made up of people, all in similar garb.

A stage had been erected at one end, and ten people sat on chairs, five men and five women. Below them, an audience of around fifty listened to their discussion, occasionally raising their hands. Below their bizarre headwear, all of them wore the same rags as Alamy, but some had weapons attached to their belts: spears, knives, metal chains; one even carried a crossbow. As the council's discussion continued, heads bobbed and shook like giant puppets.

'She should be thrown back out to where she came from,' one man in the audience shouted. 'She came from the Dark Man, so send her back.'

'It is true she has turned his eye again towards us, but I don't believe she is one of his followers,' answered one of the women from the stage. 'She is barely more than a child.'

'His followers come in all shapes and sizes!' another man shouted. 'Don't you remember that boy who appeared three years past?'

A group of people stood up, arms raised, some shouting for attention.

'He was dealt with as he needed to be dealt with,' came Trobin's voice, and she saw Alamy's partner standing to the side of the stage, apart from both groups, as though he occupied a separate position. 'He was infected. We had no choice but to cast him out.'

'And we lost Leon as a result!' another person shouted.

'Leon had become dangerous,' Trobin said. 'He could have turned away. He had a choice.'

'Whose choice, Trobin?' shouted a woman from near the back. 'His departure worked out well for you, didn't it?'

'Order!' shouted someone else, a woman Miranda had not previously noticed sitting on the other side of the stage. 'Personal matters are personal. They don't belong in the council chamber.'

'I say we keep her,' one of the council members, a man with a huge, white rabbit's head, said. 'There are sixty-four of us, yet just nine children. Our Sleeper community has weathered every storm Endinfinium could throw at us; it must not be allowed to die out. The scouting parties have brought in three more Disillusioned this year alone.' He pointed at a young man near the front. 'John, remind everyone of our value.'

'They cast you out,' the young man said. 'Sure, you can stay there and while away your life, or you can join one of the farms supplying them with food, but otherwise, they don't care about you. We're not equipped to survive outside of Endinfinium High. I'd be dead if it wasn't for the hunting party which found me. Now I have a wife, and a child on the way.' He turned and smiled at a woman who sat beside him. 'The Sleepers, they saved my life.'

'Thank you, John. You see?' The man waved his hands. 'The girl is confused, hurt. Give her time.'

A woman stood up. 'What if she's infected? What then?'

'Then we have no choice but to cast her out!'
'Send her on her way!'
'Offer her to him!'

The sudden vitriol left Miranda stunned. She shrank back, wondering whether to make a break for the surface. To escape from these people, she needed to find Enchantress, and eavesdropping on their meeting gave her the best chance, so after a moment to steady her thundering heart, she peered back around.

'His airships still circle overhead,' one of the men on the stage said. 'Even disguised, we dare not go above ground until they have gone. If the Dark Man discovers us here, he could send an army to wipe us out.'

'What about that thing that brought the girl?'

Miranda's ears pricked up.

'That reanimate?'

'Don't say that word,' shouted the previous woman. 'Such a dirty word.'

'It's caged in one of the surface caves,' Trobin said. 'A strange creature, unlike anything I've seen. It's made of paper. I believe we could use it as an offering to draw his attention away.'

'An offering?'

'Under darkness, we take it down to the shores of the Dark River and set it alight. It will draw his airships away, and perhaps trick him into thinking the girl is dead.'

'Do we have the means to transport it?'

Trobin nodded. 'It can easily be contained. If necessary we could chop it apart and move it piece by hideous piece.'

Miranda bit her tongue to stop herself crying out. Fists clenched so hard she thought her bones might break, she watched as the woman on the stage stood up. 'Then I second the motion. All in favour?' Most hands rose. 'Against?' One solitary hand rose.

'John?' The woman frowned, then looked around at

the others as though stunned by this single act of defiance. 'Are you seriously against this motion?'

'I don't believe the death of the creature will solve anything,' he said. 'Better to set it free, let it take its chances. It doesn't appear affiliated with the girl, and in flight, it would likely draw the airships away anyway.'

Murmurs of dissent came from the back of the crowd. 'John…,' the woman began slowly, 'you are aware of our policy towards these things?'

John nodded. 'I accepted your oath upon my arrival, and my feelings haven't changed. But this … this is savagery.'

The murmurs became shouts of dissent. Several people stood up, shouting abuse at John. Miranda was wondering whether now was the time to flee when a door opened behind the stage and Alamy appeared.

'Miranda,' the woman gasped, crouching down as she struggled for breath. 'She's gone.'

16

SNOUT

'Come on, there must be somewhere else,' came the whine from outside Snout's dorm room door as the clack of Gubbledon Longface's hooves on the landing signaled the arrival of their housemaster. An arbitrary knock was followed by the door swiftly opening, and the reanimated racehorse corpse, wearing his customary purple satin shirt, stepped inside. Despite his stunningly bizarre looks, Snout was more shocked by the face of the boy standing behind him.

Derek Bates.

His second worst enemy, possibly first now that Godfrey had a privileged room in the teachers' tower.

'You can't make me room with him,' Derek whined. 'I'd rather sleep outside.'

'School policy won't allow that,' Gubbledon said, the stutter that often infected his speech absent during practiced school matters. 'Your spare bed is absent now Godfrey's moved out, and Snout's been on his own for a while. We need the downstairs room for incoming first years. Don't be difficult now. You'll get on fine.'

Snout, who'd been sitting at his desk by the window and trying to do his science homework, just gulped, his throat too dry for speech.

'Simon, your bed is the lower bunk, is that right?'

'Yes,' Snout croaked.

'So, Derek, you'll be in the upper. These drawers are yours, so bring your stuff up this afternoon, please.'

Derek made a face like he had seen a ghost. His lower lip worked soundlessly, then, in a hollow, frail voice, he said, 'I can't do the upper bunk. I'm afraid of heights.'

'We're on the building's third floor, so you'd better get used to it,' Gubbledon said.

'Local heights!' Derek wailed. 'There's no way I could sleep on the upper bunk with that drop so close.'

'There's a rail,' Snout muttered.

'Look at you trying to bully me and I haven't even moved in yet,' Derek said, giving an exaggerated sniff. Gubbledon, to his credit, just rolled his eyes.

'Simon, would you really mind moving to the top bunk?'

Snout shrugged. 'Sure, if that's what Derek wants.'

'Oh, Simon, you're such a friend,' Derek said, giving an elongated sigh. 'And when you're done moving your dirty bedclothes, would you be so kind as to help me move my things up from my room downstairs? I hurt my shoulder in gym class yesterday.'

'We were doing football drills.'

Derek glowered. 'And as any decent player knows, you have to use your whole body, don't you?'

Snout sighed. The day, which had begun too well with a pretty sunrise and a decent breakfast, had taken a sudden turn for the worse.

∽

'Move your desk over to the corner,' Derek said. 'I want the window view.'

'But my desk's always been there,' Snout protested. 'And all you have to do to see the view is turn your head.'

'Do you want me to get neck strain?' Derek glared at Snout, his eyes narrowing. 'And do you want me to tell Godfrey that you're causing me trouble? How will it look to the teachers if my test scores go down straight after I moved in with you? You know there's more cleaning to be done than the school can handle. You might get moved down to the lockers permanently.'

Snout sighed and dragged his desk away from the window, into a corner where the light barely reached. Anything for a quiet life.

'And put your shoes outside the door. They smell bad.'

Snout, despite being unable to detect any scent whatsoever from his shoes, did as he was told, and as he did so, cast an angry glance at Derek's three pairs of muddy shoes lying strewn across the floor.

Derek sat down on his bed. 'Well, decent digs you have here, eh, pig boy? A shame I have to share, but I guess you can't have everything how you want it, can you? Didn't you have a friend to share with?'

'I was sharing with Neil Davis from Year Seven,' Snout said. 'He got moved in with a couple of his rugby mates on the second floor.'

'Oh, so he did. I suppose we're just stuck with each other, aren't we?'

'I suppose so.'

Derek grinned. 'Don't worry, pig boy. We'll be the best of friends.' He frowned suddenly, then punched the underside of Snout's bunk. 'I really wish they made these things a bit taller, don't you? I have a terrible tendency to kick out during the night.' He shrugged. 'Bad dreams, I think. You can't help but have them here, can you?'

Snout just shrugged. 'I suppose not.'

∼

'So what are you going to do?' Tommy Cale said over lunch, as Snout leaned despondently over his salad bowl. 'He's going to make your life a misery.'

'He's only been in there a couple of days and I think I'd rather sleep on the beach already,' Snout said. 'He was kicking my bed all night, right in the middle of my back. When I complained in the morning he started crying and ran downstairs to tell Gubbledon I was bullying him. Gubbledon told me if it happens again he'll refer the matter to Ms. Ito.'

'They're taking over,' Fat Adam said, stuffing a heaped spoonful of mash into his mouth while eyeing up Snout's barely touched bowl as he did so. 'Godfrey and him. Now that Benjamin, Wilhelm, and Miranda aren't here to keep them in check, they're taking over. We all know Dusty's on their side, but it looks like they'll soon have Speckles and Captain Wideload in their pockets too. Did you hear Godfrey's campaigning for evening math homework sessions for first and second years because he thinks their test scores are too low?'

'Didn't hear that,' Snout said.

'Doesn't bother you, you're a third year,' Fat Adam said. 'Me and Tommy, we're both Seconds. Can you believe that?'

'I doubt the teachers want to sit around after hours and supervise,' Snout said. 'I wouldn't worry if I were you.'

Fat Adam shook his head. 'No, it's not them that'll supervise. It's *him*.'

'Godfrey?'

'Yeah. That's his new thing. He's acting like a teacher and he's only, what, fourteen?'

Snout frowned. After school compulsory math classes? It didn't seem very likely, but with Godfrey, you just couldn't tell.

∼

Mistress Xemian, their towering Amazonian warrior of a math teacher, was writing on the board. To say 'writing' was an understatement, though. More like inscribing, her hand, wrist, and forearm moving with the grace of a ballet dancer as she wrote out a date and time.

'This is only for the second years among you,' she told the assembled joint Second and third year class. 'At least for now. It has been suggested among the school council community that in order for joint classes to continue—something for which, due to limited staff resources, the teachers are keen to maintain—the first and second years need to catch up. Your first program of supervised self-study will begin at eight p.m. tonight.'

Cherise raised her hand. 'Miss?'

'Yes, Cherise?'

'I'm a third year but I got the second lowest score in the class in the last test. Do I have to go?'

Mistress Xemian gave a deep frown as though it was a situation she hadn't considered. Then, just as it appeared every pupil in the room was holding their breath, the teacher shook her head.

'No, it's just for the first and second years,' she said. 'At least for now. If the situation changes, I'll let you know.'

Cherise turned to her friend, Sophie, and gave a subtle fist pump under the table. 'Result,' she hissed.

'But, if you were looking to fill some free time, there's plenty of work to be done down in the locker room,' Mistress Xemian said, her face offering just the hint of a smile, reminding Snout of the models in the clothing catalogues which occasionally washed up on the beach. He glanced around and was pleased to note that he wasn't the only boy staring with almost pious devotion at their divine teacher.

'Um, no, I suppose I could do some private study,' Cherise said.

'That would be even better,' Mistress Xemian said. 'You could even show me what you did at the beginning of our next lesson.'

Cherise looked pained. 'Okay, Miss, sure.'

Mistress Xemian clapped her hands together, creating a beautiful musical note of sound. 'So, it's time for dinner. Class dismissed.'

The girls got up and hurried out. As always, the boys took a lot longer, each wishing their teacher well on their way out.

～

Dinner was over, the first and second years had gone off to their first catch-up maths lesson, and Derek was mercifully out, perhaps helping Godfrey or perhaps doing something else. Snout didn't care. He was grateful for the peace and quiet.

Without Derek's constant distractions, he got his homework done quickly and went downstairs. Some other kids were sitting around in the common room, reading comics or playing board games. Gubbledon was sitting in one corner, reading a novel about horse racing, a lopsided smile on his decayed face.

Officially the doors were locked at nine, but it was still only eight-thirty and Snout was feeling brave. He told Gubbledon he was going back into the school for a quick walk, then headed out, grabbing his shoes and a scatlock cape before hurrying across the precarious causeway to the school.

As he closed the door, took off his cape and hung it up in the cupboard on the other side, he realised he wasn't sure where he was going. He had said something to Gubbledon about returning a book to the library, but it was in the bowels of the school on the far side, and would practically require a run to make it there and back in half an hour. Instead, he headed for the main entrance, cutting through corridors lined with generic classrooms used for teaching languages, history, and geography. One door near the end was open, several cleaners inside, spraying a group of reanimated desks with chamomile spray. The desks, bucking and leaping like wild sheep, knocked one cleaner to the ground, but the reanimated corpse simply stood up, retrieved his sprayer, and continued as though nothing had happened.

Snout shrugged and hurried on.

It was near to the main entrance that he felt the first sensation that something was wrong.

It had taken him a long time to understand his feelings. Even before he had come to Endinfinium, the family he could now barely remember had always told him he was nervous, fidgety, likely to change his mood with the weather. He had believed them, for what else could it be, the sudden, unexpected feeling that something was wrong, something bad was going to happen, something that shouldn't be here was right around the corner, about to wreak havoc?

And then after falling over in the forest he had woken

up in Endinfinium, and the feelings that had been little more than itches that need to be scratched had become glowing lights burning in the dark.

And one of them was standing at the end of the corridor ahead of him.

No mirrors, no cupboards now. The slender girl with the bright green, her hand lifted, stood in the middle of the corridor, beckoning him forward, imploring him to follow.

Every pore in his body told him to turn and run, but he found himself hurrying forward as though pulled on a string, running to catch up with her, even as she ducked out of sight around a bend, the light that had illuminated her vanishing too.

He reached the end of the corridor and turned. The girl was ahead, but closer than before. He made out her features, overlarge, glowing eyes, the elongated smile, the bony arms protruding from a dirty T-shirt which were little more than sticks covered with skin.

'Come. Follow.'

His stomach felt knotted, his palms damp through terror, but Snout found himself hurrying after as she turned and ran.

Her feet made no sound as she descended a flight of stairs to a lower level of storerooms. Snout reached the bottom just in time to see her feet disappear up another flight at the far end.

Standing in the gloom of the subterranean chamber, he stopped.

Chanting came from behind one of the doors.

The maths catch-up club … or was it?

Snout crept up to the door.

'We must try harder,' came the chant from inside. *'We must not fail. To fail is to fail ourselves. To fail is to fail the school. To fail is to fail the one who watches over us. To fail is to fall beneath his*

eyes. My brothers and sisters will protect me. And when he comes he will protect me. He is coming soon. He is coming soon.'

Snout pressed his ear against the wood, only to hear a shrieking, 'Class dismissed!' which could only have come from Godfrey. He shrank back into a nearby alcove as the door opened and pupils came streaming out.

He recognised Fat Adam and Tommy Cale, Sally Jones and Becky Denton from the among the second years. There was also Steve Dean and Emily Castonbury, two new first years who had both joined his horticulture club. Among them were a few others he didn't recognise in the shadows or whose names he didn't yet know. More than fifteen in total, all shaking their heads and frowning as though unsure what was going on.

'I think I learned a lot,' Fat Adam said to Becky Denton as they walked away. Becky Denton just muttered something monotone about getting a definite A in her next maths test.

The pupils disappeared up the stairs, heading back in the direction of the main entrance. Snout stayed where he was, two other voices still audible inside the room.

'Not long now,' came Godfrey's reedy voice.

'We're close, aren't we?' came Derek's reply, his eagerness to kiss Godfrey's butt clearly evident in his tone. 'I mean, you can talk to him, can't you? You know when he's coming?'

'When he can,' Godfrey said. 'And when he comes, he'll reward those of us who stood by him. We'll have all the power we can imagine, and all the toys we'll ever need. Can you imagine that, Derek? No more school. No more foul school lunches. No more stupid cleaning, or putting up with those stupid teachers. Video games all day long. People bringing us pizzas and hamburgers whenever we want. Sounds awesome, doesn't it?'

Derek gave a moronic snort. 'Yeah.'

The hard crack of a slap came, followed by a yelp from Derek. 'Well, wake up, then. You think he's just going to let us do what we want? Our work isn't finished, not by a long shot. He's angry because he's trapped, and only we can free him. Once he's free and he's back in control, we'll get our reward. But there's danger everywhere. Forrest and his cronies might have gone, but there are others we have to beware of, others that might try to stand up in his place. We have to stamp them out.'

'Yeah!'

'Come on, we've done enough for tonight. Get back to the dorms before that idiot suspects anything.'

Snout didn't have much time to ponder who 'that idiot' might be. Both himself and Gubbledon were prime front-runners for the label, he thought, though why he might be considered a threat, he didn't know.

They started to walk away, but after a few steps, Godfrey stopped, his head tilting.

'Do you smell something?'

Snout crouched down, his heart starting to race. He felt that tingle that he sometimes got when he was near people like Godfrey, or those orange-eyed things people called ghouls, or the teachers, or even Benjamin and his gang. Sometimes it was hot, sometimes it was cold, sometimes somewhere in between, pulsing hot and cold as though it couldn't decide which to chose.

He had once wondered what it was, but he could now label it as reanimation magic. Some of them had it, some a lot more than others, and it came in two shades, light and dark. Godfrey's was definitely on the wrong side of light, and it was spreading out, feeling all around.

Snout closed his eyes, concentrating. All around him he felt an invisible sheet lifting up, shielding him. Not far away, he heard Godfrey say, 'Probably just some filthy rotting cleaner. Let's go.'

As their footsteps receded, Snout let the sheet go, his magic vanishing into the earth. Sweat soaked his brow, and he could still hear the thousands of little voices that always called him when he did what he had done, asking if he wanted them to come. He still didn't understand his ability with the magic that infiltrated all of Endinfinium, but it was different to that of anyone else he had ever met. They would come for him if only he asked, and they would protect him.

As he hurried back to the dorms, he didn't like to think about whether that made him good or bad. It was better just to not know, to keep his head down as much as possible, to not think about Godfrey and his supposed maths catch-up class, the girl who was taunting him, and all the other stuff that kept happening that made him afraid. Best to just concentrate on the smallest thing, and the smallest thing was Derek being his new roommate.

Or was it?

For when he reached the door out onto the causeway, he found it locked from the other side. Snout groaned. He had no way back to the dorms without asking for someone to come with a master key and unlock it.

With a sigh, he turned and headed for the teachers' tower, planning to find Ms. Ito and discover how many cleans his latest transgression was worth.

17

BENJAMIN

'It started with the toys,' Sebastien Aren said, settling into a favourite armchair. Benjamin and Wilhelm sat opposite, on a comfortable old sofa, both holding a steaming mug of hot chocolate, while on the coffee table between them and Sebastien, a plate overflowed with fat, inviting cookies. A single standing corner lamp lit the cozy living room, its dim glow mixed with the flickering of an open log fire crackling behind a grate.

'At the time it felt like an attack on childhood, and it was so terrifying that at first the army was deployed to deal with it. The government thought it was some kind of crazy invasion, all these old toys standing up suddenly, dusting themselves down, and making their way towards London. People would get up on a Sunday morning and drive out to the countryside to watch it.'

'The toys walked?'

Sebastien smiled. 'It depended on the toy.' He shrugged. 'Walked, flew, drove, rolled … you name it.'

'They were alive?'

'I wouldn't say alive,' Sebastien said. 'That's a funny

way to put it. You could pick one up, put it in your pocket, and it would immediately stop whatever it was doing and become inanimate again.' He sighed. 'There were some bizarre sights, that's for sure. Soldiers gunning down child-sized teddy bears as they climbed over fences and ran across fields. They could be blown apart, yet the pieces would still keep moving. It took a few weeks for the authorities to realise that they weren't a threat, that they were simply moving towards a special place like metal filaments attracted to a magnet.'

'It must have been a little freaky,' Wilhelm said.

Sebastien nodded. 'You can't begin to imagine it. One night I got up and drove out to the edge of one of the quarantine zones, where fences had been erected, back when they thought it was the land that was causing it. I climbed over, and stood in a field beneath the full moon and watched an army of toys moving past me. I stood among them, watched them approach, watched some veer past me, others literally climb over. It was incredible, the most surreal experience a person could have. By then, of course, people were starting to understand the phenomenon.'

'They knew why?'

'The sudden reversion to an inanimate object was a big clue. It took a while, but eventually people figured it was a question of ownership. These weren't beloved toys marching across the countryside in their tens of thousands. They were the unloved, the abandoned, those thrown away.'

'So you decided to collect them?'

Sebastien nodded. 'I was already an antiques dealer, but I quickly realised that we could be facing a cleaning out of the cupboard of history, that if I didn't do what I could as soon as possible, all those beautiful toys made over the years ... they could all be lost forever.'

'How long ago was this?' Benjamin asked.

'Twenty years, give or take. It took a while for Dr. Forrest and his scientific theories to gain traction, but the evidence was indisputable and it was clear that the world had changed and couldn't be turned back. After he was freed from prison, things were allowed to take their natural course. Their new natural course.'

'Dr. Forrest?'

'Dr. Ben Forrest. The man who explained everything.'

Benjamin shared a glance with Wilhelm. Wilhelm gave a brief shrug, then lifted an eyebrow and pouted.

'He's, um, famous, is he?' Benjamin said, his throat dry.

'Famous and infamous, if you like. Famous for how his discovery has changed the way the world looks at rubbish. Infamous for its sheer robustness, that something is either encompassed by it, or not, and all the ethical problems that come with that.'

Benjamin glanced at Wilhelm, who was staring at the coffee table, his eyes wide. Benjamin didn't know what to say, even though a thousand questions burned on his lips. No doubt Wilhelm felt the same, but the sheer weight of what they were learning was holding them down.

'Well, I guess it's getting late,' Sebastien said, glancing up at the clock, which showed nearly ten p.m. 'It's probably a good idea to get some sleep. We can figure out what to do with you in the morning.'

'Are you sure it's okay for us to stay?' Wilhelm asked.

'I can hardly throw you out on the streets, can I? And a larger part of me than I'd like to admit is interested to hear the rest of your story.'

'And you're not going to quietly call those dog-catchers?'

Sebastien laughed. 'And have them trash my shop while they're chasing you two about? Not a chance.' He leaned forward. 'I am, however, concerned about that boy who saw you in my shop, and others who might be outside. Those Miscreants are a bit of a pest from time to time, and it wouldn't be the first time I've had someone try to break in. I shall be making sure the shutters are locked and the doors bolted. Two runaways are quite enough to deal with for one day.'

'Thanks,' Wilhelm muttered. 'We knew we could count on you.'

'Well, don't count on me just yet,' Sebastien said. 'You've only just got here, and there are eyes everywhere out there.'

Benjamin raised a tentative hand as Sebastien started to get up. 'Just one last question,' he said.

Sebastien smiled. 'Sure. And then it's bed for the lot of us.'

'Where does it all go?'

Sebastien let out a dry chuckle. 'London. Or near enough. A sinkhole opened up in the West End, and all those tumbleweeds just dropped right in. Made a bit of a mess of the city, it did, when they started rolling along, but they've got it organised a bit better now. London resembles something of a wagon wheel these days, though, with all the boroughs amended into triangular spokes with great swathes cut for the tumbleweeds to roll along. And there, of course, is where he sits, watching over everything.'

'Dr. Forrest?'

'The very same.'

Benjamin nodded. As he stood up, he caught a sly

glance from Wilhelm, but he shrugged it off. 'Any chance I can brush my teeth?' he asked.

∼

Wilhelm was gently snoring in his bed against the far wall, but Benjamin was unable to sleep. After Wilhelm had fallen asleep, he had gotten up and pulled back the curtains, so now he could see a full moon slowly tracing a path across the sky. He had too much to think about to be able to put things into any kind of hierarchal order, but his namesake, Dr. Ben Forrest, was up at the front of his mind.

Sebastien Aren knew a lot of things, but as more memories came back, Benjamin knew only one man would have all the answers.

The man who had tried to kill him on multiple occasions, the man whose influence hung like a raincloud over the world Benjamin had recently left behind.

Dr. Forrest.

Doctor Ben Forrest.

∼

'Are you all right?' Wilhelm asked, talking around a mouthful of cornflakes. 'That's the fifth time you've yawned in the last minute.'

Benjamin shrugged. 'Bed was a bit hard,' he said.

'Huh. Felt like I was lying on a sponge cake. Are you sure there's not something else?'

'Only everything.'

Wilhelm looked like he might blush, then he gave Benjamin a light punch on the arm. 'As Miranda might have said, hang in there.'

Benjamin laughed. 'She'd tell me to stop blubbing and stand up straight.'

'Yeah, she would.' Wilhelm sighed then gave a little sniff. 'I miss her. Not that I'd ever want her to know that.'

Wilhelm had told Benjamin what he remembered of the last time he had seen her, but they preferred to hope rather than dwell on what might have happened, and it had become a topic best left unspoken. He smiled. 'Me neither. And she'd say the same about us, I'm sure.'

'Finished?' Sebastien appeared through a door from the hall. He carried a jacket over one arm and a bag in the other. 'It would be good to get on the road before the traffic gets too heavy.'

'Where are we going?' Benjamin asked.

Sebastien smiled. 'Well, it's Sunday and I usually shut on Sunday. Normally I might fill my time with some leisure pursuit like hunting through the dump'—an awkward wink left Benjamin unsure if he was joking or telling the truth—'but since I have rather interesting guests, I thought it might be nice to take a drive out to one of the local sights.'

Benjamin stared. 'Please not Stonehenge. I went there on a school trip and it was so boring. Just a bunch of old rocks—'

Sebastien laughed. 'Oh no, this is very much more alive. In a sense, at least. And its temporary ... also in a sense. At least it'll be a lot further away if we wanted to go next weekend, and with electric cars taking over the world, petrol isn't cheap for my little vintage out there.'

'The tumbleweed?' Wilhelm asked.

Sebastien sighed. 'I was going to keep it as a surprise. Come on, let's get going. More likely we'll avoid any dog-catchers out wandering the streets. Although'—his face took on a stern look—'you'll be safe as long as you stay close to me.'

~

Half an hour later, they were rattling through the countryside. Sebastien took a scenic route along dozens of narrow lanes to avoid the congestion he claimed would clog the main roads. Whenever a tumbleweed appeared, some organisation was required to let it pass safely, and the damage its passing left behind often caused huge tailbacks, especially if it passed across a busy motorway.

'One thing no one ever talks about is what Dr. Forrest's discovery did for employment,' Sebastien said, glancing back at the boys as the car raced through winding lanes. 'Especially in the construction industry. Made the refuse collection industry obsolete, but at least all those workers had a job to go to as long as they could work a spade or drive a lorry. Near bankrupted the councils, but tourism's starting to kick in now, which should keep them going for a while.'

Benjamin glanced at Wilhelm. 'Tourism?'

'Tumbleweed-viewing is more popular than whale-watching,' Sebastien said. 'Although it'll be temporary. A few have started to appear in Europe, some in France, a couple in Italy. All coming this way, as there's still only the one big sinkhole. Not sure how they're going to cross the Channel, but a couple of smaller ones have been spotted offshore, made of ocean rubbish.'

'That's incredible,' Benjamin said.

Sebastien shrugged. 'You wait until you see one up close.'

'Are we there yet?' Wilhelm said, throwing a grin at Benjamin.

'Not yet, but here's something.'

Sebastien slowed the car as they passed a series of warning signs instructing them to lower their speed. One sign said: ROAD UNDER RECONSTRUCTION. They trundled around a corner, and Benjamin gasped. Up ahead, the road, fields, and hedgerows had been squashed flat across an area as wide as a football field. The road's former route had been cleared, filled in with gravel and marked with red barrier tape, but the hedgerows were a crushed tumble of rocks, mud, and plant matter. From the way some clumps of grass had sprouted, it had happened some time ago.

'This one came through in the spring,' Sebastien said. 'It was half the size of the one I'm taking you to see, and moved much quicker, a few miles a day. You see what I mean?'

He pulled the car out onto the gravel and slowed almost to a stop so they could see the line of destruction stretching away into the valley. Above them, it cut right through a patch of woodland and disappeared over a hill. Below, it angled through farmland, leaving a brown smear, vanishing behind a wooded hillock.

'You see that pile of rubble down there? That was a farmhouse. The people got out, I believe, but this tumbleweed was moving too quickly to be diverted. Trying to keep the things from causing too much damage is a whole industry in itself.'

They started moving again, and soon found themselves back on the original road. Sebastien, permanently smiling as though he'd waited years for someone to talk to and then two people had come along at once, hummed as he hacked the rickety old car around sharp corners and down steep, meandering hills, laughing as they plunged through fords and grimacing as the car struggled with steep upward climbs. Then, at last, they came over the brow of a hill and they saw what he had brought them to see.

'Wow,' Benjamin said, peering out the window. 'That's quite something.'

Sebastien pulled the car to a stop in a little parking area on a hill overlooking the monstrosity moving slowly through the valley below. They all climbed out and stood for a few minutes, taking everything in.

Even from their vantage point, the tumbleweed towered over them. It was simply enormous, higher than most buildings Benjamin had ever seen, and while it looked like a rough circle from a distance, close up, it was more of a shifting shape, constantly contracting and expanding as it slowly turned, rubbish thrown off regrouping to rejoin at the back or sides.

'Is that a hotdog stand down there?' Wilhelm asked.

Sebastien gave a sheepish grin. 'This is a slow one,' he said. 'Therefore, it's attracted quite a circus.'

The industry spreading out around the tumbleweed was almost as impressive as the moving mountain itself. The thing, for all its size, was moving at a relatively slow pace. Around its foot was a vast, moving entourage. First were the crane construction crews regularly firing large grapple lines into its midriff and attempting to steer it along a path that had evidently been rolled flat by previous tumbleweeds. Outside of them were lines of security: both people running to keep up and jacked-up police cars bumping over gravel laid alongside to provide a temporary roadway. And outside them came the mass-market: the food and drink stalls, the tour guides offering constantly elongating sightseeing walks around the tumbleweed's foot, the souvenir stands—selling what manner of souvenirs, Benjamin couldn't see from here—and even, set back into the fields, helicopter crews offering aerial tours. Milling among it all were hundreds of people, their cars left in car parks set up in nearby fields along the route, cameras clicking, hot dogs held to lips. Every so often a scream would come as someone got too close or an overlarge piece of rubbish fell off the main body like a calving iceberg, then a collective *ooh* would sound as whatever danger passed without incident.

'That's incredible,' Benjamin said. 'And there are more?'

'About thirty across the whole of the country,' Sebastien said. 'There are websites set up to track their progress, if you like that kind of thing. There's all sorts of jargon connected to them, too. This one is a mega-load, one of the largest types. I think the tallest ever measured reached a hundred and eighty metres just before it dropped into the sinkhole. This one is roughly a hundred and twenty, but we're a fair way out from London, so it'll grow a bit yet. However, as you can probably guess, there's not the bulk of rubbish that there was in the early days. Used to be they'd get all the plastic bags chucked out of cars, or the old TVs dumped in forests, but all that's gone now. It's only what's actively thrown away. In recent years, smaller ones—genesis-loads—have sometimes rumbled across the country and dropped into the sinkhole before reaching fifty metres.' Sebastien smiled. 'For better or worse, the country is definitely cleaner than it was a few years ago.'

'That's good, isn't it?' Wilhelm asked.

Sebastien shrugged. 'Good in some ways, bad in others.'

'Where are the TV crews?' Benjamin asked. It had been bugging him what seemed to be missing, and he had finally figured it out.

Sebastien laughed. 'Oh, the tumbleweeds became old news ten years ago. You'll never see them mentioned unless they do something unexpected, like crush a listed building or veer wildly off course. Since the major route lines were established and a whole industry developed to nudge them in the right direction, most people don't even notice them. They'll rumble past while you're sleeping and you'll not even realise.'

'Can we take a closer look?' Benjamin asked.

'Sure, why not?' Sebastien winked at Wilhelm. 'The little guy's looking hungry.'

Wilhelm patted his stomach. 'The little guy certainly is. The food here's a lot better than it was where I came from.'

'Not the continent, then?' Sebastien said, smiling as though it was a joke. 'English food's a running joke over there.'

'I'd live off hot dogs if I had a chance,' Wilhelm said.

'I suppose we'd better go and get you one, then.'

They all piled back into Sebastien's car and began another circuitous route, this time to get in front of the tumbleweed. After being stuck in a car park queue for half an hour, Sebastien finally found them a space about a mile ahead of the massive moving ball of rubbish. The food and trinket stalls which were actually little mobile carts, were already in place, so they got refreshments then found a comfortable patch of grass to sit on while they waited for the monstrosity to roll past.

'Here,' Sebastien said, passing them both a handkerchief. 'Sometimes they smell bad. Depends what kind of rubbish is on the outside.'

The huge tumbleweed groaned as it approached, slowly tumbling over, rubbish breaking off and falling, only to be crushed back into the body as it rolled on. Benjamin realised too now that the tumbleweed was still constantly growing, as objects flew through the air to assimilate with the main body. Most were light, plastic bags, pieces of food waste, ripped cardboard boxes, but occasionally something massive would approach. Not far away, a commotion grew among a small section of the crowd as they parted to let a sofa come tumbling through. It bounced into the shadows beneath the tumbleweed, which rolled and it was gone.

'Back, back!' shouted a man waving an orange flag as he came running along the crushed causeway, flapping his free hand at anyone sitting too close. 'She's bigger than she looks, and there's a section near the top that's unstable!'

Sebastien led the boys back a short distance, where they took up a new position in the corner of a field now missing its lower hedgerow. The crowd around them was swelling as people further down the line ran to get in front of the tumbleweed as it approached.

As it came level with them, Benjamin saw what the man with the flag had said: On the uppermost part, a great corner of the tumbleweed appeared to be made only of old furniture, all crushed together. As it revolved, a huge whoop went up from the crowd as a house-sized section came crashing down ahead of it, spreading out across the ground in front. Then, as the tumbleweed turned, those pieces which had fallen out of its line began to move by themselves, scraping along the ground and rolling over until they were once again part of the main body.

'And there we have it, folks,' came the amplified voice of some tour guide. 'A cycle of birth and rebirth. It's like a miracle all over again.'

Benjamin rolled his eyes as a section of the crowd further down the slope cheered and clapped. It really was a circus. A part of him was transfixed and couldn't look away, but another part just wanted to go home ... wherever that now was.

It was easy to get used to the constant background noise. Wilhelm had finished his hot dog and was now tucking into a box of popcorn as the tumbleweed creaked and groaned like an old ship caught in rough weather. The crowd *umm*ed and *aah*ed, and the surrounding circus added a cacophony of machine sounds. Benjamin found himself slipping into a kind of trance as the tumbleweed came level ... and stopped.

A ripple of excitement was spreading through the crowd. The tumbleweed began to creak again, but this time its bulk was shifting around, turning away from the pre-crushed causeway that would take it all the way to London, its front end moving to face upslope.

And then, with a roar of collapsing rubbish, it began to move again.

'Get back, get back!' shouted another amplified voice. 'Give it space! What we're seeing is unprecedented. Cameras rolling ... cameras, are you rolling?'

People were screaming, pushing past them to get away. Someone a few rows in front was whining about having to pack up a picnic table, while someone else was shouting about how the tumbleweed had stolen their sandwich. As the crowd parted, Benjamin saw a man jump out of a hot dog van's window moments before the tumbleweed rolled over it. Another crane was on its side, and a ticker table set up to mark the route now made luminous, veinlike streaks across the tumbleweed's front as it creaked and groaned uphill.

A hand fell on his shoulder.

'We really should get out of here,' Sebastien said.

They pushed through the crowd, heading in a rough direction for Sebastien's car. The tumbleweed groaned as it moved upslope, the crowd parting around it in a deafening cacophony of screams, as many people excited as terrified. Other people were climbing over each other to get into their cars as the monstrosity headed for the nearest car park, creating a massive logjam of people and vehicles as they all sought to leave at once.

'We'll never get out,' Sebastien said. 'Head for the woods. We'll walk over to the nearest town and catch a bus if we have to.'

'What about your car?'

Sebastien looked pained. 'I'd rather escape with my life,' he said. He fixed Benjamin with a long stare until a sudden crash from behind made him turn. The tumbleweed had crushed the first line of cars, and the now-flattened vehicles had been assimilated into its mass and were rising like colourful giant playing cards up its rear side as it turned.

They reached the edge of the field and ran into the first of the trees. 'Keep going,' Sebastien said. 'Don't look back.'

Of course Benjamin did, and he noticed Wilhelm repeatedly throwing glances back over his shoulder too. The ground below them was grassy and leafy, the forest old, the trees spread out. It was easy to run, but as they did so, Benjamin noticed the ground shifting in places, years of mulched leaves ripping apart as long-buried plastic bags and other rubbish broke free, flapping away behind them, back in the tumbleweed's direction.

They raced down a valley, Wilhelm in the lead, Benjamin hurrying behind. Along the valley floor trickled a small river, only a few feet wide but enough to make Wilhelm hurry to a stop. Benjamin stopped behind him, breathing hard. He looked back up the valley and saw Sebastien moving more carefully down through the trees, frowning as he climbed over protruding tree roots.

'Can you still hear it?' Wilhelm asked.

Benjamin shook his head. 'I think it's gone.'

Wilhelm stared at him. 'You know what just happened, don't you?'

Benjamin swallowed. 'Yes.'

'It came for you.'

'I know. Do you think Sebastien noticed?'

Wilhelm shrugged. 'I'm not sure. But I think it would be a good idea to keep you away from those things from now on, wouldn't it?'

18

MIRANDA

Miranda inched back the curtain and peered out. The corridor was empty, but just as she began to crawl out of the cramped cleaning space, she heard footsteps. Hurrying to get back in behind the row of buckets and brooms, she dropped the curtain back just as two shadows rounded the nearest corner.

'She must have got out somehow,' came Alamy's voice.

The man who answered was unfamiliar. 'All the entrances are guarded. And no one has been near that thing. No, she's down here somewhere. We'll have to wait her out.'

'But the tunnels run for miles.'

'She'll get hungry and try to thieve something. That's how children's minds work. They're simple, predictable. We just have to think one step ahead.'

Miranda rolled her eyes, wishing she could punch the man for being so condescending. As soon as the chase had started, Miranda had learned from her long, hungry journey with Enchantress and made a detour for Alamy's kitchen. She had enough bread rolls stuffed into her pockets to keep her going for a couple of days if necessary, but finding the exit was key. She had found one, but someone had been guarding it. The man had talked in plurals, though, so there had to be another.

Alamy and the man moved off. Miranda waited until their footsteps were out of earshot, then crept out of her hiding place and followed after them, walking on the sides of her feet to avoid making any footfalls, at the same time tentatively feeling for her magic.

She had just come around another corner when she heard more voices, more numerous than before. Unlike Alamy and her companion, these voices were carefree, excited, even.

Children.

Around the next bend a gated chamber had a wooden sign over its entrance with SLEEPERS PRIMARY painted on it and illuminated by glowing battery lights on either side. Through a closed wooden gate that rose to Miranda's chest, a small group of children was visible, playing with boxes of wooden toys. A man sat at a desk in a corner, leaning over a pad of paper, his back turned as the children played.

Miranda crept closer. Desks lined one wall, pushed aside for playtime. A timetable written on a blackboard fixed to one wall announced lessons of English, math, P.E., science, and music, with short breaks in between and an hour for lunch. A clock hung above it, reading eleven-fifty. The next class started at twelve.

Sitting on her own, playing with two toy horses, Rosa was almost directly behind the teacher, out of view. Miranda squatted down, squinted at the horses, and concentrated. Feeling a weak tug of power, she made one twist its head up to Rosa and smile. The girl gasped, then giggled. She started to turn to a friend, but Miranda made the horse shake its head. Rosa frowned. Miranda made the horse lift a leg and point at the gate. When Rosa looked up, Miranda gave a short wave.

Rosa hurried over. Miranda tried to stay back in the shadows, but she had only moments before the other kids spotted them talking.

'You're up,' Rosa exclaimed. 'You know you'll get told off if they see you moving stuff around. It was really funny, though.'

'I'm sorry. I didn't want to call out. I want to talk only to you.'

'Are you taking a walk around?'

'Kind of.' Miranda shrugged. 'I wanted to visit my friend, but I heard she's being kept on the surface somewhere.'

'You mean that big bird made of paper?'

'It's a swan,' Miranda said. 'But yes, that's the one.'

'Oh, we're not allowed to talk about that. Mummy said its one of those naughty things that sometimes come down from the mountains.'

'Well, in that case, I just wanted to get some fresh air. How can I get up to the ground above?'

'Oh, you'd have to ask Mummy.'

'But your mummy's in a meeting with some other people.'

Rosa frowned. 'Well, when we go on a school trip up to the chamomile fields, we go up the left stairs.'

'The left stairs?'

'Yes. They're down the second left if you turn out of here to the right.'

'The second left to the right, and the left stairs….?'

Rosa beamed. 'That's it. You've got it. They come out in the caves. Teacher says it's so we can check outside to make sure the coast is clear.'

She said this last phrase with a sense of pride, as though they had learned it in their last English class.

'Thanks, Rosa. Now, don't tell anyone you saw me. I don't want them to be worried—'

'Rosa? Who's that you're talking to?'

Another little girl had stood up and was looking at the gate. Disturbed, the teacher turned.

'No one!' Rosa hooted, flapping her hands, a big grin on her face. 'No one at all!'

Miranda didn't stay to find out what happened. She bolted into the dark, hoping she was going in the right direction, but already unsure. The second stairs to the left, or the right? Or was it the second door?

Running feet came from behind her. She was still wondering which way to go when she noticed a glow up ahead and saw steps leading up. Was this Rosa's staircase? Miranda didn't bother to consider it. She ran for the steps, vaulting up two at a time.

Voices came from below her, but Miranda didn't recognise them. The staircase got steeper and steeper, the rock underfoot turning to buried, calcified metal, as though she were running up a fossilised fire escape.

She was nearly out of breath when she reached the top and found herself faced with a heavy wooden door. A rusty handle turned but the door was locked. Miranda concentrated, searching for her magic, finding it there but weak, suppressed. The door had been chamomile-soaked, making it resistant, but there was more, some other force holding it still—a magical ward.

Below her came the clatter of ascending feet. Miranda gritted her teeth and concentrated. Her magic was there, hidden by the chamomile's overwhelming presence and suppressed by a magical ward which permeated everything, but it was still present. The door hadn't been doused in some time, and whoever had laid the ward hadn't reckoned on a Channeller trying to break through. With a sharp jerk, the lock moved.

Miranda pushed out through the door and found herself in a dim tunnel. Quickly she squeezed the door shut and worked her magic to push the lock back into place. The tunnel went in two directions, but she chose the one heading towards the light and soon found herself seeing real daylight for the first time in what felt like months.

The tunnel ended in a rock crevasse that opened out onto a steep hillside. Miranda took a few tentative steps outside and found the world opening up into a panorama of rolling hills in every direction. Far to the northeast, a pencil line of fogbank obscured the lower slopes of a line of mountains, the peaks of which jutted up into the sky.

Behind her came a loud thump. Someone was trying to get through the door. Miranda let out a gasp and started down the slope, unsure where she was going. Below, what she had at first thought was grass, she now realised was thousands upon thousands of chamomile plants, all swaying in the breeze, the scent different from what she was familiar with, fresh, untouched. She ran a little further until she reached it, finding the plants rising around her waist.

From here, she could see past the outcrop she had emerged from. Others rose around her, craggy hillocks topped with lumpy rock formations, some hiding caves. In the nearest, she spotted a dark entrance, so she pushed through the chamomile plants towards it.

The entrance was flatter and wider than the one she had exited, and just inside, something glinted as it caught the sun. A cage. Something round and white lay in the middle, a mound of soggy paper, soaked through by a continuous trickle of chamomile tea which ran from a tap protruding from the rock face and down across the floor.

'Enchantress!'

Out of the globule of what was left of the bird, a waxen head lifted. Eyes blinked and a beak opened.

'Oh, Miranda, dear, there you are,' came Enchantress's weak voice. 'I did wonder where you'd gone.'

Miranda gripped the bars. 'What happened to you?'

'I guess they want to keep me subdued,' the bird said. She lifted a wide flap of paper. 'My wing is fixed, don't you know? I only need to dry out in order to fly again.' The bird cocked its head. 'But don't worry, dear. I'll be fine.'

Miranda opened her mouth to speak but footsteps from inside the tunnel made her turn.

'Stop!' Trobin shouted, as the man with the dog-headdress appeared out of the gloom. 'Get away from that cage!'

'I'll come back for you,' Miranda hissed, then bolted out into the sunlight.

A few feet down the slope she stopped. A line of oversized animal heads appeared out of the grass below, spreading out to surround her. Bears, rabbits, cats, even a lion. At first the shock of seeing them rooted her to the spot. Then, as Trobin's voice came from behind her, she remembered.

The Sleepers with their bizarre disguises had found her.

'Miranda, wait!'

Miranda glowered, lifting her hands. These simple magic deniers would not contain her again. They had no right to hold her underground, and what they had done to Enchantress bordered on barbaric.

'I will not be your prisoner!' she shouted, concentrating, reaching for her magic. Out here in the open, it was far stronger than it had been underground, the effects of the ward far weaker. She could fight them off with ease, free Enchantress, and together they could escape.

'Wait! Don't do it! The airship!'

She turned. Trobin, face only just visible below the massive lolling dog's head, pointed to the north. There, a tiny, dark oval hung in the sky. At this distance mistakable for some kind of bird, she knew it was anything but.

The Dark Man was still searching for her.

Panic began to rise. Enchantress was damaged, unable to fly, and the Sleepers were closing in. On foot, she wouldn't get far, but in any case she couldn't bring herself to leave Enchantress behind, not with these people, these savages—

'We have children!' Trobin shouted. 'We've been hiding here for generations! If he finds us, he'll send an army to wipe us out. Don't use it. Please!'

Miranda turned to face him. The magic was still there, at her fingertips. She wanted to pick him up and throw him over the hilltop, smash some sense into him. These people were idiots, denying what was all around, what was right in front of their faces.

Realisation shook her like a hard gust of wind. They were no different really to the teachers at the school. They had denied the existence of reanimation magic until they had no choice, but even now it was tentatively taught, explained with care, its use prohibited outside of class.

Why?

To protect the children. And wasn't that what these people were trying to do? Protect children like Rosa, growing up in the shadow of the Dark Man?

If she channeled her magic to fight off these people, she would draw the Dark Man's attention, and the children who knew nothing of the world in which they existed would be threatened with great danger.

Death, she remembered, wasn't the worst that could happen.

With a sigh of resignation, she let her magic go.

Almost immediately, invisible arms clamped around her, pulling her to the ground. Her body rolled as she slid through the grass, moving upslope until she lay at Trobin's feet. He looked down at her and smiled. 'Thank you for your cooperation.'

'What did you do? You told me—'

Trobin smiled again. 'Your use of magic is so immature,' he said. 'When you've lived with it as long as I, you'll learn how to disguise it.'

'The wards—?'

'Of course. Someone has to keep these people safe.'

The others had reached them. Trobin instructed them to bind her and take her inside. Miranda felt for her magic, but now a ward surrounded her alone. She could feel it, pushing in, and while her magic was there, it was suppressed, hidden so deep she couldn't find the strength to pull it free.

'Where do you want us to take her?' one of those holding her arms said.

'She can't be allowed to escape again,' Trobin said. 'Take her to the cells.'

19

SNOUT

THE TICKER CLICKED OVER TO ZERO. SNOUT GAVE A long sigh then picked a pencil off the conveyor and did one last clean, just for luck.

Eight hundred. By his count he had now broken three thousand already this term, and they were only a couple of weeks in. He knew a couple of the Fifth Years did an unofficial competition with prizes awarded to the pupils who did the most cleans. Everyone knew that legendary Fifth Year misfit Tony Burns was way out in front, but according to sources, Snout was lying a close third behind a first year boy who had somehow managed to set fire to his school uniform.

Third wasn't bad, although he'd rather be sitting on the same fat zero as at least half of the other kids, even if to survive the whole year without doing a single clean was almost unheard of.

When he reached the top of the stairs leading down into the basements, he found Tommy Cale lingering in the corridor.

'Hey, Simon, I figured you must be due out by now.'

Snout shrugged. 'Yeah, took my time, I suppose. What time is it?'

'Just after eight.'

Snout breathed a sigh of relief. He had a teachers' pass card from Ms. Ito proving he had a reason to be in the school after nine, but he still had to ask for someone to let him through the door. Just being in the presence of the teachers these days carried the very real threat of additional cleans.

'What are you doing in here, anyway?'

'Maths catch-up club.'

Snout smiled. 'Oh, I forgot you're a second year. How is it?'

Tommy Cale looked down. 'I want to stop going.'

'Why don't you?'

'Because Mistress Xemian said we have to make over sixty in the weekly review test in order to be exempt. 'Last week I got fifty-eight, but this week I was back down to fifty-seven.'

'You're close.'

'The thing is, I don't think I'm ever going to make it.'

'Why's that?'

'Because Godfrey doesn't teach us maths. He just stands at the front, prattling on about stuff most of us don't understand. If we even look down at our textbooks, we get balled out for not paying attention. It feels like he's trying to hypnotise us.'

Snout had felt something similar when he had overheard one of the afterschool classes.

'Perhaps we should go to Professor Loane and tell him,' he said.

Tommy Cale gave a bitter laugh. 'Yeah, Godfrey would like that. Remember, the teachers all disappear at night into their tower. I don't feel much protection from Gubbledon, do you?'

Snout frowned. His own policy had been to keep his head down. In many ways, going down to the lockers after dinner was better than going back to the dorms, where Derek was making his life a misery.

Tommy Cale's lip was trembling. 'There's something else.'

'What?'

'I feel kind of stupid after me and Adam took the mickey out of you ... but I've seen a strange girl.'

Snout jerked around. 'You mean—?'

'Like you said you saw in that closet. Kind of creepy-looking. Always runs away, but she keeps telling me to follow her. She doesn't make any noise, and her voice is weird, like it's in my head.'

'Where did you see her?'

'Outside the gym on the third floor. I left my shorts behind so I went back after dinner yesterday to get them. She was outside when I came out of the changing rooms.'

'How close?'

'Down the corridor, in the dark, you know, waving at me.'

'Did you recognise her?'

'No, but she looked kind of familiar. I felt like I should.'

'What do you mean?'

Tommy Cale frowned. 'Well, I thought she might be one of the cleaners. You know how most of them disappeared after that trouble a few weeks ago? Well, there were some new ones too, weren't there? I was wondering if she might be one of those, but that she's not really a cleaner, just pretending, you know?'

Snout shrugged. 'You read a lot more books than me, so I suppose you'd know.'

'What do you think?'

'I think I'm losing my mind, and it sounds like you're losing yours now too.'

Tommy was quiet for a few seconds. Then he said, 'Adam saw her too.'

'Really?' Snout lifted an eyebrow. 'He never said.'

'He told me, but he didn't want to tell you because of the same reason. He didn't want to look like a muppet for laughing at you.'

'When?'

'A couple of nights ago.'

'Did he follow her?'

'He said he did, but she disappeared. He said she was leading him towards the old science block on the east wing's third floor.'

'The abandoned one?'

Tommy nodded.

'He said he followed her up to those doors, which are kept locked, but when he reached them, she'd disappeared.'

Snout grimaced. 'This could be serious. We really should go and talk to Professor Loane, or at least Professor Caspian.'

'And do you really think they'd know what to do? You know as well as I do that the only one who might care is Ms. Ito, and she'd just send us to the lockers to keep us out of trouble. What was it she said? "Wandering thoughts get into tricky situations."'

'We need to talk to Adam,' Snout said. 'Come on, let's head back. I don't want to get locked out all over again.'

They headed back across to the dormitory building. Gubbledon was waiting outside the dormitory's main entrance, one hand tapping his wrist as they hurried across the causeway.

'What time do you call this?' he groaned in a kind of half-horse, half-human voice. 'I was just about to lock the doors. There's a storm coming in from the west. Another ten minutes and you'd have been washed off.'

'Cherise White is still in the locker room,' Adam said. 'And Derek Bates.'

Gubbledon nodded. 'Well, I hope they're on their way back. If they leave it much longer they'll have to bunk down in reception for the night. Come on, get inside.'

In anticipation of the coming weather maelstrom, many of the other kids had brought pillows and blankets downstairs and had taken up residence by the common room's bay windows. As Snout and Tommy came in, Gubbledon tried to get them to go to bed, but was met with the same refusals his tone suggested he had been hearing all evening.

'But Housemaster, what if the upper floors blow away?'

Snout looked around for Fat Adam, but he was nowhere to be seen, so he waved Tommy after him and together they climbed the stairs. They found Adam sitting by the bedroom window he shared with Tommy, gazing out at the sea.

'Hey, guys,' he said, briefly turning around. 'Have you seen it? The sky's going crazy out there. Looks like it's going to dump down at any minute. The wind's getting up too.'

Tommy sat down on the edge of his lower bunk and Snout took a spare stool. Adam ignored them, watching the sky as great, dark clouds billowed in, many lit up by jagged lightning. A minute after Fat Adam had predicted it, the heavens opened, and rain began to drum so loudly on the roof above that Snout could barely hear himself think.

'Tommy told me what you saw,' he said, practically shouting. 'You know, the girl.'

At first Fat Adam ignored him, then he slowly turned back. 'Oh, so let me guess, you've come to have a joke.'

Snout shook his head. 'No. We've all seen her, and perhaps we're not the only ones.'

'Who is she?'

Snout shrugged. 'I have no idea.'

'Do you think we should tell the teachers?' Adam asked.

'What about Godfrey?' Tommy said.

'What about him?'

Tommy gave a nervous laugh. 'I'm far more scared of getting in trouble with him than with the teachers.'

Adam nodded. 'And they're in his pocket, anyway.'

Snout didn't want to admit it, but he agreed. Telling the teachers would get them nowhere, but if all three of them had seen the girl, it could mean others had too. And what if she was leading kids into something dangerous?

Not for the first time he wished Benjamin, Wilhelm, and Miranda were here. They would have stormed off like heroes and figured out what to do.

'Come on, Simon,' Tommy Cale said. 'You always know what to do.'

'Since when?'

Fat Adam flashed a nervous smile. 'Since now.'

'Well,' Snout began, not entirely sure what he was going to say. 'We have to figure out what's going on, don't we? We can't just sit around and wait for Benjamin and his mates to show up and help us.' Far from feeling brave, Snout was literally shaking with nerves.

'And how do we do that?'

'I've seen her twice,' Snout said. 'I didn't know where she was trying to lead me, but now that I look back, it was in that direction, wasn't it? The old science block. She's in there.'

'Or something else is in there,' Fat Adam said. 'Something that might eat us all.'

'Stop thinking about food,' Tommy said.

'It might!'

'I know, but don't keep talking about it, just in case it comes true.'

'We have to go in there and face her,' Snout said, so quietly that at first neither Tommy Cale nor Fat Adam realised what he had said. 'We have to be brave, and go in there, and see who she is, and what she wants. That's what Benjamin and Wilhelm would have done, but they're not here. They could be dead, but bad stuff keeps happening. And'—he punched a fist into his other palm—'we have to stand up and be heroes.'

He glanced up, but neither Tommy nor Fat Adam was looking at him. Both were staring at the doorway.

Snout turned, his heart lurching as he found Derek Bates leaning through the doorway. His hair was wet as though he'd caught the beginning of the storm in his rush across the causeway, but his face was split by a massive leer.

'Ahaha, listen to you three chumps!' he bellowed. '"We have to be heroes." What a load of muck! You three? Heroes of what? Carrot-planting club?' Derek wiped a hand across his eyes. 'Oh, brother, I don't think I've ever heard anything so ridiculous. I can't wait to tell Godfrey.'

'Go away,' Fat Adam said. 'This isn't your room.'

Snout, his cheeks flushed, wondered how much Derek had overheard. 'We're just, um, playing a roleplay game,' he said.

Derek laughed so hard he spat on the floor. 'Oh, what fun!' he wailed. 'Let me guess, Fatboy over there is the mother pig, you're the father pig, and Cale is the runt?' He suddenly dropped to all fours and shouted, 'Oink, oink! Oink, oink!'

Footsteps came on the stairs outside as Derek continued his pig impression. Gubbledon appeared, a frown on his long, partly decomposed horse face.

'Whatever is going on up here?'

Derek jumped to his feet. 'Oh, I'm sorry, Housemaster. We were just playing charades. Were we too loud?' He turned to the others. 'Come on, wasn't it obvious? Three Little Pigs.'

With another howl of laughter, he pushed past Gubbledon and headed up the stairs.

'Keep the noise down,' Gubbledon said, glancing at each of them in turn before heading back downstairs.

For a few seconds, no one spoke. Then Fat Adam said, 'I don't think he heard everything.'

Snout, his cheeks burning, was too humiliated to speak, but Tommy Cale smiled. With one eye on the door, in case Derek made a sudden reappearance, he whispered, 'I say we do it. I've always wanted to be a hero.'

20

BENJAMIN

The tumbleweed, after veering off course for an unprecedented mile of destruction, had gradually returned to its original route, eventually returning to the carved channel along which its progress had been predicted, according to the BBC news. Despite no longer needing to fear that it would come and roll over them during the night, Benjamin was certain he would find sleep hard to come by for the next few days.

After settling them down in front of the TV, Sebastien had gone back out, taking a taxi he said, back to the site where he had been lucky enough to find the tumbleweed's brief course alteration had missed his beloved car. On his return, Sebastien hadn't said anything openly about what had happened, and Benjamin had made Wilhelm promise not to say anything, but the look in the old man's eyes told Benjamin he suspected what had happened.

The tumbleweed had come straight for Benjamin, and had they not gotten out of its range, it would have rolled them pancake-flat, just as it had done to several hundred parked cars.

At least that seemed more likely. It was evidence, if nothing else, that Benjamin was who he said he was, but after gaining Sebastien's trust as an imposter, he was unwilling to fight once more for his original assertion, afraid of being cast out. While he felt that he and Wilhelm should be doing more to find a way back to Endinfinium, or at least find out what was really going on, it nevertheless felt nice to sleep in a real bed.

But it couldn't last, and he knew it.

He sat up and slipped out of the bed, then made it up as neatly as he had found it. His clothes were folded up on a chair by the window, so he quietly dressed, peering between the curtains at the street outside, bathed in cool moonlight.

Wilhelm was still snoring. Benjamin gave his friend's shoulder a quick squeeze then slipped out of the room, closing the door behind him. Further down the hall, he passed Sebastien's bedroom, the door open a crack. Benjamin glanced inside, making sure the old man was fast asleep before descending the stairs to the ground floor.

On Sebastien's desk he scrawled a brief note on a piece of headed paper, and tucked it under a paperweight. Then, he opened the till and took out just enough money that he thought he would need.

In the kitchen, he assembled a small bag of fruit and bread which he hoped would last him a couple of days. His cheeks burned at the thought of being labeled a thief, so he went back and amended his note with an apology.

Then he headed for the door.

The front door had two bolts and a Yale lock. Benjamin unlocked it and stepped outside. Standing on the step with a cool breeze ruffling his hair, he held onto the door for a long time, aware that once it was closed, he was locked out, and there was no way back. With a frantic nod of stoicism, he clicked it shut. Now, he was truly on his own again, but at least Sebastien and Wilhelm would be safe.

And he knew what he had to do.

~

The streets were unfamiliar, having changed a lot in however much time had passed since he had woken up in Endinfinium, but the general town layout was the same and soon he found himself at the end of a wide street which ended in a turning circle outside Basingstoke's little train station.

It was a little after three in the morning, and to his dismay the earliest commuter train for London wasn't until five a.m. The station had a sign outside to say the main building was closed until half an hour before the earliest train, so Benjamin had no choice but to wait in a sticky-warm pre-fab waiting room tacked onto the outside edge of the station's east exit. A couple of overnighters were bunking down on the only bench, forcing Benjamin to stand. The room smelled of cigarettes and urine, and after ten minutes, Benjamin had had enough. He pushed out through the door, back into the cold.

It was only an hour. Wishing he had the option to go back to bed for a bit longer, he rubbed his hands together until his palms gained a semblance of warmth, and then took off for a circuit of the town centre to get a bit of heat into his legs.

Most of the shops were new, but as he walked, taking everything in, a sense of familiarity began to grow, as though his own memories were adjusting to accommodate this new situation. It made him feel uncomfortable, as though his own reality was shifting backwards, making false what he had grown up with and recreating the past. After a few minutes, he could really believe that the Primark next to the HSBC where his mother had always shopped for his school uniform had never existed at all, that it had always been a Costa coffee-and-book shop, or that the little greengrocer which had once sold him an apple with a worm in it had always been a specialist shop selling expensive wood burners. The more he thought about it, the more that greengrocer faded, until he was unsure if he had ever eaten that apple at all.

Frustrated, he headed back towards the station, not wanting to taint his memories any further, in case he found that they began to erase his family, just like the construction company which had built the playground had erased his house. He was losing his sense of belonging a little more with each step. He had to get out of Basingstoke while he still had some of his identity left.

A station worker had unlocked the building's main entrance and was propping up a couple of signboards outside when Benjamin returned. He could now go inside, get a ticket, and maybe even a hot cup of tea from a machine he could see just inside, its buttons flickering with lights. He hoped Sebastien and Wilhelm were still soundly asleep, but he wouldn't feel really comfortable until he was racing away on a train.

'Hey! Hey, you!'

The voice stopped him in his tracks. He turned, bringing his hands up, expecting to see a team of dog-catchers, but instead he found himself looking into the eyes of the boy he had saved a few days ago, the boy who had spied on them inside Sebastien's emporium.

The boy was sitting on the step of a war memorial, wrapped in a thick duffel coat which framed his face with grey fluff. Benjamin took a quick stock of his clothes, noting the scuffed knees of the boy's trousers, the ragged shoes, and an unwashed smell which lingered whenever the breeze dropped.

'Hey,' Benjamin said. 'It's Ray, isn't it?'

The boy's face lit up. 'You remembered? Must have left as great an impression on you as you did on me. Thanks for what you did the other day, by the way. You saved my life.'

'No problem. What are you doing out here?'

Ray shrugged. 'Foraging, wandering, the usual. This is my world, out here. Me and a few others. Don't like to sit still too long. Got to keep moving, see?'

'Why?'

Ray grinned. Benjamin felt a sudden warming of the air around them, and a breeze whipped up around his feet. A piece of newspaper, caught in a crack in the pavement, suddenly broke free and began to swirl in the air between them as though caught in a microcosmic tornado.

'No one wants us. Because of what we can do. Because of what happens when we touch something.' Ray grinned again, this time revealing a gap in his teeth. 'They call us Miscreants.'

'Who does?'

'Everyone.' Ray spread his hands. 'And we get hunted, see? Hunted like stray dogs, and taken away. You saved me. I saw what you did, you and that mate of yours. And that power you had … I ain't never seen anything like it. Could help us, you could.'

Ray took a step forward, grinning again. Benjamin took a step backwards, and tripped on the edge of the pavement. As he fell back into the road, he felt hands behind him, catching his arms. At first he felt thankful, but then something wiry fell over his face.

'Gotcha. Quick, get him out of sight.'

'Get off me!' Benjamin shouted. He started to struggle, but the net was too heavy. He felt instead for his magic, planning to throw it off, but something sharp jabbed into his back. His body shook from a sudden jolt of electricity, and then everything went numb. He was still awake as he was dragged into a side street, but his legs felt like jelly and his arms hung limp at his sides.

'Quick, get him to the camp before it wears off.'
'Just give him another prod.'
'The battery's nearly flat.'
'I told you to recharge it!'
'I did, but the power keeps going on and off.'
'You're an idiot.'
'Shut up!'
'Both of you, zip it or someone might hear!'

As they carried him, Benjamin tried to concentrate on the voices, to estimate how many kids were there. His head was lolling and his vision was blurred, his hearing fading in and out like a worn-out CD. When they turned corners he occasionally caught glimpses of the sky and glitters of light to the east, the sun slowly moving into a position from which to begin its attack on dawn. They were carrying him down residential streets, frog-walking him, keeping him in the middle of the group to avoid the attention of early morning joggers or dog walkers. While they might be surprised by a rabble of shabbily dressed children, they wouldn't suspect a kidnapping.

'Quick, get him inside. Give him another jab if there's enough juice, in case he gets any ideas.'

Something prodded Benjamin in the back again, but this time the jolt of electricity was weak, barely topping up the numbness he still felt.

A tall door with dirty glass window panes opened wide, scraping on the floor with a chilling screech. The group carried Benjamin inside, through a second door and down a gloomy corridor that smelled musty, not unlike Sebastien's shop but with more of an unwashed taint.

'Quick, put him in the common room.'

'Ray, the floor's getting jumpy again!'

'There are some buckets by the door. Quick, slosh one over it then tell Lulu to go and fill them up.'

'She's still sulking because you wouldn't let her come.'

'Tell her to stop sulking, this is important!'

Benjamin bounced down on a sofa which smelled of unwashed feet. His head lolled again, but someone stuffed a cushion behind it to hold him up. Someone else drew back a curtain covering a skylight to let in the first colour of the morning sun. Benjamin stared at the group of dirty, disheveled kids standing in front of him.

'Huh?' he said, not sure what word he was trying to say but unable to make his tongue form anything more meaningful.

Ray stepped forward, a beaming smile on his face. 'Welcome,' he said. 'I don't think I ever got your name, so let's have some formal introductions. I'm Ray Summers, as you know.' He waved a hand at the three kids standing beside him. 'This is Big Don,' he said, pointing to a beanpole of a boy, all height and no width. 'He eats too much. Beside him is Dorothy, and on the end is Kevin.' A girl with an electrical frizz of blonde hair and a chubby ginger boy with freckles nodded. 'And in the other room, sulking because I made her stay behind, is my little sister Lucy, although she likes Lulu.' He shrugged. 'Not sure why.'

'Huh,' Benjamin said again, sure that this time he meant to say 'hello.'

Ray spread his hands. 'We're the Basingstoke Miscreants, and proud of it. Not a dog-catcher in the land which can get us. Welcome to our camp, whatever your name is.'

'Ben … Ben … um, Ben,' Benjamin said, sounding not unlike Gubbledon Longface during an attempt at anger. Giving up on saying anything else, he just tried to smile, but his face felt like putty, leaving him unsure what kind of shape he had made.

'Well, welcome, Ben,' Ray said. 'Sorry about our little kidnapping, but there were two reasons for it. One is kind of selfish.' He shrugged. 'After you helped me get away, I thought it might be a good idea to keep a tab on you. I put the word around until someone spotted you again.'

'That was me,' Big Don said proudly, raising a hand.

'After that we followed you. I ain't never seen power like you have. Kids like you are few and far between, but what I do know is it ain't safe for you to be out there wandering about.'

The others all nodded, muttering their agreement.

'And secondly, is that I saw you hanging around the station while I was out having a scout around. You really ain't from 'round here, are you? Dog-catchers are all over that place. Anywhere people might try and travel, see? They're all over it, picking us up, taking us off to god-knows-where. Only last week, Jake, a boy who hung with us, he was picked up, and he's gone now.'

The others tutted. At the end of the line, Kevin sniffed.

'So, you see, we had to get you to protect you. See? So, where you from, because you definitely ain't from 'round here.'

The numbness in Benjamin's face had finally receded enough that he felt capable of speech. With a delirious laugh, he said, 'Endinfinium.'

21

MIRANDA

'Here's your food. You can eat it or not. It's up to you.'

Miranda glared at Trobin through the hole in the door. 'Just let me out and I'll leave and you'll never see me again.'

'I'm afraid I can't do that. You're too dangerous.'

Miranda glowered. 'You haven't seen anything. Although I could say the same of you—you're lying to these people, aren't you?'

Trobin rolled his eyes. 'Do you want your food or not? Stand back against the wall and let me open the door. I'll count to five. If you don't do it, I'll take it away.'

'Take it away.'

Trobin shrugged. 'As you wish.'

He picked up the tray of food, turned, and disappeared up the corridor. A door slammed at the far end, and as if on cue, her stomach started to rumble. 'I've changed my mind!' she shouted, but no one answered. Frustrated, she sat down against the wall, folding her arms across her chest.

She'd been sitting no more than a couple of minutes when something cold and wet beneath her caused her to jump up. She stared at the ground, disbelieving, then realised it was what she thought it was: a trickle of water slowly spreading out across the cell floor.

As the smell reached her, she realised. Not water: chamomile tea.

Soon, the smell of the stuff pervaded everything. Miranda was quickly coming to hate that which brought calm to everything in Endinfinium and wished it would just go away. There were days when she would take everything jumping up and down over this irritating, all-encompassing smell.

Frustrated, Miranda banged against the door, but of course got no answer. There was nowhere for her to sit now, so she leaned against the wall, wishing she'd noticed the trickle of tea before sitting in it. Now the seat of her trousers was wet, and in these dark, sunless rooms, nothing would dry quickly.

She wondered what the Sleepers planned for her. They had said nothing since locking her up except to bring food and tell her to stand back. Twice Trobin had come, still wearing the ridiculous dog's head mask, while the other times had been people whom she didn't know. She had taken the food from the others, but knowing that Trobin was a liar and a cheat, she couldn't bring herself to accept anything from him.

And now her stomach was punishing her for it.

The chamomile and Trobin's ward were to keep her magic subdued now that her strength was back. Trobin, while not having the brute power of a Summoner, was at the very least a powerful Channeller, and had far better control of his magic than she. The ward was far stronger than one Channeller could have made alone, so the others

—most likely all Weavers, even if they didn't know it—had to be in league with him. Far from being free, many of these people were prisoners too.

If only she could get out. The door had a heavy lock. Without her magic she needed something to pick it with, and she had nothing—

A bump in her pocket made her jump. She lifted the flap over the top and saw the little plastic rhino running back and forth. Having been subdued by a dousing they had given her after bringing her to the room, it had now dried out and reanimated.

Miranda stared. Was it small enough to fit into the lock?

She lifted it out and cupped it in her hands. 'Hello,' she said, lifting it up. 'Do you think you could do something for me? I want you to move a couple of levers so I can open the door.'

If the rhino understood, it made no obvious sign. It simply charged back and forth across her palm, butting into the lower curves of her fingers.

It was a risk. If it simply ran off, she would never get it back, and it might even alert Trobin and his cronies to her escape attempt.

But, while it was perhaps only a simple creature, it had stayed with her when it could have climbed out and run off at any time.

She held it up to the lock. The opening was just large enough for the rhino to squeeze inside. At first, however, it just butted the edge of the door, as though sizing up an enemy.

'Just push the levers,' Miranda said. 'Then come back. Please?'

The rhino charged. This time, instead of lowering its head, it leapt upwards, disappearing into the lock. Its feet were left poking out for a few seconds then it disappeared inside. Miranda heard it shuffling about. The lock was barely large enough for it to fit and she worried about it getting stuck. If that happened, she might never get out. Then, just as she was beginning to sweat, something clicked, and the rhino's back appeared as it shuffled out backwards. It returned to butting her fingers and running wantonly across her palm.

Miranda nudged the door with her foot. The lock was loose.

Thanking the rhino, she put him back into her pocket and quietly opened the door. She stepped out into a corridor lined with other doors that looked to be storerooms. This section definitely wasn't part of the old train station she had seen above, so she wondered if she wasn't in an ancient, fossilized prison.

At the end of the corridor, she found another door that opened onto a carved stone tunnel, one that looked hand-dug. It connected to another smooth-walled corridor that ended at stairs leading up. Miranda climbed to another door and peered out.

She had reached the bottom levels of the buried underground railway station. Dusty, cracked tiles lined the floor and in some places the walls were adorned with the shredded remnants of old posters. She heard footsteps and ducked out of sight as someone she didn't recognise strolled past.

Waiting until the corridor was empty again, she took a left turn, and hurried along until she heard voices again. She found herself outside a door with a frosted glass window behind which light shone. She was just about to pass it by when a voice said, 'I'll go and check on her. She has to eat sometime.'

'I doubt Trobin will care if she dies.'

'He thinks she's a threat, but if we do as Robell suggested, the airships will go and we'll be free to go above ground again.'

What had Robell suggested? Miranda's ears burned, but she heard someone stand up, a chair scraping back.

'I'll be back in a few minutes,' the first person said.

Miranda turned and ran. She panicked, thinking she had missed the stairs she had come up, before spotting a dark space along the corridor wall. She raced down them, tripping once and scuffing her jeans, then bolted back through the carved tunnel and down the corridor to her cell. She had just got inside and closed the door when she heard the other door opening and footsteps on the stone floor.

'Miranda, are you awake?'

Miranda's heart was pounding and she didn't trust herself to speak without giving away her exhaustion. 'Uh, oh, sorry … I just woke up,' she muttered, hiding her lack of breath beneath the pretense of sudden wakefulness.

'I've brought you some food.'

Miranda waited a few seconds until she was sure she could speak without breathlessness. 'That's great, thank you. I'll get away from the door.'

A key jostled in the lock, the woman grunting with exertion. Miranda realised with a flash of panic that she hadn't locked it again, but she heard it click once and then again before it opened and a young woman's face appeared. Miranda recognised her from the crowd at the meeting.

'Hello, young lady. My name's Lisa.' She shrugged. 'I've thrown a bit of extra in there because I heard you didn't eat your last meal.' She gave Miranda a smile, as though to apologise for her current living conditions.

'Thanks. When can I get out?'

Lisa gave an awkward shrug as she closed the door and locked it, giving a surprised grunt at how easily the key turned this time.

'You can get out when you agree to stop causing trouble,' she said.

'But I haven't caused any … well, apart from trying to escape. You're keeping me prisoner.'

Lisa sighed. 'You don't understand how fragile life is here for us. We live in the shadow of the High Mountains. The Dark Man could send his people at any time.'

'Then come with me back to the school. The teachers could protect you.'

Lisa gave a bitter laugh. 'Oh, like they've protected so many others? You don't get it, do you? You're still young, running around the corridors of that dusty old place, having your adventures, acting like Alice in Wonderland. I don't know where you came from, but you didn't wake up in a dream. You woke up in a nightmare.'

'We can protect you.'

Lisa shook her head. 'We protect ourselves. Every single adult you see here was cast out from that place. Oh, I know they call it triangulating, or something silly like that, but the action is the same. We were schooled in lies and secrets, and we walked away from that place with no purpose, nowhere to go, and no understanding of how to protect ourselves. How many died, I can't imagine, but some of us banded together and formed our own community. We have children of our own now, and these children are pure born, children of these lands. They came from nowhere else, and they have nowhere else to go, so it is our duty to protect them. Both from *him* … and from *them*.'

'Things are changing.'

'Are they now? Says a twelve-year-old girl on the run

from the Dark Man himself? You are one to be believed, are you not?'

Miranda decided to ignore the woman's mistaking of her age. 'He sent his forces to attack the school a year ago and again only a few weeks back, and my friend, he beat them both times.'

'Who is this friend of yours?'

'Benjamin Forrest. He's a great Summoner.'

Lisa's eyes drew guarded as though some flower of memory had just poked its head through the snow of her misunderstanding. 'I think it's time to end our conversation,' she said. 'Trobin warned us to keep away from you. The tongue is as dangerous as any magic wand.'

'Wait!'

Too late. Lisa had turned on her heels and marched briskly away. A door slammed, leaving Miranda alone.

Miranda started to sit down, but then remembered the water running across the floor and sighed. She stood up to eat the bowl of stew the woman had brought, leaning against the wall as the water sloshed around her shoes. In her pocket the little rhino charged back and forth. Miranda wondered whether to undertake another reconnaissance mission, but if Lisa had noticed something amiss about the door, she might send Trobin or one of the others down to check. It would be better to stay in place, her escape route assured if she needed to run.

She was so hungry that she didn't care how the food tasted. From the smell she knew it had been cooked in chamomile and was fully aware it would dull her grip on her magic, but all she wanted to feel right now was something in her stomach. And when the bowl was empty, she realised that, by turning it upside down, it was just high enough to form a little seat to keep her out of the water trickling across the floor.

She positioned it in a corner where two walls could prop her up, then sat down, leaning her head against the cold stone. She thought about her predicament, and when she was tired of feeling sorry for herself she started wondering what had happened to Benjamin and Wilhelm. Had they survived their ordeal, and were they back at the school, waiting for her, or were they both dead? Even worse, had they both come back as cleaners?

She closed her eyes. Her magic felt weak, but it was still there, a knot in her stomach. She had always been able to feel their presence from their magic, as though each of them had a length of thread they could send out, searching for others. Miranda concentrated, but there was only a void around her, one in which Trobin's magic ward waited, blocking hers, holding it in. But even as it existed, it was porous like a sponge, and it wasn't hard for Miranda to thread her own magic through, sending it out into the world to search for others.

If they were out there, she couldn't find them. It was as though both Benjamin and Wilhelm had disappeared over the edge of the world.

There were others, though, and as she drew her magic back in, she felt another tiny thread, flicking and teasing around her own, as though testing it, trying to understand.

It was close by.

Rosa.

Miranda's eyes widened in surprise. No wonder the girl hadn't seemed fazed by the sudden movement of her toys when Miranda had needed to get her attention. From the strength of her thread of magic Miranda could tell the little girl was a Channeller. Growing up in this place, however, where these people calling themselves Sleepers denied all existence of magic, the little girl was coming to terms with a secret ability she couldn't name. She perhaps wasn't even aware it existed.

Trobin, however, was aware. Miranda could feel the ward he had placed around Rosa, subduing her magic, keeping it hidden. But the little girl, as though playing blindfolded in a box filled with holes, had found ways out, her magic threading undetected out into the world.

'Rosa,' Miranda whispered . 'Can you hear me?'

The tendril of magic began to flicker and dance like an excited firefly. Perhaps Rosa didn't understand what she was hearing, but she had certainly heard it.

'Rosa, it's Miranda. Can you hear me?'

Miranda knew, of course, that Rosa would never be able to hear her voice, but it helped her visualise the image she wanted to present. She felt Rosa's magic plume, spreading out to wrap around hers as though someone was giving her a hug. She wiped a tear away from her eye.

A door slammed. Miranda jerked upright, losing her hold on the magic. She opened her eyes and listened as footsteps rang out on the corridor outside.

Miranda stood up as a light came through the little hole in the door, suddenly blocked by Trobin's face.

'I have some news,' he said, his voice sounding empty, as though he couldn't decide whether to be happy or sad. 'The council has voted, and a decision has been made. Tomorrow you will be returned to where you came.'

'Where I came?'

'Yes. You came from the sky. You will be returned to the sky, as an offering to the Dark Man. When you go, you will take those airships with you, and the Sleepers will know peace once more.'

Miranda tried to answer but her throat was dry. She stared at the ground, disbelieving. When she looked up again, Trobin had gone.

22

SNOUT

'Just trust me,' Fat Adam said, pouring the bowl of custard into the bag nestled in his lap. 'It'll work.'

Tommy Cale looked disgusted as a lumpy chunk overflowed the plastic bag's edge and began a rolling march down Fat Adam's trouser leg, only for Adam to reach one podgy finger down and scoop it up. With a grin, most of it disappeared into his mouth. The bit that missed trickled down his chin and found a new home on the floor.

'This is the stupidest plan I think I've ever heard,' Tommy said.

'Do you have a better one?'

'Give me a few minutes to think,' Tommy said, his voice becoming suddenly loud as though it was a horse running away in his mouth. Snout reached out and jerked his arm.

'Shut up! Godfrey'll hear.'

Over on the edge of the teachers' table, Godfrey half turned. Snout's custard bowl suddenly upended itself, pouring onto his lap. He scowled as he jumped up, knocking the rest of it to the floor. From the teachers' table,

Professor Caspian gave Godfrey a glare that only Snout noticed, but Ms. Ito stood up and called him over.

'Boy!'

Snout, his trousers dripping with yellow gunge, went to stand in front of her, head bowed.

'Your disruption is getting out of hand,' she snapped. 'And I'm getting tired of punishing you. Are you not aware of the shortage of staff we currently face?'

Snout mumbled something, but even he wasn't sure what it was.

'I'll make this simple. How many cleans do you deserve?'

Godfrey was staring at Snout with a look of triumph. At the adjacent table, Derek was making pig noises as he spooned down the remainder of his dinner, occasionally throwing glances in Snout's direction.

'Uh ... a thousand?' Snout muttered, certain Ms. Ito would double it.

Ms. Ito, however, lifted a manicured eyebrow. 'Well, I was going to give you half that for a simple misdemeanour, but I wouldn't like to look soft now, would I? Instead, perhaps you could choose a friend to share your punishment?'

Snout looked around. Behind him, Fat Adam and Tommy Cale were both eating in silence, their faces barely above their bowls. Either one would do, but Snout remembered Fat Adam's madcap plan. It was also true that it would be easier for the boys to pull it off if certain obstructions were out of the way.

'Um ... I think my roommate would help, Miss,' Snout mumbled.

'Speak up, boy! Name!'

'D-D-Derek B-B-Bates,' Snout stammered.

'Derek Bates.' Ms. Ito swung around in her chair. 'Your

new roommate, is he? A fine choice. A bonding experience.'

You're a dead man, Derek mouthed as Snout turned around. Ignoring him, Snout fixed Fat Adam and Tommy Cale with a glare, hoping they understood. *Get it done*, that glare said.

'Do you have some other reason to be standing there?' Ms. Ito snapped, and Snout stepped quickly back out of range of her sweeping plaster cast. 'Get cleaned and get cleaning. Now!'

∾

'You know, I had to go back to the dorm to get something, and while I was there, I had a sandwich, just because this punishment you roped me into might go on late. And while I was in our room, I accidentally tripped and knocked a whole pot of pepper all over your bed. I mean, I tried to brush it off, but it was proper ground in to your pillow and your sheet. I hope you don't mind….'

Snout tried to ignore Derek's ongoing monologue from the next cubicle. Every time he got sucked in to some torture method or punishment that was surely coming his way, he stopped focusing on the cleans. After two hours, his ticker was only at a hundred and eighty. It was looking like a late finish.

'You know, the teachers are thinking about appointing a beach monitor, someone to patrol along the beaches at night just in case anything interesting gets washed up. Godfrey wasn't sure who to recommend, but I suggested you'd do a great job. Godfrey's only waiting for approval from the teachers now. Just think, at this time next week you could be alone on the beach with just the stars and the red sun for company. Oh, and the haulocks, and the turtle-cars, and whatever monstrosities from the sea that decide to flop up on the beach ... but I'm sure you'll be fine—oh, that's me done!' A shuffle of movement, then the click of a door opening. 'I'll see you back in the dorms, my good friend.'

Snout sighed. Gasbagging the entire time obviously worked for Derek, but Snout was less than halfway through. He glanced at a little alarm clock beside the ticker counter. Just after nine. While he would get a pass for being out so late, he would need to request a master key from whoever was on night watchman duty. He hoped it was Mrs. Martin from the office: she was stern but kind. Often it was Old Cleat, the librarian, who was a little too spooky for Snout's liking. Other times it was one of the teachers, who would invariably give him a lecture about his behaviour on the way back. The worst was Captain Roche, who would make him do twenty-five press-ups before handing over a key.

It was short change before midnight when Snout finally finished. Derek had obviously horded the easy items to clean while simultaneously distracting Snout, who had found himself left with the endless hassle of cleaning Filofaxes, water filters, wicker baskets and plastic tissue holders, all of which kept jumping out of his hands and required several coats of chamomile spray before they could be calmed down. His arms and shoulders ached as he finally left the cubicle and went to inform the sin keeper he was done.

Instead of coming out of his booth to meet Snout, however, the sin keeper remained seated on his chair, only lifting his head as Snout let himself out.

'Are you all right?' Snout asked, feeling strangely uncomfortable without that curved sword waving in his face.

'You have been absolved of your sins,' the sin keeper muttered, not looking up. 'Be on your way.'

Snout turned and took a few steps, but then stopped. 'Shouldn't you berate me or threaten me or something?' he asked, turning back.

The sin keeper didn't respond. His helmet lifted up and down as though he were breathing heavily through the empty cavities behind his armour. Snout shrugged, starting to turn, just as a piece of metal fell away from the sin keeper's shin and bounced across the floor.

The sin keeper made no move to retrieve it, so Snout tentatively reached down and picked it up, handing it back. The sin keeper didn't move to take it, so Snout rested it on his leg armour then quickly stepped back in case the sin keeper suddenly leapt to the attack.

The reanimate, however, didn't move.

Snout frowned as he walked away. His nose felt tickly as though Derek had brought some of the pepper down here with him. The sin keeper, too, despite being a reanimated suit of armour, had smelled funny. Where there was usually a metallic scent of steel and copper, today there was something almost spicy. Snout couldn't place it, so he just shrugged as he headed for the stairs leading up out of the basements.

His luck was in, and Mrs. Martin was on night watch. With a frown, she reached into a box of sand and handed him a temporary master key. It felt grainy to the touch as Snout pocketed it, careful not to touch it too long for fear of eroding the edges which might be needed for the doors out onto the causeway and into the dorm. The school had perfected a clever way of making late-night master keys which couldn't be stolen—they were short-lived reanimated lumps of sand which lasted for approximately fifteen minutes. If Snout wasn't back in the dorms by then, the key would fall apart and he'd have to go back and ask for another, a misgiving that came with a mandatory additional one hundred cleans. Snout had spent enough time in the locker room for one evening, so he hurried back to the dorms, dropping his key into a bucket of sand inside the door once he was safely inside.

This late, the common room was empty. It was after midnight and with breakfast at eight, Snout could only hope Derek was snoring away if he wanted a decent night's sleep. On the second floor landing, however, he saw a light on underneath Tommy Cale and Fat Adam's door. Unable to suppress his curiosity, he gave a little knock.

The two boys were sitting in the middle of the floor with a bucket between them. Both grinned as Snout entered.

'You took your time,' Tommy said, keeping his voice low. 'Derek came back hours ago.'

Snout shrugged. 'He left me all the hard stuff.'

'Sounds about right. Check this out, though. Adam was right. It worked.'

Snout peered in the bucket. A lump of soap floated in a bucket of ice. 'What is it?'

'We sneaked Cherise's science block key while she was at history club,' Tommy said. 'We made a cast with it out of soap, returned it, then put the custard Adam stole in the cast. It's now frozen hard. We're going to leave it until morning to make sure its solid.'

Snout nodded without really being sure why. 'A key made out of custard?'

Tommy grinned. 'We mixed it with a bit of superglue from the art room. It'll be rock hard, don't you worry.'

'Great. When shall we get in there to take a look?'

'There's a self-study period tomorrow afternoon,' Fat Adam said. 'We're supposed to go to the library or one of the self-study rooms near the main entrance. Tommy told Ms. Ito we'd be going to the library, but I told Professor Caspian we'd be going to the study rooms.'

The boys exchanged a glance. 'And we included you.' Then, with a sheepish grin, added, 'We told them both you were our study leader, since we're both second years, and you're a third year.'

Snout frowned. 'So, if we get caught lying to either teacher, we'll likely all get sent to the locker room, but I'll probably double down because I'm the official leader.'

'It's a risk,' Fat Adam said.

'But you said how important it was that we find out what might be going on in there,' Tommy Cale added.

Snout gave a resigned nod. 'Tomorrow afternoon it is then.'

And he headed off to bed.

When he got there, though, he found a snoring Derek had been true to his word and had ground pepper into Snout's pillow. By the time he had taken it and his bed sheets down to the laundry room, replaced them with new ones and also found enough clothes to stuff into a pillow case—all in complete silence so as not to wake his new roommate—it was so late it was barely worth going to bed. He hit his makeshift pillow like a sack of bricks, but then lay in the dark for a while, worried about sleeping so heavily he snored and woke Derek, cajoling his new roommate into some fresh, as-yet undeveloped form of revenge.

Eventually, though, he was just too tired to care.

∼

He awoke in a sudden shock as cold water soaked him. He

opened his eyes and saw Derek standing beside his bed with an empty bucket.

'Oh, heavens I'm thankful,' Derek said, dramatically loud enough that anyone in the corridor might hear. 'You were sleeping so deeply I really thought you were dead. I apologise—my good friend—for such a dramatic way to wake up, but my heart was in my mouth.'

Snout, who thought his own heart was also in his mouth, just stared, unsure if this was reality or a cruel dream.

'Come on,' Derek said. 'We need to get to school. Class starts in ten minutes. You've missed breakfast but there might be some scraps in the dormitory kitchen.'

And with that, he was gone. Snout struggled out of bed, rushing to find his uniform and books for the day. During his slumber, it seemed Derek had moved everything about. When he got downstairs, he found Gubbledon waiting for him with hooves planted firmly on decaying hips.

'Simon, there you are. Well, it looks like you're feeling better.'

'Huh?'

'Derek said you were sick and didn't want breakfast.'

'Oh.'

'Well, run along or you'll be late. If you're still feeling poorly, ask your form teacher for a pass to visit the nurse.'

'Okay.'

'Wait.' Gubbledon thrust a paper bag into his hands. 'I saved you some fritters from breakfast, just in case you got your appetite back.'

Snout had never felt so much like hugging the reanimated racehorse as he did now. Even then, though, it was a horrifying proposition, so he just gave Gubbledon a smile of thanks and ran for the door.

∼

'You look tired,' Fat Adam said as Snout leaned over his custard-clad lunch, eyes drooping. 'You know they don't like us to waste anything, so if you want, I'll finish it for you.'

Snout sighed and pushed the bowl across the table. 'I've got a stomachache,' he said. 'I think it's nerves.'

Tommy Cale looked up at a big ticking clock on the wall, one that had recently been returned after a spell in the lockers for reanimating and shouting 'tick!' through a tiny mouth in its lower surface. 'We have thirty minutes before lift-off. Do you think we'll get found out and sent to the lockers? And what happens if we figure out what to do early and have to come back, and we have to choose whether to go to Ms. Ito's room or Professor Caspian's? What do we do then?'

Snout sighed. 'Let's worry about that after we've finished worrying about what's happening in the old science block,' he said. 'Come on, Adam. Eat up. Let's get this over with.'

Derek smirked at Snout as he got up and left with the others. Snout ignored him, glancing briefly at Godfrey, but the curly haired boy was deep in conversation with Captain Roche, who looked desperate to get away.

Together, Snout, Fat Adam, and Tommy Cale headed for the maths department, but just before reaching the doors leading to the line of classrooms, they ducked into a small alcove, went through a door used only by the cleaners, and descended a narrow flight of stairs that brought them out into another alcove in a corridor that led to the old science block. One rainy afternoon a year ago, Wilhelm Jacobs had taught Snout a few of the secret passages through the school. A good way to escape a rampaging Godfrey, he said.

A metal barrier stood in front of the double doors with *science department* written on them in red lettering. A DANGER: KEEP OUT sign had fallen to the floor and lay collecting dust. Snout stared at it, realising that the dust adorned the sign alone, that the floor around it was clear. There was another double door behind them which was the limit of where the cleaners went, so this section had been tidied artificially, most likely by someone wanting to hide their passage.

Snout's heart was thundering. He turned to the others, both of whom looked equally terrified.

'Okay, are we ready?'

Fat Adam reached into his pocket and held out the key. 'You're the … leader.'

'Thanks.'

Snout closed his eyes, as Professor Caspian had once taught him in a private science catch-up class. 'You can feel it,' the science professor had said. 'If you can use it, you can feel it. Close your eyes and imagine yourself surrounded by a bubble. Push it outwards until it meets resistance. Is that resistance warm or cold? Does it move when you push harder? That's how you feel it. With practice you'll be able to identify where it comes from.'

Snout, with a seemingly unique ability, had never really practiced. It was far easier to just ignore all the crazy things going on around him and hope it all went away, but there was no denying he could feel it if he really tried. Now, though, he felt nothing, just a regular, simple lock.

He walked around the sign and opened the doors, the copy of the master key made from custard and glue doing a perfect job. The lock, though, wasn't stiff at all. For a department supposedly off limits, it felt often used.

Through the doors, the corridor was dark. In a couple of places, the ceiling had collapsed, and reanimating pipes shifted and slithered like nests of snakes. They gave every damaged area a wide berth, as though some terrifying reanimate would come bursting through. Tommy Cale clutched Adam's arm, and Adam walked so close to Snout he kept stepping on the back of Snout's trainers. On the fifth or sixth time, Snout turned around and hissed at him to take a step back.

The first part of the corridor passed storage rooms. A couple of doors were open, and inside, a rattling cacophony of reanimating beakers, test tubes, gauzes, and utensils created a skeletal orchestra of discordant sound. Inside one, a wheeled vacuum cleaner with a suction pipe like an elephant's trunk rolled to the entrance and peered out, so Snout nudged the door shut with his toe to relieved gasps from Tommy Cale and Fat Adam.

Beyond the storage rooms, the corridor made an abrupt right turn, passing a line of windows on the left side, classroom doors on the right. Here they found the main reason for its abandonment: in places the left-side wall had collapsed, leaving the corridor open to the cliff-face, the floor interspersed by triangles of shingle where it had begun to erode. Snout squatted down on the last patch of crack-free floor and peered out. The drop, while not sheer, was a steep scree slope falling a hundred or so metres to a grassy bank where a narrow footpath passed around the cliff-side. From there, however, was another straight drop down to the beach.

He gulped and stepped back.

'What's this?' Tommy Cale said from behind him. Snout turned. Tommy reached for something hanging from the ceiling in the shadows near the inner wall. It was black and shiny, and looked like a folded plastic cape.

'No!' Snout hissed, grabbing Tommy's hand a moment before his fingers closed over it. He pulled Tommy back as the sleeping haulock shifted slightly, flexing one wing before setting back to sleep.

'They eat people, don't they?' Fat Adam said, his voice a mousy squeak.

'Only at night, when they wake up,' Snout said, barely able to keep his own voice from trembling, realising there were a dozen more haulocks sleeping in the shadows behind the first. 'Best to let them sleep.'

They ducked down to creep past. Suspended haulocks lined the inner wall where the shadows were deepest, so once they were past the collapsed section, Snout kept them near to the windows as he led the others past several abandoned classrooms. Through the window of one he saw a group of reanimated desks dancing around in a circle, wooden stools clumping together like revelers clapping hands.

The corridor ended at another pair of double doors. Snout stopped outside, certain this was where they would find what they were looking for. A sign on the door read AUDITORIUM.

'Be ready in case we need to run,' he said.

'What's behind that door?' Tommy Cale asked, to which Fat Adam tutted and Snout rolled his eyes.

'If we knew that—'

'Shhh,' Snout said, a finger to his lips. 'Let's get this over with. If it's really bad, we'll go find a teacher straight away.'

'What about if it's only a bit bad?'

Fat Adam gave Tommy a light push. 'We'll just tell Gubbledon.'

'What will he—'

'Shh!'

Snout stepped forward and leaned on the left side door until it opened a crack. Immediately he smelled the mustiness of age mixed with the sweat of human bodies. There was something else, too: the coppery scent of dried blood.

The auditorium was dark. Light following Snout in through the door only illuminated the first ten rows of seats before petering out. He stood at the top of a side entrance, with a main entrance likely out of sight to his right, perhaps accessed by doors from another abandoned block. The stage was in front and slightly to his left; from his memory of the school's outside shape, it was jutting out over the sea on an outcropping section of cliff.

'It's dark,' Tommy said.

'Open the curtains, Simon,' Fat Adam said, pointing to the left, where Snout realised great black drapes hung across windows twice as high as himself. 'Go on, you're at the front.'

'Adam, you hold the door. Tommy … just don't do anything.'

Snout closed his eyes, wishing he was as brave as Benjamin Forrest or Miranda Butterworth, but aware that if something terrifying hid in this room, he was the only one who might be able to stop it. He cursed them under his breath for disappearing, wishing the worst he had to worry about was finishing his maths homework before tomorrow's class.

He inched back the nearest curtain and a knife of light cut across the lines of chairs, reaching the bottom of a stage. As the gloom lifted, something large and square revealed itself as a glass tank of some kind. Nudging back the curtain a couple more inches revealed it as filled with grimy water.

'Ooh, a fish tank,' Fat Adam said. 'I wonder if they're

growing anything for the kitchens? Perhaps it's an experiment to see if something is safe to eat.'

Tommy hissed at Adam to shut up as his voice echoed across the chamber. Snout jerked the curtain right back, filling the auditorium with gloomy light. The glass tank on the stage was easy to see now. About the size of a phone box, it was filled with grey-green water, with a crud on the top surface as though they were looking at a cross-section of a stagnant pond.

'Is there anything in it?' Tommy Cale whispered.

Snout shook his head. 'No one puts a tank full of green water on a stage in the middle of an auditorium for no reason,' he said. 'I'm not going near it.'

'Perhaps it, you know, reanimated and jumped there,' Tommy Cale said, blushing, as though what he suggested were the height of ridiculousness.

Snout just shook his head. Unsure what he had expected to find, this was certainly not it. Now that they were here, he had no idea what to do. He closed his eyes, thought outwards like a bubble, then staggered as it suddenly burst, struck by a object so frigid it made him break out in goosebumps.

The tank.

He opened his eyes just as Fat Adam reached up to touch it.

'Don't!'

The water swirled, something inside shifting, pushing through the murk to gaze out, something horribly ancient with dead, mummified eyes as it peered through the glass just inches from Fat Adam's face.

And then the world twisted. Snout was no longer sure if he was on his feet or not, as a thousand voices seemed to rage from everywhere at once. He was sure one belonged to the spectral girl, but there were others, some screaming, some crying out with terror or pain, others bellowing with laughter.

'Do something!' Fat Adam screamed, and Snout had a vision of him rolling across the floor and sliding up the surface of the glass, ankles first as though invisible hands were pulling him up, while all the while the leering skull clacked its jaw and silently laughed.

'Help!' screamed Tommy, and Snout imagined him rolling over and over, stretched by a thousand hands, drawn up into the air and carried towards murky water which would douse him and drown him and strip the skin from his bones, leaving him as soulless as the monster now taunting them.

And in his own terror, in an attempt to save them all, he did what only he could do.

He called the ghouls.

23

BENJAMIN

'Look, I know you want me to stay, but I have to get back to my friend.'

Benjamin started to stand, but Ray backed up against the door, holding up both hands as though Benjamin was a tiger about to spring to the attack.

'Whoa, wait a minute. You can't just get up and leave. And what's all this about your friend? You were quick enough to run out on him.'

'I don't want to put him in danger. And if I'm here, you're all in danger, too. Plus, there's something I need to do.'

'And what's that, may I ask?'

Benjamin thought about confessing that he believed he was a younger version of the man who had caused all these bizarre happenings, caught in a strange alternative reality. Even with everything going on, he doubted he could make it sound credible, so he just shrugged and said, 'I need to meet someone.'

'Well, you ain't gonna get far trying to go by train. You know they can quarantine the whole thing if they think there's one of us onboard?'

'The dog-catchers?'

'Yeah. They're a government agency, we reckon. Means they can do what they like.'

'What happens to the kids they catch?'

Big Don, standing in a corner, said, 'We don't talk about that.'

'Why not?'

'Because we don't know,' said Dorothy, suddenly pushing through the door, knocking Ray aside. 'None of us know anything except they don't come back.' She turned on Ray. 'Are you threatening Ben again? It's your turn to go and scavenge for breakfast.'

'I—'

'I'm getting hungry?' Dorothy pouted. 'Yeah, me too. And Lulu's going to start sulking again if we don't eat something soon.'

Benjamin gave a sad smile. Her frizzy blonde hair might be a polar opposite of Miranda's long, straight crimson hair, but their personalities were uncannily similar.

Ray scowled. 'Just don't let him leave before we've told him what we know. If they catch him, God knows what'll happen. I've never seen anyone do what he did before. It almost looked like he could control it.'

With that, Ray waved Don after him and went out. The tall boy gave Benjamin a smile as he closed the door behind him, leaving Benjamin and Dorothy alone.

Dorothy sighed. 'He just wants to keep us all together,' she said. 'When Jake got caught, Ray was mortified. Blamed himself.'

'Isn't there any way to stop it?'

Dorothy slumped down on a sofa. 'Stop what? Did you just wake up yesterday?'

Benjamin smiled. 'More or less.'

'Where'd you say you were from again?'

'Endinfinium.'

'That up near Shropshire?'

'Probably a bit further. Look, I don't know who you guys are, but I really need to get to London. I think it could be important. I think I might be able to stop all this and get the dog-catchers off your tail.'

Dorothy lifted an eyebrow. 'You really think you're something, don't you?'

'I'm not sure yet. I don't really know what's going on.'

The door opened and Kevin entered. His T-shirt wore sweat rings under his arms and grime slid down his cheeks.

'I've done the buckets,' he said. 'Should be enough to keep the school quiet for another day or two.'

'What's up with the school?' Benjamin asked.

'It wants to go,' Dorothy said.

'Go where?'

'Where all the other stuff goes. I don't know, London? I mean, we're using it, but that's not enough. It's not official. It's quiet for a few days but then it starts trying to move. We have to be careful; if the dog-catchers notice it's abandoned but still sitting here, they might get suspicious and come to check. Then we'd have to move again.'

Benjamin shook his head. 'None of this makes much sense.'

Kevin exchanged a look with Dorothy.

'Says he doesn't know what's going on,' Dorothy said.

'Were you born yesterday?'

Benjamin flapped his hands. 'Look, this will sound stupid, but I just woke up here a few days ago. I used to live in Basingstoke but I woke up in a strange country and stayed there for a year or so—I'm not sure how long because it doesn't really have seasons.'

Dorothy scoffed. 'Neither does England. Unless it's called "rainy season."'

Benjamin rolled his eyes at her attempted humour. 'Anyway, something happened, and I woke up here again. Although it's not the same place I left.'

'Sounds like you're better off not going to sleep,' Kevin said. 'I suppose we could try to steal you some energy drinks.'

Benjamin wasn't sure whether to scream or laugh. 'I've seen stuff no one would believe, and I can do stuff that even I can't believe just by thinking about it … but here, I really have no idea what's happening. Who are you guys? Where are your parents?'

Dorothy exchanged a glance with Kevin. 'Don't have none,' she said. 'At least none that I remember. Went through a couple of foster places but I got in a bit of trouble because I started setting fire to things.' She grinned. 'Don't worry. I'm through that phase now.' With a shrug, she added, 'More or less.'

'Same,' Kevin said. 'Not the burning things bit, but I was in a kid's home for some reason or other. Not really sure why, but I've never met my real parents.'

'They threw him away because he's ginger,' Dorothy said with a smirk.

Kevin grinned. 'Too hot to handle,' he said. 'She tried to set fire to me, but the fire wasn't hot enough.'

'If you look up spicy in the dictionary, you'll find a picture of Kevin,' Dorothy said, reaching out to give Kevin a high-five.

'If you pour water over me it evaporates,' Kevin said.

'He's the reason for global warming,' Dorothy added.

'I once went to the Sahara on holiday,' Kevin said. 'But in those days it was called Green Hills.'

'He can't never go in the sea when he goes to the beach because when he goes near it, it runs away,' Dorothy said.

'Only person to ever walk to America,' Kevin said. 'Or I would be, but I can't be bothered.'

They both broke down into sniggers. Benjamin suddenly found himself missing Wilhelm, and felt a pang of guilt that he'd left his friend behind. He sat down on the sofa again, and the others sat on another opposite.

'You ended up here?' Benjamin asked.

Dorothy shrugged. 'We met in Torquay, down Devon way. Met on the street. Dog-catchers caught wind of me setting something on fire in the home I was in and came looking. Kevin saved me and we ran together. We met Ray and his sister outside Exeter after basically walking there. They'd escaped another home and so we hung out together. Met a couple of others on the way but they got caught. Ended up staying here because Big Don was already hiding out here and it seemed like a cool enough place. Been here a couple of months now, I suppose.'

'Kind of gives us a bit of stability being together,' Kevin said. 'We help each other and that eases it.'

'Eases what?'

Dorothy glanced at Kevin. Together they looked at Benjamin, both frowning.

'The pull. Don't you feel it?'

'What pull?'

'The one drawing you to *him*. To Dr. Forrest. When I was living on my own, and weird stuff started to happen, I didn't know what it was at first. I kept wanting to run away, but I wasn't sure why. Then I met Dorothy and figured it out, because she felt it too.'

'London,' she said. 'That's why Ray found you by the station. You were trying to get to London.'

'I have to…' Benjamin trailed off. He wasn't sure what

he had to do, only that he had to go. The pull was intense … like a rope wrapped around his waist.

'You feel it, don't you?' Kevin said.

'London.' Benjamin nodded. 'I have to go.'

'We all figure out some kind of reason, that we'll find answers there as to why we're different, but it's not that, is it? We're no different from those tumbleweeds. We have our own minds, that's all.' Dorothy shrugged. 'And they're trying to stop us from being thrown away.'

All three were silent for a moment. Then Benjamin looked up. 'It's less the more of you who are together, isn't it?'

The others nodded. 'It's like we're safe,' Dorothy said. 'We're wanted, so we don't need to go.'

'It's still there a bit, though,' Kevin added. 'Every now and again you feel it like a lump in your tummy, like a hand reaching in and trying to drag you.'

'And sometimes we meet kids who just wander off again,' Dorothy said. 'They stay for a few days and then just disappear.'

'We don't want you to disappear,' Kevin said. 'You seem kind of, you know, okay.'

Benjamin looked at each of them in turn. 'I'm just trying to figure out what's going on.'

'Strength in numbers,' Kevin said. 'Although it's not all roses because that makes us easier for the dog-catchers to spot.'

'Come on,' Dorothy said, standing up. 'Let's go check the place out, make sure it's not getting jumpy.'

Benjamin followed them through the door and along a corridor to a another door that led outside. Lining up against the wall were a couple of dozen metal buckets filled with a brown-tinted liquid. Benjamin recognised the smell immediately.

'Chamomile,' he said.

'Calms it down,' Kevin said. 'Don't ask me why. Some chemical reason, but I didn't go to school.'

'And I burned mine down,' Dorothy said, laughing, leaving Benjamin unsure whether she had made a joke or not.

'Ray steals the powder from the tanks up by the dump,' Kevin said. 'We mix it up here. Someone forgot to turn off the water mains.'

'Let's go,' Dorothy said, picking up a bucket and heading around the corner. 'We'll check the outer walls first, see where it's been trying break up.'

Benjamin picked up a bucket and followed the others. Sure enough, around another corner, against a wall that bordered a toilet block, the concrete had split and the wall was lifting and falling a few inches as though some invisible beast were trying to break it free. Dorothy and Kevin began pouring the chamomile into the crack. Benjamin copied them, and after a couple of minutes the wall fell still.

'It'll stay quiet for a while,' Dorothy said. 'Then it'll start again. Come on, next place.'

A sports equipment shed on the far side of a playground had almost broken free and was rattling back and forth like a snake with its tail caught in a trap. Dorothy poured what was left in her bucket into the most active corner, while Kevin ran for more. Benjamin finished his bucket just as a door broke off its hinges and went sailing up into the sky, nearly cutting him in half in the process.

'Wow, that was close! Are you all right?'

Benjamin stared at a scratch on his T-shirt, his heart thundering. 'Yeah, just about.'

Together they watched the door as it twisted and

turned, flying low over the nearby houses until it disappeared out of sight.

'I hope nobody saw it,' Dorothy said. 'They might come and check this place out, and if they find us here—'

She didn't finish as Kevin came running back, his face flushed. Benjamin stared at his empty hands as Kevin said, 'She's gone!'

∼

Dorothy was cursing far worse than Benjamin had ever heard from a twelve-year-old as they ran up and down the school's dusty corridors, searching for Lulu.

'Not in here,' Kevin said, poking his head into an empty storeroom.

'Or here,' Dorothy said from across the corridor, leaning into a large, empty lunchroom with an attached kitchen.

Benjamin, wanting to help, peered through the door of an adjacent classroom, but it was empty, no sign of Ray's missing sister. The girl, last seen an hour before by Kevin, still inside a sleeping bag in the old teacher's room where the group had their makeshift bedroom, had vanished.

'Better wait for Ray and Big Don,' Dorothy said, as they reached the end of the corridor with still no sign. 'She could be anywhere.'

'If she's gone outside, the dog-catchers will pick her up,' Kevin said.

'It's not the first time,' Dorothy added. 'The girl keeps running off.'

They went out to the school's front gate until they saw Ray and Big Don come running up the street. Smiles as Ray held up a basket of fruit faded as Dorothy explained what had happened.

'We were outside dealing with the jumpy bits. Kevin went to see if she would come and help, but she was gone. We've searched everywhere.'

Ray stamped his foot. 'You should have watched her! You know what she's like!'

'She's your sister, not mine!' Dorothy snapped. 'If she attracts the dog-catchers it'll be your fault.'

'Calm down,' Big Don said. 'We'll find her. Where did she go last time? The bus station, wasn't it?'

'She got on a coach to Reading,' Ray said to Benjamin. 'She tried to hide in the luggage compartment. The driver spotted her before they left and threw her off.'

'At least he didn't call the dog-catchers.'

'He tried, but she blew up his phone.'

'Blew it up?'

Ray shrugged. 'She can make electrical things explode. She doesn't know how she does it, but it's terrifying. That time, we managed to find her, but we were lucky.'

'If she went there once, she'll go there again,' Big Don said.

'I'll go and look,' Ray said. 'You guys stay here. It's nearly lunchtime so the dog-catchers will be everywhere.'

'We can't just do nothing,' Dorothy said. 'Kevin and me will check the town square.'

'And I'll go have a scout down by the park,' Big Don said. 'She went down there once, remember? We found her playing on the swings.'

Benjamin realised everyone was looking at him. He shrugged. 'I can—'

'You come with me,' Ray said. 'If the dog-catchers show up, you can blast them or something.'

Benjamin didn't have time to reply as the group scattered, and he found himself running to keep up with Ray. He remembered that the old bus station had been in the centre of town, but he had passed the spot with Wilhelm a couple of days before and it had been replaced by a car park. Instead, he found Ray leading him up a gentle hill that led out of town to a large, modern bus station.

'She's trying to get to London,' Ray said breathlessly as they came to a stop.

Benjamin thought about what Dorothy had said, how the draw was less the larger a group they made, how none of them had families. He frowned.

'She's your sister,' he said. 'Shouldn't that make a difference?'

'Foster sister,' Ray said. 'We shared the last couple of homes together. She's two years younger than me and I always tried to look after her because she kept getting in trouble. The others don't know. Don't tell them, please. They don't like her because she's too unpredictable, but she's just young.'

'Why are you telling me something you won't tell them?'

Ray turned to look at him. 'Because … you're different. I can just tell. You can find her, can't you?'

'You're expecting a lot of me, aren't you?'

'Look, I saw what you did. No one else can do that. No one else has nearly that much control.'

Benjamin didn't want to admit that compared to how he had used his reanimation magic back in Endinfinium— and even that had been borderline life-threatening at times —trying to control it here in England was like riding on the back of a giant, thrashing dragon. Ray's eyes shone with desperation, though, and he figured he could at least try.

They squatted down on a grass verge behind a crash barrier on the corner into the bus station. Benjamin closed his eyes. He hadn't felt for anyone's magic since he had come here, but now, as he let his thoughts drift in the way Grand Lord Bastien had taught him, he saw the tendrils of other nearby users snapping back and forth. One, the closest, was writhing violently, as though unable to find peace.

He opened his eyes and pointed at a window halfway along the main building. Posters advertising crisps and drinks were pasted to the window. A door alongside opened suddenly and a man came out, tucking a newspaper under his arm before throwing a glance back over his shoulder and giving a bemused shake of his head.

'She's over there,' Benjamin said. 'Inside that building, by those windows.'

Ray nodded. 'That's the gift shop. She's waiting for a coach. How did you know?'

Benjamin shrugged. 'I can feel her. It's difficult to explain. Once, I had someone who taught me.'

'I'd love to meet that teacher of yours,' Ray said. 'All I know is that when I touch stuff, sometimes it jumps up in the air. I don't know why or when it's going to happen, and I can't control it.'

'Let's go and get her,' Benjamin said.

Ray started to stand up, but ducked back down as a van came roaring around the corner, banking so hard its right-side wheels cut across the grass verge, leaving skidding tyre tracks in the soft mud.

'Dog-catchers,' Ray said.

The van skidded to a stop outside the bus station's main building, alongside the gift shop. The back doors swung open and five men jumped out. Two ducked down by the shop's door. A third ran along the pavement and went through another door leading into a ticket office, while the last two went left and right respectively, running around the building's corners and disappearing from sight.

'They've brought a posse this time,' Ray said. 'Someone must have called them in. Come on, we have to stop them.'

Ray bolted from cover, heading across the parking area. Benjamin could do nothing other than run after him as the taller boy dodged out in front of buses simultaneously coming into park and trying to depart. A horn blared as a bus braked sharply, the driver winding down his window to shout obscenities in Ray's direction.

People were gathering outside the gift shop. One of the dog-catchers shoved open the door, and in the moment before it swung shut, Benjamin caught a glimpse of a dozen chocolate bars spinning in midair while Lulu stood among them, gazing up, a vacant smile on her face.

'Don't move!' came a dog-catcher's muffled voice from inside. Through the window, Benjamin saw Lulu standing still, not reacting, her face still turned upwards to view her creation, a rapturous smile on her lips.

The other dog-catchers readied their electrical prongs. Ray had ducked down behind a parked bus and was peering out. He glanced back at Benjamin, who had stopped on a small traffic island midway across the parking area.

'Help her!' he hissed. 'Please help her!' Then, as though to set an example, he touched the side of the bus he hid behind, gritted his teeth and groaned, as though willing it to do something—*anything*—to keep the dog-catchers away from his foster sister.

Benjamin closed his eyes for a moment and felt for Ray's magic, finding only a ball of confusion. Dark reanimate mixed with light, and Benjamin understood that Ray, who would be considered a Channeller in

Endinfinium, similar in power to Miranda—had no understanding of a power that was both suppressed and influenced by its surroundings. Magic didn't work here like it did in Endinfinium; it couldn't be easily controlled. Unlike Ray, however, Benjamin at least understood some of what he possessed.

He glanced up at the bus and saw it was empty. Feeling for his magic in his gut, he reached out and pushed.

The bus jumped about thirty feet in the air, where it hung, rocking from side to side. Nearby, people began to scream.

'I did it!' Ray screamed, lifting his arms in triumph.

'Get out of the way!' Benjamin shouted, running forward and dragging Ray aside as the bus came crashing back down, its bumpers scattering, spraying the surrounding area with debris which immediately began to rise up into the air and flutter off like grumpy, just-woken birds. After a few seconds of indecision, the bus also began to move again, lifting up at one side.

'I'm not doing anything!' Ray shouted, still clearly stunned by what he presumed were his own actions. Benjamin just pulled him back out of range, slapped him across the face, and pointed at the gift shop.

Lulu now stood outside, her eyes turned upwards, a dog-catcher on either side, making no attempt to move or escape. The dog-catchers presumably believed she had caused the bus to rise, and were having their own difficulty understanding the situation. Two of them shared a glance as though wondering what to do, then one jabbed the electrical prod into Lulu's back. The girl's face creased with pain and she slumped to her knees. Cajoled back into action, the other dog-catcher threw a net over her. Together, they bundled her into the back of the van as the others came running over.

'They're getting away!' Ray shouted, grabbing Benjamin's arm. 'Save her!'

Benjamin felt for his magic, but the effort of lifting the bus had taken far more out of him in this world than it would have done in Endinfinium, as though using the magic at all was going against the natural law of the world and had to break down a barrier of resistance before anything could be done. A few remaining pieces of shrapnel lifted off the ground, but nothing else happened, and Benjamin slumped to his hands and knees, exhausted.

The last dog-catcher jumped into the back of the van and pulled the rear doors closed. As the bus finally made it airborne, dropping shrapnel on the bus station's roof as it moved slowly off across the roofs of the nearest houses.

'They've taken her!' Ray shouted as the van sped past them and accelerated up the street. With a deep frown, Ray clenched his fists and glared after it, but nothing happened. Benjamin sensed the same confused ball of ineffectual magic fighting against itself, and put a hand on Ray's arm.

'We'll get her back,' he said, noticing tears in Ray's eyes. 'Where will they take her?'

Ray gave a hoarse, nervous laugh. 'Only one place: London. Funny, isn't it? That's where she wanted to go anyway.'

Benjamin smiled. 'That's where I was planning to go too,' he said. 'Let's go.'

24

MIRANDA

Miranda couldn't be sure it was night, but it had been several hours since anyone had come to visit her, so she urged the little rhino back into the lock and made another attempt to get out. This time, however, she found that the second door leading out from her containment corridor had been bolted shut from the outside, and no amount of jostling would open it. She tried to use her magic but found a fresh ward in place, holding it firm. This time Trobin had been thorough.

She explored the corridor, looking for an alternative way out, but there was only a line of other cells, each leading nowhere. Miranda returned to her own miserable, tea-soaked cell and sat down on the upturned bowl, leaning her head back against the wall.

Tomorrow they would give her back to the skies.

Whatever that meant.

These crazy people, they—

—*Miranda?*

She sat up. The word had come from nowhere.

—*Miranda? Can you hear me?*

This time it was clearer, and Miranda knew.

Rosa.

'Rosa, can you hear me?' Miranda whispered, voicing her thoughts.

—*Yes! Wow, how are you doing this?*

'It's a kind of magic,' Miranda whispered. 'It's hard to explain, but we both have it. Your people deny its existence to protect you, but it's everywhere. It's the reason this world exists.'

—*The reason for the flowers?*

Miranda frowned. Then she realised. The chamomile flowers. 'Yes. They help to calm it. To make everything more stable.'

Rosa's voice went quiet, and Miranda began to fear the girl had been discovered. Then: —*Mum said you're leaving tomorrow. That you have to go home.*

Miranda frowned. 'Yes, so Trobin said. I'll … I'll try to visit you again one day.'

—*My dad left and never came back.*

'I'm sorry.'

—*I think maybe he's never coming back. I think maybe he's dead.*

'Don't say that.'

—*I'm worried that if you leave, something bad will happen to you. Mum said we're not allowed to watch. That only the big ones can go to say goodbye.*

Miranda wrinkled her brow as she tried to think of some way to respond. Rosa clearly had a child's blinkered view on something sinister, and now that situation included her. She very much doubted Trobin and his followers would just let her leave.

'Thanks for worrying about me,' Miranda said, reluctant to get the girl involved. 'I'm sure I'll be fine.'

—*We meet lots of travelers, but not all of them stay. Sometimes they want to stay, but Trobin tells them they have to leave. And they do. Usually with a ceremony only the big ones can watch.*

Miranda grimaced. She felt more and more certain that she was headed for some kind of human sacrifice.

—*I'm going to sneak out this time,* Rosa continued. —*I know a secret way. There are tunnels in the rock all over the place, and me and my friends made a secret door.* Miranda felt a titter that could have been a laugh. *We can go outside any time we like.*

Miranda knew the danger she might put the girl in if she got Rosa involved, but it might be her only chance. She looked down at her feet, at the tea pooling around her, quelling her magic, and remembered poor Enchantress, reduced to a blob of mushy paper. If she had any chance of getting away, they both needed to dry out.

'The tea—the water—is there any way to turn it off?' she asked.

—*Easy. There's a big tap. It comes from a tank in the rock above us. I saw it once on a school trip. They pour the flowers into the water, and the rain fills it up. There's a tap on the side.*

'Do you think—'

—*I could turn it off? Of course.*

Rosa's thread suddenly went still, and Miranda imagined two things might have happened: one, that the girl had jumped up and enthusiastically run off to help; the other, that she had been caught communicating with Miranda via their shared magic. She waited, but Rosa's thread had vanished back through the ward trying to block Miranda out. With a sigh, Miranda leaned her head back against the wall again, patted the little rhino still jumping about in her pocket, and closed her eyes.

Without meaning to, she slept.

∼

She opened her eyes as the door opened. At some point she had fallen on her side in the night, and as she sat up, massaging her cold, stiff shoulder, she saw Trobin standing in front of her, preposterous dog mask lit by a glowing paraffin lamp. At his shoulder, Alamy stood, her own head adorned by the giant papier-mâché visage of a cat.

'Where is she?' Trobin said.

'Who?'

'My daughter,' Alamy spat. The woman took a step forward, but Trobin put out a hand.

'I'll deal with this,' he said.

Despite feeling a flush of guilt, Miranda knew that if Trobin found out she had been communicating with the girl, things could be worse for both of them. She had to trust that Rosa was clever beyond her years and could keep herself out of trouble.

'I don't know anything,' Miranda lied.

'Don't think I don't know what you are,' Trobin said. 'You, bringing your poison in here, putting every one of us in great danger.'

'I asked you to let me go,' Miranda said. 'You refused.'

'Because you're too stupid for your own good. You don't know what you're doing. In any case, the council had decided, and it's time now for you to leave … on our terms.'

Miranda felt magical arms encircling her, but she called her own magic, fighting them off. 'Get off me!' she shouted. 'You don't own me. You can't treat me like this. You're a liar. Do these people know what you are?'

'That mouth of yours is dangerous,' Trobin said. He reached out and took Alamy's hand, and the magic suddenly intensified. Alamy's expression didn't change. The woman had no idea she was a Weaver, but Trobin did, and now he used her to hold Miranda still. She fought as hard as she could, but her magic was no match for their combined strength. As she gave in, she felt the ward tighten, closing her magic down. She stumbled forward, exhausted, and Trobin caught her. He looped a chain around her arms, fastening it with a padlock which was an arbitrary addition to the dark reanimate Miranda felt flowing through it, locking it around her as tight as a snake around its victim. She could barely breathe as he pushed her out through the door, pausing for a moment to frown at the floor where she had been lying, no longer wet, but bone dry.

~

Miranda's eyes hurt when two of Trobin's followers pushed her out through the door into the bright sunlight. The sky above was a clear blue, the yellow sun high overhead, the red sun off at an angle to the east. To the northwest, great dark clouds billowed over the distant peaks of the High Mountains, occasionally emitting the brief flash of a lightning bolt.

In the tall grass around her, the overlarge heads of three dozen papier-mâché animals bobbed, appearing for all the world like the bizarre inhabitants of this land, leaving no trace of the humans hidden beneath.

As those holding her pushed her forward, Miranda sensed an unusual amount of unease among those assembled. Several threw muffled but scathing comments in her direction, blaming her for bringing horrors to their doorstep, for letting in a taint that they had tried so hard to keep away. She tried to regain her strength, but even as Trobin's ward slowly weakened, she felt the chains tainted with dark reanimate grow stronger, throwing off tendrils of magic which snaked up into the sky.

Far to the northwest, four black dots appeared out of the clouds.

Her captors led her to a towering pedestal of rock a few minutes' walk from where their community was hidden. The sheer weight of the chains was buckling Miranda's knees as she was pushed up a steep, winding path to the outcrop's flat top. There, she found a hand-carved stone altar. Trobin, his dog's head pulled right down over his face to connect with the flowing fur jacket he wore and leaving Miranda with no idea how he could see at all, instructed her captors to lie her flat on the rock. By now, the tendrils of dark reanimate extended high into the sky, reaching out, searching for those looking for her.

In the distance, the four black dots, closer now, were clearly identifiable as the massive, reanimated airships.

The Sleepers made a circle around the altar, and Trobin instructed them to join hands. Miranda felt a sudden surge of power as Trobin took control of the unwitting Weavers all around him.

'We have gathered here today to expel this fiend from our midst and send it back to where it came,' Trobin said. 'We offered our hospitality and our kindness, our understanding, and we asked only that our rules be accepted and obeyed.'

Miranda tried to open her mouth to argue, but found it held shut. Bonded, she could barely even struggle and could do nothing but stare at the bizarre figures surrounding her, wishing this was just a dream and that she was merely a player in some bizarre pantomime.

'We will not have our community threatened. As we have done with fiends and infidels in the past, we shall offer this one an onward journey. We shall not shed her blood nor break her skin, but merely offer her a path back the way she came, into the arms of He who sent her, and beg that He take His mercy and offer His punishment, and that our part be considered played, and that we be left to continue our lives in peace.'

Trobin lifted the two hands he was holding over his head, and the others followed suit. Together they began to hum. Miranda felt the cold of the stone beneath her back vanish and realised she was rising slowly into the air. She passed the heads then the raised arms of the Sleepers, then she was rising, rising, rising, higher and higher, until the land below was a play mat laid out beneath her. Wrapped in the chains, she had no control, but beneath her she felt the press of magic, as Trobin drew on the power of his band of Weavers to push her far higher than his own magic could have done alone.

Soon, she was so high that any fall meant certain death, even if she could find her own magic and use it to cushion her. She thought at first that they meant to dash her on the rocks, then the wind buffeted her and she saw four dark shapes approaching through the sky.

The airships. The dark reanimate resonating out from the chains Trobin had used was calling them. Calling them to claim her and take her into the grip of the Dark Man.

Miranda struggled, reaching for her magic with every ounce of strength she could muster until she thought she might vomit with the exertion. She found herself rolling over, seeing at once the airships, then a view of the ground, then the blazing suns above her, then something white and billowing—

She rolled, losing it from her vision, but she had thought—

She twisted again, and there it was, coming up beneath her, something white and shiny, its long neck stretching out, huge wings on either side flapping gracefully to lift it on the wind.

Far below, she sensed Trobin was at the end of his strength. The massive airships bore down on her. A huge whale's maw opened on the front of the nearest, enveloping her with a gust of stale heat. Inside, she saw only blackness outlined with a distinct orange glow.

She rolled again.

'Enchantress,' she gasped.

The bird rose up below her and Miranda found herself cushioned by soft, papier-mâché feathers. As the maw snapped shut, Enchantress banked, barely avoiding serrated steel teeth as they clamped down, claiming a couple of tail feathers. The great swan banked again, cutting over the top of the nearest airship, avoiding water cannons as they swung towards her, flying along its upper surface to keep out of view of the others to either side. She rose up over a massive, spinning propeller and dropped down in a great arcing glide into the slipstream created behind. Engaging her wings again, she flapped hard, increasing the distance as the four massive reanimates struggled to turn.

As Enchantress banked gently northwest, Miranda caught a glimpse of the ground. Far behind, she thought she saw a group of strange animals running through the tall vegetation to one of the rock stacks. She tried to twist her head then realised the chains still held her, and that something was holding on to them, keeping her from sliding off.

'Hello,' Rosa gasped, her hair billowing out around her. 'This is quite something, isn't it?'

25

WILHELM

'He's gone,' Wilhelm said. 'I know it. Ah, he has a habit of doing this. Running off to save the world on his own, always scared he'll get us in trouble.' He slapped a hand against his forehead. 'And look who has to go and save him? Me, of course.'

Sebastien shrugged. 'Perhaps he just went out for a walk. I know he was a little unnerved by what happened yesterday. Perhaps he went to clear his head.' He crossed the shop, saw something lying on his desk, and then frowned as he picked it up. 'Oh, well, perhaps not.'

'What's that? A little "sorry I had to run off and save the world but I don't want to endanger anyone but myself" note?'

Sebastien gave Wilhelm a wry smile. 'I can tell you two are extremely good friends.'

Wilhelm sighed. 'I thought so. Does it say where he's gone?'

'No. Only that he's sorry.'

'Typical. I have to go and rescue him now. I don't suppose you could lend me enough for a bus ticket? I only have a couple of quid, and I'm guessing I'd struggle to get out of the town with that.'

Sebastien sat down and waved at another chair, even though Wilhelm ignored him and continued to pace up and down, occasionally jerking his elbows in to avoid knocking anything off the crowded shelves.

'Let's not be hasty,' the old man said. 'We have to figure out where he might have gone. You say he had no money? It's unlikely he would have been able to get aboard a bus or train.' His calming smile faded. 'Unless….' He opened the drawer of his cash register and frowned. 'Okay, maybe he could have.'

Wilhelm glanced up at the clock. It was a little after nine in the morning. He had overslept, as usual. Had Sebastien gone down to his shop at the normal time, he might have noticed the note earlier, but leaving the boys to sleep, he had gone out to a workshop to do some maintenance on some damaged toys he had found. Only when Wilhelm had come rushing in to tell him Benjamin had gone had he realised.

'He's gone to London,' Wilhelm said. 'Of course he has.'

'For what reason do you suppose?'

'To find Doctor Ben Forrest. You don't get it, do you? Benjamin *is* this Doctor Forrest. At least, we both think so.' Wilhelm shrugged. 'Somehow or other.'

'Impossible. I know the world has changed a lot over the last few years, but there are certain things that just aren't possible.'

'See, I would have thought that flying junk, kids that can do magic, and massive sinkholes in the middle of London might have been considered, you know, just a bit weird. But perhaps that's just me?'

Sebastien laughed. 'There's no need to jump up and

down. We'll find your friend. We just have to be logical about it. He has no transport of his own, not even a bicycle. That leaves him three ways to get out of Basingstoke: by bus, by train, or by hitching a ride. I very much doubt he would have done the latter due to the fact that he, um, borrowed some money from my till. That leaves us with the train and the bus. It might be wise for me to make a phone call or two. Just stay here and relax for a few minutes.'

Sebastien went into a back room, and after a short pause, Wilhelm heard him talking on the phone. Unable to control his urge to do something, Wilhelm went to the front windows and peered outside, afraid of seeing a dog-catcher van parked up in the street. When he saw nothing, he opened the door and went out, pacing up and down as people walked past on their way to work, some offering frowns or bemused smiles as he muttered to himself.

'Benjamin, you muppet, what are you playing at?' he said to himself, grimacing, wishing he had thought to do something drastic like tape their door shut so Benjamin would have woken him up while trying to get out. It wasn't the first time Benjamin had run off, and if Wilhelm could find him this time, it probably wouldn't be the last.

'Ah, there you are,' Sebastien said, coming out of the shop, the bell tinkling over his head. 'I made some calls. No one has seen him, but I don't think we'll do any good sitting around here, so I think it might be best to take the car out and have a look. Can you come inside and stay out of sight while I go and warm her up?'

There was something of a note of excitement in Sebastien's voice, as though he were about to set off on a grand adventure. Wilhelm reluctantly did as he was told, waiting inside while the old man locked the front door.

'I won't be a moment. Perhaps you could run back into

the kitchen and make us some sandwiches? It takes a while for the engine to warm up on cold mornings.'

Wilhelm rolled his eyes at the absurdity of the request, but did as he was told anyway, running into the kitchen and hastily stuffing some slices of ham between some slices of bread. As he reached for the plastic bag the bread had come in to wrap it all up, he was dismayed to find it had begun to move, lifting up at one end as though preparing for takeoff.

'And I thought Endinfinium was weird,' he muttered, stuffing his bag of sandwiches under his arm and heading back to the shop floor.

'Ready!' Sebastien shouted from a door that led out to a yard and then a workshop and car garage. As Wilhelm hurried in the direction of the voice, he wished the old man would stop sounding so excited. It reminded him of how he used to feel, before everything got so dangerous.

∽

They drove up and down Basingstoke's residential streets, peering out of the windows for any sign of Benjamin. Once, when they saw a group of boys on their way to school, they pulled over and asked, but none had seen a boy matching Benjamin's description. At the train station, they left the car idling outside and went to talk to the ticket inspector. Only two trains had left for London that morning, but again, no one of Benjamin's description had been seen. The next train was due to leave in an hour, so Sebastien suggested they try the bus station and then double back.

At the bus station, they were directed into a short-stay car park and found themselves in a spot right near the back. Sebastien told Wilhelm to wait in the car, but

Wilhelm refused, so the old man reluctantly let him tag along as they hurried across the car park and through a door at the bus station's rear.

They found themselves in a long corridor with three doors heading off. One was signposted WAITING ROOM, with another TICKETS, and the third ANDREW'S CONFECTIONARY AND GIFTS.

'Just stay here,' Sebastien said, indicating a line of chairs in the corridor. 'I'll go and ask in the ticket shop if anyone's seen him and what time the next coach leaves.'

Wilhelm took a seat, but a chilly wind was blowing through an open door at the end, so he got up and peered into the waiting room. There were no free seats, so he headed for the gift shop.

A few people stood along one side, reading magazines. Wilhelm's eyes lit up at the sight of so much reading material that hadn't been water damaged. He picked up a model railways magazine, then discarded it for one about vintage cars. He was flicking through the pages, trying to see if he could find Sebastien's car, when he realised something strange was happening beside him.

A young girl, no more than ten years old, was staring straight ahead into space. Around her head revolved a number of magazines. As Wilhelm watched, they began to move faster and faster, spinning until they became a kaleidoscopic blur.

And then suddenly they stopped. The girl grinned as the magazines moved smoothly back into place.

'Even Benjamin can't control it here,' Wilhelm muttered to himself. He started to move forward, but the girl turned around, facing the confectionery rack. Almost immediately, a cluster of chocolate bars rose into the air and began to spin around.

Other people had noticed now, too. An older couple

muttered something about sorcery as they exited through the door Wilhelm had entered by. Another older man just shrugged as he tucked a newspaper under his arm. Behind the counter, a middle-aged shop assistant was talking on the phone while staring at the girl.

Something was about to happen. 'Hey!' Wilhelm hissed to the girl, but she paid no attention. He reached out to touch her arm, but at the same moment, the screech of tyres came from the parking bay outside. The girl didn't move, but afraid of dog-catchers, Wilhelm dived down behind a rack of foodstuffs as the door burst open.

Three men entered. Two carried the usual electric prongs. They stared at the girl in disbelief, then one shouted rather redundantly at her to stay still. One made a move towards her, but at that moment, there was a sudden grinding sound from outside. Wilhelm lifted his head just far enough to look out through the window and saw a bus balancing in midair while around it people screamed in terror and scattered out of the way. With a sudden groan, the bus crashed to the ground, debris exploding everywhere.

'Come on,' one of the dog-catchers snapped, waving his prong at the girl. The girl sighed, the chocolate bars falling to the floor, and turned to follow them. One held the door, while the first waved her outside. Wilhelm lifted his head again and saw one jab her with the electrical prong and another throw a net over her. A van was waiting at the curb, and they bundled her inside before driving off.

Wilhelm was frozen for a moment. The bus had gone, taking off and floating away over the top of the bus station, pieces of debris following in its wake. The girl, he felt certain, had not been responsible, so that left the question of who had?

He ran to the window and peered outside. A crowd

was gathering, and he looked from face to face, searching for Benjamin. No one else could have done that, he felt sure. He was just about to go outside when a hand fell on his shoulder. He jumped, but it was only Sebastien, face etched with a worried look.

'Did you see that?' the old man asked.

'It happened right in front of me.'

'I was standing in line at the information desk, when a dog-catcher came pushing past,' Sebastien said. 'He told the clerk they'd come to investigate a possible sighting of a Miscreant.'

'There was a girl right here, making magazines and chocolate bars float in the air, but she had nothing to do with that bus,' Wilhelm said.

'It was an attempt at distraction. Could your friend have done that?'

Wilhelm remembered the van Benjamin had turned into an insect, and the playground climbing frame he had turned into a cage.

'Absolutely,' he said.

'Then he's near. Let's go.'

Wilhelm started towards the door out into the bus parking area, but Sebastien shook his head. 'There might be other dog-catchers. Alone, you're a prime target. Stay with me and you can pass off as my grandson.'

Reluctantly, Wilhelm had to accept the old man was right. They headed back to the car park, but found themselves stuck in a log-jam of vehicles trying to get out. Wilhelm thumped the dashboard in frustration as Sebastien held the wheel so tight his knuckles whitened.

When finally they made it out onto the road, Wilhelm felt sure they were too late. Sebastien drove back down the hill towards the town, while Wilhelm scanned the connecting roads on either side in search of Benjamin.

They were just coming past a school when they saw a tall boy climbing over a fence and running across a weed-strewn playground.

'That place is abandoned,' Sebastien said, frowning.

Wilhelm didn't reply. He let instinct take over, opening the door and rolling out before Sebastien had even brought the car to a full stop. He took off after the boy, leaping over the fence in a single motion, running hard across the playground and reaching the boy as he pulled open a door that led into an old classroom.

Grabbing him around the legs, Wilhelm tackled the boy to the ground. The taller boy cried out and aimed a kick at Wilhelm's face. Wilhelm ducked to the side, scrambling forward as the boy's momentum left him vulnerable. Wilhelm twisted him face down, lying across his back, pinning the boy to the ground.

'Get off me!'

'Where's Benjamin?'

'Who?'

'My friend. Benjamin. I bet you know, don't you?'

The boy struggled. Wilhelm grabbed his elbow and twisted it around, pushing the boy's arm up behind his back.

'Benjamin, where is he?'

'You mean Ben?'

'Is that what he's calling himself? Yeah, Ben. Benjamin. Benjamin Forrest. He's my best friend, and he ran off. I know you kids go creeping around, and I bet you all know each other. Spit it out.'

'He went off with Ray.'

'Who's Ray?'

'My friend,' the boy grunted. 'He's our leader. They went off after Lulu.'

Wilhelm was getting confused. 'And who's Lulu?'

'Lulu—Lucy. Ray's little sister.'

A terrible realisation dawned on Wilhelm. 'About ten years old?' He lifted a hand. 'About this tall?'

'That's her. She ran off to London. She does it a lot.'

'And where did they go to look?'

'The bus station.'

Wilhelm sighed. He climbed off of the taller boy and brushed himself down, before reaching out and helping the taller boy up. Standing, the boy towered over him.

'Sorry,' Wilhelm said, sticking out a hand. 'I'm Wilhelm. I'm Benjamin's friend.'

'Don,' the taller boy said. 'We poached him early this morning.'

'Poached him?'

'Yeah. Ray spotted him hanging around the station. Bad idea, that. Dog-catchers everywhere, always watching for runners. We brought him back here, but then Lulu went and ran off again. We split up.'

Wilhelm was shaking his head, trying to order all the random things Don had said. 'So where are they now?'

Don shrugged. 'Did me reccy down the park, no sign, so came back.' The boy frowned. 'Did you say his name is Benjamin Forrest?'

'Yes.'

'Why on earth's he called that?'

Wilhelm rolled his eyes. 'Because that's his name.'

'What, like the same as Doctor Ben Forrest? Bit weird, that.'

'It's complicated. When will they be back?'

'Don't know. Hey, here's two of the others.'

Two other kids came climbing over the fence, a girl with frizzy hair and a ginger boy with freckles. They approached Wilhelm and Don, frowning as they saw Wilhelm.

'Who's this?' the girl asked.

'He just showed up. Looking for Ben.'

'My name's Wilhelm,' Wilhelm said. The others introduced themselves as Dorothy and Kevin. 'I'm looking for my mate, Benjamin. I was up at the bus station and I saw this girl I think was your friend Lulu. She got caught. Someone threw a bus up in the air, but I didn't see who. I'm guessing it was my friend, as he can do stuff like that. Now, will he come back here?'

The girl, who clearly had authority over the two boys, shrugged. 'Yeah, unless they got caught, too. We'll have to wait. Hey, who's the old man?'

Wilhelm looked up. Sebastien was painstakingly trying to climb over the fence that the kids had all hurdled with ease. Wilhelm smiled.

'That's my grandad,' he said. 'Don't worry, he's cool.'

Sebastien, limping, stumbled over to the group. 'Are you children living in here?' he asked.

'That's right,' Dorothy said. 'What business is it of yours?'

'None, none at all. I suppose that explains why it hasn't taken off and joined one of those terrible tumbleweeds.'

'We have to live somewhere,' Dorothy snapped. 'Nowhere else wanted us.'

'Believe me, I sympathise,' Sebastien said. 'Terrible times we live in.'

'Says you in your sports car.'

Sebastien gave a tired chuckle. 'I'm guessing you haven't seen it? Car, for sure. Sports … I suppose it depends on the definition.'

Dorothy gave Wilhelm a sour look as though to express her anger at him for allowing a grown-up into their child's world, then turned back to Sebastien. 'You're still better off than us,' she said.

'I suppose, if you consider one wheel to be better than none.' He spread his hands, offering a smile. 'While we wait, I don't suppose you have anything you could define as tea?'

Kevin flicked a thumb back over his shoulder. 'Buckets of the stuff round the back, if you don't mind it cold.'

26

SNOUT

THEY WERE BURIED DEEP IN THIS SECTION OF THE school, but they came regardless, digging and clawing their way up through the rock, some creating new forms as they came, drawing their human souls into the folds and bends of their part-machine, part-organic bodies, taking on shapes that could run, jump, fight, destroy. As Snout scrambled back into the corridor outside the auditorium, barely pulling up before he stumbled down the scree slope where the floor had collapsed, he saw the cliff face bubbling with them, hundreds of tons of rock breaking off and crashing down into the sea as an army of dark reanimated creatures rose from the earth.

Tommy Cale was screaming over the top of a blaring alarm. Snout reached out and a hand closed over his, but then they were both falling, sliding among the rock as they slipped down the steep cliffside, huge rocks bouncing around them.

'Help!' Snout screamed at no one, and something broke through the rock above them, something flat and wide like an office table with crablike pincers and a human skull embedded into one side, with an orange glow emanating from its eye sockets. It rose to shield them as a boulder as big as a chair smashed against it and deflected away, leaving a crack in its body wide enough to see through.

Others came forward to reach for Snout's arms, pulling him and Tommy aside, dragging them across the slope and away from the worst of the rock fall, onto a path shielded from above by a jutting corner of the cliff.

'Where's Adam?' Tommy cried as Snout pushed the smaller boy behind him, trying to protect him from both the falling rock and the dozens of ghouls now clambering up the cliff towards the passage into the school. 'What happened to him?'

Snout just shook his head, unable to find the strength to speak. He stared at the mayhem he had caused, dumbstruck, mind reeling, and was still staring when a figure dressed in white stepped out of the shadows of the old corridor to stand in front of the gap in the school's wall above.

Wild hair danced in the wind as her arms lifted, fingers stretching out like claws.

'Back!' Ms. Ito howled, sending a barrage of hot air buffeting down the slope. Ghouls tumbled backwards, some dropping off the ledge below into the sea. Snout ducked out of sight then peered back, catching sight of two other teachers standing to either side of her: Mistress Xemian to her left, Professor Caspian to her right.

The ghouls, unsure of what fight they had been called to join, were quickly in disarray as the three teachers scoured the hillside. Rocks rose unnaturally to pummel back down, knocking the ghouls off of the cliff.

Snout, keeping Tommy beside him, closed his eyes, and without knowing quite how, willed the ghouls to leave. He felt a great gust of wind inside his gut, and when he opened his eyes, the creatures were sinking back into the earth, burrowing back into the rock, or rolling down to the beach where they stumbled into the waves, breaking down into their component parts as they went.

In moments the hillside was calm, only the distant call of some kind of bird breaking up the soft crunch of waves over the shingle of the shore below.

When Snout glanced back out, the three teachers had gone.

'What happened to Adam?' Tommy whispered. 'Did you see? I think it took him into the tank.'

For a few seconds Snout couldn't find his voice. Finally he muttered, 'I don't know.' He was about to say something else when the hiss of a loudspeaker came from upslope.

'All pupils are to report to the Great Hall for roll call. Repeat: all pupils, report to the Great Hall. Immediately.'

Tommy looked about to cry. Snout, who felt little better, squeezed the smaller boy's hand. 'Come on. We'll come back and find him later.'

The path led around the side of the cliff, through a few tunnels carved through particularly dangerous sections, and came out on a section of beach below the main entrance. As they began the arduous climb up a meandering cliff path to the school, Snout became increasingly aware that they had no chance of making it to the Great Hall in time.

In fact, when they finally stumbled through the door, exhausted, the entire school turned to stare at them. Professor Loane stood on the podium in the middle of the stage, with the other teachers—along with Godfrey—lined up on one side. On the other were a number of reanimates who helped out around the school, including Gubbledon

Longface, the sin keeper, and the old gatekeeper—a reanimated David Brown tractor. Ms. Ito glared at both of them as they sheepishly joined the end of their respective lines.

'It's nice of you two to join us,' Professor Loane said, not bothering to hide his irritation. 'That leaves just one boy missing. Has anyone seen Adam Kimber?'

There were murmurs from the assembled pupils. Snout kept his head down, while Tommy glanced over his shoulder, eyes wondering if Snout was prepared to speak up.

'No one?' Professor Loane cleared his throat. 'In that case, we will organise a search. However, in light of the unexpected attack on the old science block by ghouls, we teachers will carry out the initial search ourselves. All pupils will remain under supervision in the dormitory building until further notice. No exceptions. Is that clear?'

No one answered. Professor Loane looked around him at the other teachers. Professor Eaves raised a hand.

'I would like to remind all of those present, that such actions as these will not be tolerated. This school does not allow for theft or vandalism of personal or club items. Those responsible for this despicable act will be both found and disciplined. I don't need to remind you that blatant, repeated disregard for the school's rules holds a maximum penalty of expulsion?'

Snout glanced at Ms. Ito just in time to catch her roll her eyes. Standing on the other side of Captain Roche, Godfrey looked triumphant, his chest puffed out and his green eyes beaming above a wide smile. As Professor Loane dismissed everyone, Snout leaned close to Cherise and whispered, 'What happened?'

'Trust you to miss everything. Where on Endinfinium where you? Someone broke into Dusty's club room and stole something important. He won't say what, because it's "private club matters,"'—Cherise theatrically made quotation marks with her fore and middle fingers—'but it's apparently really important. Who cares, when we just got attacked by ghouls?'

'Me and Tommy got stuck behind a door that had reanimated,' Snout said, coining an excuse he doubted would get past Ms. Ito. 'That's why we were late.'

'Good luck explaining that,' Cherise said, nodding to Snout's nemesis, who stood by the exit, glaring at him as he approached.

He knew not to bother trying to avoid her. He reluctantly met her eyes and turned as she gave a sharp twist of her head to indicate he should stay behind.

Sullenly, he stood a couple of paces away with his head down as the rest of his class filed out. 'You're in for it now,' Derek whispered as he passed, the briefest of grins appearing on his face.

Most of the pupils had gone. Snout didn't look up until Ms. Ito prodded his arm. He found himself facing Professor Loane and Professor Caspian.

'Don't waste time lying to me,' Ms. Ito said. 'I'll give you a thousand years of cleans if you make even one attempt. Only you can call the ghouls up from the ground like that. Why?'

Snout sniffed then wiped his nose. 'Me, Adam, and Tommy went to the old science block,' he said.

'How did you get in?'

'Adam and Tommy borrowed Cherise's key and we made a copy out of reanimated custard mixed with glue.'

'Huh. Three points for ingenuity,' Professor Caspian said.

'Quiet,' Ms. Ito snapped, then rounded on Snout. 'Why?'

'Because we'd all seen a strange girl around the school, and we thought she came from in there.'

'What girl?' Professor Loane asked. 'A new arrival?'

Snout shook his head. 'No, more like a ghost. She kept calling to us, beckoning us to follow her. We reckoned she was coming from the old science block ... from the ... the Dark Reanimate Society.'

'The what?'

'Eaves,' Professor Loane said. 'We have to be careful here. That twit Godfrey has him in his palm. They say that group of theirs is harmless, but we all know that boy's history. Did you really think he didn't still have his loyalties with the Dark Man? It's pretty obvious now, isn't it?'

'We should have cast him out when we had a chance. Now his taint's rooted too deep, and if he goes, he'll take half the school with him.'

Snout got the impression they were talking over him about things pupils shouldn't know. He lowered his head and tried to pretend he was somewhere else.

'Without Benjamin here, there's no balance,' Professor Caspian said. 'He had a habit of shaking things up, but I believe we'll have to handle this one ourselves.'

'Forrest was a royal thorn in my backside, but I'd grudgingly admit he and his little chums had a habit of averting a crisis. We have to be careful, Caspian. The boy is dangerous.'

In the midst of their conversation, Snout raised a tentative hand.

'What, boy, what?' Ms. Ito snapped.

'Did you find Adam?'

'Kimber? That overweight boy?'

'Plump,' Loane said. 'We're supposed to call them plump.'

'He's fat. There's no other way to describe it, and you

know how much I hate all this faffing about correctness.' Then, turning to Snout, she snapped, 'No, we didn't find him. Where was he last seen?'

'In the auditorium.'

'Doing what?'

'Looking into a glass tank. There was something in it. I think it might have come out and caught him.'

Ms. Ito scowled. 'Anywhere else and I might think you were reading too many fairy stories. However … I can tell from the sweat dribbling down your face that you're not telling me porkies, are you?'

'No, miss.'

'You see, we have a little problem. Someone has put a dark reanimate ward on that room. None of us have the power to break through it, and such is its nature that if we try, it'll spread out and damage the rest of the school. To what extent, we won't know, unless it happens, but it's not likely to be good, is it?'

'I, um, don't—'

'Don't worry, Simon, we're not expecting you to know,' Professor Caspian said. 'But I'm afraid your little investigation has triggered something dangerous which we're at loggerheads to understand.'

'I'm sorry, sir.'

'Quit your sniveling.'

'I'm sorry, miss.'

'What did I just say?'

This time Snout simply lowered his head again.

'It's all right, Simon,' Professor Loane said, patting Snout on the arm. 'We'll find your friend. We're just not sure how. Unfortunately, we've got quite a few problems to deal with right now.'

The teachers moved into a group of their own, leaving Snout standing on the outside. After a few minutes in which he thought he had been forgotten, Ms. Ito suddenly swung around and flapped an arm in his direction. 'Dismissed, boy. I'll figure out your full punishment when I have more time to think, but for now, you're on a hundred cleans per night until further notice. Is that clear?'

'Yes, miss,' Snout said.

He filed out of the Great Hall with his head still lowered. He was halfway along the corridor, when two figures stepped out in front of him.

'Pig Boy, there you are.'

Godfrey's snake-like eyes glittered from beneath his curly mop of jet-black hair. Unlike the rest of the pupils—who had to stick to their graded blue-grey uniforms—Godfrey had taken to wearing what he liked, and now sported a black-and-gold frilled waistcoat over a pair of crimson trousers. At his shoulder stood Derek, a smug smile on his lips made comical by his own dirty blue sweatshirt and trousers.

'What do you want?'

Snout felt a sudden surge of magic that was quickly suppressed. He shivered, aware Godfrey—the only known Summoner in the school now that Benjamin Forrest had disappeared—could probably cut him into slices with a flick of his fingers. While the teachers still passively tried to dampen down the pupils' latent ability to use the magic that had created the world around them, Godfrey openly practiced his and didn't care who knew it.

And there was no one in the school who could stand up to him.

'I want to know what you thought you and your idiot mates were playing at, breaking into our clubroom like you did.'

'We got lost.'

'You got lost through a locked door?'

Snout shrugged. 'Things move about on their own here, don't they?'

Godfrey rushed forward, grabbing Snout by the scruff of his shirt and pushing him up against the wall. Derek glared over Godfrey's shoulder, his eyes glowing with triumph.

'Not through a door I've locked, they don't. I'm warning you, Pig Sty Boy, I could make you disappear. I made Benjamin and his little friends disappear, didn't I?'

'You had nothing to do with that!' Snout protested.

Godfrey's eyes narrowed. 'Oh, didn't I? Are you so very sure?' He stepped back and pushed Snout to the floor. As Snout started to get up, Godfrey put a foot on his shoulder and pushed him down again. This time Snout relented, turning over to sit looking up at the two bullies standing over him.

'All I'll say is if it wasn't for what you can do, you'd be gone already,' Godfrey said. 'As it happens, someone even more powerful than me has use of you. Keep looking over your shoulder, Grunty. Sooner or later you'll find me there.'

He turned and strode away. Derek, clearly feeling like he needed to impose some authority of his own, tried to spit on Snout, but he didn't juice it enough and it dribbled down his shirt instead. He glared at Snout, wiped it angrily away and turned to follow Godfrey.

Snout watched them go, his heart racing. If they hadn't been his enemies before, they certainly were now.

27

BENJAMIN

They had just turned the corner into the street on which the school stood when Benjamin caught sight of Sebastien's car parked by the curb. He put out a hand, stopping Ray.

'We can't go back,' he said.

'Why not?'

'The man I was staying with, he's there.'

'Is he a dog-catcher?'

'No, but—'

'So he might help us.'

Benjamin shook his head. 'I don't want anyone hurt. I'm going to London. If you want to come and find your sister, you can come too, but I don't want anyone else involved. You have no idea how dangerous this could be.'

'Which is why I have to find Lulu.'

They backtracked until they were out of sight, then Benjamin came to a stop. 'How can we get to London without using a bus or a train?'

Ray shrugged. 'We fly? You can make those vans fly through the air. Perhaps you could make one carry us.'

'I didn't have much control over it. I suppose we could steal a car.' Even as he said it, he realised both that it was the best idea and also one that would confirm him as a criminal. The temptation to turn around and walk back to the school where Sebastien and Wilhelm were likely waiting with Ray's friends was so overwhelming that he put out a hand to stop himself, gripping the edge of a stone garden wall a little too hard. A piece of tile broke free, clattered to the ground, then rose back into the air, flying away westward. Benjamin watched it go until it was out of sight.

'I have an idea,' he said. 'Trains and buses aren't the only things going to London.'

Ray frowned. 'I don't understand.'

'The tumbleweeds.'

'What? You don't think…?'

Benjamin shrugged. 'It's worth a try. First we need to find one.'

They headed back into the centre of town, keeping to alleyways where possible, following a route Ray and his Miscreants had often taken to get around town without being seen. Ray led them around the back of the train station to where a line of buses was parked.

'The tours,' he said. 'They pick up parties off the train and drive them out to the nearest tumbleweed.'

'The big one?'

Ray smiled. 'The biggest.' He put a hand on Benjamin's arm. 'Wait here.'

Benjamin hunkered down in the shadows as Ray sneaked out across the car park, first around the backs of the buses and then blending into the crowd milling around the front. As he passed a group of school children all wearing matching hats, Benjamin noticed for the first time how his dirty, ripped clothes made Ray stand out. The dog-catchers wouldn't just go on obvious uses of magic, he realised.

Just as Benjamin was starting to panic, Ray appeared through the crowd and came running back over.

'We're in luck,' he said. 'The current tumbleweed is about to pass out of this tour's range, so today is the last day for a couple of weeks until the next one comes past. For that reason they've got extra buses running, but being typically British, they're understaffed, and the place is a mess.' Ray held up two strips of paper. 'I got us tickets.'

'Tickets?'

'Well, unless you'd prefer to ride in the luggage compartment.'

'How on earth did you do that?'

Ray looked hurt. 'I didn't steal them, if that's what you mean. Well, not exactly. I just nipped behind the ticket counter and tore them off a roll.'

'And no one saw you?'

Ray glanced back over his shoulder, then smiled. 'Doesn't look like it. Are you coming or not?'

He started running across the car park. Benjamin hurried to catch up. 'Which bus are we on?' he asked as Ray came to a stop.

'Number Three. Let's go.'

They climbed onboard among a throng of late-middle-aged to elderly people. A few people baulked at Ray's obvious unwashed state, but the boy wore a wide grin as he waved the tickets at the driver and took a seat halfway back, moving over to the window so Benjamin could squeeze in beside him.

'This feels like a school trip,' Ray said. 'I've never been on one, so I'm quite excited.'

Benjamin said nothing. He stared out through the

window, wondering how in the world they were going to use the tumbleweed to get them to London.

~

An hour later, the bus pulled into a crowded car park. Benjamin recognised the same chaos as before, but this time it seemed to have an even greater urgency, as though soon the tumbleweed would pass on, and their chance to view it would be lost forever. As Ray pointed out during their journey, all it meant was that it passed into the region controlled by a different tourism board, and Basingstoke's would have a lull for a couple of weeks while they waited for the next one—currently, according to overheard conversations, just passing Exeter—to appear.

Once, of course, they might have used that time to clear up the mess. Now they no longer had to.

Benjamin and Ray squeezed through the crowds until they were standing behind a safety barrier keeping them about fifty feet back from the muddy, rocky channel carved by previous tumbleweeds. A rumble in the ground announced its approach around a hill to the southwest, and people began to gasp as it came into view, a towering, cascading wheel of rubbish and debris moving up the channel in a motion that wasn't quite rolling, but more of a constant folding in upon itself, like a giant washing machine drum let loose to roll across the countryside.

'Okay, Benjamin,' Ray said, patting him on the shoulder. 'What's your plan?'

'Still working on it,' Benjamin said.

'Well, you have about five minutes.'

Benjamin grimaced. Even if his magic worked like it did in Endinfinium, there was no way he could control something like that. It was like a living ball of everything, constantly evolving, and as people further down the line began to scream, he knew it was coming for him.

A loud speaker mounted on a pole nearby announced a sudden change in the tumbleweed's direction. People began to scream and push backwards. Benjamin grabbed Ray's arm and held him tight so as not to lose him, but the panic in Ray's eyes said how badly he wanted to run with the rest of the stampede.

'It won't hurt me,' Benjamin said, as the speaker announced that the tumbleweed had moved two degrees to the north and threatened the vehicles in two lower car parks. 'It wants me, but it won't hurt me.'

'Oh, I'm pretty sure it will,' Ray said. 'Unless you're made of elastic.'

The tumbleweed, still half a mile distant, already towered above them, like a veritable moving mountain. Benjamin stared into the tumbling, crashing depths of its oncoming front. At such a size, it had to weigh a million tons. A million tons of moving rubbish throwing up a wave of scree at its front end as it carved its path across the landscape.

'The bus,' Benjamin said.

'What?'

'Back to the bus. Well, a bus or a coach. Either will do.'

'You've got to be joking.'

Benjamin turned and started running across a now-empty field. Over his shoulder he shouted, 'Well, you're welcome to wait there if you don't believe me.'

Ray caught up with him as he reached the lowest car park. Further up the slope, a few people were trying desperately to get away, creating an even bigger log-jam as a hundred vehicles pushed and shoved. Those lower down, however, had already been abandoned. Benjamin ran up to the first coach he found which was pointing in the right direction and had its doors still open. The keys had been left in the ignition, so he sat down in the driver's seat and started the engine.

'We're trapped, Benjamin!' Ray shouted, still standing on the entrance steps. 'Where are you expecting to go?'

Benjamin smiled, but inside his heart was thundering. 'London,' he said, trying to sound confident. 'Do you want a lift?'

Ray was half laughing, half crying as he climbed up into the seat behind Benjamin. 'You're crazy,' he said.

'Put your seat belt on,' Benjamin said. 'I've never driven a coach before. Or should I say, surfed?'

'Surfed?'

Benjamin leaned out the side window. The tumbleweed was bearing down on them, pushing a mountain of displaced earth a hundred feet high ahead of it.

'That's the idea….'

'You're out of your mind.'

Benjamin laughed. 'Oh, I went out of that a long time ago.'

Around them, cars began to bump and roll aside. Those that were damaged immediately fused with the tumbleweed behind them. Benjamin turned the steering wheel as the coach's rear began to lift then stamped the accelerator. Ray howled in terror. They were thirty feet off the ground before the wheels gripped, then they went sliding forward, only to be dragged back up again.

'It's speeding up!' Ray shouted.

Benjamin, barely able to speak through the terror he felt, was aware the tumbleweed was moving back towards its original channel as it bulldozed them along in the shadow cast by its immense size. But as something heavy crashed down on them from above, making the roof buckle, he knew he had to concentrate. One slip and they could be dragged over the scree pile and into the tumbleweed itself.

'It's going faster!' Ray shouted, as though Benjamin wasn't already aware. All around them was a deafening roar, and objects hitting the coach's roof came more frequently now. Benjamin could only imagine what they must look like: an increasingly battered coach surfing along at the tumbleweed's base, with two terrified boys sitting in the front.

Like an endless loop on the world's most unstable rollercoaster, they bumped and jumped along. A couple of times the coach rose high up the slope, once nearly falling end over front, and another time the front flipping upwards as the back got caught. Both times Benjamin shut his eyes and did *something* with his magic. With no way to control it, once they surged forward down the scree slope, actually bumping across scoured earth on wheel rims long-relieved of their tyres, and another time jumped high up in the air, executing a dramatic twist which revealed the churning wall of the tumbleweed in all its heart-stopping glory, before crashing back down.

Ray just hung on for dear life to the back of Benjamin's seat, while Benjamin himself clutched the long-useless steering wheel to his chest like a favourite teddy bear. Whenever the view was stable enough to get a glimpse of the world outside, he spotted helicopters hovering in the air ahead of them, and wondered if some sort of optimistic rescue attempt was in progress. As the coach began to crumple and break up around them, the windows cracked and muddied, the roof buckled in a dozen places, the back emergency door ripped off to allow a steady flow of muck to slide inside, his chances to see outside became less and less.

And then, without warning, everything stopped.

All around them, the world became still. From somewhere outside came the steady beating of helicopter blades, but behind them, the giant tumbleweed had fallen silent. A lump of mud landed on the windscreen and slid down it, actually clearing more dirt than it left, reminding them of the tumbleweed's presence, but as Benjamin leaned forward and peered through the broken side window to see a city spread out ahead of them with a great muddy streak cutting its way between tall office blocks, he knew it had gone calm.

The helicopters were keeping their distance, perhaps trying to see if anyone was still alive. Benjamin glanced up and saw a vertical wall of rubbish, like a town dump lifted on end, towering over him so high he couldn't see the top. He watched it for a moment, realising something else nearby was making a rumbling sound, then craned his neck to look.

Up ahead, another tumbleweed was coming in from an adjoining pathway to enter theirs. Like planes coming into an airport, it seemed even mountains of rubbish could form an orderly queue.

He glanced back at Ray, only to find the other boy leaning over his shoulder.

'What in the world is that?' Ray said, pointing out through the window.

'I think it's London,' Benjamin said.

'Yeah, I know that, I've seen pictures. What's that glowing orange thing?'

Benjamin squinted. Ray was right, something semi-circular in shape hung over the middle of the city, visible between office blocks at the end of the pathway's gentle arc. As he stared at it, it began to morph into towers and jutting buttresses, like a castle, one suspended in the sky.

'I think that's our destination,' he said.

28

MIRANDA

'I DON'T THINK WE WERE EVER FORMALLY INTRODUCED,' Miranda said, having managed to position herself a little more comfortably on Enchantress's back, with Rosa positioned in front. To her credit, the girl showed none of the fear Miranda might have expected of one so young. While she was still getting used to the experience herself, Rosa appeared to enjoy soaring so high that the ground looked like a giant bedspread stretching out below them.

Rosa smiled. 'You go first,' she said. 'Then I'll know what to say.'

'Well ... my name is Miranda Butterworth. I'm thirteen, I think, although that's mostly just a guess. I grew up in a cloning factory but woke up one day in Endinfinium, about a year and a half ago. I chose my name myself because before that it was just a number. I picked it off a book I found in the dormitory at my school.'

'What's a cloning factory?'

Miranda shrugged. 'To be honest, I have no idea. I only know that there were lots of other girls who looked exactly like me. We were in groups, or batches, as we were called. Each batch had a different colour hair.'

Rosa reached out for a strand that had fallen over her shoulder. 'Is it real?' she asked. 'It's like paint.'

'Completely real,' Miranda said, feeling a certain sense of pride at the girl's wondrous expression. She had a lot of misgivings about her personality and looks, but had always been rather proud of the flowing crimson hair that fell almost to her waist.

'I wish I had hair like that. Mine's a really boring brown.'

'It's not boring,' Miranda said. 'And if you think it is, I can plait it or something. That'll make it look more interesting.'

Even after she said it, she hoped Rosa refused. After all, what would Benjamin and Wilhelm think if they knew she was going around plaiting people's hair? They'd probably tell her she should form the frilly dress appreciation society.

As a sudden tear sprang to her eye, Miranda realised she gladly would if it meant seeing her two best friends again.

Rosa, though, was still beaming at her. 'I'm seven,' she said. 'And I was born here. I've heard people say they weren't, but I've never really believed it. I mean, how can you just appear out of nowhere?'

Miranda shrugged. 'If only we knew. For the longest time I thought it was all a dream that I would wake up from. By the time I came to terms with it all, I realised that I'd actually rather be here than where I was before.'

'Mother said that we live in paradise,' Rosa said. 'Whatever that means. I don't like the tunnels. They smell bad, and the light makes my eyes hurt. I don't see why we can't live outside, but Mother said it's too dangerous.'

'Hardly paradise then, is it?'

'But we're free. Nobody tells us what to do.'

'Except Trobin.'

Rosa shook her head. 'Mother says he's just a spokesperson for the council.'

'Then they tell you what to do.'

'They're just trying to protect us.'

Miranda sighed. 'Rosa, do you know what reanimation magic is?'

Rosa shrugged. 'Magic's something in books. We've got some books in the school library, but not many. I've read all of them at least twice.'

Miranda shook her head. 'Reanimation magic is what made Enchantress come to life,' she said. 'Otherwise she'd just be a pile of paper.'

'I am listening, you know, dear,' the giant swan said, arching her elegant neck and peering around at the two girls perched on her back. 'Just so you know. But yes, I imagine you could say there's a little magic involved.'

'You know,' Rosa said, 'I've always felt a bit different from the other kids. I mean, we were talking to each other with our minds, weren't we? And when I want the doors to open, they just, you know, do.'

Miranda nodded. 'How can you control it?'

Rosa shrugged. 'I just tell it what to do.'

Miranda remembered that Rosa had been born here in Endinfinium. Perhaps the rules were different for her. Miranda had struggled to control her Channeller's power since the day of her arrival, eventually being taken under the wing of an old hermit called Edgar Caspian who had helped her learn how to use it. Edgar, who it turned out had once been a teacher at Endinfinium High but left due to an objection to the suppression and denial of reanimation magic, had described Miranda as a Miscreant, an untrained magic user. Even now, over a year later, the magic that resided inside her felt like an animal fighting to get off a chain.

Enchantress banked northwards again, and Miranda peered out at the skies to the east. Four black dots hung above the horizon at regular intervals across the sky, like dirty raindrops which refused to fall.

The airships.

'They're blocking our route to the east,' Miranda said. 'If we try to head back to your community, they'll converge on us.'

'I don't want to go back,' Rosa said.

'But you can't stay with me,' Miranda said. 'It's too dangerous. You need your mother and father.'

'I only have Mum,' Rosa said, sulkily crossing her arms, even though it meant she was no longer holding on. 'Trobin sent Dad away.'

'Sent him away?'

'He got returned, like you,' Rosa said. 'That's what some of the older kids said. Trobin told Mum that he ran off to the High Mountains, but kids always know the gossip, don't they? Trobin didn't like him.' Rosa scowled. 'Almost as soon as Dad was gone, he moved in, saying he needed to protect Mum from whatever taint Dad had left behind.'

Miranda frowned. 'I didn't like Trobin.'

'No one likes Trobin. But he controls everything. And if you don't do what he asks, he puts his secret hold on you to make you.'

'His secret hold?'

Rosa shrugged. 'Like he did to you.'

'He's a Channeller, like me. He's just a lot stronger. And his magic is tainted by dark reanimate.'

'Yeah, it always felt bad whenever he put his hold on

something. We used to sneak out of school during breaks sometimes, but then one of the kids got caught and so Trobin put his secret hold on the door. If you touched it during school time, it made your skin tingle and feel weird. Loads of kids cried. They said it felt like someone was chewing on their arms.'

Miranda gave a slow nod. In a community where magic was denied, it had been easy for one strong magic user to take control. She wondered what Trobin's aim was? Just to move in with Alamy, or something more?

'Where are you planning to go?' Rosa said.

'Back to Endinfinium High School. It's on the coast, and where my friends are. I'm worried about them. There was a big attack on the school a few weeks ago. Something happened, and I woke up in the woods near the High Mountains. I've been trying to find my way back. An old hermit called Olin helped me by finding Enchantress, but the airships have been on our tail ever since.'

'Can you take me there too?'

Miranda grimaced. Bringing Rosa along hadn't been part of her plan, but now that the girl was with her, she had little choice. She couldn't go back to the Sleeper community for fear of the airships.

'Perhaps someone from the school could send a messenger to your mother to say you're all right,' she said.

'Yay! So you'll take me?'

'I suppose so.'

'Great!'

'But we have to worry about those airships first. And I'm getting hungry. What about you?'

Rosa patted her stomach. 'I missed breakfast.'

Miranda leaned over Enchantress's side and peered down at the ground far below. Was there anywhere safe they could land to forage for food? They were close to the

High Mountains but still far south of the Shifting Castle. If they landed and hid for a while, perhaps the airships would forget about them and give up.

'Enchantress,' Miranda said, leaning forward to pat the swan's neck, 'can you take us down? Find a stand of trees where we'll have shelter. We need to find some food.'

'There is a river running through a valley a short distance to the northwest, dear,' Enchantress said. 'I suspect you might find something there which you can eat.'

'Great. Let's go.'

~

Half an hour later, Enchantress brought them down in a narrow, secluded valley where towering, overhanging cliffs offered some shelter from above. Enchantress landed in a thicket among a stand of trees, announced she would take a short rest, and then ducked her head under her wing. Miranda, aware the yellow sun was beginning to fade towards the horizon, leaving behind the chill of the eternal twilight cast by the weaker red sun, took Rosa to gather firewood. With a couple of armfuls each, they headed back, dug a pit, and got everything ready. Then they went foraging for food.

Finding edible vegetables and fruit would be easy using magic, but Miranda was reluctant, in case it drew attention. First, they checked the trees for fruit, then nearby bushes for berries. In the nearby river, they found some fish they were able to catch by using rocks to trap them in the shallows. Miranda remembered how fish had been a rare delicacy at Endinfinium High, but these looked like the regular fish she'd seen in books, so she figured it was worth the risk.

On the way back, they found some wild carrots that

tasted as bland as those Miranda was used to, followed by a patch of far tastier wild strawberries. Content with their haul, they returned to the thicket, where they started a fire with a quick, guilty burst of magic, and then disguised the flames with a pile of rocks.

The fish tasted better than anything Miranda had eaten in months, and even the carrots had a familiarity about them which made her pine for the labyrinthine corridors of the school and the endless chatter of kids in the dorm. After they were finished, Miranda told Rosa stories of her life at the school, of her friends, the oddball collection of teachers, the unnervingly blank-faced cleaners, and the even stranger reanimates who populated the school's hidden regions. Rosa listened, her eyes never leaving Miranda's, her face rapt with excitement. Later, in turn, she told Miranda of her life among the Sleepers, unable to avoid mentioning frequently how boring it was to live in a collection of old subway tunnels hidden deep underground.

'Trobin controls everything,' she said, shortly after letting out a long yawn, signaling to Miranda that it was time they got to sleep. 'We even had to say a prayer to him after school each day, thanking him for protecting us from the evils of the world.'

Miranda, who had faced some of the various evils of this world and barely survived with the clothes on her back, was torn between hating the dog-mask-wearing weirdo and offering him grudging respect. In the end, she decided she'd sleep on it and see what the morning brought. With Enchantress offering to keep watch during the night, both Miranda and Rosa drifted off to sleep.

Enchantress nudged Miranda awake. The pile of twigs and grass that had served as a bed appeared to have turned into rocks overnight. Feeling a momentary panic, she looked around for Rosa, and finally located the girl, sleeping soundly beneath Enchantress's other wing.

'Poor dear got cold during the night,' the swan said. 'You could have woken me. I have two wings, you know.'

Miranda brushed a piece of twig out of her hair and smiled. 'Thanks. I'll remember that for tonight. Did any airships come across during the night?'

'Three times. However, we were concealed. They didn't spot us, dear.'

Miranda let out a sigh of relief. She nudged Rosa awake, and offered the girl a piece of leftover fish from the night before which she had left to smoke on a twig above the fire's embers.

'Did you sleep okay?'

Rosa frowned. 'I had a funny dream. At least, I thought it was a dream, until you woke me up, and I realised it was still there.'

'What kind of dream?'

'About my dad.'

Miranda cocked her head. Even Enchantress swung her graceful neck around to listen.

'What happened?' Miranda asked.

'He was calling me. He was telling me where to find him, where he's been trapped all this time. He was asking me to find help to free him.'

Miranda narrowed her eyes. 'And you said it was still there when you woke up?'

Rosa smiled. 'It's still there now. I can hear him calling me, like you called me in the tunnels. Because Trobin's not around putting his secret hold on everything, it's really clear, as though my dad's shouting at me from over the top of those hills.'

'And, um ... where exactly is he?'

Rosa's smile faded. 'He said it's like a castle, but that it keeps moving around. Do you know where that is?'

Miranda shared a look with Enchantress. 'Yes, I do,' she said. 'I suppose it's not that far from here, really. Not by the air.'

Rosa beamed. 'Great! Do you think we could go and rescue him? Perhaps we could take him back to your school as well. Perhaps we could even go and get Mum and all go together. Wouldn't that be fantastic?'

Miranda gave a reluctant nod. 'I suppose it would be. However, I'm not sure it'll be that easy. The place you're talking about is very dangerous.'

Rosa's smile dropped. 'But we have to! Dad said something bad's going to happen to him, that he doesn't have much time left.'

Miranda looked at Enchantress, but the swan just cocked her head. 'You're the boss, dear.'

Miranda gave a reluctant nod. 'We can try,' she said, wishing there was something else she could say.

29

WILHELM

No one appeared to know what to say. Wilhelm looked at the assembled faces, mentally trying to recall each of the names he had been told.

Don. A towering stick insect of a kid, fourteen years old but nearly six feet tall already as though something invisible had hold of his head and feet and was gradually stretching him like a piece of elastic.

Kevin. The one that would definitely get bullied if it wasn't that he could make things explode just by looking at them. Fat and freckly. Being the runt of any perceived litter himself, Wilhelm felt a certain level of kinship with the jovial thirteen-year-old.

Dorothy. While Wilhelm would never—ever, even under pain of death—tell her to her face, Miranda was something of a beauty, with her flowing crimson hair and lab-created features. Dorothy was nothing of the sort; sour-faced, unnecessarily snotty, frizzy hair tied in a frustrated ponytail that could spring back around and engulf her head at any moment. Fifty years old before she was fifteen,

Dorothy was the girl who ran the school library club, constantly railing on anyone who brought a book back late.

'Well, it's nice tea,' Sebastien said at last, sipping from a cup with a crack down the side, one of just a handful the kids had salvaged from the school kitchen before the rest took off. 'You make it with rainwater runoff, you say? Well, it adds a certain kick.'

The three Miscreants just stared at Sebastien, resentful at an adult entering their domain yet stunned that one would accept it so readily.

'When are they supposed to be back?' Wilhelm asked, looking around the three faces in turn. Dorothy scowled, Kevin looked at his feet, and Don shrugged.

'We don't really have a set schedule,' the tall boy said.

Wilhelm wanted to kick something, but there was nothing in range except a few ankles, and he doubted that would help the situation. Sebastien seemed content to wait with the kind of frustrating patience that old people had made into an art form, while the three Miscreants looked keen for everything to go back to normal.

'I'm going to go and look for him,' Wilhelm said at last, the inactivity getting the better of him. He turned to the door, but Sebastien put up a hand.

'Where do you plan to go? Try to clear your thoughts, young man. You won't get anywhere by rushing around in a circle. Suppose your friend comes back while you're out looking? You'll forever be chasing each other's tails.'

'I can't just stand here and do nothing,' Wilhelm said, gritting his teeth to prevent himself from shouting. 'Benjamin's out there somewhere and he could be in trouble.'

Kevin put up a chubby hand like a shy kid at school volunteering for the first time. 'Perhaps we could check the news?' he said. 'If they've been captured, there might be some word.'

'On what TV?' Dorothy snapped.

'I don't mean the TV. There's an old radio in the staffroom which works. It's fitted into the wall so it hasn't flown away yet.'

Dorothy gave a familiar scowl, while Don just shrugged. Sebastien looked at Wilhelm. 'And there comes your voice of reason,' he said. 'Like a breeze through an open window.'

'Come on, then,' Wilhelm said, throwing the old man a glare. He marched out into the corridor before realising he had no idea how to find the staffroom. He stopped and waited awkwardly for the others to catch up.

Kevin was right. In a room at the end of the corridor they found a large electronics bank fitted into the wall. Once, bells, fire alarms, and announcements would have been made from it, but many of the dials and fixtures were now missing, not to mention the labels which had once said what everything did. The brown-yellow stain of old Sellotape had left its residue behind.

'How does it work?' Dorothy said.

Kevin gave an awkward shrug. 'It doesn't until I touch it.'

Wilhelm watched as the fat boy touched his finger against the machine. At once LEDs switched on and a digital clock flashed out of the display.

'Can you do that to anything?' Sebastien asked.

Kevin shrugged again. 'Dunno. Never tried.'

'How on earth do you do it?'

'Dunno.'

Despite brushing off what had happened, Kevin's brief smile held a suppressed delight at having his ability praised. Wilhelm felt both envious and relieved that he had no such anomaly to deal with.

'It works like this,' Kevin said, twisting a knob. Static broke from a speaker overhead, making them all jump back. Kevin frowned and adjusted the volume, then tweaked another dial until a voice emerged out of the crackle.

Wilhelm frowned at Sebastien as a posh woman's voice gave instructions to a man about how best to peel potatoes, but the old man just laughed.

'*The Archers*,' he said. 'Wrong channel, young man. Give it another tweak.'

Kevin adjusted it again, and this time found a news program. They waited through a cycle of sports and weather until local headlines came on again.

'The incident this morning at Basingstoke's bus station is being dealt with by the appropriate authorities,' came an obnoxious man's voice. 'There is no cause for alarm and regular services should be running again by this afternoon. At this stage the malfunction is being attributed to a fault in the engine of the bus.'

Wilhelm gave an incredulous gasp as Sebastien just chuckled. 'Weren't they there?' he said. 'It jumped twenty feet into the air. I didn't realise an engine malfunction could do that.'

'Old habits die hard,' Sebastien said. 'Despite everything, the general authorities are reluctant to blame any such incident on … unnatural causes.'

'I'm guessing by appropriate authorities they mean the dog-catchers?' Don said.

'Pigs,' Dorothy spat.

'They must have captured Benjamin and Ray,' Wilhelm said. 'We'll have to go and bust them out.'

Sebastien raised a hand for quiet. 'Don't be hasty,' he

said. 'There's also the importance of maintaining public order. They probably don't want to give the impression there are fugitives on the loose.'

'And the strange case of the tumbleweed continues,' began the newscaster again. 'Its speed has increased, pushing it over thirty miles an hour. The coach caught in the debris around its base remains in position. The safety of the two passengers seen inside can no longer be confirmed due to the deteriorating state of the coach. At this stage, while a rescue attempt is still underway, it has been downgraded to a medium priority level unless evidence reappears of the passengers' continued survival.'

Sebastien looked around at the others. 'Does anyone in this room have any doubt as to who these two trapped passengers are?'

'Probably a couple of old people who were eating their sandwiches,' Kevin said, receiving a scowl and a nudge in the ribs from Dorothy, which reminded Wilhelm fondly of his relationship with Miranda.

'No!' the girl shouted, stamping her foot just for good measure. 'It's clearly Ray and Benjamin.'

Wilhelm nodded. 'It's the kind of ridiculous situation Benjamin would end up in, that's for sure.'

'Well, let's not stand around here debating it,' Sebastien said. 'We can do that on the way.'

'On the way?' Don said.

'There's only one place those tumbleweeds go,' Sebastien said. 'I think we'd better get going if we're going to catch it up. My car can be a bit slow to get moving on a chilly day.'

'Your car?' Wilhelm said. 'We're not all going to fit in that.'

Sebastien winked. 'It's a lot bigger than it looks.'

~

Pride, perhaps, had been talking. With Kevin, politely referred to as broad, given the front passenger seat, Wilhelm found himself squashed into the middle of the back seat, an irritatingly purposeless lump pressed into his lower back. Dorothy sat scowling on his left, while Don was constantly leaning into his line of view on his right.

Sebastien, when he wanted to, could drive far faster than necessary. At least it certainly felt that way with the old man laughing and howling as the old car swerved and careened its way through Basingstoke, collecting horn blares and annoyed shouts wherever it went.

Once they were out on to the M3 and heading for London, things only got worse. The speed that had felt excessive in the town turned out to be amplified by the car's quaking and shuddering. On the open road they struggled to hit fifty miles per hour, and the car was the continual target for tailgating lorries and groups of laughing yobs, windows wound down, hands waving. While the four kids hid their faces out of a repeating sense of shame, through it all Sebastien appeared unconcerned.

'Oh, got a chancer now,' Sebastien laughed, as a huge, articulated lorry came up behind them, closing the distance and then pulling out to overtake, its horn blaring non-stop. 'I think he wants to take us on, don't you?'

'No,' Wilhelm shouted over the roar of the lorry as it pulled alongside before slowing up, 'I really think he doesn't. We should just slow down, let it pass.'

'Speed up!' Dorothy shouted. 'Take it on, Grandad!'

'I'll have you know, I'm no one's grandad,' Sebastien said. 'In fact, I could get away with being your father.'

Don, on the nearside to the lorry, was cowering in his

seat, hugging Wilhelm's arm. 'It's going to run us off the road,' he moaned.

'Oh no, it's not!' Dorothy shouted. She leaned across Wilhelm, crushing him against the seat, and shouted, 'Leave us alone!'

As though on cue, the lorry's brakes squealed. It dropped away behind them, the driver blocking all three lanes as it tried to pick up speed. A huge cacophony of horns began to blare as the road behind them became entirely blocked.

'What on earth did you do?' Sebastien said, glancing behind him.

Dorothy looked terrified. 'I just got angry at it,' she said.

Wilhelm, who had felt a little warmth in his palms as the lorry's brakes tightened, knew otherwise. In another world a long, long way away, Dorothy would be considered a Channeller, and she had unknowingly used his Weaver ability to boost her own.

However, he reasoned, if he told her that, he'd probably have her clinging to him all day long. 'You should be a bit more careful about throwing your anger around,' he told her with a grin. 'Although we've got a nice clear road for a while now.'

As they headed towards London, connecting junctions began to add traffic again, but for a while they enjoyed a peaceful country drive in the middle of a three-lane motorway. With Sebastien humming an old show tune in the front and Dorothy dozing against the window, Wilhelm had been enjoying a period of relative calm, when Don abruptly patted him on the shoulder.

'Got one of them coming up behind.'

'Where?'

'On our tail. Closing in.'

Wilhelm twisted around, inadvertently awakening Dorothy and receiving a snapped reprimand for his misdemeanour. Lights flashed on a van coming up the central lane.

'Dog-catchers,' Don said.

Wilhelm turned back around and leaned forward to pat Sebastien on the shoulder. 'Can we go any faster? We've got dog-catchers on our tail.'

Sebastien peered at the mirror. 'They might not be after us,' he said, pulling into the inside lane. 'They might be after someone else.'

'Like who?' Wilhelm said, hitting the back of the front seat. 'They've heard about the lorry, I expect.'

'Careful with your hands, young man,' Sebastien said, as the dog-catcher van pulled in behind them, flashing its headlights to tell them to pull over. 'They're not the law, you know. They hold no authority. I'm pulling over out of common courtesy, but I would suggest that you four keep quiet and let me do the talking.'

Sebastien kept the engine idling as two men approached the driver's window. A third went around to the passenger side and stood a few steps back, holding a metal stick across his chest while wearing a defiant scowl, like a man who had turned up at a Medieval costume party without most of his costume. For the first time Wilhelm was able to study them up close. They wore baseball caps with Department of Civil Safety written in an arc across the front. Their uniform was a burnt orange.

'D.C.S.,' Don muttered. 'Say it quickly. Not the letters. Read it.'

'D. ...' Wilhelm had a moment of clarity. 'Ah ... I get it.'

'About sums it up,' Dorothy. 'Don't open the window, Grandad.'

'I'll deal with this,' Sebastien said, cranking a window handle that was so stiff it made veins stand out on the back of his neck. He leaned out, frowning at the two men standing alongside the car.

'Yes? Can I help you?'

The nearest leaned threateningly over the front of the car, peering inside. An ID card announced him as CHADWICK LOATES – D.C.S.

'Are these children yours?'

Sebastien looked abashed. 'Excuse me, young man, but what kind of question is that?'

'We had reports of an unusual disturbance four junctions back along the M3.'

'I don't know what you're questioning me for. You should be questioning the lorry driver who needs to go back to driving school.'

'Are you sure these children are yours?'

'I'm their grandfather, I'll have you know.'

'They look nothing like you.'

Sebastien rolled his eyes. 'You noticed? Like I'm not the butt of jokes at every party. The tall one, my first daughter's second husband was a real beanpole. Hit his head on the marble ceilings in his mansion, can you believe? And the runt … well, my second daughter's third husband was so short he could slide underneath doors. A right odd couple, they made.'

'The fat one is ginger.'

'I prefer strawberry blond, if you don't mind,' Sebastien said. 'Let's keep it civil. My son's wife was Scottish. Should have seen her, like a wildcat. Got run over facing down a steamroller. Quite a sight. They had to write the thing off. And his second wife wasn't much better. Welsh lass, wild hair, hence the girl. Plays rugby union for Wales. The men's team. At least nine times the size of you, and her daughter has sights on playing in the scrum at school. So, if I were you ... I'd scramble back to your van on the double and let us be on our way.'

Wilhelm looked around at the others. All at once, they began to cheer. The dog-catchers backed away, glancing at each other as though uncertain what to do. Chadwick looked about to order his minions off, when the one at the back suddenly shouted, 'Oi, Chad! Kid in the back is the same one Les said was hanging round the playground that turned into a cage. Looks just like him!'

Chadwick's look of uncertainty turned to one of anger. 'I'm afraid, sir, that we need to inspect these children a little more closely.'

He moved forward, reaching for the back door handle, but Wilhelm pressed down the lock. Sebastien began frantically winding at the window handle, but it was even stiffer to go back up and was only halfway up when Chadwick's cattle prong poked in through the window, angling towards Wilhelm in the middle at the back.

'Leave my kids alone!' Sebastien shouted, turning around and grabbing it, just as a sudden spark came from the end. He jerked, his eyes rolling back, and then slumped down across the middle seats.

'You've killed him!' Wilhelm shouted, pushing himself forward. He grabbed the cattle prod and twisted it out of a stunned Chadwick's hands.

'Watch out with that thing!' Dorothy shouted, as Wilhelm tried to turn it around in the tight confines of the car. Chadwick was reaching into the half-open window, trying to reach the lock on the inside. Kevin and Dorothy batted at his hands as Wilhelm tried to line the cattle prod up, pushing Don against the window as he turned the handle around.

He had just managed to get the danger end up past

Dorothy's back when Chadwick backed away, and the second man, identified as ROYSTON WHEELER, approached, brandishing his stick.

Kevin, leaning over Sebastien to try to wind up the window, got a direct hit in the middle of the back. He jerked violently before slumping down over the old man. Royston, with Chadwick shouting at his shoulder, attempted to thread his prong into the back seat, but Wilhelm batted it aside. Royston stabbed at Wilhelm, who responded by trying to poke the dog-catcher's body. On one side, Dorothy was trying to avoid both prongs, while on the other, Don was shouting ideas for how to get the thing to work. It had five buttons, four more than Wilhelm had expected, but just keeping Royston's point away from his chest was proving hard enough.

'The other one's on the phone!' Dorothy shouted, twisted around so her back was against the seat in front. 'He's calling for backup, I bet. We have to do something!'

'Can't you do what you did before?'

'I don't know what I did!'

'Try! Or you do something,' Wilhelm shouted at Don. 'Just grab my arm when you do it!'

'Why?'

'Just trust me!'

Don grabbed Wilhelm's arm. Royston's prong came in, jabbing into the seat as Wilhelm twisted aside, fizzing against the upholstery and leaving a burn stain. Wilhelm felt a small tingle in his hands, but it was from Don's attempt to use magic, not the prong.

'I don't know what I'm doing!'

'Nor do I, but something's happening!'

'What's happening?' came a terrified shout. Chadwick was rising up into the air, his legs flapping. Royston abandoned his attack and turned to help his boss, as the third man dropped the phone and came running around.

'Nice one,' Wilhelm shouted. 'Now, Dotty, get in the front and drive. You know how to do it, don't you? Just turn the key and press the pedals.'

'My name's Dorothy,' the girl snapped, slapping him across the face with a half-hearted pat which reminded Wilhelm so much of Miranda he could have cried. He grinned at her, but received only another scowl in return as she climbed through the gap in the seats, hauled Kevin to one side and Sebastien to the other, before leaning across to twist the key in the ignition.

The car started with a welcoming grumble.

'Quick, take off the handbrake and put it into gear,' Wilhelm said.

'How?'

Sweat was pouring down Don's face, his knuckles white as he gripped Wilhelm's arm. Wilhelm was only too aware that soon Chadwick would fall the fifteen feet into the arms of his waiting colleagues and the battle would be on again, but with another of his troops exhausted. 'Push down the stick and push forward the other stick!' he shouted.

Dorothy flapped her hands, but the car suddenly lurched forward, tyres squealing. Kevin groaned as he opened his eyes. He looked around then closed them again, and the car came to a sudden, jolting stop. Wilhelm glanced back and saw the dog-catchers about a hundred metres behind them. As Don let out a gasp, Chadwick fell out of the sky to land on top of the others, and all three crashed to the ground in a farcical heap. Within moments, however, they were back on their feet and running after Sebastien's car.

'Quick!' Wilhelm shouted.

Dorothy scowled. She kicked something, jerked

something else, and then let out a triumphant cry as the car's engine caught and they bumped forward.

'You've got it!' Wilhelm shouted, patting her on the shoulder.

'Don't touch me!' she shouted back, but there was a hint of amusement in her voice. Leaning over the unconscious Sebastien, she pressed the accelerator and they began to gain speed. Behind, the dog-catchers had given up their chase and were returning to their van. Wilhelm pointed at a junction leading off the motorway.

'That way,' he said. 'We'll lose them on the back streets.'

Dorothy took the slip road, which ended in a roundabout, the car narrowly avoiding an oncoming lorry as Dorothy zigzagged across the road. Hanging on to the front seats, Wilhelm glanced back over his shoulder.

No sign of the pursuing van. However, Sebastien was barely breathing, and both Kevin and Don looked groggy and useless.

'Which way?' Dorothy asked.

'London,' Wilhelm answered.

'Which way is that?'

Wilhelm gave a tired shrug. 'I have no idea,' he said. 'Let's just keep going straight and hope for the best.'

30

SNOUT

HIS HAIR SMELLED OF VINEGAR. SNOUT RUBBED HIS EYES, wondering why he was alone in the room with the pervading stench. Peering over the side of the bunk, he saw Derek's bed neatly made, his shoes gone. Snout's uniform drawer had been upended on the floor, while his own shoes sat by the door, the laces tied together.

He climbed out of bed, for a moment forgetting it was forbidden to open the windows during the day. If one scatlock could get in, they all could. At night, a crack was allowed, because the giant haulocks which inhabited the nocturnal hours couldn't fit, and the day-dwelling scatlocks would be roosting.

Down the hall, he found the shower rooms empty, so he washed the vinegar out of his hair as best he could, wondering first where Derek had got it from, and second, why they couldn't use it at mealtimes to improve the taste of the food. Then, after tidying his uniform drawer and untying his shoelaces, he got dressed and went downstairs.

Gubbledon Longface looked up from a dog-eared,

water-damaged horse racing magazine, his eyes registering a look of surprise.

'Oh, Simon, what are you still doing here? Derek told me you went over at first light to swat up.'

'Swat up on ... what?'

Even as he said it, he knew. Today's mid-term science test. He would look more decomposed than Gubbledon did if he was late.

A clock hanging over a bookshelf read five minutes to nine. With a sudden lazy clunk the minute hand clicked forward one more minute.

Four minutes to get to the science block.

Snout ran.

He didn't bother with a scatlock cape—an offence worth five hundred cleans if he was spotted—as he raced across the precipitous path to the main school building. He hit the stairs to the new science block at a full sprint—another five hundred—then burst through the double doors without checking for people coming the other way—five hundred more—on to the corridor lined with classrooms. He burst in through the door without knocking—a nominal hundred, but at this point he was so deep in cleaning debt he didn't care—and hit his seat a moment before Ms. Ito's spindly arm slapped a test paper down.

'Cutting it fine, aren't you, Simon?' she said, glaring at him with no hint of the conspiracy he now felt part of after the escapade in the old science block.

'Forgot my pencil,' he muttered, reaching into his pocket and finding that his pencil was, thankfully, there.

'Forgot my pencil, what?' Ms Ito said.

Snout felt a momentary confusion before remembering. 'Forgot my pencil, Miss,' he corrected.

'You just took a hundred cleans off your late attendance penalty,' she said.

This one, Snout remembered, had no set number but was set at the discretion of the teacher. He waited as the briefest of smiles touched Ms. Ito's lips before vanishing like a butterfly buried in snow.

'You're down to just nine hundred,' she said. 'Plus one for each question you get wrong.'

As Ms. Ito continued her languid movement from desk to desk, the stump's thud announcing her arrival at each, Derek leaned across from the adjacent desk.

'Sorry, old boy,' he said. 'Was sure your bed was empty when I got up this morning. Now, be a good sport and make sure you keep your left elbow out of the way of your answers.' Suddenly frowning, he added, 'Or you're as dead as your blubberface friend.'

At the reference to Fat Adam, Snout felt a flush of anger. The ghouls were far below, but it wouldn't take much to draw them forth to gobble up Derek. They fed on his anger; he could feel it. If he pulled them with a little hate on his side, they would run amok with jovial abandon.

Derek, though, could wait. There were bigger battles to be won.

Two rows in front, Tommy Cale glanced back and gave Snout a gentle smile. He still had one ally, at least.

The test began. As with most tests, it was pretty easy for Snout, but his concentration was elsewhere. When the bell rang to signal the end, he had completed barely half of the answers, and to his left, Derek was scowling. *You're in for it*, he mouthed as Ms. Ito called a halt, then began collecting papers while the pupils sighed and relaxed.

A couple of minutes later, Ms. Ito gave the order to leave. Derek elbowed Snout in the ribs as he went to get up, then pushed past him and headed out. Snout, head bowed, was last in line, but as he reached the door he heard a barely whispered, 'Wait,' from behind him.

He turned to find Ms. Ito glaring at him. At his back, the door snapped shut with a gust of reanimation magic.

'I do not appreciate tardiness to my classes,' Ms. Ito said. 'However, in light of certain circumstances, I will overlook it this time.'

'Thank you, Miss,' Snout said, not looking up.

'And I would appreciate a little favour done by yourself to aid the teaching staff.'

Snout looked up and reluctantly met her eyes. 'Yes, Miss? Um, of course. Er, Miss.'

'You are aware, of course, of the unusual events that transpired in the old science block. We, the teachers, continue to work on a plan of action to both safeguard the school and recover your friend, Adam Kimber. We are aware that some pupils might actually be involved, so therefore we have to tread carefully. What would help us most was if we had someone on the inside.'

'Me, Miss?'

Ms. Ito's already narrow eyes narrowed further. 'Yes, Simon, you. We would like you to buddy up to your roommate, Derek Bates, in an attempt to find out what is going on. We are aware that you have a certain ... skill. This is a skill which might make you attractive to the so-called Dark Reanimate Society. Do you follow, boy?'

Snout nodded. 'Yes, Miss.'

'Superb. Begin today, please. We would like as much information as possible, but don't worry about coming to us. We will come to you when we are ready. Dismissed.'

The sharpness of the final word caught Snout unawares, and he hesitated. 'Um, Miss? Does this excuse me from my cleaning duties?'

Ms. Ito gave a bitter laugh. 'Oh, young man, what a fool you are. *Of course* it doesn't. And if you question me once more, I will double what you are currently required to do. However, you do have my greatest appreciation.'

Snout nodded. 'Thank you, Miss. Your leniency is greatly appreciated.'

'Of course it is, boy. Of course it is. Now get out of here while I'm still in a good mood.'

This time Snout didn't hesitate.

⁓

'So, you're basically a slave to the teachers?' Tommy said as they sullenly ate lunch together at the end of a bench, several seats obviously left between them and the next group, Cherise and some of her friends. From time to time, one of the girls would turn and flick something in the boys' general direction, then melt back into the midst of the group, tittering and hooting.

'That's about it,' Snout said. 'I'm in a bit of a fix, really. I can't win either way.'

'Better to be in Ms. Ito's good book than her bad one,' Tommy said. 'Even if it's pretty hard to tell sometimes which one is which.'

'I have to suck up to Derek,' Snout said. 'That's the hard part. I'm quite happy down in the locker room. It's quite peaceful and you can daydream there, I suppose. You know I'm only five hundred cleans behind Tony Burns? I've had fifth years nudging me all day, telling me they'll make it worth my while if I get into some kind of mischief.'

Tommy Cale ducked his head, not meeting Snout's eyes. 'I believe in you,' he muttered. 'Got three Spiderman comics resting on it.'

Snout rolled his eyes. 'Thanks for having faith. I'll do my best to get into yet more trouble.'

'So what are you going to do?'

Snout shrugged. 'What I have to, I suppose. Anything for an easy life.'

~

After lunch, the pupils had a period for club activities. Instead of going to the horticultural club as he had planned, Snout pretended to have a stomachache and headed back to the dorms. There, he polished Derek's shoes, and then borrowed an iron from the kitchen downstairs and ironed all of Derek's clothes. Finally, he made Derek's bed and even corrected a couple of sums on some maths homework left lying on Derek's desk.

Afterwards, he wanted to take a long bath, or hide his head under a towel in shame, but if everything worked out, it would be worth it.

So he hoped.

With his mind set to a task, he could complete it pretty quickly, so he still had time left to reach the Horticultural Society's club room and catch the tail end of the meeting. Today, they were discussing the wild tulip breeds found on the moorland around the school, and Snout had been looking forward to it all week. In a hollow just inland from the school gardens, he had found what he thought was a pure specimen of a Queen of the Night, a black tulip variety he hadn't seen in Endinfinium before. One of the fourth year members had promised to bring a book from the library they both hoped would clarify its identity.

Downstairs in the common room, Gubbledon was lying across two sofas, his eyes closed. He looked less like a reanimate and more like the dead racehorse he really was, and Snout found himself a little creeped out, despite the lemon yellow velvet scarf wrapped around Gubbledon's decomposed neck.

'Feeling better, are you?' came the horse's voice, making Snout pause. 'Wish I could say the same.'

Snout turned. 'Aren't you feeling well? I thought reanimates didn't get sick.'

'Nor did I. A little under the weather. Perhaps something's going around.'

Snout wasn't sure what to say, so he just wished Gubbledon well and then headed on his way, managing to make it to the club meeting just as the vice-chairman, Oliver Pipe, was wrapping things up. He gave a frustrated shrug as Snout took his chairman's seat, before wishing everyone a good weekend.

Apparently the tulip hadn't been a Queen of the Night but a daffodil which had reanimated with a printer ink cartridge, the discovery of which had left the whole group on a downer. Snout sighed as they filed out, shoulders slumped.

'Thanks for coming,' Oliver said, giving Snout a rather forced smile before closing the door and leaving Snout on his own in the meeting room. He wanted to cheer himself up, but he still had his daily quota of punishment cleans to do, and if he could get them done before the next class began at five p.m., he would be able to go straight back to the dorms after dinner. Ever since Fat Adam's disappearance, Snout had felt more at home in the locker room than he had in his own bed.

Downstairs, the sin keeper was surprisingly absent from his post. In all the time Snout had been coming down to perform his punishment, he had never seen the booth by the entrance empty, but now he simply went inside and found an empty locker.

An hour later, when he emerged, the booth was still empty. With a shrug, Snout made his way upstairs, but he was still a level below the main school corridors when he heard a scuffle of feet coming up behind him.

'There he is!' someone shouted. 'Get him!'

'He's been down there trying to outdo Tony!' shouted another. 'Let's sort him out!'

For a few important seconds, Snout stood dumbstruck and rooted to the spot as four boys from the fifth year, two of whom played in the school rugby team's scrum, came rushing towards him.

Despite everything, despite his unique ability, despite the inherent craziness of Endinfinium, Snout was nothing more than a schoolboy about to get crushed by a bunch of irate big kids. He let out a feminine, high-pitched shriek, turned on his heels, and fled.

He had no chance. Captain Roche coached the rugby team, and even though there were no other teams to play against, he drilled his boys hard on the off-chance an international touring team came floating down the Great Junk River. The two boys at the front dropped into formation as they closed on Snout, while the two at the rear hung back, ready to run him down if he managed to slip through the oncoming juggernaut.

With less than a ten-pace advantage, he cut down a narrow corridor, hoping it was a shortcut through to the maths department where he might find protection behind the towering legs of Mistress Xemian, but instead found it was one of the school's many infuriating dead ends. Skidding to a halt, he mentally prepared himself to beg for his life as he lifted his hands to avoid slamming into the wall and giving his face a pre-meal tenderisation.

When he opened his eyes, however, he was alone, and

facing down a dusty, brick-walled corridor which was poorly lit by candelabras protruding from the walls. At his back he heard muffled voices, and turned to find a solid wall behind him. Pressing his ear to it, he heard someone say, 'Now, just where did he go?'

He was still wondering what had happened, when a dinner plate with arms and legs bounced out of a doorway to his left, gave him a brief glance, then bounced away through another doorway to his right. With a sigh of relief, Snout realised where he now stood.

Underfloor.

He had heard Benjamin, Miranda, and Wilhelm talk about it, but had little experience of it himself. Underfloor was a world which existed behind the walls of Endinfinium High's corridors and classrooms, entire blocks hidden from the people who lived and studied in the school. While there were numerous hidden physical entrances, most were metaphysical, with Underfloor accessible only with a little touch of reanimation magic in the right place and at the right time. While some kids—Benjamin and Wilhelm claimed to come and go from Underfloor at will, for example—were familiar with it, most had no idea of its existence, and their only experience of its inhabitants was of the few who worked around the school, and those troublesome ones they encountered outside the school's walls.

Underfloor was the domain of the reanimates, those inanimate objects brought to life by Endinfinium's magic. Some, such as Gubbledon Longface, the sin keeper, and the Gate Keeper, were well known, but most kept themselves to themselves, enjoying a life of pleasure and simple delight. While keeping out of the affairs of the other half of the school's inhabitants, unlike simple objects, which tended to reach a maximum level of reanimation rarely beyond making a nuisance of themselves, the reanimates of Underfloor were equally as —and often more—intelligent than those humans with which they co-inhabited the school.

Apart from the jumping dinner plate, there seemed to be no one else around in this particular part of Underfloor. Snout moved cautiously forward, calling out to alert anyone nearby to his presence, concerned that surprise would find him at the end of a sword point, or worse, the blade of a chainsaw.

'Hello? Is anyone here? I think I came in here by accident, and was wondering how I could get back out?'

A groan came from through a door to his right. He peered around it, at first seeing only a bed lying on its side, before realising that the groan was coming from the bed itself.

'Are you all right?' he asked, carefully making his way around the bed to where a shape in the headboard suggested a face wincing in pain. 'I'm sorry to intrude, but I was just looking for the way out….'

'Is that Simon?' A pair of eyes snapped open. A curl in the headboard's floral carving design opened and then crimped up like a mouth wincing. 'We heard about what you did over in the old science block. What on earth were you playing at?'

'It was an accident.'

'You broke something, do you know that?'

'What? I'm sorry—'

'Too late for that.'

'I didn't mean—'

'Go on, get out of here. There's a door that leads into a cleaning cupboard at the end of the corridor.'

With his cheeks burning, Snout retreated, leaving the bed to its pained groans. In the next door he found himself facing a towering creature that looked like a refrigerator with stumpy arms and legs. A face set into its upper door scowled at him and turned away. Again, Snout retreated.

He had found the door leading into the cupboard and was just plucking up the courage to sneak through when he heard something moving behind him. He turned to find a motorbike standing on its rear wheel, its front wheel revolving to reveal a series of different facial expressions, while an elongated kick-start lever gestured like the arm of a Tyrannosaurus.

'Simon, there you are. I heard from Frank that you'd appeared.'

'Frank?'

'Frank the Fridge. You just passed him?'

'Yes.' Snout hesitated. 'It's Moto, isn't it?'

The motorbike's revolving face spun to one revealing a smile, even as its voice came from nowhere, as though the face were just that of a ventriloquist's doll. Simon tried to calm himself, remembering that, unlike the ghouls, the reanimates were—in the majority, at least—friendly.

'You remember. It's been a long time since we saw you. We all heard what happened, though.'

'What's going on? Why are you all sick?'

'There's a taint,' Moto said. 'Dark reanimate. I don't know why, or how, but it's affecting all of us. Something's in the school that shouldn't be, and I fear what might happen if we can't get rid of it.'

'In the old science block,' Snout said. 'Adam, Tommy, and me found something. A kind of tank filled with gunge. There was a girl in it.'

Moto's front end tilted in a nod. 'It could be coming from there. We're not magic users, Snout. We are created by it, but we have no control over it. Find out what that thing is, and what can be done. Quickly. We are getting weaker … and weaker.'

As though to emphasise his point, Moto stumbled, his lower wheel slipping. His chassis cracked back against the wall.

'I think we're dying, Simon,' he said.

31

MIRANDA

'You have to try not to use it,' Miranda said. 'Every time you use your magic, those airships can feel it. They're tracking us the same way a dog follows a scent.'

'I don't know how,' Rosa said. 'It just happens without me thinking about it.'

Miranda frowned. She had noticed the way Rosa used her magic for simple things like climbing off Enchantress's back or tying her shoelaces. She did it without thinking, the same way Miranda would cough if she had something stuck in her throat. For the girl, born here in Endinfinium, the magic was as normal as breathing.

'Every time you do something, think about how you're doing it,' Miranda said. 'And try to use your hands. Think of magic as cheating.'

'Like using it for school tests?' Rosa giggled. 'I used to lift up the answer sheet when the teacher wasn't looking so I could see the answers.'

'Well, I suppose like that,' Miranda said. 'Just try not to use it unless we're in danger.'

Rosa grinned and patted Miranda on the arm. 'I wish

you were my big sister,' she said. 'Mum was always like, "No, no, no," all the time.'

Miranda squirmed but forced a grin. 'I imagine that's what mothers are supposed to do,' she said. 'Not that I'd know.'

'So you never had one?'

Miranda shook her head. 'I had a serial number.'

'Mums can be a pain, but they're your mum, right?'

Miranda nodded. She remembered how Benjamin had always pined for his family, trying to find a way back home at every possible opportunity. Neither she nor Wilhelm—who had come from an orphanage—had ever understood it. Except for one time, of course, when she had nearly been tricked, but that was a long time ago. Despite its inherent craziness, Endinfinium was the best home she had ever had, even if, from time to time, she longed for the kind of family you saw in storybooks: a mother cooking the breakfast, father with a kind smile as he left for work, a little brother playing with the dog in front of the TV … she shook her head.

Don't be stupid, Miranda.

'Don't be stupid about what?'

Miranda jerked. 'Did you hear that?'

'I thought you were talking to me.'

'No, I … was just … you know, thinking.' Even as she said it, she reminded herself not to visualise her thoughts too much, if Rosa's mindreading ability was as strong as it seemed. She couldn't trust herself not to think something she wanted to keep hidden.

Below them, rolling forests interspersed with bare hilltops with outcrops or patches of moorland eased by. To keep out of sight of the four airships searching to the east, Enchantress was flying low to the ground, sometimes barely higher than the treetops. Every few minutes she would rise high enough for Miranda to see over the nearest hills, to check on their pursuers to the east and the mountains rising to the west. Rosa still claimed she could feel her father's thread, but if Miranda was going to find him, she needed to make sure the girl could control her magic, otherwise it would shine like a beacon in a dark room. Putting a ward over it to protect the girl was the best thing, but it wasn't a skill Miranda had.

She needed help.

'There!' she said at last, pointing to a rocky knoll she recognised. 'We're near now, I can tell. Enchantress, take us down.'

The great swan swooped low, alighting in a small clearing halfway up a hillside. Miranda climbed off, helping Rosa down behind her, the girl scowling but pointing out to Miranda that she had indeed managed to keep her magic in check.

A path led away into the woods. Miranda asked Enchantress to keep out of sight and stay safe from the wraith animals haunting the woods, before turning to Rosa.

'We're going to meet an old friend,' she said. 'Stay close to me, and if I happen to fall into any traps, feel free to use your magic to help me out. Otherwise, keep it hidden. There are creatures in these woods which can feel it, and aren't friendly at all.'

'Like those airships?'

'Well, a little smaller, but just as dangerous.'

'Got it.'

Miranda nodded. 'Then let's go.'

The trees closed in quickly, but Miranda remembered these routes from before. She kept Rosa close and moved slowly, afraid of any traps. Aware now of what she was looking for, she spotted a couple of snares just off the path, and a pit dug in between the trees which had been covered with reeds.

'Ooh, look at that,' Rosa said, grabbing Miranda's arm and pointing off into the trees. 'I've seen one of those in a book.'

Miranda felt a tickle of fear. 'Where?'

'There, by that tree.'

Miranda let out a sigh of relief. It was only a rabbit, grey and white, hopping through the grass. In fact, it looked just like rabbits she had seen in books too, before it suddenly turned and scaled the nearest tree trunk with the speed and agility of a squirrel, metallic claws gleaming in a beam of light cast down through the canopy.

'Didn't know they could climb,' Rosa said.

'Me neither,' Miranda answered, peering up into the boughs overhead, aware that something unsavory could drop onto their heads at any moment. It was still day, and the branches looked empty. Even so, she quickened her pace.

A few minutes later they emerged at a clearing on the side of a hill. Miranda smiled, recalling fond memories and even fonder meals, then suddenly frowned. The lines of vegetables were no more, the plots dug over and ripped up, the plants nothing more than ashes.

'Did someone have a bonfire?' Rosa said. Then, grabbing Miranda's arm again, she hugged the bigger girl close and shivered. 'But it's cold here, like something bad happened.'

Miranda swallowed a lump in her throat. 'Come on,' she said. 'We have to hurry. You might be right.'

Down a path at the bottom of the clearing she led Rosa, moving in a jog now, aware this path was free of traps but worried enough that she no longer cared. Breaking into a smaller clearing, she saw the knoll up ahead. For the briefest of moments she thought everything was fine, then the door, caught in a light breeze, sagged back, hanging from a single hook, revealing a chaotic jumble of belongings inside.

'Olin!' she shouted. 'Olin! Are you in there?'

'What is this place?' Rosa said, frowning again.

'A friend lives here,' Miranda said. 'Or at least he did.'

She pushed past the door and climbed inside, scrambling over collapsed tables and chairs, overturned cupboards, all the while shouting Olin's name. No answer came, and by the time she reached the small living room at the back of the house, her heart was thundering, her hands clammy despite the cold.

'He's gone,' she said.

'Who?'

'My friend. Olin Brin. He helped me. He gave me Enchantress.'

'Are you sure he's not here?'

'He must have run or been captured. His house has been ransacked. Perhaps the wraith animals took him back to the Shifting Castle.'

Rosa shook her head. 'No, he's still here. Hiding.'

'You can feel him?'

'Everything's dark and cold, except for one place.' She climbed over an upended table and pulled a wall-hanging curtain aside to reveal a small door, barely waist high.

Miranda dropped to her knees. She felt the door handle, but it didn't open. Closing her eyes, she sensed a magical ward holding it shut.

'Rosa, give me your hand.'

Rosa was a Channeller like herself, but perhaps if they combined their magic, they could break the ward together. She concentrated, imagining the air pushing and pulling, condensing into a device strong enough to rip through Olin's ward.

'On three, pull that door,' she said. 'With your magic. One ... two ... three!'

The door popped open, and a cramped, bundled shape tumbled out to land at their feet. Miranda took a moment to recognise Olin's bearded face, because his eyes were closed, his skin so pale. She reached down and touched him, his skin cold to the touch.

'Is he dead?' Rosa asked.

Under Miranda's fingers came a faint pulse. She stepped back, scowling, then aimed a slap at Olin's face. With a groan, his eyes opened.

'Wake up!'

'Huh?'

'Those things, they've gone. You're safe.'

Olin lifted a hand and tried to rub his head, but it scratched vainly at the air before dropping back to the floor. Miranda and Rosa helped him sit back up against the wall. Slowly he came to his senses, first looking around him, before fixing them one by one with a confused look.

'What are you doing here?'

Miranda shrugged. 'Things didn't go according to plan. Looks like I could say the same of you.'

Olin's face abruptly changed, his expression losing the confusion and hardening. 'They came sweeping through ... they were looking for you. They destroyed everything. I feared my taint wouldn't protect me, so I hid, using a ward to protect myself, but I pulled it too tight, putting a binding on myself too. If you hadn't come ... I'd have rotted away to nothing.'

'It's my fault,' Miranda said, lowering her gaze. 'I went to have a look, but they saw me.'

'You went where?'

'To have a look at the Shifting Castle.'

Olin sighed, leaning his head back against the wall. 'You stupid girl,' he muttered, sounding too tired even to be angry. 'I survived for years by not drawing attention to myself. His gaze isn't like the gaze of others. Once he's seen you ... you can't be unseen.'

'I'm sorry.'

'It's too late for that. Everything is gone. I have to move. I have to start again.'

'I need your help.'

Olin groaned again. 'Why would I ever want to help you?'

'This is Rosa,' Miranda said, turning to the girl. 'She was born here in Endinfinium. She lives in an underground community of people who call themselves Sleepers. They deny the existence of magic. They captured me, but Rosa helped me escape. We're trying to find her father.'

Olin frowned. 'What madness ... you're crazy, girl. Just leave me alone.'

'He's in the Shifting Castle. Rosa thinks he could be part of something dangerous, something the Dark Man is planning.'

Olin closed his eyes. 'And what on Endinfinium does that have to do with me?'

Miranda glanced at Rosa. 'We're both Channellers,' she said. 'But I'm still a novice, and Rosa is a child. It's too dangerous for us to go alone.'

'Go where?' Even as he asked the question, he seemed to understand the answer. 'Oh, please tell me you're not serious. You're not really going there, are you?'

Miranda forced a smile, shaking off the creeping sense of dread that hung on every word. 'We have to. We're going to get inside and free Rosa's father, and whoever else the Dark Man has taken captive. And we want your help.'

This time Olin didn't answer. He simply let out a long sigh, leaned his head back against the wall again, and closed his eyes.

32

BENJAMIN

'Take my hand!'

Benjamin, leaning half out of the coach, reached for Ray's stretching fingers as, looming over them, the tumbleweed groaned. Up ahead, the tumbleweed they had been following had finished its journey, dropping away into a white halo surrounding the floating castle.

Benjamin's fingers closed over Ray's, and he dragged the bigger boy free. Together, they scrambled down the heap of accumulated earth and rocks, reaching the cleared ground below them just as the tumbleweed began to move.

'Quick, we have to get out of range or it'll follow me!'

They scrambled up a steep ridge alongside the tumbleweed's route, clambered over onto an old road, and dashed away between two rows of abandoned houses. The tumbleweed initially began to turn, forcing itself up the curved earth wall of the carved channel it had been following like a spider attempting to escape from a dish, but as the distance between it and they grew, it slipped back down and started to move forward again. Once it was safely back on its original course, they stopped, breathing hard as it rolled away in the direction of the floating castle and its enormous surrounding halo of light.

'What is that thing?' Benjamin asked when he was finally able to speak without gasping for breath.

'Us Miscreants call it the Pit of Oblivion,' Ray said, sounding equally exhausted. 'No idea what it's actually there for. From what I've heard, it's been there longer than I've been alive, and by all accounts it's getting slowly bigger year by year.'

'And what's that thing above it?'

'That's where he lives.'

'Who?'

'Doctor Forrest. The man who built it all.'

Benjamin nodded. He had expected as much. From now, he had only one option, to face the man in the castle … to face himself. He frowned at the thought, unsure whether he should be excited, scared, or simply confused.

Far away, over the roofs of the nearest houses, something hung in the air. Benjamin squinted, recognising a helicopter. He had vague memories of one trying to get close as they made their dramatic way here, but now the tumbleweed had gone, there was no reason for it to hang back. He asked Ray.

'We must be in the quarantine zone,' Ray said. 'Can't see anyone round here, can you? Nothing's allowed inside. The edges of the pit tend to collapse without warning, so they have a big fence around it which they keep moving back.'

'If these houses are abandoned, why haven't they fallen into the pit?' Benjamin asked, walking up to the nearest house and putting his hands against the walls. Instead of touching cold stone, though, he felt slight warmth under his palms.

'Perhaps because by being so close, they're pretty much

already in the pit,' Ray said, looking around him and pointing at an empty crisp packet sitting by the curb. As they watched, it suddenly stood up and began walking on its own.

'It's reanimated,' Benjamin said to himself, too quietly for Ray to hear.

They watched it go, skipping and twisting as it ran, like something out of a kids' TV show.

'Let's follow it,' Ray said.

They trailed it to the end of the street, but at the next corner, they found themselves facing a direct line into the pit. The dancing crisp packet, its legs scurrying faster and faster, lost its balance, tripped, and continued its route in an increasingly fast, ungainly tumble.

'The pit's drawing it in,' Benjamin said, pushing Ray back behind the nearest house. He closed his eyes, trying to visualise everything around him in a different way. A confusion of colours surrounded everything, reminding him of the mess of streamers that had come out of party poppers at children's birthday parties.

But within it—

Like a vicious, snapping snake, a streamer of dark reanimate rushed out of the confusion, heading straight for his face.

He jerked back out of range, his eyes snapping open. 'Don't let it get hold of you—'

'Benjamin!'

He looked around, but Ray was gone. Spinning around in desperation, he spotted his new friend further up the street, tumbling over and over like the crisp packet had, bouncing across the ground as though something had a hold on his foot and was dragging him away. Benjamin started after him, but Ray disappeared around a corner, his voice cutting off.

Panic rising, Benjamin closed his eyes again, searching for the tendrils of darkness. Now that he knew they were there, they were everywhere, sifting and searching through the colours, but from him they kept their distance, tentatively sneaking forward before withdrawing out of range.

As though they were afraid.

He had to keep moving or they would eventually overcome their fear and attack him. Roughly following the pit's perimeter, he jogged through the streets, trying to locate where Ray had been taken. Here, the remaining buildings were hollowed shells, their walls warm but devoid of any fixtures or fittings. He had a sudden memory of the school, that deep in its bowels it was the rock that was the most stable, unable to reanimate further than gaining a gradual, comforting warmth. Every building he passed was stripped bare of any plastic, wood, or glass, leaving behind only bare concrete.

Without trying, he was gradually getting closer to the pit, which was now less than half a mile ahead of him, glowing with an orange incandescence, like a lava pit made of children's sweets. The building he had seen from afar was somewhere above it, occasional shapes and angles behind a screen of mist and smoke.

Up ahead came the sound of something else: an engine. Benjamin turned a corner and found himself facing a tall fence. Behind it was a long, squat building which reminded him of an airport terminal. On one side, to his left, were lines of orderly parked dog-catcher vans. Beyond them was another fence, a double-gate in its middle, and outside it, a large crowd.

The people appeared to be in a state of open battle. Police lines pushed between two milling groups of protesters, attempting to keep them separated, occasionally forcing them to part to allow another van to come through, at which point the shouting would intensify on both sides. Benjamin caught sight of the slogans on some waving placard boards, offering contrasting opinions. Some proclaimed Doctor Forrest the saviour of the world, the other the devil. In some opinions he was freeing the world of the unwanted, in others he was stealing its heart. Benjamin wondered how he ought to feel, bearing in mind that in some version of reality he was the person they were both praising and berating in equal measure.

'Help!'

Ray's voice came from the other side of the fence. Benjamin spotted the boy now held in the arms of two dog-catchers, the men struggling to hold him. Benjamin ducked back behind the nearest row of buildings, made his way further along, and then peered out again.

His jaw dropped at the sight in front of him.

'Oh, my....'

He now faced the back of the terminal-like building. Double doors opened out onto a flat area which then separated into two. Twin lines of dog-catchers—armed with the same electric prongs but with different uniforms— guarded the area on either side. Behind them, two rows of children walked trance-like in the direction of the great pit. One line, however, rose up over a strange translucent bridge, its detail impossible to clarify inside the orange glow which encased it. The children walked upwards until it flattened out, then disappeared into the glow as it led across to the shifting angles of the great castle looming over the chasm.

The other line dropped straight over the edge.

Benjamin squatted down, keeping out of sight. Then, closing his eyes, he felt outwards again for the cold tendrils of dark reanimate.

They were all around him, but from the two lines of children they rose in a great wave. The dark reanimate was coming from inside them, radiating outwards. From the line walking calmly over the edge into the pit, however, there was no resistance. Within the other, there was an invisible conflict going on, a battle between the warmth of light reanimate and the freezing dark. Unseen to the children, Benjamin recognised it as waves of heat and cold pulsing against his heart.

He nodded, understanding. Those with an ability to use reanimation magic were sent one way, those without, another.

The question he couldn't answer, however, was what his namesake wanted with all of the children.

There was only one way to find out.

He backtracked again, heading back around the fence. Here, so close to the pit, his magic felt strong, and he felt in control. He felt as though within this space, he could make it do anything he chose. Remembering the day he had first met his old friend Edgar Caspian, he felt outwards, feeling for his magic. Then, pushing and pulling with his mind, he had it condense below him to lift him up. At the same time, he made it condense in front of him, making the air so thick, nothing could be seen beyond it, rendering him effectively invisible to the crowd of protesters, as well as the dog-catchers and police trying to control them.

He let the magic lower him down on the other side of the fence, barely a stones' throw from where the two lines of protesters berated each other over the suffering police. Releasing it, he felt his feet touch down, but he maintained the ward around him, and the wall keeping him from sight.

Unseen, he walked calmly into the terminal building, and found himself in the middle of an even more chaotic scene than that outside.

Dog-catchers wrestled children back and forth, some in cuffs or bonds, others with their arms flailing as though seeking to break free. Every so often something unexpected would happen—a person would rise into the air, something would catch fire, something would move without warning—and the dog-catchers would converge on the child they deemed responsible, electric prongs sparking, while others would rush from cubicles in the wall, carrying fire extinguishers, nets, buckets or water in long, oversized syringes. Other than the children and the dog-catchers, the room was sparse with almost no furniture or fittings—clearly to minimalise the potential damage—with only two sets of doors entering at one end, and two leading out at the other.

The children were wrestled to one of the two sets of doors. Other dog-catchers would pull them open, and the child would be pushed through, the doors slammed quickly behind them.

At first it seemed the dog-catchers were merely trying to get the children from one side of the room to the other. Then, as Benjamin closed his eyes again and felt for other users of magic, a different scenario presented itself.

On the open floor, the children were being baited by teams of dog-catchers, encircled and chided into a response. Stunned, Benjamin watched the barbaric procedure, noting that those children who fought back with magic were dragged through one door, those who battled with only hands and feet through another. The dog-catchers, in superior numbers, seemed to be in control of things, but when a child appeared too powerful, another team would rush forward to provide back up, and one by one, each child brought in was assigned to a door, and a pathway.

The magic users went over the bridge, the others

straight into the pit as though they were nothing more than rubbish.

'Where's my sister, you pig?'

Ray's voice came from the other side of the room. Two dog-catchers had a hold of his arms and a third was trying to avoid his kicking feet long enough to prod him. Ray, bigger than Benjamin, was putting up a decent fight. Benjamin began threading through the crowd towards him.

He had nearly reached his friend when the doors opened and the latest arrivals came in. Two dog-catchers stood either side of a stretcher with a girl strapped to the top. Her eyes were wide open but she made no move to struggle or escape.

'Lulu—' Ray's shout was cut off as the dog-catcher's prong finally found its mark. Ray slumped into the arms of the other two, his head drooping. Benjamin paused, barely a few steps away, overcome by a sudden helplessness.

'No.'

Lulu's head lifted, her bonds falling away as though they were no more than tissue paper. Benjamin felt a sudden wave of magic emanating out of the girl, but there was no malice or anger in it. It spread out across the room like a puddle of melted butter, sweeping dog-catchers and children alike to the floor where they lay, trance-like.

In moments, only Benjamin remained standing. Lulu climbed off the stretcher and walked calmly towards him.

She was no more than seven or eight years old, barely tall enough to reach his shoulder, but her eyes held a calm maturity far beyond her years. Her eyes met his and she gave him a sad smile.

'Hello,' she said, and her voice was as much in his head as outside of it. 'I've been wanting to meet you for so long.'

Benjamin said nothing. He opened his mouth but could think of no appropriate response.

'Can you save us?' she asked. 'Can you save us all?'

'I … don't know,' he whispered. 'I'm not even quite sure … who I am.'

Lulu smiled again. 'One day you'll find out,' she said. A hand reached up to touch his cheek. She smiled, and a wash of heat rushed through him. For a moment the pain was so intense he couldn't even breathe. Then, as though a veil had been lifted, the world began again. Children, freed from the hold of the dog-catchers leapt up and made their bids for freedom, while the dog-catchers themselves howled with anger and swung their prongs indiscriminately. Lulu had fallen limp again; two nearby dog-catchers had taken hold of her arms and were dragging her towards one of the doors. Ray was crying out in pain, and someone was shouting at Benjamin.

'That one there! Get him!'

He turned as a dog-catcher closed on him. He brought up his hands, thinking to send the man bouncing away, but where moments before he had felt in total control of his magic, now it felt locked deep inside again, as though Lulu's touch had stolen it away.

He could do nothing but flail his arms as the dog-catcher's prong jabbed into his stomach.

The pain was intense, but worse was the sudden numbness that spread out through his limbs. His legs and arms felt useless, and he slumped into the grasp of a dog-catcher coming up behind him. He couldn't even groan as the first one said, 'Pit Line. This one's empty.'

They dragged him towards the second door. Benjamin was nothing more than a passenger, barely with the strength to move his eyes. Feeling was beginning to return to his extremities in a series of tingles, but he could do nothing other than twitch his fingers and toes, and the magic that had felt so strong had vanished.

One dog-catcher held him as another two opened the doors. The first pushed him upright, into a glowing light cascading down from above. Immediately he felt caught in some sort of hold, his body held upright despite the lack of any feeling in his arms or legs. Ahead of him, a line of other children moved serenely forward.

'Man, I hate the way they do that,' came a voice from behind him. 'Creeps me out every time.'

'Just shut up and do your job,' said another. 'At least you've got one.'

'Where do you think they go?'

'Don't know, don't care. At least Forrest wants them. Perhaps he starts fires with them, who knows?'

'Mate told me there ain't no one in there. That's it's all just some government cover up. Got these kids training up for some war or other, but it's all a big secret.'

'Whatever you want to think.'

'Well, you know what—'

The voice was cut off by a door closing. Despite being at the end of a line of children, Benjamin felt suddenly alone. Feeling had returned enough to allow him to turn his head, and he glanced across at the other line, walking serenely in their own orange glow, heading for the bridge rising up out of the mist to extend over the pit. Benjamin had a sudden moment of panic: *I'm in the wrong line.* He glanced ahead, and saw a boy at the front step calmly over the edge of the pit and drop out of sight. Far off around the pit's curve, a massive tumbleweed fell in, sending a plume of orange sparks high into the air.

Not one of the children in either line reacted. They continued to walk slowly, calmly forward in their two ordered lines, heading without any kind of concern towards one of two destinies.

There were nine children in front of Benjamin. Unable to move, he could do nothing but wait until it was his turn to drop over the edge of the pit into oblivion.

33

WILHELM

THE OLD WOMAN LEANED CLOSER TO THE WINDOW. 'What did you say happened to your grandfather?'

Dorothy started to repeat her previous confession about Sebastien drinking too much wine at a funeral, but Wilhelm pushed in front of her.

'He had a turn,' he said. 'We're taking him home. Which way is London?'

The old woman wrinkled her brow then glared at Dorothy sitting in the driver's seat. After some deliberation and considerable effort, they had stopped and transferred the unconscious Sebastien into the back seat, where he now sat propped up between Kevin and Don.

'Are you sure you're old enough to be driving?' the old woman said. 'You don't look a snip over ten years old, girl.'

'I'm twelve!' Dorothy shouted, and then stamped on the accelerator in frustration. The car lurched forward, leaving the old woman shaking a fist in the rear mirrors.

'Best drive on for a bit, then try someone else,' Wilhelm said.

'Are we there yet?' Kevin said, sniggering. Dorothy

twisted in the seat to glower at him, the car swerving out across the road, only avoiding an oncoming van because Wilhelm yanked the wheel back straight.

'Can you please concentrate?' he said. 'If we wreck Sebastien's car, we'll never get to London.'

'I just saw a sign!' Don shouted.

'Where?'

'Back that way.'

'What did it say?'

'Can't remember.'

Wilhelm slapped his forehead. Things were going from bad to worse. They were low on petrol, and while they had so far managed to avoid any more dog-catchers, it had been half an hour since they had last seen a sign pointing to London.

'I'm hungry,' Kevin said.

'Do something useful and eat Don!' Dorothy shouted, slamming on the brakes to avoid rear-ending the car in front, then hacking sideways and only narrowly avoiding the hedgerow on the passenger side.

'There's another sign!' Don shouted.

'Where?'

'There. Look. London!'

'How far?'

'Thirty-six miles.'

Wilhelm sighed. 'That's better than the fifty-four the last one said. We're getting there.'

'That was an hour ago,' Dorothy snapped. 'It doesn't take an hour to go fifteen miles.'

'Eighteen,' Kevin said.

'Shut up!'

Wilhelm glanced back at Sebastien. The old man's eyes had rolled a few times, and he groaned from time to time, but he still hadn't woken up. Wilhelm's fear for him was only lessened by his fear for Benjamin. Wherever his friend was now, he was close to out of reach.

'Problem!' Dorothy shouted, so loud Wilhelm bumped his head on the window out of surprise.

'Where?'

'Right ahead. I suppose we'll have to go round.'

Standstill traffic blocked the way forward. 'What is it?' Wilhelm asked. 'Why are they all stopped like that?'

'Must be rush hour,' Don said. 'Happens every day.'

Kevin banged the back of Wilhelm's seat. 'Nope. It's a tumbleweed coming through. Look at that.'

Over the line of the nearest hedgerow Wilhelm saw the top of something massive moving in the distance. It wasn't quite as large as the one Sebastien had taken them to see, but it was still an impressive sight. And as it rolled, something rectangular rolled up its back towards the peak.

'Wow, it's got an entire house on its back,' Kevin said.

He was right. The old house reached the peak, appeared to pause for a few seconds as though admiring the view, and then came crashing down.

'That's the end of that,' Don said.

'The traffic's waiting for it to pass,' Dorothy said. 'We could be stuck here for hours.'

Wilhelm punched the dashboard. 'No!' he shouted. 'There must be something we can do. Don't you lot have any magic we can use?' he turned to Dorothy. 'You made those men hang up in the air. Can't you do that with this car?'

Dorothy shrugged. 'I can't just tell it what to do,' she said. 'I have no idea what's going to happen.'

'Push and pull,' Wilhelm said, remembering something Miranda had told him. 'All you have to do is push and pull.'

'What's he talking about?' Don asked Dorothy, as though Wilhelm had ceased to exist.

'I have no idea.'

'Just try it,' Wilhelm said. 'Hold on to me. I'm a Weaver. I'll make your magic stronger.'

'What's a Weaver?' Don asked.

'It's hard to explain,' Wilhelm said. 'But put your hand on Dorothy's shoulder, just in case you're one, too.'

Dorothy looked distraught at the idea of being touched by Don, who rested a tentative finger on the shoulder of her sweater. Whether it was close enough, Wilhelm had no idea. Kevin reached out and touched Wilhelm's arm, so they were all technically connected. Wilhelm swallowed down his terror and nodded.

'Right. Do something,' he said.

Dorothy frowned. Her knuckles went white on the steering wheel, and the car's engine screamed as she hit the accelerator.

'It's not in gear,' Don said.

'It doesn't need to be if it's going to fly, does it?' Dorothy snapped.

'Well, it might help—'

The car's front lurched upward, throwing them all back. 'Don't let go!' Wilhelm screamed as his head bumped back against the headrest.

With a squeal of tyres dragging on the road, the car rose up into the air. For a moment Wilhelm thought they might actually be flying, but then it dropped, bumping off the roof of the car in front. Someone started shouting at them, but they were moving forward, bumping over the tops of the other cars in the line, scratching off the paint, sending showers of metallic sparks up into the air.

'Can't you steer it?' Don gasped, sounding as though he were about to throw up.

'I can't do everything, can I?' Dorothy shouted. 'He said push and pull. I'm pushing and pulling!'

They bumped over the top of a land rover and found themselves behind a lorry. The car rose up, but a wing mirror struck a corner of metal and snapped off. Then they were bumping over the lorry's roof, down over the cab, and onto a saloon car in front, dipping with a sudden lurch like a rollercoaster about to enter a free fall.

To their left, the tumbleweed was getting closer. It was rumbling along its channel, with cars lined up at a policed gate to let it pass. Wilhelm was watching it coming closer when the car suddenly bumped high up into the air, made a gradual downward arc, and came to rest in a heap of soft mud in the tumbleweed's pathway.

'Well, I suppose at least we jumped the queue,' Don said.

'We're going to die!' Kevin wailed. 'It's coming. Look!'

The tumbleweed was bearing down on them. The channel carved by previous tumbleweeds dropped ten feet below the level of the surrounding countryside, like a dry river channel. At the end of each section of severed road was a metal contraption that looked like a fold-out temporary bridge. A handful of police and engineers stood on either side, patiently waiting for the tumbleweed to pass. As Wilhelm glanced over his shoulder, he saw the men looking down at them with confused expressions on their faces.

No one came to help. The tumbleweed continued to approach, a massive, rolling ball of rubbish.

'Get it moving!' Kevin shouted, but with a long sigh, Dorothy slumped in her seat.

'I'm tired,' she said, struggling to keep her eyes open.

Aware the magic had used the last of Dorothy's energy, Wilhelm turned to the others. 'Can't one of you do something?' he said. 'One of you must have some magic.'

Don shrugged. Kevin looked uncertain.

'I've never tried to control it before,' the freckled boy said.

Wilhelm twisted in the seat. He put a hand on Kevin's arm and pointed with his other hand. 'We have to go that way,' he said, trying not to let his voice go too high-pitched through fear. 'We have to go that way, and we have to go that way right now!'

'That way,' Kevin said, frowning. 'That way.'

'Now...!'

Kevin closed his eyes. He gritted his teeth and moaned under his breath. Beside Wilhelm in the front, Dorothy had fallen asleep.

'Nothing's happening,' Kevin said.

'What about the old man?' Don asked. 'Hold his hand. Perhaps that'll make a difference. Perhaps he's a Binder.'

'A Weaver,' Wilhelm said.

'I don't want to hold his hand,' Kevin said.

Wilhelm frowned. Sebastien Aren, known in Endinfinium as Grand Lord Bastien. He had ended up there somehow, but only part of him. The rest of him had stayed somewhere else—

'Got it,' he said, clicking his fingers.

'Got what?' Don asked.

'The only adults in Endinfinium arrived as kids and grew up there,' he said, patting Don on the shoulder. 'Sebastien had to have had some kind of power which set him apart.'

'What on earth are you talking about?' Kevin said.

'It doesn't matter. Just take his hand. Pull!'

Kevin frowned. 'It's heavy.'

'Not his hand. Pull his *mind*!'

'How—'

The car lurched. Kevin looked terrified. Wheels spun, lights flashed and the engine roared like an animal trying to escape a cage. As the sun vanished behind the looming tumbleweed, they shot forward like a lead ball from a cannon's barrel, plowed into a bank of mud, and came to a grinding stop.

'That's it!' Wilhelm shouted. 'Do it again, but point us a bit more upwards.'

The car lurched again, throwing off the mud bank and bouncing forward.

'Slow down!' Don shouted as they glanced off a rock and spun around, but Wilhelm knew Kevin had no more control than Dorothy had had. The car raced forward, its wheels spinning in all directions, but carried by an unnatural momentum that had nothing to do with physics or Kevin's sense of direction. The car, in a way that Wilhelm didn't think he'd ever truly understand, had been brought to life.

In moments they had left the tumbleweed and the stunned police officers behind. Rushing along the carved channel, the world was a blur around them as the car swung and rolled, dipping and diving, with each moment threatening to slam them face first into something that would reduce them to component parts. Wilhelm could only hang on to the seat, one hand holding tight to Kevin, whose face was ghostly white, while Dorothy lolled in her seatbelt and Don struggled to hold Sebastien in place.

And then, as quickly as it had begun, it was over. The car's speed dropped, and they bumped and skidded across a wide car park, coming to an abrupt halt inches from another car.

Wilhelm gasped. Behind him, Kevin had slumped back against the seat, groaning as he wiped sweat off his face.

Don was staring pale-faced out of the front, while Dorothy, slowly waking up, looked confused.

'Oh, you found a parking space,' came a voice from behind him, and Wilhelm looked back to see Sebastien blinking as though he had just woken up.

'Yes,' he croaked. 'We're here, I think.'

'Where are we?'

'I'm not sure.'

Wilhelm made to open the door, but it fell off, bumping on the ground. A cool breeze tickled his face, and he realised he was sweating.

'I think perhaps you three should stay here,' Sebastien said, sitting up. He wiped his brow, then frowned as though unsure what was going on. He glanced around him at the four kids then grimaced at the cracks in the windows, the missing wing mirrors, the bonnet that was buckled, and the roof which had been partly torn off.

'You made quite a mess of my car,' he said.

Don got out, then reached back to help Sebastien. The old man looked shaky on his feet. He leaned against the car, picking away a piece of loose paint with his fingers.

'I suppose she wasn't likely to pass the next MOT anyway,' he said.

Wilhelm got out and looked around. The car park was at the back of a long, flat building. Apart from Sebastien's wrecked classic car, all the other vehicles were dog-catcher vans. He turned to the others, but Sebastien gave a shrill laugh.

'I think we're in the staff parking area,' he said. 'I'm sure that will take some explaining, but we won't worry about it until someone asks. Come on, this way, young Wilhelm. You three stay with my car. If anyone asks, tell them your grandfather has gone to buy ice cream.'

Dorothy, Don, and Kevin all nodded in turn, their expressions still appearing stunned by everything that had happened. Kevin wiped sweat off his brow then looked unwilling to wipe his hand on his own clothes, so he surreptitiously patted his hand dry on Don's shoulder. The tall boy paid no attention, just continued staring straight ahead.

'That's the place,' Dorothy said suddenly, her voice hollow. 'That's where we have to go. That's where he is.'

Don and Kevin straightened. Don smiled. Kevin, after a moment of confusion, nodded, his face adopting a calm serenity.

'What's going on?' Wilhelm asked, turning to Sebastien.

The old man frowned. 'Can't you feel it? Even I can, and I've only ever been a boy in my mind. This is the place where the disassociated go, the unwanted. They're tired, they can't fight it anymore.'

Dorothy, Don, and Kevin began walking across the car park towards the low building, ignoring Wilhelm's shouts to stop. He ran a few steps after them and tried to pull Kevin back, but the fat boy just shrugged off his arm without looking back.

'Sebastien, what's going on? And why isn't it doing anything to me?'

The old man shrugged. 'Perhaps, because if the tales you tell me are true, you've already come this way once before.'

'Come on, we have to stop them.'

'I think it's too late for that,' Sebastien said, but Wilhelm shook his head. He started running after the three Miscreants as they walked calmly towards the building on the other side of the car park. They passed the last line of parked vans and started across an open space. Wilhelm reached it and started after, then stopped. He looked up to the right, and felt his knees buckle.

Beyond a fence bordering the car park was something he could barely comprehend. A pit of glowing orange stretched out before him. Hanging over it was what appeared to be a constantly evolving castle, towers and balustrades and battlements relentlessly on the move, rising and falling, folding and unfolding. As he watched, a tumbleweed rolled up to the edge of the pit and dropped over, sending up a cloud of orange which briefly obscured the immense building before falling to earth like a glittering fireworks shower.

'The Shifting Castle,' Sebastien said, coming up behind Wilhelm and putting a hand on his shoulder. 'That's where your friend's namesake, Doctor Ben Forrest, can be found. By all accounts, he tired of explaining himself and created an abode in the one place no one could get to him.'

Wilhelm pushed away from him and ran up to the fence. He peered through the links at the world inside. It looked like something out of a giant science experiment, an explosion moving in slow motion. The ground around the pit was scoured clean, a field of gravel and sand. Every few seconds something like a piece of plastic or wood would billow over his head, revolving over and over, and then fall into the pit.

'Help!'

The cry cut off almost as soon as it sounded. Wilhelm turned to the left, looking at the space beyond the flat building where the others had gone. At first he wasn't sure what he was looking at: shapes appeared through the mists, figures moving slowly towards the pit. At one point the line appeared to separate, and Wilhelm realised he was looking at two lines, not one. The line behind the first was climbing up a stairway onto a bridge which led across to the shifting castle. The line in front was walking straight to the pit's edge.

Children.

All of them calm, serene, accepting of their fate.

Except one.

A boy in the nearest line, forced into walking in unison with the others, but still fighting to get out.

A boy Wilhelm recognised.

'Benjamin…!'

34

SNOUT

'I must say, you've done a good job,' Derek said, lifting a shoe and turning it over. 'However, you did miss a bit down here in the corner. I used the toilet up in the math block yesterday and I'm afraid I stepped in something that had crusted into the floor. Could you pick it off for me? If you can't do it with a needle, use your fingernails.'

Inside, Snout was as angry as perhaps he'd ever been. On the outside, he remembered his promise to Ms. Ito.

'Sure,' he said. 'Maybe I'll have to use my teeth if it's really ground in.'

'You're a mate,' Derek said, grinning. 'I'll ask Gubbledon to hold back some cold breakfast for you.'

Before Snout could reply, Derek bounded out of the room and down the stairs to breakfast. Snout stared at Derek's shoe, wishing he could just pitch it out the window into the sea far below.

It was for the good of the entire school, he reminded himself. He was to blame for Fat Adam's disappearance, even if the discovery had alerted the teachers to a new threat. For all he knew, Fat Adam could be dead, and it would be his fault. Even if all his friend was doing was wallowing in a tank of stinking gunk, it was still something for which Snout had to make amends.

So he retrieved Derek's shoe and began to pick away at the brown chunk caught in the tread.

And when he was finished, he made Derek's bed, and then folded all of his roommate's clothes.

By the time he went down for breakfast, he felt as soulless as the cleaners. A single cold bowl of mashed vegetables sat on a table. The spoon, however, had fallen onto the floor, somehow lodging itself into a crack in the flooring. Snout sighed as he bent down to pick it up, then baulked as he stood back upright.

Gubbledon was leaning in the doorway to the small dormitory kitchen, one skeletal front leg lifted, a hoof pressed against the frame. He wore the usual ridiculous outfit—this time a silver satin shirt and lemon yellow trousers enlarged and adapted to fit his horsey frame, but beyond the gaudiness of his attire he looked like a dead horse dying over again.

'No school today, Simon?' he muttered, staring at the floor as though no answer would matter.

'This morning is self-study,' Snout said. 'We had tests last week and they're still in for marking. I was supposed to meet Tommy to do some maths revision but I, um, decided to tidy Derek's half of the room instead.'

Gubbledon nodded. 'Derek's told me how kind you've been recently. He very much appreciates it. He likes that, despite everything, you're keen to put your differences behind you and become friends.'

Snout forced himself to shrug. 'We just had some teething problems, I suppose. It's like that when you get a new roommate.'

'That's nice.'

Gubbledon moved to sit down, but slumped, his awkward frame slipping forwards. One hoof knocked Snout's bowl out of his hands and sent a shower of gunk spraying across the neighbouring table.

'Oh, bother.'

Snout stood up. 'Don't worry, I'll clean it up. Are you all right?'

Gubbledon slumped down onto a chair and leaned forwards over the table. 'Just a little under the weather, I think,' he said, resting his big head on his front legs.

'I, um, bumped into a few of your reanimate friends a couple of days ago,' Snout said. 'They didn't look too well, either. Perhaps something's going around?'

'I'm sure that's what it is,' Gubbledon said. 'Just a bug. I never thought us reanimates could catch bugs like you humans, but I suppose you learn something new every day.'

Snout nodded his agreement, but was already lining up who he could tell about the affliction passing around the reanimates. While they might not be natural in the way he thought of as natural, their sickness was decidedly unnatural. A motorbike come back to life shouldn't be able to get flu or something worse.

After cleaning up the mess as best he could, then brewing some chamomile tea for Gubbledon to calm the old horse's nerves a little bit, he headed across into the school. He didn't have any classes before lunch, but didn't think he could concentrate on studying anything. He needed information, however. Unsure of where else he might find it, he headed down into the bowels of the school to visit the library.

Old Cleat, the crusty, ancient librarian, looked up from

his desk, scowling and raising an eyebrow at the sight of Snout pushing in through the door.

'Well, well, what do we have here? Someone come to study? That would be a first.'

Snout glanced around and saw all the study tables inside the library were empty. He gulped and stepped inside. It wasn't so much that pupils didn't like to study, it was that most of them were afraid of Old Cleat. On organised class trips they would come, but one by one … they needed a special reason to brave the spiky librarian's domain.

'Um, I was wondering if you had any books on the school's history?'

Cleat, wild-haired, rheumy-eyed, stubble-faced, and dressed in attire that looked like pieces of a hundred sacks cut up and sewn back together, waved a hand at the towering stacks of books.

'In there somewhere.'

'Isn't there some kind of cataloguing system?'

'This ain't the New York Book Repository, son,' Cleat snapped. 'Can you be a little bit more specific?'

Snout came inside. Before closing the door he glanced back down the corridor to make sure he was alone.

'I'm trying to find out a bit more about the reanimates,' he said.

Cleat grinned. Jagged teeth looked like the rocks at the end of the world. 'Ah, now you're getting there. Reanimates? Sure, people have done studies. Not sure where. Local history section, most likely.'

'Whereabouts would I find it?'

Cleat spread grubby hands and grinned again. 'You're looking at it. Fire away. I'll tell you what I can, if I can remember. That's not much, mind you. Things tend to … drift away over time.'

'I want to know if the reanimates have ever gotten sick before. I found myself in Underfloor the other day, and it looked like a hospital. And Gubbledon, our housemaster, is also sick.'

Cleat's smile dropped and he gave a sage nod. 'Sick, you say? Those things can't get sick, not as we know it. Only one way it's possible. There's a taint got in.'

'A taint?'

'Dark reanimate. You know all about that, don't you?'

'Well, what we've been taught.'

Cleat rolled his eyes. 'Which probably isn't very much. Sit down.'

Snout turned to look at the chairs, but one came rushing towards him, stopping at his back. He slumped down and felt warmth under his bum.

Cleat lifted his hands and cracked his knuckles back, then grinned. 'Been a while since I've done anything like that for fun,' he said. 'Feels good. Might do some practice.'

'You can use the magic?'

'I'm a Channeller,' he said. 'At least, by the labels of those up above. I suppose you've realised by now that no one is quite the same, that those of us who can use it have quite different skills.'

Snout thought about his own ability to call ghouls up from the earth. According to Ms. Ito, no one else had ever shown the ability to do it. He didn't like the thought of being unique, but at the same time, it was rather cool.

'It's all still a little new to me,' Snout said.

Cleat sat back down at his desk and leaned forwards. 'You keep telling yourself that, son. It'll keep you safe. Don't ever play with what you can do. It's like fire. Keep it in a glass cup and its all good, but a paper cup … that's a different matter.'

Snout nodded. 'I see.'

'Reanimation magic is split into two,' Cleat said. 'Dark and light. What most of us here in the school use is light. We can manipulate, and we can create. It's like playing with clay. Fun, if you're careful.'

'Right.'

'But there's the other side, too. The dark. Isn't that the case for everything? Night and day, light and dark, up and down.' Cleat's smile dropped. 'Dark reanimate is sometimes called deanimation magic. It's used to destroy, to taint, to take things away. I use my light reanimate to give life to an inanimate object, and someone else uses dark to take it away. Simple. When life is so easy, it makes it less special, ain't that right?'

'I suppose,' Snout said, feeling that agreement was the best thing to do, even though Cleat was slowly losing him.

'Only that's not the only way it is, is it? Wouldn't that be so simple?' Cleat sighed. 'It's the grey bit in the middle that's the troublesome side of things. The bit where you're never quite sure what's going to happen. That's when things go boom.'

'Boom?'

'Boom,' Cleat said, the lights above suddenly darkening, making his face appear skeletal, spectral. Snout jerked back, tingles of fear running up his arms.

'When someone starts playing with what they don't understand,' Cleat continued, 'that's when danger arises. When a kid plays with fire, people get burned. Unfortunately, there are some kids in this school who are very good indeed at playing with fire. And, of course, far worse.'

'Someone's playing with something they shouldn't be? Is that what you're saying?'

'This school has always been a safe haven,' Cleat said. 'That's the reason for its existence. Its founders created it to keep out the Dark Man and his ghouls and protect the children waking up here in Endinfinium with no clue where they were, what was going on. Many years before you or me was ever born, they pushed back the dark, set up wards to protect the school and the regions around it, and pushed the Dark Man and his influence back to the edges of the world. Unfortunately, time passes, even here. People forget. People lose the knowledge they learned that protected them. This school, as it stands, is like a cracked pane of glass. At any moment it could shatter, and dark reanimate could take over everything.'

'And what would happen then?'

Cleat shrugged. 'No idea. Judging by the history of all worlds, a few would benefit to the detriment and enslavement of everyone else.'

Snout nodded, slowly making sense of Cleat's words. 'Someone is trying to draw dark reanimate into the school,' he said. 'That's what that thing my friends and I found was doing. I'm not sure how it worked, but it was like a conductor. We might have disrupted it for a bit, but it's still there.'

'Like a spot on the school's backside that needs to get popped,' Cleat said, lifting two fingers and squeezing them together. 'And if it isn't, it'll infect everything around it.'

'So what can I do about it?'

Cleat grinned. 'Squeeze it. As soon as you can.'

∼

Derek was sitting in the languages study room with Tony Burns. Snout peered through the glass then cautiously slipped inside. He had heard on the gossip grapevine that Tony Burns was back out in front on the cleans league after throwing one of Professor Loane's shoes over the cliff.

As long as Snout stayed out of trouble, he had a good chance of avoiding a beating, a flushing, or worse.

'*Bonjour*,' Tony said, waving his hands about. 'Come on, repeat it.'

'Bon … Bon … Bon….' Derek threw down his pen. 'I hate languages.'

'Look, it's easy. Try this one: *J'ai un petit hund.*'

'What the hell does that mean?'

'I have a small dog in Frog.'

'Is it in the test?'

'How would I know?'

Snout slipped in through the door. 'Actually, "*hund*" is German,' he said, unable to help himself. 'The French word is "*chien*."'

Derek glared at him. 'Do you want your butt whipped? What are you doing here?'

'Yeah,' Tony said, grinning. 'Can't you see we're in the middle of a mentoring session? Derek only got nine out of a hundred on his French test so Mistress Castillo asked me to step in. He has to get more than twenty-five or he gets put back in next year's first year class with all the runts.' Tony started laughing, slapping his knees at the same time. 'He'll be about double their size and the only one without a squeaky voice.'

'Shut your mouth,' Derek said. Tony took no notice, but Snout felt a tremble in the floor which suggested Derek was about to use his magic. He took a step back in case things got worse, but the trembling came to a gradual stop. It was a school rule that no magic should be used against another pupil. The penalty was immediate expulsion. Even Derek wasn't about to risk being kicked out.

A bell rang, startling all three of them. Tony jumped up out of his seat and scooped up his books.

'Session's over,' he said. 'I'll leave you two girls to talk about handbags.'

He bounded out of the room, slamming the door behind him. Derek gathered his textbooks and turned to glare at Snout.

'If you tell anyone about this, you're worse than just dead. I'll make every day of your life hell.'

'I won't,' Snout said.

'What do you want, anyway?'

'I came to tell you that I went to Captain Roche and volunteered to do the two hundred cleans he gave you for being late to gym class last week. I told him you needed the time to prepare for the next tests.'

Derek narrowed his eyes. 'Why?'

Snout smiled. 'Because I'm trying to be a mate.'

'I don't want to be your mate. I'd rather live forever and never speak to another person again than be your mate. I'd rather scrape the gunk off my shoe, name it Billy, and be mates with it forever than be your mate.'

It was the reaction Snout had expected. He lifted an eyebrow, trying to look confident. 'Well, it couldn't be because I'm only a hundred cleans behind Tony, and if I win the book the fifth years are running, he'll swap rooms with me.'

Derek looked surprised. 'Meaning you'll no longer have to share with me? Oh, how I'd miss you so much.' His eyes narrowed. 'Not.'

'Well, whatever. But you don't have to go to the locker room tonight.'

'And you expect me to say thanks? You know you'll never beat Tony. He'll have another thousand by the end of the day, I guarantee it.'

'You know what would make sure I won, don't you?'

'What?'

Snout was literally shaking as he said, 'If I did that … thing. That thing that only I can do. If Ms. Ito found out, I'd be stuck in the locker room forever.' He took a step forward. 'But, you know, I'd have to do it a lot. Like more than before. And I wondered—'

'What?'

'If you and Godfrey could help me.'

'What? Why would we help you?'

'Because I know what you're doing in there, and I know you want me to help.'

Derek took a step forward. 'All this to get a better room?'

Snout forced himself to put on a tough face, even though inside he was trembling like a little girl facing an angry dog.

'No, not just that. I'm tired of everyone thinking I'm such a … such a … goody-goody.'

'Is that so?'

'Yeah. You and Godfrey think you're so bad and tough, but you're not. I'm … way tougher than either of you.'

Derek, his eyes wide, nodded slowly. Then, so suddenly it made Snout jump, he started laughing.

'You? Don't make me laugh, you grotty worm. You're nothing. You're less than nothing. You're so nothing that you're a puddle of turd under my foot.'

Derek started forward and for a moment Snout thought he'd instigated a fight. He didn't remember much of his life before Endinfinium, but he was pretty sure he'd never been in a fight. At the last moment, though, Derek slapped him across the stomach with his French notebook then dropped it on the floor at Snout's feet.

'I'll tell you what, though, pig-face. If you don't do my French homework right now, I'll go straight to Ms. Ito and tell her everything you just told me. I'll tell her you accused me and Godfrey of doing something bad in the old science block, and that you want to damage the school. Then I'll go to Tony and his mates and tell them that you're trying to fix the cleans book. After that, you'll be pleased to get expelled before the fifth years get you. Do you hear me? And not just my French homework. All my homework, every day, until the end of time.'

He made to headbutt Snout, then stopped at the last moment and laughed into Snout's face, the laughs quickly turning into pig-like grunts. As Snout watched, Derek began to run in a circle around him, grunting and squealing like a pig. With a final laugh, Derek pushed through the door and slammed it behind him.

Snout looked at the closed door, then down at the notebook lying by his feet. Unsure of whether or not he had achieved what he had set out to do, he bent down and picked it up. Then, with a long sigh, he sat down and got to work.

35

MIRANDA

'I must be out of my mind,' Olin said, shaking his head.

'Come on, you owe me.'

Olin pushed aside the boot he was slowly re-threading a lace into and turned to glare at Miranda. 'Excuse me? I owe you? I did everything I could to help you, and what did it get me? My house and gardens destroyed, and almost killed.'

Miranda pouted. 'Well, I did just save you.'

'You saved me from my own stupidity. Why couldn't you have saved my vegetables from the trash hounds or my house from the tar bears?'

'Well, I—'

Olin sighed. 'Look, I'll help you. Of course I will. Not like I have anything left to stay here for, is it?'

Miranda couldn't keep the grin off her face. She grabbed Rosa's hand and jumped up and down in delight. Only at the look of surprise from the younger girl did she recover her composure.

'Thanks,' she said, trying to look solemn. 'It's for the good of all mankind.'

'Well, let's hope so. Now, do you have any sort of plan as to how you're going to get into the Shifting Castle without being eaten alive by tar bars, turned into a ghoul, or utterly and comprehensively destroyed in some other way I haven't thought of yet?'

'I thought we could wait until it got dark—'

Olin flapped his hands. 'There are two suns. It never gets dark. And even if it did, do you really think the Dark Man uses his eyes like the rest of us? He sees in other ways. You haven't got a chance of getting in there unless he wants you in, and if he wants you in, then you haven't got a chance of getting out.'

'Then what do you suggest?'

Olin sighed. 'There's only one way where he won't be watching, but it's the hardest way of all.'

'And what way's that?'

It was Rosa who answered, the little girl standing up from her chair and pointing. 'Underground,' she said.

~

'Mr. Mead? Are you there?'

'Who is it?'

'It's your old friend, Olin Brin. And I've brought along a couple of other friends with me.'

The old recycling plant's window eyes opened. The upper part of the frames curved into a frown. 'Who do we have here? Miranda Butterworth?'

Miranda stepped forward. 'Hello again, Mr. Mead. Do you remember me? I gave you that fetching makeover.'

The blue walls below Rilston Mead's window eyes appeared to darken as though the reanimate was blushing.

'Oh yes, I remember you,' he said. 'Such a fine young lady. I trust you made it back to Endinfinium High School all right?'

Miranda winced. 'Well, not exactly. Since you created such a wonderful companion for me, I decided to have a few adventures.' She glanced back over her shoulder at Enchantress, who was sitting with her wings neatly folded up a short distance behind them. The elegant swan lifted her head and nodded to Rilston.

'Lovely to see you again, dear,' she said.

Rilston's eyes turned to Rosa. 'And who's this?'

'My young companion, Rosa,' said Miranda. Rosa stepped forward and gave a little curtsy.

'Pleased to make your acquaintance.'

'And yours.' Rilston looked back at Olin. 'So, while I appreciate the social visit—a rarity, I might add, despite us residing so close—I'd like to know what you want from me this time. There's certain to be something, isn't there? Not like you to traipse so far north'—Rilston rolled his eyes—'just to pay your respects, is it, Olin?'

'I'm afraid we ran into a little trouble.'

'Oh? So you want me to build you something with which to flee with the tail between your legs? Perhaps a rocket ship? Give me a moment—'

'No, wait.' Olin lifted a hand. 'We felt it necessary to repent for our failings. We decided to do something more dramatic, and pay the Dark Man a visit.'

For a few seconds Rilston didn't move, and Miranda could believe he had suddenly lost his magic and become nothing more than a face painted on the wall of an old shed. Then his eyes slowly widened until the darkest shades of blue at the centre were ringed by a pure white.

'Have you lost your tiny human mind?'

Olin gave Miranda a frustrated glance. 'Well, not all of

it. You see, Rosa here has a special reason to go into the Shifting Castle. She believes her father is trapped inside.'

'Go on.'

'And it appears the Dark Man has captured him, and perhaps some others, and might be using them to do something bad.'

'A whole lot of speculation in there,' Rilston said. 'Are you sure you really know what you're talking about?' His eyes swung back to Miranda and Rosa. 'You two seem like nice children. You should spend more time hanging around with reanimates than these old fools who've been wandering around too long. You'll get a lot more sense out of us. We tend to say it as we see it.'

Miranda smiled. 'And tell the best jokes.'

Rilston beamed. 'What do you get when you cross a recycling plant with hip-hop music?'

'No idea,' Miranda said.

'Bubble wrap.' At their confused expressions, he added, 'It's in the spelling.'

Rosa gave a sudden laugh. 'That's the best joke I've ever heard!' she said, clapping her hands together, then giving Miranda a sideways frown to suggest she had no idea what Rilston was talking about.

'Why, thank you, young lady,' Rilston said.

'Mr. Mead,' Olin continued, 'I'm afraid that, foolhardy or not, we have to get into that castle. And there's only one way that might work.' He pointed at the ground.

'On foot? So what do you want me for? I'm sure you can find some decent hiking boots buried near the river. Just check to make sure they've not reanimated yet.'

'Um, no—'

Rilston's eyes rolled. 'I'm teasing you, fool. You want me to build you something that can burrow right underneath the Shifting Castle. Something that can burrow through solid rock?'

'Um, yes.'

'How many weeks do you have at your disposal?'

'Well—'

'Rock is rock. It doesn't react well to magic, and digging through it is as tough as you might think. However, there's an alternative.'

'What?'

'If you can get down there, the ground below where we stand is similar to Swiss Cheese. It's full of holes. And if you know the way, I'm pretty sure you could find your way to the Shifting Castle and get up into its basements.'

'But we don't know the way.'

Rilston's eyes lifted up and down in an expression that suggested a nod. 'It's lucky that you're not my only friend, isn't it?'

~

When Olin returned, Miranda and Rosa were sitting on the ground, playing a scratched game of connect four in a patch of dirt while Enchantress leaned over Miranda's shoulder, occasionally offering advice. Rosa had won nine games in a row, but Miranda felt certain she was going to break her duck soon. Rosa was starting to get cocky, barely even thinking before scratching her circles in the dirt. Miranda was sure overconfidence would get the girl in the end.

'This will keep us alive,' Olin said, dropping down a bundle of vegetables. 'A good job one of us knows how to forage, isn't it?'

Miranda gave him a disarming smile. 'Thank you,' she

said. Then, glancing over her shoulder at Rilston Mead, she asked, 'Do you think he'll take much longer?'

The reanimated recycling plant hadn't moved in more than an hour. Informing them that he needed to make some enquiries, his eyes had closed and all movement from inside had ceased. Miranda had begun to think he was waiting for them to leave.

'If you try to hurry him, he'll only resent you and purposely take longer,' Olin said. 'It's best to wait.'

Miranda nodded, trying to hide her frustration as Rosa won yet another game. She swiped away the dirt and drew out another grid. 'Best of twenty-one,' she said.

A few minutes later, she was on the cusp of an eleventh straight defeat when a groan from behind her announced the end of Rilston Mead's long rest. The huge window-eyes opened and turned towards where Olin sat on a rock beside Miranda and Rosa.

'You can come inside now,' he said, his front doors swinging open.

'Inside?' Olin said, frowning.

'I've dug you a little hole,' Rilston said. 'Of course, to keep it out of sight of anyone unsavoury who might be watching, I dug it inside. It goes a fair way down, but I've arranged a guide to lead you to your destination, and, all being well, back out again.'

'Thank you so much,' Miranda said, running over to Rilston and hugging the wall. 'You're a great friend. Olin never had praise high enough.'

'It's a shame you can't come with us,' Rosa added. 'I'll miss the jokes.'

Rilston blushed again. 'I'll save some for your return.'

'Thanks, old boy,' Olin said, following the others and patting Rilston on the wall.

'While I'm sure you're aware that we reanimates won't

take sides in any altercation, I hope that whatever you're planning to do, you bring these two young ladies back in one piece each. They possess a charm that you sadly lack.'

'I'll use my time in their company to work on my etiquette,' Olin said. 'But thanks anyway.'

'Look after yourselves, dears,' Enchantress intoned, lifting her graceful head. 'When you return, I'll be waiting to fly you back to wherever you need to go.'

Miranda ran over and hugged the swan around the neck. 'I'll miss you,' she said. 'I hope we'll be back soon.'

'I hope so too, dear,' Enchantress said. 'You take good care of little Rosa in there.'

'I will.'

Rilston's eyes had begun to revolve at the length of their goodbyes. One door flapped as though indicating they should get a move on.

'Your guide won't wait forever,' he said. 'He's prone to wander off if his mind isn't occupied.'

Miranda went inside, with Rosa at her shoulder and Olin following behind. She hadn't been sure what to expect of the inside of a reanimated recycling plant, but a vast empty space with a ceiling that pulsed and shifted like the inside of a giant animal's stomach hadn't been quite it. In the centre of a wooden floor, a ladder poked out of a hole a couple of metres wide. There was no indication of how Rilston had dug it, but when Miranda leaned over the side, she saw the ladder stretching far down until it ended in a dim circle of light.

'Have you got torches down there for us?' Olin asked.

'Your light source has been sorted out,' Rilston replied, his voice coming from everywhere at once. 'I suggest you get a move on. I'm not fond of that hole—it's creating quite a draft. Don't tempt me to close it back up.'

Miranda glanced at the others. Neither looked keen, so

she gulped and nodded. 'This was my decision so I'll go first. Rosa, you come behind me. Olin, you know you don't have to come—'

Olin flapped a hand. 'Just get moving. I'll be right behind you.'

Miranda grinned. 'And Rilston ... thank you.'

'It's Mr. Mead to you. Now get out of here and leave me in peace.'

Miranda patted the floor of the old recycling plant, and then climbed down onto the ladder. Only as she put her hands on it did she realise that the ladder itself was made of tightly woven paper. As she started down into the hole, she prayed it would hold, particularly once Olin got moving down.

She descended a few rungs, then called to Rosa. When she glanced down she could still see the glow far below them, but the shaft itself was in darkness, and she was climbing by sheer guesswork, hoping that Rilston had created the rungs an equal distance apart. On a few occasions, however, she found her fears realised, her fingers clutching at nothing where she guessed a rung should be. Each time, she took a moment to pause, assure her position on the other rungs, and then feel around for the next one, usually slightly up or down. Only a couple of times did she have to lower her feet a depth of where two rungs should be, each time calling up to warn the others.

The glow below never seemed to grow in size. Around her, the air cooled, but drafts were coming up from below, bringing occasional warm gusts of air, as though the ground had its own subterranean heating system. After climbing for some minutes, however, she realised that the shaft descended far deeper than she had first imagined.

She was nearly at the bottom when she realised the light below was moving. Not so much even flickering as moving back and forth, as though whatever emitted it was shuffling around, waiting for their arrival. Rilston had said about sorting out their light source, and now Miranda began to imagine all kind of strange creatures living down here in the tunnels.

When she finally reached the bottom and found hard ground under her feet, however, the sight before her was something she could never have imagined.

'You took your time,' came a squeaky voice, and Miranda found herself staring into the blind eyes of a giant plastic rabbit, grey and flecked with black, glowing from some flickering light inside its body. It bobbed back and forth on a flat bottom, ears creaking as they twitched.

'Um, hello,' she said, reaching out a hand.

The rabbit, its front paws moulded into its body, dipped forward, one ear bending to touch her hand.

'On the side!' it shouted, its ear twisting around. 'Down, below, you're too slow!'

Miranda gave it a polite smile. 'My name is Miranda Butterworth,' she said, as Rosa climbed down behind her, eyes going wide at the sight of the giant plastic rabbit. 'This is Rosa, and up there is Olin Brin.'

'Pleased to make your acquaintance,' said the rabbit. 'My name is Squeaker, and I'm your guide.'

36

BENJAMIN

THE CRY OF HIS NAME CAME FROM BEHIND HIM. Benjamin craned his neck to look, his body aching from the effort. There, beyond a tall fence, Wilhelm stood beside Sebastien. Wilhelm's fingers threaded through the links in the fence and he was shaking it with all his might to get Benjamin's attention.

Benjamin opened his mouth. He tried to shout something back, to tell them to leave, to tell them to save themselves, but no words would come. He could only watch as Wilhelm, boosted by Sebastien, scaled up the fence and dropped over the other side.

Stay away, he screamed in his mind as Wilhelm began running across the gravelly open space towards the two lines of entranced children. He tried to break free from the line, but his legs were defying him, moving him forwards as more children came behind, all of them blank-faced, accepting of their fate. He watched with horror as Wilhelm, at first running hard, began to slow, his movements taking on an exaggerated, slow-motion appearance, arcing him gently away from Benjamin despite the horrified look on Wilhelm's face, moving him towards the back of the line.

'No—'

The word came out like a cough. One of Benjamin's feet slipped out of its preordained position as he half-turned. The chains of pure thought that shackled him were momentarily loosened, jerking away as though scalded with a hot iron.

'No!'

This time it was a scream, and he broke out of his position, lost his balance, and fell to his knees. The boy walking behind him stepped forwards to take his place, making no acknowledgment of Benjamin, his face serene as he followed those in front. In his mind, Benjamin felt the world closing in around the boy like a bubble sealing a hole, but briefly rejecting him as he scrambled out of its grasp.

Even as he crawled towards Wilhelm, the invisible force regrouped and came for him again. It was like a thousand hands on his body, trying to drag him back into position, and it was all he could do to take just one movement forwards. He paused to take a breath, and his body slid back through the gravel, hard stones scraping his knees.

'No!'

He closed his eyes. He couldn't fight it; whatever force held him was too strong. He stopped seeing with his eyes and started seeing with his mind, imagining a vast sphere pluming outwards from the castle floating over the pit.

The castle of Dr. Ben Forrest. The castle that, in one version of this world, he himself had created.

And surely, if he created it, he could also destroy it.

Instead of trying to push the magical force away, he began to draw it in, wrapping it around himself, letting it seep into his skin. His body felt suddenly strong, his mind as powerful as a sledgehammer. As more and more of the force flowed into him, it began to lose its hold on the two lines of children. Their footsteps began to falter, one or two to stop entirely. A flying plastic bag suddenly dropped out of the sky, while around the curve to the east, a massive tumbleweed paused in its progress.

Who are you? What are you doing?

Benjamin ignored the voice which had come on the threads of thought energy he was drawing into himself. He let his mind drift, no longer caring about his physical body being dragged back into its line. He sent his own thoughts out towards the castle, searching for Forrest, searching for himself.

What are you doing here?

The voice came from everywhere now. Benjamin sought it, pulling it inwards, making it the only sound in the world.

You cannot be here. Why are you here? How?

Let my friend go. I will come if you let my friend go.

You cannot be here! It's not possible! I set you adrift! I let you go!

Suddenly everything felt so easy. The world was no longer a plume of a single sensation but a million threads each linking a child who had come, who would come, who had come and gone, each with some link to the place in which they would one day discover a new form of existence.

Ultimate power rested on his fingertips.

I can destroy everything you have created. I can set everyone you enslaved free. All I have to do is pull.

You cannot! You will destroy yourself. You will destroy me. You will destroy us.

Let me see you. Let me see me.

The world changed. Benjamin saw everything from above. Two lines of children, one again climbing slowly into the castle, one walking forward into the pit. In the depths of that cavern itself, he saw a maelstrom of orange, a great furnace in which all the world's unwanted was absorbed. And above it, a shifting halo of light and energy which solidified into shapes which became towers and galleries and balustrades, alive in themselves, and confused about their existence.

∼

The man was sitting on a chair which had outlines but no substance. He wore nothing, yet, like the chair, was only a series of outlines, like the imaginings of a sketch on a sheet of white paper. He stood up, bowing, and then extended a sketched hand, the lines of which were constantly redrawing themselves.

'I never believed you could exist. You are my past, and my other side. I sent you away with everything else no longer wanted. I set my mind free of you.'

Benjamin had to glance down at himself to make sure he was real, but while he still wore clothes, to his horror, he had taken on a translucency and could see through himself to the castle floor, and through that in turn to multiple levels of shifting rooms below him.

'I'm not sure I do exist.'

'Oh, you do. In a certain way. You are my past. I am your future. In a certain way. In another, we have no connection. We are separate paths.'

'Which is it?'

'I do not know.'

'Why did you bring me here?'

'I didn't. You came of your own accord. I sent you away. I sent you into the darkness, leaving myself free for the light. And now you have come back. You are my chains, the chains I thought I had escaped, returned to enslave me once more.'

Dr. Forrest shifted on his seat. The outlines of his body readjusted, creating a human in a sitting position. Benjamin's eyes began to ache.

'I don't understand where I am. When I am. Only that I had to come. I was in Endinfinium, and I escaped.'

'Endinfinium…?'

Benjamin stared. 'Everything that you're destroying, it goes there. I don't know how, or why, but you have created an entire world. And you live there too; but a different you, one who wishes to destroy everything.'

'I have had dreams—'

'It's not a dream! There are people there, places, creatures, my friends—'

'And your family?'

Benjamin thought of his brother, David, lying ephemeral inside a glowing capsule, and phone calls to his mother, both of which now felt like a million years ago. Until his return to Basingstoke, he hadn't even thought of them in months.

'No, not them.'

Dr. Forrest let out a great sigh. 'As I thought.'

'That's what started everything, isn't it? Your—our—family died, and you—we—tried in some way to avenge it.'

Dr. Forrest's shape became a series of shifting colours. 'I give the unwanted freedom,' he said. 'I allow them to begin again. Endinfinium, you call this place? It is an interesting word.'

'You don't know of it?'

'How could I? I am here, not somewhere else.'

Benjamin frowned. 'Then who is the Dark Man?'

Dr. Forrest shrugged his shoulders as the colours began

to fade. 'That's a question you'll have to ask yourself. It seems you know more than me.'

'No! You created Endinfinium, you are the Dark Man, and you are me!'

'If you have the answers, why the need to ask questions?'

Benjamin felt his anger rising. Dr. Forrest was nothing more than a light shadow, an empty silhouette. Everything that he could have been he had purged himself of, leaving nothing left.

'Why do they come here? The children?'

Dr Forrest shifted on his chair. 'They come to find a better place. They are unwanted, unneeded, everywhere, except here.'

'But what is here?'

'Here is the end of everything. Where everything becomes one again. Where everything shares its experiences and joins together. Where all sadness and misery is spread so thin that it can no longer cause harm.'

Benjamin stared at the man he would one day become. 'You're insane,' he said.

'Proclaimed by the younger version of myself yet to go through the suffering that will turn you into me. Said with such authority. You'll see, young Benjamin. You'll see, young me.'

Benjamin shook his head. 'I don't—'

But even as he began to speak, he looked down at himself and found that the translucent outline of his body had begun to pixelate, pieces of him slowly unravelling like pulled threads, floating across the space to enter Dr. Forrest's body where they slowly began to form again into the colours, contours, and textures of a man.

'What are you doing?'

'I'm letting you see. I'm letting you see everything. You

came to me. I can set you free of the suffering you feel. I have freed so many, but I have waited for you for so long. Don't worry, dear Benjamin, soon your fears will be my fears, and then there will be no fears at all.'

'Stop—'

'Benjamin, don't fight it. We are the same person. Why trouble ourselves with a joust of questions when we can easily understand the answers?'

Benjamin looked down at himself. His legs were gone, and the threads were unravelling up his waist and over his stomach. Sitting across from him, Dr. Forrest's outline was beginning to fill with shapes and features. The eyes took on a blue colour, line-drawing sketched cheeks filled out with a flushed reddish pink. Teeth formed; a jawline, hair.

'Thank you,' Dr. Forrest said. 'I have felt hollow for so long. Now, at last, I can find peace.'

37

SNOUT

Tommy Cale's teeth were literally chattering with fear. 'Come on, Simon, can't we go back? I'm scared.'

'Look, I know what happened to Adam was my fault, but you were with me. We're in this together. Plus, if anything happens to me, I want you to run back to the dorms and tell the others.'

'Tell who?'

'Anyone who'll care.'

'Like who?'

Snout shrugged. 'I don't know ... Gubbledon? He might care for at least five seconds if I disappear.'

'He's been sick in bed for three days.'

'Which is part of the reason why we have to find out what's going on. Reanimates never get sick.'

'If we get busted breaking curfew to spy on a teachers' meeting, we'll never get let out of the locker room ever again,' Tommy said.

Snout took a deep breath. 'Then let's hope we're not.'

They carried on down the corridor, Snout leading, Tommy following at his shoulder, muttering under his breath. At the end, Snout led them up a flight of stairs, emerging on another long corridor with a high, vaulted ceiling and candelabras flickering in alcoves in the wall.

'There,' Snout said, pointing to the large, double wooden door at the far end. 'The entrance to the teachers' apartments.'

'And how do you suppose we get inside?'

'We're not going to.'

'Then what?'

'This way.'

Snout led Tommy through a barely noticeable side door. They found themselves in a narrow, cramped corridor with almost no natural light besides a faint glimmer through a couple of arrow slits in the walls through which a cool breeze was blowing.

'Where are we?'

'Service corridor. Cleat told me about it.'

'Cleat? The librarian? What, is he your best mate now or something?'

'No. He was telling me about how when he was a pupil here, the kids used to use the service corridors to get around under the teachers' noses. I hunted out a map.'

'Uh, Snout—' Tommy suddenly gasped, gripping hold of Snout's arm and swinging him around. Snout barely had time to slap a hand over his mouth to stifle a cry of terror as a ghostly faced cleaner came stumbling past, pushing a cart loaded with glass bottles stoppered with rags and all tied together with a piece of rope around the outside. The cart made a sudden musical jingle as the cleaner pushed it over a bump in the stone floor, and then the reanimated corpse was gone, disappearing out of sight around a gradual bend.

'Service corridor,' Snout muttered, his voice shaking. 'Got to remember that. The cleaners use them too.'

Tommy was rocking from foot to foot, eyes wide. 'I almost wet myself,' he said. He lifted a hand until it was a couple of inches from his face. 'He was right here, and he didn't even glance at us.'

Like most of the kids, Snout had gotten used to seeing the reanimated corpses wandering about. Devoid of their souls, they had reanimated enough that they could perform simple tasks, but even so, seeing one close up was still a shock.

'We have to follow him,' Snout said, recovering his composure. He led Tommy in pursuit, and not long after, they caught up with the cleaner, who reached a narrow wooden door and stopped outside. Instead of going in, though, the cleaner just parked his cart and then withdrew a bottle and pulled out the stopper. As they watched, he poured some of the liquid onto the rag and then began wiping the door down.

'The door must have started to reanimate,' Snout said. 'They can't send fixtures and fittings down to the lockers so the cleaners have to do it.'

'Is that the way in?' Tommy asked.

'Yeah.'

'So we're stuck until he's finished.'

Snout frowned. 'Unless … come on, I have an idea.'

'What?'

'Just follow me.'

With Tommy muttering again at his shoulder, Snout went up to the cleaner and tapped the reanimated corpse on the shoulder. It had once been a man, but when it turned towards him, he saw black lumps where its eyes would have been, and opened its decayed lips in a grin to reveal a blackened line of teeth inside, Snout could only see it as a thing, not something that had once been a person. He was shaking so badly his knees were knocking together as he pointed at the door and croaked, 'We got locked out. Can you let us in, please?'

The cleaner's grin widened further. With a nod, it reached out and stuck a fat key into the lock. It turned with a rusty grating sound and then the door swung inwards. Snout nodded thanks, then was about to go inside, when he had another idea.

'Um, we won't be long,' he said. 'Can you wait for us? I'll knock when we're ready to come back out.'

The cleaner's head rose and fell. A piece of rotting flesh dropped off its cheek and splatted on the floor.

'Did it say yes?' Tommy hissed, clutching Snout's arm.

'I think so,' Snout said. He smiled at the cleaner despite the knotting of his stomach and a growing wave of nausea, and then stepped inside, pulling Tommy with him. The cleaner pulled the door shut and Snout heard the lock click.

'We're in,' he said.

'I'm going to be sick,' Tommy said, doubling over. 'Did you see the way his bones were poking out of his neck? I don't think that was his original head.'

'Look, just hold it together. We have work to do.'

They found themselves halfway up a gloomy stairwell with turns on either side. A strange contraption bolted to the outer wall appeared to be a pulley system for lifting goods up and down.

'Which way?' Tommy asked.

Snout shook his head. 'Your guess is as good as mine. I'd think they'd be more likely to sleep higher up, wouldn't they? Let's try down.'

Snout went first, with Tommy as usual tight at his shoulder. Snout tried to shrug him off, but Tommy kept leaning against him, as though afraid Snout might vanish into thin air. Snout was on the verge of telling him to pack it in, when a glow appeared below them.

A few steps further on, the stairwell opened out into a storeroom. Piles of clothing, bedding, cleaning materials, boxes, and trays filled shelves on three sides. On the fourth, a door led out.

It wasn't locked. Snout opened it and took a peek, finding himself at the back of a stack of books.

He had heard of the teachers' library, where they kept all the most important books discovered in Endinfinium. As he read the spine of one turned the wrong way around —*Mathematics for Idiots*—he guessed they wouldn't be popular in the main library anyway.

'Come on, Loane, get a move on. Let's get this meeting started.'

Snout froze. Ms. Ito's voice. She was only a few steps away, on the other side of the bookshelf. Snout peered through a narrow gap in the rows of books and saw the other teachers assembled there too: Captain Roche, Professor Caspian, Mistress Xemian, Professor Neale, Mistress Castillo, and half a dozen others he had seen around the school but didn't have classes with. Through an arch on the other side of the room, Professor Loane appeared, carrying a steaming kettle. He set it down on a table in the centre and began pouring it into cups.

'It's from the fields down by the old botanical gardens,' he said, handing a cup to Captain Roche. 'It has a much more pungent flavour than the stuff that grows on the cliffs.'

'Am I the only one taking this seriously?' Ms. Ito said. 'Can we please stop wasting our time talking about plants and get to the point? Eaves could be back from his society meeting at any moment.'

Professor Eaves. The only noticeable absence, apart

from Grand Lord Bastien, who no one had seen in some time. Snout put a finger to his lips and glanced at Tommy, in case the smaller boy was starting to panic, but Tommy had knelt down and was clutching Snout's knee like a precious teddy bear.

'Okay, let's get this started,' Captain Roche said. 'Nice brew, Loane. A shame there's no sugar. So, what choices do we have? We close their society down?'

'We have to be so, so careful with this,' Professor Caspian said. 'Godfrey Pendleton is dangerous. He's the only Summoner in the school now that Benjamin Forrest has disappeared—'

'He's dead, Caspian. Just say it,' Ms. Ito snapped. 'Him and his two friends, Butterworth and Jacobs. As regretful as it is, let's not mince our words. The boys went over the edge of the world. They're not coming back. And no one's seen the girl since either.'

'I'm afraid she's right,' Mistress Xemian said. 'Runners have been sent to look for Miranda to all points of the compass, as far south as the river, as far north as the Bay of Paper Dragons. No one has seen her. She's gone.'

'But let's not forget what they did for us,' Professor Caspian said. 'They saved the school.'

'And without them, it falls to us,' Ms. Ito said. 'Enough of the sentimentality. Thanks to that unfortunate Patterson boy we know what they're doing in there, even if we were too quick to turn a blind eye ourselves. That curly haired twit and his cronies are trying to draw the Dark Man into our school. And Eaves, well. I thought better of him. He's as blind as the rat he resembles. All this equality rubbish. Dark reanimate has no place in a school built to protect people against it. That boy has our idiot professor wrapped around his fingers. Good riddance to both of them, I say.'

'You were part of this,' Professor Caspian said. 'It was

you who wanted Godfrey as a prefect, to let him take rooms in the teachers' tower.'

'So we could keep an eye on him!' Ms. Ito snapped. 'Because over there in the dorms we have no idea what he's doing. And even though we did he's got away with running around under our noses. We've been tied in a knot and if it hadn't been for Patterson and his meddling—much as I hate to admit it—we'd never have known what was happening until it was too late.'

Snout couldn't help but smile. From Ms. Ito, it was high praise indeed.

'A shame that fat boy got caught in the crossfire. It looks like he'll have to be sacrificed for the common good.'

'You can't be serious?'

'What else do you suggest? We can't start a war, Loane. We'll lose if we do, and then everything we stand for, everything we protect, will be lost.'

'So what do you suggest?'

Captain Roche stepped forward. 'We calve it,' he said.

'We do what?'

'We sever that wing of the school, the old science block, everything. We send it into the sea, with Eaves and his society and Godfrey all in it together. We hold a ward over it until it's dropped over the edge out of harm's way. We wipe them out, and then we rewrite the rules. We tighten our control over everything and we make sure it never happens again.'

There were a few seconds of silence before Professor Loane spoke. 'You're suggesting … murder.'

'We're suggesting a sacrifice for the greater good,' Ms. Ito almost shouted before getting control of herself. 'This school exists to protect the children of Endinfinium from the Dark Man. He wants to destroy us because what we protect is the calm and order in the chaos he so loves. If we do not protect the children in their great hour of need, if we let Godfrey and his Dark Reanimate Society bring the Dark Man into our school and destroy it from the inside out, then we will have failed them.'

'We will need to consult the Grand Lord on this,' Professor Loane said.

'The Grand Lord is sick, like all the reanimates!' Ms. Ito said. 'It's already almost too late. If the Dark Man's power seeps into our school, if Godfrey harnesses it, there will be no school left. We'll be sitting on a blackened pile of wood and rock. We have to act now!'

'This is not a decision which can be taken lightly,' Professor Caspian said.

'And it hasn't been, fool,' Ms. Ito snapped. 'I've barely slept in a week. Do you think I'm enjoying this?'

Loane let out a little cough, hiding the delay in Professor Caspian's response.

'You fools playing your high castle games,' Ms. Ito said, shaking her mop of pepper-coloured hair. 'Every one of us grew up in this school, and every one of us was protected from the dangers of Endinfinium until we were old enough to deal with it. We have to pass that protection on. Don't you remember what happens to those who don't make it? Those who get lost? Open your windows before dawn once in a while, and you might hear the screams drifting off the Haunted Forest if the wind's right. And look around the faces of the cleaners. Anyone you know? The girl who stands third from the left at lunch used to be called Jenny. She was my best friend when I went here, but one night she went out for an adventure. She never came back. Fourteen years later she was found wandering in the forest, her body a decomposing wreck, only a shred of her mind left. What happened to the rest of it, I'll never know. So. When I say this decision hasn't been taken lightly, I mean it.' She stood up. Snout hadn't even realised she had been sitting down. 'A vote. Do we do this thing or not?'

A couple of hands went up reluctantly, but in the end they all went up. Ms. Ito looked around the group. 'Good. At least we agree on something. The only question we have to answer now, is when.'

'Neither Professor Eaves nor Godfrey must hear a word about this,' Professor Loane said. 'Eaves is a fool, but Godfrey is more dangerous than anyone in this school. He has no idea just how much power he can control, and its best that we keep it that way.'

'Agreed. I suggest we wait until they're in position to perform their little stunt, when their minds will be most occupied,' Ms. Ito said. 'Our timing is paramount. I have a spy among them who will inform me when they're ready to do what it is they plan.'

'Patterson?'

'Yes.'

'Do you trust him?'

Ms. Ito shrugged. 'The boy's too simple to rebel against my orders.'

Snout's cheeks burned.

'He wields a great power,' Professor Loane said. 'An uncharted one.'

'Like Godfrey, he has no idea just how great,' Professor Caspian said. 'He's barely touched the surface of what he's capable of doing.'

'Then let's not inform him otherwise,' Ms. Ito snapped. 'Keep him in the dark and we'll keep ourselves and the rest of the pupils a lot safer. Right. I think we're done here. We'll gather again two nights from now to see what developments have been made. Everyone okay on that?'

There were mumbles of agreement.

'Good. In the meantime, Loane, try to have a word with Bastien. If he's unresponsive, just leave it.'

'I'll try.'

One by one they mumbled their goodbyes and headed off. Snout and Tommy crouched down behind the bookshelf until they heard Ms. Ito stumping up the spiral staircase in the library's centre. As the thuds of her cast on the stairs reached the floor above, the lights suddenly went out, plunging the room into darkness. Snout clapped a hand over Tommy's mouth before the smaller boy could cry out. As soon as he felt Tommy relax, he pulled his palm away and wiped Tommy's spittle on his trouser leg.

'That didn't sound too good,' Tommy whispered.

'We'll worry about what to do after we get out of here,' Snout answered, keeping his voice low. 'Come on.'

The cleaner was still there. With a light tap and a whispered request, the door swung open to reveal a grin beneath vacant eyes. As they slipped past, the cleaner—a cloth in one hand—continued to polish the doorframe to an imperious shine.

Tommy yawned several times as they headed back to the dorms. Snout, however, was too wired from what he had heard to feel even remotely sleepy.

They were planning to send the entire science block over the edge of the world.

And that meant Fat Adam, if he were still alive, would go with it.

38

MIRANDA

Much to Miranda's frustration, Squeaker, their giant, plastic, glowing rabbit-guide, insisted on taking his new friends to visit his subterranean family en-route. Following the luminous blind rabbit down a series of crumbly tunnels which looked set to collapse at any moment, they emerged into a chamber where several other plastic rabbits of varying sizes bounced around in seemingly contented abandon.

'My wife, Flopper,' Squeaker announced, indicating a plastic bunny which had one ear missing, huge teeth marks in the plastic edging suggesting she had narrowly escaped the presence of some terrible beast. Flopper performed an awkward bow which made her plastic body creak. 'And these are my children,' Squeaker continued, indicating the numerous other plastic bunnies bouncing around. None looked remotely like their parents, but were a collection of oversized toy rabbits from various production backgrounds: one was made of wood, another some kind of sponge, a third apparently cut glass, but getting a good look at its features was difficult due to the way its shape reflected the glow of its alleged father.

'These are my younglings,' Squeaker said. 'Bouncer, Hopper, Leaper, Jumper, and'—indicating the cut glass rabbit—'Shiner. Welcome to our home. I'd love to offer you food but unless you're a fan of earthworms, there's not a lot to be found down here.'

'We packed a lunch,' Olin said quickly, patting the bag slung around his waist.

'But thanks anyway,' Miranda added, quickly putting a hand over Rosa's mouth as the girl prepared a groan of disgust.

'It's been so long since we had visitors,' Flopper said, shifting from side to side, her face lit up with delight. 'I do wish you could stay.'

'We're a bit busy,' Olin said.

'We're on a mission to rescue my father and save the world,' Rosa added.

'Oh, how delightful,' Flopper said. 'I do wish you the best of luck. Come on children, let's get back to our embroidery.'

Miranda saw, to her delight, that the five smaller rabbits and their mother had actually been in the process of embroidering something. Balls of yarn, needles, and pins filled two baskets on a low table, and half of a colourful rabbit had been embroidered across a cushion cover, a little blue jacket covering its shoulders. It looked familiar from somewhere Miranda couldn't quite place, but she didn't have time to linger because Olin was tugging her sleeve, pulling her after him.

'It's this way,' Squeaker said, bouncing ahead, his light flickering off of the cave walls. 'At least it was last time I wandered over there for a look. Sometimes the tunnels move above, because they're not all tunnels, you see.'

'Um, what are they?' Miranda asked.

'Giant buried reanimates,' Squeaker said, then squealed as though making a joke, the sound piercing enough to make both Miranda and Rosa cover their ears. Olin just grimaced.

'Do they wake up very often?' Miranda asked, when the ringing in her ears had stopped.

'Oh, they're not asleep,' Squeaker said. 'They're just resting. The bigger they are, the more relaxed they tend to be, but from time to time they feel the need to fidget. The nicest will give us a heads up, but the family live in regular tunnels, so we're generally safe.'

'That's nice to know,' Olin said, throwing Miranda a sarcastic look.

'Mother always said our tunnels were part of some giant sleeping creature,' Rosa said. 'She would never say it in front of Trobin, though, as he'd tell her it was rubbish. From time to time we'd try to tickle the walls, and sometimes we'd see them tremble. One day, though, it told me to stop.'

'It spoke to you?'

'In here,' Rosa said, tapping the side of her head. Olin, turning back, lifted an eyebrow. 'So I told all the others we should perhaps leave it alone. I think it was worried about sneezing and destroying all our homes.'

Miranda thought about Rilston Mead, an entire reanimated recycling plant. When she considered his scale, it wasn't so hard to believe that entire train stations or buildings could have been buried and then reanimated. She remembered how small items at the school would reanimate and move frantically until sprayed with the chamomile to calm them down. It made sense that larger reanimates would do everything more slowly. She also remembered something Benjamin had heard in

Underfloor and told her and Wilhelm: that the more complex a reanimate, the more intelligent it could become. She wondered what knowledge these giant reanimates might have if she knew how to ask.

'Looks like we're all good through here,' Squeaker said, bouncing onwards, with each step giving a little squeak through an air hole in his underside.

'How do you know where you're going?' Olin said. 'I mean, no offense, but you don't see too well.'

Squeaker twisted his ears right round like two radio antennae. 'Sound,' he said. 'You'd be amazed what you can hear when you really listen.'

'What can you hear?' Rosa said.

Squeaker's face creaked as his rabbit mouth grinned. 'A couple of miles below us, a family of reanimated snakes are hunting out another ladder to finish up the creation of a giant game. Behind us, my littlest, Jumper, is complaining about bumping his foot. And above us, Rilston Mead is snoring.'

'You can hear all that?'

Squeaker's ears twitched. 'That and a thousand other things.'

'Can you hear what the Dark Man's doing?' Rosa asked.

Squeaker's smile dropped. 'I choose not to listen,' he said. 'Perhaps you've heard by now that reanimates take no interest in the lives of humans?'

'It's been mentioned,' Miranda said with a wry smile.

'We know of his existence, but we prefer not to interfere. You remember your life before, don't you?'

'Before Endinfinium?'

'Yes.'

'Some,' Miranda said. 'It wasn't the best, so I try to shut it out.'

'We do too,' Squeaker said. 'In a different kind of way. I have a family now, a wife, children. A few friends here and there down here in these tunnels. I had none of that before, so why would I risk something which might take it away?'

Miranda nodded. While she understood his logic, she still found it frustrating. 'But if you wanted to, you could listen right into the Shifting Castle and find out what's going on in there?'

'Some, perhaps,' Squeaker said, but abruptly ended the conversation by bouncing ahead, calling for them to follow.

'Try not to annoy him too much,' Olin said, glancing back. 'Do you really want to be stuck down here without a guide or any light? I'm not too keen.'

'Sorry,' she muttered, but Rosa took her hand and gave it a squeeze. 'Thank you,' she whispered. 'I know you're trying to help me find my dad.'

As they walked though, Miranda felt increasingly sure she wouldn't need Squeaker's help to find Rosa's father when they finally reached the Shifting Castle. Whenever she closed her eyes, she felt a pervading sense of discomfort pushing in at her senses. It wasn't the caves or the air, it was the taint of dark reanimate which ran through everything. It was getting stronger, thicker. Soon it would be all around.

'Are there ghouls down here?' Olin asked, as Squeaker paused for them to catch up. 'I hope we don't run into any.'

'They're sleeping,' Squeaker said. 'They won't wake unless called.' Then, with another squealing laugh, added, 'Best not to call them.'

The tunnels stretched on. Sometimes they were stone caves, other times they were earth or gravel. A few times they passed through bricked sections or areas of packed plastic which were warm to the touch. Once in a while Squeaker would pause, his ears twitching, peering into tunnels to either side, then nod and carry on, Olin, Miranda, and Rosa hurrying in his wake.

Time passed, but it became impossible to know how long they had been travelling. At one point they came to an immense moving walkway, where they stood for some minutes, resting their legs, while a conveyor beneath their feet carried them for what felt like a couple of miles. As they reached the end and Squeaker bounced away into another rocky tunnel, Rosa leaned down to give the conveyor a pat.

'He said he was happy to help,' she said, looking up at Miranda.

A couple of times it was Olin who called a halt, waving Squeaker back and then passing out chunks of unnamed vegetables to Miranda and Rosa, then offering them a drink from a metal flask he had brought. Every time they stopped, Squeaker would bounce around them, appearing increasingly agitated, as though keen to get the job done. One time Olin had to point out that two girls and an overweight man didn't have the same endless supply of energy that the reanimates had, to which Squeaker grinned and suggested they change their diet. As Olin scowled, Rosa laughed, and Miranda found herself warming to the giant, glowing rabbit.

Finally, Squeaker came to a stop in a chamber about the size of one of the school's gyms. Here, his glow wasn't the only source of light; high up in the cavern's walls, old light bulbs buried in the rock glowed and shook as they reanimated inside their rock prisons.

'This is as far as I can take you,' Squeaker said. 'Through that door at the end, there's a passageway that leads upwards. If you follow it, you'll find yourselves in the basements of the Shifting Castle. I've heard that the basements are fairly stable, being made of solid rock. The further up you go, however, the more you'll encounter that issue which gives the castle its name. I wish you luck. I will wait here for you, should I be needed.' He tapped one foot on the ground. 'There are plenty of worms down here to keep me busy.'

'I thought reanimates didn't need to eat,' Olin muttered.

'Oh, we don't,' Squeaker said, grinning. 'We do it purely for enjoyment.'

Miranda exchanged a look of disgust with Rosa then turned to the giant plastic rabbit.

'Thank you so much,' she said. 'If there's anything we can do to repay you, consider it done.'

'Just come back in one piece,' Squeaker said. 'Or at least, few enough that it's still possible to be mended.'

'We'll try.'

With one last glance back at the rabbit, Miranda took the lead, heading for the double doors at the end of the cavern. Rosa held one hand and trailed after, while Olin came behind. As they reached the doors, Miranda took a deep breath.

'Right,' she said. 'Are we all ready for this?'

'Absolutely not,' Olin said.

'Only if you are,' Rosa said, looking up at Miranda.

'I don't think I ever will be,' Miranda said, 'but what the hell? Let's do this.'

Giving the doors a defiant glare, she reached up and pushed them open.

39

WILHELM

He could do nothing but walk calmly forward towards the edge of the pit, following the line of kids in front as, one by one, they stepped over the edge. He didn't feel fear of what might happen, because some part of him sensed that he wasn't about to die, only change places, or end up transformed into something else. Instead he felt a massive sense of frustration that his attempt to rescue Benjamin had failed, and that his best friend was now lost.

What had happened made no sense. One moment Benjamin had been in front of him in the line, the next he had been crawling through the gravel in Wilhelm's direction. And then, slowly, what had been Wilhelm's best friend began to unravel. First, Benjamin became translucent. Next, the colours began to fade until he was only a sepia outline of a boy. And then, finally, the lines began to unwrite themselves, until there was nothing left of Benjamin but a few depressions in the gravel where his hands, knees, and feet had been.

Wilhelm's friend was gone, vanished into the air.

Up ahead, he recognised Don at the front of the line.

Wilhelm tried to shout to the lanky boy but his mouth felt full of a thick jelly from which no words could escape. Even the effort of opening his mouth sent shudders of weariness through his body, and if the jellylike sensation wasn't all around him, holding him up, he might have fallen to the ground, to lie as useless and inert as the gravel below him.

Don, lifting his head slightly as though to give a nod to the floating, formless castle, stepped forward and disappeared over the edge. Wilhelm tried to scream, but again, no sound would come out. He turned his eyes to the left, looking towards the rising bridge leading to the castle, upon which he recognised Ray, Kevin, and Dorothy. Further ahead of them walked a girl he also recognised, ghostly, translucent, as though part of her had already gone. The closer she came to the castle, the less of her was visible, until she stepped down on the other side little more than an outline.

Lulu.

She paused for a moment, glancing up at the castle, before vanishing into the air.

A penny dropped, and Wilhelm understood. Don was a Weaver, like himself. Dorothy, Ray, and Kevin were all Channellers.

And Lulu was a Summoner.

The castle needed those who carried magic for its life force, but those with nothing were sent onwards, into the pit and beyond.

So why had Benjamin, a powerful Summoner, been in the line of Weavers?

Wilhelm didn't have time to think about it. His legs moved him forward another step. Another step closer to the pit. To his left, he saw Kevin reach the far side of the bridge. In a flash of light bright enough to make Wilhelm wince, Kevin shuddered, a glow flaring around him. Then he slumped to his knees, ducked his head, and rolled forward over the edge, into the pit.

High above, the castle gave a single brief pulse.

That queue was moving faster than his. He saw a girl begin to struggle as she stepped forward, lifting her hands suddenly. The castle pulsed, but the girl remained. She started to turn but she slipped, dropping into the pit like falling stone.

Lulu.

Dorothy was two places back. When her turn came, she tried to struggle, but didn't have the strength. Like Kevin, she shuddered, releasing a plume of energy, then fell into the pit. The castle pulsed, and she was gone. Ray, two spaces behind her, stepped up for his turn. With a sudden twist, he appeared to break free from the magical hold. He leaned over the pit, then the castle drew him back. It held him for a moment, shook him in its grip, then tossed what was left of him away.

Wilhelm frowned as much as his invisible shackles would allow. He sensed that in some way he was viewing the selection process for the children who ended up in Endinfinium. There had always been far more Weavers in the school than the others. Each year had three or four Channellers—many unaware of it due to the school's policies of concealing and denying their magical abilities—but Summoners were rare. That anyone knew, only Benjamin and Godfrey of the current pupils had fallen into that category.

He remembered how he had woken up in Endinfinium, feeling as though he had been lying, partly buried, in the ground for decades. For the first few hours he had felt barely capable of thought, as though his body had been reawakening from the longest of all sleeps.

The lines of discarded, unwanted children snaked back to the exits from the dog-catchers' facility. How many there were, but how few ended up reaching the relatively safety of the school.

With a sudden jolt of horror, he wondered how many children lay in eternal sleep, undiscovered, part of the fabric of Endinfinium's world. And how, if what power they possessed was shaken from them here, how there could be Channellers and Summoners in the school, still in possession of great power.

There are other ways in. The voice was like a whisper at the back of his mind.

Lost in his thoughts, he was still staring at the bridge and its line of children when he realised the child in front of him was gone. Only the chasm yawned in front of him, and his gaze snapped away from the bridge to regard a maelstrom of orange-and-grey churning far below. Among great rolling waves he saw thrown away items bobbing and circling, from tiny pieces of litter to entire lorries, parts of buildings, even what looked like a swimming pool, still intact. Rather than terror at what was about to befall him, he only felt a sense of peace, as though finally, at long last, he had found something that wanted him.

Welcome, a voice said, seeming to come from everywhere, and Wilhelm smiled, lifting his foot to step forward into its calming, welcoming embrace.

'Oh no, you don't—'

Arms encircled him, pulling him out of the queue. Hard gravel dug into his back as he fell back hard, scratching his elbows. The hold on him had vanished, and he scrambled up to his knees as a hand fell on his arm.

He looked up into Sebastien's face as the old man gave a grim smile.

'Keep a hold of me,' he said. 'I'm going to need you if we're going to save him.'

The ground below them began to shake. Sebastien had a stoic look on his face, kindly eyes turned hard as they stared at the castle looming over the pit. Where it had once been pure white, now colours flickered across its walls, dancing and flashing.

'What are you doing?' Wilhelm gasped. 'I thought you said—'

Sebastien let out a bitter laugh. 'I have no idea what I'm doing,' he said. 'Only that I'm doing it. Whatever it is that Doctor Forrest unleashed in the world, it doesn't only affect kids. It wasn't until I started trying to save the toys that I began to feel it, but over time it grew inside me. Things would move when I touched them, get hot, even reanimate a little. I quickly realised how dangerous such a thing could be, and I always sought to suppress it, to keep it hidden.' He gave Wilhelm a grim smile. 'Until now.'

Wilhelm stared at the ground around him. Gravel was spreading out in a circle around his feet, leaving behind bare earth as it rose into a growing rampart. It struck the line of children, pushing through them as they fell back, growing until it was several metres high, moving slowly but like a destructive wave. Behind him, it struck the side of the containment building, breaking through the wall. Dog-catchers fled, the children they were dragging with them abandoned, left to save themselves.

From the pit, lights started to flicker. Wilhelm gasped as the swimming pool he had seen came rushing up into the air and crashed down between him and the containment building. Tiles exploded outwards, but even as they settled, massive stone arms and legs grew out of the remains, the pool reanimating in front of Wilhelm's eyes.

'Sebastien, what on earth is going on? Sebastien?'

He glanced back at the old man, but Sebastien had fallen to the ground, his face pale, a trickle of blood running from the side of his mouth. He stared at Wilhelm, his eyes faltering as though he were on the verge of unconsciousness.

'It's up to you, now,' he said, his voice barely more than a whisper. 'I've done for you what I can.'

'Wait—'

Even as Sebastien's eyes closed as his body slumped to the ground, Wilhelm felt that something had happened beyond simply the old man's death. He turned, and as he did, he felt like something turned with him, a shadow, one so close to his body it could be considered part of him.

'You're there, aren't you?' he said, addressing the shadow, looking down at his arms and feeling a sense of additional motion his eyes couldn't pick up. 'You gave me yourself.'

A roar came from behind him. Wilhelm turned to find the reanimated swimming pool bearing down on him, a snapping mouth filled with serrated pieces of tile lunging forward. He put up his hands towards it off, and *pushed*. With an inhuman howl, the creature flipped over onto its back, writhing with its arms and legs in the air, unable to right itself.

Wilhelm stared at his hands. He had no idea what he had done, or how he could repeat it. Was this how Benjamin and Miranda felt when they used reanimation magic? He looked around, wondering what else he could do. The huge reanimated swimming pool was still trying to right itself. The line of children behind him had scattered, but was slowly regrouping, moving back into their positions as though nothing had happened. And over in the other line, the children continued to climb up the bridge.

He turned back again, looking down at Sebastien, and

felt a thickness returning to the air, as though something were trying to grab him. 'Get off me!' he shouted, shaking himself, and found again the force moving from within him, pushing the world back. The invisible arms shifted, backing off.

Save him.

Where had the voice come from, and who did it belong to? Sebastien lay at his feet, but Wilhelm sensed again that only part of the old man was dead. Part of him lived within Wilhelm now, a passenger.

And he had given Wilhelm power.

'Benjamin!' he shouted. 'Where are you?' *Where are you? I'm here.*

The voice was faint, and it came from within Wilhelm's mind. He closed his eyes to concentrate, but instead of finding blackness, something strange was happening. He felt a sense of internal vision, and the world appeared filled with threads of colour. Those that came from the castle were pure white, those from the children a mixture of different pale shades of various colours ... and his own, a paleness flecked with sparkles of burnt orange, the same colour as that of the depths of the pit.

The same colour as the eyes of the ghouls.

Dark reanimate.

Taint.

'Give me back my friend,' Wilhelm said through gritted teeth. He turned away from Sebastien to look up at the castle. 'Let him go.'

He pulled, as hard as he could. He realised his eyes were open only when the dazzling brightness forced them closed. And there he felt the light coming for him, wanting to stamp him out, to crush him.

'Let him go!'

He pulled harder. The castle appeared to shift, turning

as though attached to a giant wheel. From behind him came a roar, and he turned just in time to see the reanimated swimming pool, now righted again, leap towards him. He jumped aside and it skidded over the edge and into the pit. A plume of orange sparks rose high into the air. Wilhelm stared at them, and he felt the magic staring back. It seemed to pause, stationary in the air, like a curious animal come to explore. Even as the light from the castle bombarded him, the glow from the pit grew as though rising up to match it.

A bridge.

I'm a bridge.

He stood up and walked forward. The edge of the pit loomed and for a second his heart was in his mouth as he stepped out into nothing. Then he was floating in the air, pulled from one side, buoyed from below. His heart raced as he walked further out over nothingness.

Then, closing his eyes, he began to push and pull all at once, drawing the world around him together.

40

BENJAMIN

It felt like a prison. Even though Dr. Forrest's eyes were his eyes, his soul his soul, his mind his mind, it felt alien. As though one day long ago when his brother had opened up a rift in the ground and pushed him through into another world, another world had also begun, and a different path had been taken. He was no more Dr. Forrest than he was Wilhelm, or Miranda, or Sebastien Aren, but here he was, shoehorned into a body which belonged to him only in name, in memory.

Dr. Forrest stood up. He lifted hands and looked down at them, turning them over, seeing real flesh and blood with only a hint of translucence.

'My innocence,' he whispered. 'Returned.'

Benjamin was nothing more than a passenger, trapped inside Dr. Forrest's body. He saw through Dr. Forrest's eyes, but it felt like looking through a train window. He was no more in control of what he saw than he was of the world rushing past.

'I thought I lost you,' Dr. Forrest was saying. Benjamin

was unsure whether his namesake was talking to him or musing idly to himself.

'You're still there, aren't you? In another time, another place. Another river flowing free through lands unscorched, untainted.'

Hands lifted to press against his forehead. 'I'll never forgive the day you left me.'

What day?

Benjamin couldn't answer. He was part of Dr. Forrest now, but he had no control over anything.

'How easy it is to throw something away. How easy to drop something into the bin, something unwanted, discarded and forgotten. Yet you torment me. If I can throw away a newspaper, an old book, why not a memory? Why do you torment me so after all these years? I have turned the whole world to forget you, but you still remain there, a taint, destroying me slowly, piece by piece.'

Riding inside Dr. Forrest's body, Benjamin wanted to frown, but the body that no longer responded to his instincts didn't react. Instead, he reacted by thought alone.

What memory?

'You should never have died,' Dr. Forrest was sobbing. '"Accidents happen," they told me, over and over again, patting me on the head like I was some kind of dog, their condolences only making worse what I had caused. It wasn't an accident. It never was. But that part, I blocked out. Why are you coming back to me now?'

Benjamin didn't understand. He felt a rage building inside the alien body he now shared.

'The taint, oh heavens, you're always with me. Even when I thought you were gone, you're still there, tormenting me.'

Dr. Forrest swung around, raising his hands in front of him, outlines now made flesh and blood curved into claws.

Benjamin tried to concentrate, tried to see what he could control, but as he was reaching out with his mind to try to flex the fingers he shared, the world lurched.

Dr. Forrest staggered as the castle shook. Lines of orange appeared in the walls as though someone had thrown watery paint over them.

'The taint....'

Benjamin concentrated ... and one finger moved.

'I thought ... I hoped ... no. I made a mistake.'

More colours were infiltrating the pure white of the castle walls. Benjamin heard a faint sound that sounded like a voice, one which might have been in his head.

'Benjamin!'

It sounded familiar.

It sounded like Wilhelm.

'Let him go!'

Dr. Forrest swung around again like some raging beast. Benjamin felt a wave of heat emanating from their shared body and the orange fled from the walls like spiders chased from a dark room.

'Get out! I shed you! I cast you off! Leave me alone!'

As Dr. Forrest raged, Benjamin could do nothing but remain party to what was going on. He felt certain his alter ego was a madman, yet at the same time this madman had once been the boy playing among the trees with his little brother when orange lights began to appear.

He was as much Dr. Forrest as Dr. Forrest was him.

Closing his eyes, he stopped trying to fight. Instead of battling to escape, he looked inwards, into the mind they now shared, searching for answers even as, on the outside, the body in which he was trapped continued to rage.

He saw wanderings, study, decades of learning, investigation, scientific experiments, thought experiments, mental examinations, and finally the understanding of the great power he had unleashed.

A power that could cleanse.

And Dr. Forrest had begun with himself.

Where was all the torment, the anger, the suffering which Benjamin himself felt as he battled for survival in Endinfinium? Even as a boy of thirteen he struggled with his own decisions every day, yet here, Dr. Forrest was a blank canvas, the only frustration, loneliness, anger, and self-pity coming from the soul of the boy who now tainted him.

Dr. Forrest had wanted his innocence back, but it came with a price: the layers of everything he had cast away.

But where had it gone?

In the deepest depths of Dr. Forrest's empty soul, Benjamin found the answer.

Another bridge.

One into another world, and another form, one who shared their name.

The Dark Man.

Everything Dr. Forrest had shed away, layer upon layer of his soul. Hoping to cleanse himself of every last regret, Forrest had embraced the magic he had discovered, but in doing so had left little of himself behind.

The pain ran too deep.

The Dark Man was taking over.

'Let him go!'

The voice felt right in front of him. Benjamin and Dr. Forrest opened their eyes. They gasped. There stood Wilhelm, a boy only one of them knew, his body trembling with a power that seemed to leech out of him as he stepped forward, his eyes glowing orange with the taint of dark reanimate.

'Let him go!'

The world churned. Benjamin sensed a great pulling, like a giant vacuum tugging on every fibre of his being. Before his vision blurred too much to make out what was happening, he saw Wilhelm reach down and put his hands on the floor, unleashing a flood of power as though Wilhelm was drawing on the power of every child who had walked up to the gates of this terrible place, using it to split two fused souls apart.

A moment of blackness. A loud pop, like a bubble bursting.

And Benjamin opened his eyes to see a hand reaching down for him.

'I think we'd better get out of here,' Wilhelm said.

41

SNOUT

Having entered Underfloor by mistake on the previous occasion, it took Snout some time to find a way in. With Little Tommy trailing at his shoulder, he walked along the corridors in the lower reaches of the school, tapping on walls, wishing he could remember what he had done to make one suddenly liquefy and allow him access. They had skipped out on lunch in order to give themselves time, but Tommy, as expected, was proving of little help.

'What if we see that girl?' he said.

Snout shook his head. 'I don't think we will. I think that was part of the Dark Reanimate Society's recruitment plan. If we achieved anything at all, it was to make them less bold.'

'If Adam's stuck in that tank with her, do you think they can talk to each other?'

Snout rolled his eyes. 'How would I know?'

'Do you think it's cold?'

Snout didn't bother with a reply. He quickened his pace, putting a few steps between them, continuing his frantic tapping on the walls. It was nice not to be alone down here in the gloom, but bringing Tommy as moral support was looking like a bad idea.

'What was that noise?'

'What noise?'

Tommy looked over his shoulder. 'I heard a growling sound.'

'Where?'

'Back there!'

Snout herded Tommy into a cubbyhole. At the far end of a side corridor came a flicker of light, followed by a growl.

'The incinerators,' Snout said. 'The rubbish must have reanimated again.'

He knew it happened from time to time. All the food waste and anything that had broken seemingly beyond repair was sent to a fire pit deep in the school's bowels. Unfortunately, once things began to burn, they also began to reanimate.

'What do we do?' Tommy hissed.

'Better not go that way,' Snout said, giving the side corridor a nervous glance before pushing Tommy on ahead of him.

They headed down another side corridor which led eventually to the locker room. Snout continued his furtive search for an entrance, while Tommy lingered behind, watching over his shoulder in case the creature being battled in the incinerator room should somehow escape.

Snout's stomach grumbled. He was about ready to give up when he felt a tingling sensation under his fingers.

'Tommy,' he called. 'Over here.' As the smaller boy approached, Snout reached out a hand. 'Hold on to me.'

'Do I have to?'

'Just do it. Then close your eyes if you want to. It feels

totally weird when you pass through the wall. Like you're in gunge or something.'

With Tommy holding on to him, Snout stepped forward. There was a momentary resistance before he stepped out into a corridor running adjacent to the one they had left.

'We made it.'

'Whoa, what's this place all about?' Tommy turned on his heels, taking in the dusty corridor which stretched away in both directions, half a dozen rooms' doors leading off, some open, leaving rectangles of light on the corridor floor.

'Underfloor,' Snout said. 'Where the reanimates live. I've been here approximately once more than you have.'

'Is it dangerous?'

'I don't think so, but again, don't go on everything I say.'

Snout began to move cautiously down the corridor. Even though he had been here as recently as a few days ago, something felt different. There was no sound, for one thing: on his previous visit he had heard the reanimates moving about, voices, even music. Now, nothing but silence punctuated by the occasional sound of water dripping, or the distant groan of some great internal mechanism shifting in the school's depths.

As he stepped through a door into a wide chamber, he understood. On the ground in front of him lay a sports car with eight arms and legs, like an octopus. Eyes that had once peered out of reanimated headlights were closed. Nearby was a tangled clothes horse, metal arms lying beneath a face made from a sculpture of pegs, as though it had lain down to sleep. In the middle of the room, two TVs had folded against each other like lovers frozen in time.

All around, the reanimates stood or lay in silence, unresponsive. Snout stepped among them with Tommy close behind, clutching his arm now, his breathing coming quick and sharp.

'Are they sleeping?'

Snout shrugged. 'I don't know. They look dead, but reanimates can't die. At least, I didn't think so. Not just like that, like humans can.'

'Well, they're not moving very much.'

They went out of the chamber and into an adjacent one. Through a door Snout found Moto, the motorbike, on his wheels, leaning on a kickstand. When he touched Moto's chassis, it felt cold.

'Moto?' he whispered. 'Are you in there?'

When he got no reply, he nodded at Tommy and they moved on. The next room was a wide ballroom, with a stage at one end and tables scattered about. Silent, immobile reanimates sat at the tables as though they had frozen in time, their lives switched off in a single instant. Snout felt a ghost of a shiver run down his back as he waved at Tommy to turn back.

'They've all shut down,' he whispered. 'It looks like we're too late.'

Unsure which way they had come, Snout turned down a side corridor. He took a couple of steps then paused, hearing a sound from up ahead. It sounded like coughing.

Moving slowly, he crept towards the sound, Tommy at his shoulder. They turned a corner and found an open doorway, a light glowing from inside. Another cough came, louder this time. Snout crept up to the door and peered through.

An old bureau, reanimated into curves with wooden shapes representing arms, leaned over a stack of papers on the floor. One wooden arm was darting about, scribbling down words with a pencil.

'Um ... excuse me?' Snout asked. 'Are you a reanimate?'

With a sudden squeal of alarm, the bureau jerked back and then jumped up into the air. It landed with a loud crash which threw up a plume of dust. A drop-down lid fell open and inside, two inkwells revolved like eyes.

'Who are you and what in all Endinfinium are you doing here?' came a rustling wail that it took Snout a moment to realise was caused by sheets of paper fluttering inside a thin drawer beneath the bureau's desk.

'Um, my name's Simon,' Snout said. 'I was looking for Moto, but it looks like he's not, um, working today.'

The bureau bounced up and down a couple of times, then fell still. It gave a long, juddering creak like a reanimate's version of a sigh, before rocking from side to side.

'They've gone into extended hibernation,' the bureau said. 'I, Laurel, the Historian of Underfloor, am the only one still left. And I have to say, I'm hating every minute of it. If it wasn't that someone had to keep a record of everything ... I'd be out like the proverbial light along with the rest of them.'

'Hibernating?' Snout said. 'Why?'

'Isn't it true that when a long winter comes in, all the animals back in your homeworld find somewhere warm to snuggle up and go to sleep until it's over?' Laurel said, still rocking from side to side.

'Well, some of them do, I suppose.'

'When something bad gets into our systems, that's what we do, too. There's a taint infiltrating the school. You're a human so you won't be able to feel it, because it's not in the air, or the food, or the ground, but in the magic that gives everything life. For us reanimates, it's like drinking dirty water. We'll only get sicker and sicker until something really bad happens.'

'Like what?'

'I'm not sure you want to know.'

'I do.'

Laurel bumped from side to side as though to shrug. 'Well, I can't tell you, because I don't remember. The last time it happened, I would have just been a wood shaving in my mother's eye.'

'But whatever it is, it's going to happen again?'

'No, because everyone has hibernated to stop it. However, someone has to record what happens, and that's my job. Although I'd love to be hibernating with the rest. It's extremely unpleasant being alive right now—'

Before he could finish, Laurel jerked forward, his lower cupboard doors bursting open. A spray of orange wood shavings burst out, scattering at Snout's feet. He hastily stepped back to avoid them as they glowed for a few seconds before going dark.

'Oh, my apologies, but that's better. I've been feeling queasy all day.' Laurel leaned sideways, his inkwell eyes revolving. 'What did you want, by the way?'

'I was looking for help. There's big trouble brewing in the school, and everyone seems on the wrong side. I have no idea what to do.'

'Why don't you ask that young Benjamin Forrest? He always seemed to have a knack of luck running his way at the right time.'

'He disappeared weeks ago. No one knows where.'

'Oh? It must have slipped my mind. I suppose you're on your own, then. If I can give you a word of advice, it would be to not give up. Endinfinium has been around for a lot longer than any of us—although I couldn't put a figure on how long, as the history books tend to reanimate after a while and rewrite themselves, the pesky things—but it's still here, isn't it? I'm sure it'll still be here after us reanimates are mere dust and you humans are all mindless cleaners.'

Snout grimaced. 'Thanks for the reassurance. I'll try to keep it in mind.'

'Well, I must get back to work—'

Laurel vomited again. This time Snout wasn't quick enough to avoid the expulsion of wood shavings which covered his shoes. As he kicked them off, he waved goodbye to Laurel, who had already turned back to the heap of shifting papers at his wooden feet.

Tommy, standing behind Snout, just gave him a shrug. 'Well, he said it,' he said.

'Said what? He didn't say much of anything.'

'Don't give up. He said that. More or less.'

Snout sighed. 'Well, we don't have a lot of choice. Come on.'

They headed back the way they had come. The door out of Underfloor had reanimated while they were searching, and had moved a few paces to the right, leaving them with a frustrating search before locating the way out. Back in the bowels of the school, it seemed like a chill had fallen over everything. Snout suggested they head for the library to see if Cleat could give them any advice, but Tommy appeared to be losing his nerve and muttered something about maths homework to finish.

As Tommy scampered off to the nearest stairs leading up into the world of light and relative safety, Snout felt more alone than ever. He headed for the library, but found it closed, a sign over the door announcing that Cleat would be back later. Not wanting to hang around, he headed down to the locker room, but to his astonishment found those closed too. Sliding glass doors had been pulled across, but when he peered through, Snout saw a chaos of reanimated objects milling around: pens flying about like birds, pencil cases crawling like caterpillars across the floor, metal chairs jousting and tables wrestling each other. Among the melee, several cleaners stumbled about, vainly spraying chamomile solution or trying to catch the flying objects in nets.

Snout backed off. Things were falling apart. The sin keeper had kept order in the locker room, but he hadn't been responsible for sending pupils down for punishment. Something else was amiss.

When he reached the main lobby, he headed for the reception desk, but Mrs. Martin was nowhere to be seen. A sign up on the window said she would be back soon. A spider made out of a reanimated paper clip had built a metallic web across one corner, suggesting the sign had already been there for some time.

Snout frowned. Where had everyone gone? He glanced up at the large clock high on the wall inside the main doors, but it had begun to reanimate, its hands spinning in both directions. He had never seen that happen before. Mrs. Martin had always given it a morning spray, but even had she not, it would surely last a few days before beginning to reanimate.

He turned at the sound of a rumbling behind him. At first afraid the ceiling was falling, he was relieved to see it was only the wooden banisters of the stairs to the upper lobby beginning to reanimate. His relief turned to fear, though, as the wooden posts broke free in a domino-like flurry, and a multi-headed snake reared at him, its attempted snap thwarted at the last moment by the fact that its tail was still fixed to the wall.

Afraid its next tug would break it free, Snout retreated

out of the main doors onto the series of terraces which fronted the school building.

He backed away as far as the main terrace would allow, until a low stone wall at his back was all that separated him from a bumpy tumble down to a rocky beach far below. From outside, the main entrance looked normal, a quiet lump of blocky concrete with tall glass walls. From around the headland to the south, though, came the rumble and crack of pieces of rock breaking away and falling into the sea.

Snout ran across the terraces, up and down short flights of concrete stairs, until he reached the southernmost terrace, which had a view of the south part of the main school building. From there, he could see the old science block hanging precariously out over the sea battering at the jagged cliffs far below.

It appeared to be vibrating, sparks bursting out of its roof, and from the sky above, a dark rainbow of various shades of grey flecked with burnt orange appeared to descend right into its depths. Unlike a regular rainbow, which was a static, colourful thing, this one seemed to be moving, like a waterfall of sadness pouring its grime in through the roof of the old science block.

Snout stared, his blood running cold. It came from the west, from the direction of the High Mountains.

Even Snout, who had always buried his head in the sand whenever possible, knew that the High Mountains was where the Dark Man lived.

42

MIRANDA

At first the bowels of the Shifting Castle looked no different to the lower corridors of Endinfinium High. Cold stone, sometimes carved, other times with brick or calcified plastic walls, as though great ancient buildings lay encased in the rock, soundtracked by distant dripping water and the rustle of cold, originless winds. Routes led off from all around, vanishing into the dark, only occasional reanimated lights set into the walls giving glimpses at the vast distances involved.

'Rosa, which way?' Miranda asked, after Olin had shrugged at her question.

The girl closed her eyes momentarily then pointed at the ceiling. 'Up,' she said.

'That's nice,' Olin said, 'However—'

'There's a shaft,' Miranda said, pointing. 'That bit there that's darker than the rest of the cave roof. I can feel the wind come down.'

'And how do you suppose we get up there?'

Rosa smiled. 'It's easy—'

'Wait!' Miranda said. 'If you use your magic, the Dark Man will be able to feel you. He'll know we're coming.'

Rosa shrugged. 'Not if we use his magic.'

Miranda shared a glance with Olin. 'What are you talking about?' the old man said.

'The dirty stuff.'

'You mean dark reanimate?'

Rosa rolled her eyes. 'I don't know your name you have for it, but it's the stuff that comes out of his castle.'

Olin was staring at her. 'You can use dark reanimate?'

'Don't be silly. It's not *mine*. I meant use his. It's everywhere. All we have to do is push it.'

Rosa, smiling, began to rise up into the air. Miranda concentrated, using her mind to feel for the magic, and found a condensed cloud of darkness around Rosa's feet, slowly expanding as it pushed her upwards.

Olin looked uncomfortable, but Miranda reached for his arm and pulled him close. As though rising up on a crane, the platform of darkness lifted them into the shaft above. As the cold rock walls closed in, Miranda hugged Rosa close, aware the little girl was controlling everything with a knowledge of magic Miranda couldn't begin to comprehend. Born into Endinfinium, Rosa could manipulate the reanimate as easily as if it were her own arms or legs.

A glimmer of light had appeared above them, when Rosa suddenly sagged.

'Heavy—'

Miranda grabbed her, holding her up. The press of the magic beneath her feet immediately began to loosen, only for it to suddenly tighten again and push them upwards far faster than before. As they burst out onto a rocky platform, the world seemed to groan all around them. Miranda looked up at the walls of the cavern, illuminated by grey light through openings in the walls, as well as hundreds of pinprick orange glows coming from deep inside the walls themselves.

'What happened?' she asked, as she sat up, still cradling Rosa against her.

Olin looked fearful. 'I had to help her,' he said. 'Her magic gave out.'

'Rosa, are you all right?'

The girl looked up. She blinked at Miranda and frowned, before seeming to remember where they were.

'Oh ... I felt dizzy all of a sudden, like I'd run out of air.'

From all around, came a great creaking sound. Miranda looked up and saw the walls nearby seeming to expand, great bubbles made of a thick grey tar appearing out of the stone, stretching out towards them. As the globules stretched tight, they became translucent, revealing writhing shapes trapped inside.

'What's that?' Miranda said. 'It looks like there's a person in there—'

'Get back!' Olin shouted as he climbed to his feet. He grabbed Miranda's arm and pulled her up. 'I don't think we want to know,' he said, waving at a corridor behind them. 'I really think we ought to—'

The nearest bubble exploded, showering them with lumps of stinking grey matter. With a banshee roar that felt like claws scraping the insides of Miranda's eardrums, something grey and ethereal stretched for them, its amorphous shape evolving arms and a head as it grew. A hole appeared in its head, stretching wide and deepening, a tint of burnt orange at the back of the creature's throat. With a jerk, it wailed again, sending them sprawling backwards as arms reached out, orange-tinted claws scratching at the air.

Rosa was closest. Miranda grabbed her arm and pulled her away as the claws closed over the space where the little girl's hands had been. The creature pawed at her, but a sudden howling wind rose from down the corridor behind them. Miranda braced herself as the air turned hot, forcing the creature to flinch back into the depths of its rocky prison.

'Move!' Olin shouted, sweat standing out on his brow. He lifted his hands, and the rocky edges of the burst bubble cascaded inwards, battering the creature as it struggled to escape. As the barrage subsided, it began to stretch out again, but by now they were out of range.

Nearby, however, other bubbles were beginning to rise, growing tight, set to burst. Olin pushed the girls towards the corridor, then lifted a hand. The ceiling exploded, rock crashing down to block the tunnel behind. Miranda frowned, aware the old wizard was using enough magic to reveal their position to the Dark Man, but knowing he had no choice. Through the barricade came the faint scream of the hideous grey creatures. As they emerged onto a wide internal courtyard over which massive, towering walls loomed, she was thankful for a few seconds of respite.

Olin pulled them into the shadows beneath an overhanging buttress. Miranda held a crying Rosa close and looked up at the old man.

'What happened back there?'

'The chamber of tormented souls,' Olin said. 'At least that's how it was described to me by a traveller I met years ago who was heading north. I think now he might have been one of Rosa's people, in search of adventure. He told me he found a way in, only to be confronted by those creatures. One grabbed his hand, revealing its secrets. Trapped in the rock for all eternity, they are looking for someone to replace them. Had they caught you, you would have become one and they would have walked free, restored to life. The man told me he had channeled every last drop of his magic just to break the hold, then fled for his life. When he found himself back outside the castle, he realised he was barren. All his magic was gone.'

'Luke,' Rosa said, wiping her eyes and taking a deep breath to calm herself.

'Who's Luke?' Miranda asked, leaning forward.

'A sleeper legend. We were told stories of him to get us to sleep at night. He possessed the tallest ladder in the land, but he wasn't content with it. He kept cutting down trees to make it longer, to climb higher. One day, he climbed so high he reached the clouds. He sat down to rest, but the ladder was so big it collapsed, leaving him trapped on the clouds forever.'

Olin lifted an eyebrow. 'Your people need to get more books.'

'It's just a story, though, isn't it?' Miranda said.

'Yes, but Luke was real. I could feel his trail.'

'Girl, you scare me,' Olin said.

'It's nothing much,' Rosa answered. 'People leave trails like pathways. I can feel them. Luke's always led out across the flower fields, heading north. It had faded with time, but one of the reasons we were never allowed to play outside was because some kids would wander off, following those trails, when they weren't even sure what they were following. I felt one of them in that room. It ended there.'

'Where he lost his magic,' Olin said. 'And luckily not his soul.'

'How did those souls get trapped there?' Miranda asked.

'That's a question for someone far more knowledgeable than me,' Olin answered. 'Luke—if that indeed was his name, for he never told me—claimed that the creature's touch had revealed its torment. They're souls stripped of all good, their very darkness helping to build the castle above them, as though they were part of its foundations. What I think you have to realise, is that of everything you've seen, it all ends here. The Dark Man got his name for good reason. Everything stripped of light and good and hope … it's here, a cauldron of constantly evolving suffering. I wish to all Endinfinium we weren't here, but since we are, let's hurry up and do what we have to do, shall we?'

Rosa pointed upwards. 'My father's up there,' she said. 'In that tower.'

Miranda looked up. The tower Rosa was pointing at was slowly moving along the wall, the part of the castle keep below it collapsing and rebuilding to allow its passage. It reached the end, suddenly dropped down like a needle piercing skin, before slowly rising again like a rocket preparing for take-off.

'If we had Enchantress with us, we could fly,' Miranda said. 'Unfortunately we don't.'

Olin shook his head. 'Don't even think about flying. See those things hanging from the wall?'

'Where?'

Olin pointed. Miranda noted how his finger was shaking. At first she thought she was looking at shadows beneath the tower, then she realised the angle of the light through the gloomy storm clouds overhead was wrong. The things looked like curtains, each as big as a sports field.

'Trash-dragons,' Olin said. 'They're like haulocks but much, much bigger. Industrial awnings fused with the scaffolding they used to cover.'

'Big plastic sheets?' Rosa asked.

As though to illustrate Olin's point, two massive black

wings suddenly billowed upwards from the outermost creature, stretching into the air before settling back down. As it shifted, Miranda caught sight of a thick, tube-like plastic body, at one end a maw filled with serrated teeth.

'Don't wake them up,' Olin said. 'I think it would be safer to take a route through the castle.'

The nearest door stood just along the wall. Miranda, still clutching Rosa, approached it, Olin close behind. They were within touching distance when it began to move, sliding along the wall, the rocks on either side knitting and separating to accommodate it.

'How are we supposed to get in?' Miranda snapped, unable to hide her frustration at the door moving away from them quicker than she could walk. 'I feel like we're playing some stupid game.'

Rosa shook her head. 'It's easy,' she said. She pushed away from Miranda and approached the wall. She lifted her hands and placed them on the rock, then looked back. 'These doors are for the castle's people. We need to make our own,' she said.

Miranda glanced at Olin as Rosa closed her eyes and let out a little growl of concentration. Olin just shrugged and shook his head, but to Miranda's amazement the bricks in the wall began to shift. Wood chippings appeared out of the cracks with the rustle of shuffling cards, forming into wooden beams and planks. In less than a minute, a door stood where there had previously been nothing.

'How on Endinfinium did you do that?' Olin said.

Rosa glanced back and shrugged. 'I'm not sure. I just told it what to do, that's all.'

As the little girl opened the door and ran inside, Olin turned to Miranda. 'Don't forget, she's not like us,' he said. 'She was born of this world, we weren't. She might be able to get us in, but if we lose her, we might have a hard time getting back out.'

'Is he watching us?' Miranda asked. 'The Dark Man?'

Olin glanced up at the tower, now settled into position as two smaller towers began to rearrange themselves. With a sigh, he shrugged. 'I'm not sure. I get the feeling he might be distracted. Just a thought, that's all.'

'I hope so.'

Rosa was waiting for them inside, a wide grin on her face as she stood at the foot of a staircase.

'I can feel him,' she said, bouncing up and down. 'My father, he's close!'

Rosa bounded straight up the stairs, leaving Miranda and Olin to hurry in her wake. As the staircase wound upwards, Miranda found herself tiring quickly. She reached out for the wall to take a momentary rest, only for a tickle of cold to run up her arms. Jerking her hands away, she brushed at her arms as though to shake off spiders, but it was some moments before the cold receded. Olin, a couple of steps behind, shook his head.

'Dark reanimate,' he said. 'This place was built with it. Touch as little of it as possible.'

They were nearly to the top of the stairs when they met Rosa coming back down. The hope they had seen in the little girl's face only moments before had gone, replaced by a look of terror that sent shivers down Miranda's back.

'Back down that way,' Rosa said, her voice trembling. 'They're coming.'

43

BENJAMIN

BENJAMIN HELD ON TO WILHELM'S ARM AS THEY RAN, the smaller boy waving his other arm about, creating what Benjamin could only describe as a rift through the fabric of existence. Where they came to an ethereal, translucent wall, Wilhelm waved his arm and an opening appeared like a hole melted in plastic, holding long enough for them to pass through. Where they came to a chasm between crystalline galleries, Wilhelm kicked at the ground and a molten, flowing walkway extended out of the surrounding floor to reach the other side. Running hard, soon they could see the lights of what remained of London appear through the last of the translucent walls, even as spiderwebs of orange-and-grey rose up everywhere around them.

'I think I made it sick,' Wilhelm said, glancing around them. 'I don't think Sebastien's magic was quite the same as yours.'

Benjamin, exhausted, managed a tired nod as Wilhelm bored a hole in the next wall. They stepped out onto a promenade surrounding the great pit. Ahead of them, a ring of grey marked the quarantine zone, before, some miles distant, the towers and high-rises of what remained of London began. Far below, orange lights sparkled within a sea of black, sending up acrid-smelling puffs of smoke which made Benjamin's throat burn. He gulped, trying to clear it out, but it only seemed to thicken, like oil pushing its way down his throat.

'Look at that,' Wilhelm said.

To their left, a massive tumbleweed reached the pit's edge. It paused a moment, before moving forward with a groan like an old galleon breaking up in violent waves. It dropped, breaking apart as it did so. They watched it plummet for a couple of seconds, then it vanished in an explosion of orange which had them both flinching back from the edge.

'I don't think we can go any further,' Wilhelm said. 'They're waiting for us.'

On the other side of the chasm, lines of dog-catchers crouched on the grey gravel, given away only by the sparking of their prods. They watched Benjamin and Wilhelm like an army waiting for the order to charge.

'We have to jump,' Wilhelm said. 'It's the way in, isn't it? Are you ready to go back?'

Benjamin turned to look at Wilhelm. He worked his mouth for a few seconds before he could find the strength to form words. 'Thank you for saving me,' he said. Then, with a wry smile, he added. 'I think.'

Wilhelm grinned. 'No problem.' He held out a hand. 'Together,' he said. 'Hopefully we'll wake up somewhere close.'

Benjamin gulped. He leaned forward, peering down at the maelstrom below. Wilhelm was right. It would take them back. Perhaps if he was lucky, he would wake up on the beach like he had before, when Miranda had saved him from the turtle-car, with sand in his shoes and his hair all messy, with the sensation that he had been sleeping for a very long time—

'No,' he said, turning to Wilhelm. 'This isn't it. This won't work.'

'Why not? It has to go to Endinfinium—'

'Yes, but it's too random. We have no idea when we'll wake up, if we ever will. Look at all these kids, and think about how few there are in the school. We could be buried for hundreds of years, or even end up as part of a ghoul. We have to get back to the same time and place we left.'

Wilhelm's shoulders slumped. 'And how do we do that?'

'We have to go back to where we came in.'

Wilhelm swung to face him. 'Basingstoke? How the blazes do you think we're going to get back there?'

Before Benjamin could answer, a loud crash came from behind them. They both turned to see the nearest wall shatter and collapse into a heap of glowing orange shards. Tendrils of steam rose from it. Benjamin was staring at them when a figure appeared through the haze.

Dr. Forrest. Where before he had been little more than a pencil outline of a human shape, now he had form and colour. He wore a grey suit with orange buttons, and an orange tie. Everything was charred and shredded as though he had dressed himself with the embers of a fire.

Benjamin took a step forward, but Wilhelm grabbed his arm. 'He's like the Grand Lord,' he whispered. 'You can see through him.'

The walls moved through Dr. Forrest's face as he smiled and lifted a hand. 'Come back to me, Benjamin,' he said, the soothing central column of his voice bringing with it a cacophonous grating like metal sheets being rubbed together. Benjamin felt Wilhelm clutching his arm as he shrank back, his heels teetering on the promenade's edge.

'Stay away from us!' Wilhelm shouted.

Dr. Forrest ignored him. 'I did so much good,' he said, his voice seeming to take away all other sound. 'I did so much good, and I did it all for you, boy. All to heal you. All to heal *me*.'

Benjamin shook his head. 'You're not me! Leave me alone!'

'I am what you'll become. It is not something you can change. Come back to me now, and save both of us years of suffering, of rage, of denial, of hatred—'

'Get away from him!' Wilhelm shouted, stepping forward and raising his hands. The ashes of the fallen wall plumed upwards, but Dr. Forrest lifted a hand of his own and brushed them aside. His eyes narrowed, taking on an orange tint.

'Look what you have done,' he said to Wilhelm. 'Everything was perfect until you brought in your taint, Bastien—'

Wilhelm screamed. Benjamin glanced at his friend and saw two people there: one solid, one ephemeral, a shadow moving separately to the body which carried it.

Sebastien Aren.

Grand Lord Bastien.

Benjamin looked back at Dr. Forrest. Around the man another shadow appeared. It glowed orange-and-black, wore a billowing cloak, and had eyes that were darker than the shadows in a nightmare.

The Dark Man.

Benjamin didn't think. He was Dr. Forrest and Benjamin Forrest and the thousand Benjamins in between. He was a Summoner, a controller of great magic, the magic that he himself had, in another world, helped to create. The magic that could cleanse, and create life.

And create suffering.

The itch in his hand was back, the itch caused by a long-ago night when a tainted creature had scratched him, leaving him with the ability to touch both sides of the abyss at once.

He reached out for Wilhelm and took hold of his friend's arm, then looked up at Dr. Forrest, The Dark Man, and the residue of himself.

'Back,' he said.

～

The castle was crumbling. Benjamin stared as a crystalline tower spider-webbed with orange came crashing down, vanishing into the centre of the castle's main keep. All around him rubbish billowed as a stunning wind came up from the great pit. He reached out for Wilhelm, who was crawling across the gravel, and pulled his friend close. Something hard struck his back and he groaned, watching as a crushed cardboard box from some long-removed toy bounced merrily away in the direction of London.

Beside him, Wilhelm was laughing. 'And I thought I'd made a mess,' he said, coughing, before patting Benjamin on the shoulder. 'Wow, that was something else.'

Benjamin glanced back. An entire section of the castle had collapsed across the pit, leaving a tumbling, jagged slope down which he vaguely remembered rolling. Back up in the castle, there was no sign of Dr. Forrest or the Dark Man who had briefly revealed himself as a plume of orange-grey smoke rose into the sky. Benjamin turned to Wilhelm and helped his friend to his feet.

'We have to get as far away as possible,' he said. 'I'm not sure what I did, but I don't think it'll last long.'

'We have trouble already,' Wilhelm said, pointing to the right, to the admissions building which was now missing a roof. Outside, the dog-catchers, initially scattered in the explosion, were beginning to regroup, advancing across the gravel field towards them.

No longer human, their eyes glowed dark orange.

'Ghouls,' Wilhelm said. 'They hide themselves better here than they do in Endinfinium. Come on, I have an idea.'

Wilhelm took over, pulling Benjamin around and pointing to a battered car sitting on the other side of a tall fence.

'There's our ride.'

Holding on to each other, they staggered to the fence. Benjamin, so weary he could barely keep to his feet, closed his eyes and began searching for his magic.

'Don't bother, I've got this,' Wilhelm said.

Benjamin opened his eyes. With a smile, Wilhelm lifted a hand and pointed it at the fence. Wires uncurled and drew back amidst a flurry of orange sparks, offering them a way through.

'Easy, isn't it?' Wilhelm said, winking. 'A shame I don't think it'll last much longer.'

Benjamin didn't have time to ask him what he meant. The dog-catchers at the front of the line had broken into a run, while behind them others were retreating to their vehicles. The car Wilhelm had indicated had once been Sebastien's vintage car, but now looked like a model kit hastily put together and then stamped on by a petulant child.

'That thing's not going anywhere,' Benjamin said.

'Not yet it isn't,' Wilhelm said, his eyes narrowed in concentration. 'We have to wake it up first.'

He pulled open a battered door and climbed inside, moving across to the driver's side so Benjamin could squeeze in. He managed to get the door shut just as the first dog-catchers burst through the fence and surrounded the car.

Benjamin lifted his hands. 'I won't let them take us—'

'Not them,' Wilhelm said. 'Ignore them.' He punched the dashboard. 'Help me wake it up.'

'How?'

'You're free of him now. Do what you did before.'

Benjamin closed his eyes. Wilhelm was right, it was back. Like a slowly budding flower, his magic was growing within him.

'I don't have much left,' Wilhelm said. 'I think Sebastien was kind of unique, you know, but he wasn't all-powerful like that so-and-so we just met—get away!'

The dog-catchers had reached the car and the closest were banging on the doors. Benjamin held his shut as the nearest man tried to pull it open, his teeth gritted, his narrowed eyes glowing orange.

'Quick, Benjamin!'

'What do I do?'

'Tell it where to go!'

Benjamin let go of the door handle and twisted around, grabbing hold of the old car's gear lever. He stared at the dashboard, wondering what on earth he could say to make this car do what he wanted. They were in London, but he wasn't even sure whereabouts. Perhaps if he could see a landmark or two ... he shook his head. No, it wouldn't work. How did you give directions to a magical car?

'Hurry up!'

'I'm thinking!'

'They're getting in!'

One of them had jammed his electric prong into a gap in the buckled passenger door and was trying to lever it open. Wilhelm hung on to the handle as sparks crackled and popped along the edge of the metal frame.

In seconds the dog-catchers would be inside. Benjamin's throat felt dry, his mind empty. In desperation, he put his hands on the dashboard and said the first word that came into his head.

'Home. Go home.'

The car jerked, bouncing up into the air. The closest dog-catcher screamed as he was lifted off the ground and then thrown off. The car revolved, sending Benjamin and Wilhelm into a spin, then plummeted. Just before it hit the ground, its wheels creaked with a sudden violent groan, and shiny metallic appendages appeared where its axles had been. Resembling an awkward lizard, the car spun around and rushed back through the throng of dog-catchers, knocking aside those too slow to get out of the way.

'Where's it going?' Wilhelm shouted. 'Basingstoke is behind us.'

Benjamin was about to answer when he saw a shape lying in the gravel up ahead, not far from the edge of the pit. A maelstrom of rubbish blew over their heads, and he ducked down as old cereal boxes, broken picture frames, discarded newspapers, and unwanted kitchen utensils battered against the windscreen of the reanimated vintage car.

'Sebastien!'

The car bumped down beside the old man's body, creating a barricade between the pit's edge and the man. Wilhelm and Benjamin exchanged a look, then both nodded and jumped out. Sebastien was breathing, but his eyes were closed. Together, they hauled him up and dragged him into the car's back seat, clicking a seat belt around his shoulders.

They were barely back in their seats when the lizard-car began to move again. It turned against the raging torrent of rubbish and leapt high into the air, over the heads of the dog-catchers as they tried to re-group. One thrown electric prong sparked as it struck the lizard-car's rear leg, provoking a grating roar before it touched down, coiled like a frog, then leapt back into the air.

Wilhelm, hanging on to the steering wheel, turned to Benjamin. With his cheeks pale and his eyes wide with terror, he gasped, 'I suppose we'd better put our seat belts on.'

Benjamin, realising he was still gripping the door handle with both hands, could only nod.

As the lizard-car leapt and scuttled through the streets in a direction only it understood, Benjamin felt a little comfort at the sight of other objects swiftly reanimating. They passed a bus which was standing on end like a dinosaur, a mouth formed out of its lower fuselage howling up at the sky while people who had recently been passengers fled out of range. On one street they passed, a line of black rubbish bins, strapped into place to prevent them flying away, rattled out a cacophonous harmony as they clacked their lids up and down. On another, the progress of a construction job had been halted by a scaffolding rig which had reanimated and now hung from the building it had surrounded like a giant, metallic spider.

'You've turned the world crazy,' Wilhelm said, as they bounced through a field across which hundreds of racing toy cars bashed and rammed each other in a giant, microcosmic demolition derby.

'I'm not sure what I did,' Benjamin gasped. 'Or what you did, either. I'm not even sure if we won or lost.'

'A bit of both, I reckon,' Wilhelm said. 'We got you out, but that's about it.'

'The others?'

'The Miscreants?' Wilhelm shook his head. 'I think that was their curse,' he said. 'They were part of it.'

As London faded behind them, giving way to meadows, dual carriageways, and single-street country towns, the signs of reanimation became less and less. They passed one giant tumbleweed which was rocking back and forth as though unsure what to do. A few minutes later, the car bounced down rather heavily and didn't spring back up again. Benjamin leaned out of the window and saw that the front left appendage had become a regular wheel all over again.

Finally, with one last crushing bump, they came to a stop.

'Is everyone still alive?' Wilhelm muttered, wiping dust off his brow. He peered out of the cracked windscreen and gave a gasp of surprise. 'Well, look where we are.'

Benjamin went to open the door, but it dropped off in the street. He looked up and found they were outside Sebastien's shop. Besides a few parked cars, the street was deserted, as though a sudden curfew had been called.

'Is he all right?' Wilhelm asked, nodding at Sebastien.

The old man was sleeping soundly, his breathing laboured but steady. Still strapped into his seat, it appeared he had passed the journey better than either of them.

'Let's get him inside,' Benjamin said.

The shop was unlocked. Together, they carried Sebastien out of the car, through the shop, and into his office back room. Both groaning from the effort, they lowered him down into an old armchair and arranged him so he looked peaceful. Despite patting his cheek a few times, the old man didn't stir.

Benjamin turned on the TV and found a news station. A scrolling headline announced CHAOS IN LONDON: VIOLENT ATTACK ON DR. BEN FORREST.

A distant helicopter view showed rising plumes of orange smoke above the peaks of Dr. Forrest's castle. In a split-screen shot panning around the quarantine area around the pit, they saw an endless field of rubbish, all of it rocking and shaking like the surface of an argumentative sea. Every so often, something expelled from the pit would crash down into the surface and settle among the rubbish, while larger items occasionally stood up like tourists emerging from a swim, newly formed appendages moving them through the shallows.

The shot changed, of a reporter standing on a London street, a scene of chaos behind him, as police made a barricade against a line of metal chairs advancing like soldiers.

'Covent Garden High Street's branch of Emilio's closed just yesterday,' the reporter said. 'Instead of assimilating with the nearest tumbleweed as expected, the furniture has been waging a pitched battle against police....'

'It's madness,' Benjamin said. 'What did we do?'

Wilhelm turned to him. 'I think I know,' he said. He lifted his hands and stared at them. From the moment Sebastien … joined with me, I've felt things that I've never felt before. When I pulled you back out of Forrest, I think I opened a door.'

'A door? What are you talking about?'

'All that stuff that goes in that pit, including all those kids, it all ends up in Endinfinium, right? Kind of like

Endinfinium is a dump for everything this world doesn't want. Only, I think—for a while, at least—I reversed it.'

'So, you mean stuff's started coming back through?'

'Well, maybe not stuff, but the … you know, the bad energy.'

'Dark reanimate?'

Wilhelm shrugged. 'If that's how you want to call it. Like, in Endinfinium, reanimates don't attack people, do they? They generally leave us alone. But those ones we saw, they were dangerous. The only ones in Endinfinium that are dangerous are *his* ones. The ghouls, and the other bad stuff *he* makes.'

'The Dark Man?'

Wilhelm looked down. 'I don't like saying his name. Not because I think he's you, but you know, it kind of makes me feel weird.'

'Weird?'

'Like if I say his name, he'll know. Like when Sebastien gave me his power, he gave me a connection to the, um, Dark Man, too.'

'A taint?'

'Something like that.'

Benjamin closed his eyes. He concentrated on the world around him, feeling for magic and magic users. Beside him, where Wilhelm stood, he felt nothing, but also something. And that something sparked with dark reanimate, as though someone had poured a handful of orange into a pot of blue paint.

'I can feel him,' he said. 'He's in you, but he's not part of you. He's like a passenger.'

Wilhelm grimaced. 'While I liked having a go with the magic, that's just strange,' he said. 'He'll be watching everything I do. Like when I go to the toilet or something.'

Benjamin rolled his eyes. 'I don't think he'll care about that.'

'I hope not.'

'You're right, though. There's a taint. There's some dark reanimate in him.'

'He told me some adults had it, too. Perhaps old people aren't pure like we are. Wow, that's got to be the first time I've ever thought of myself as pure.'

Benjamin was about to reply when the news report changed. A woman reporter this time was speaking from inside a car racing along a motorway. Over her shoulder, a pair of police cars, their lights flashing, could be seen through the rear window.

'While the commotion around the Exclusion Zone appears to be dying down, the hunt is on for rogue creatures which have spread across the country, to capture or neutralise them before they cause too much damage. Police and several military battalions have joined the Department of Civil Safety in hunting these creatures down. One was seen earlier today, entering the outskirts of Basingstoke, and we've received word that it was spotted just minutes ago on Remington Street, not far from the local railway station.'

As though on cue, the sound of distant helicopter blades came from overhead. Benjamin turned to Wilhelm, who was staring at the ceiling.

'Is that what I think it is?'

Wilhelm looked at him. 'They've found us,' he said.

44

SNOUT

Whatever was happening to the old science block was sending shudders through the rest of the school. Plumes of dust coated Snout as he ran back through the main lobby and up the stairs to the corridor leading to the causeway over to the dormitory building. All his fanciful ideas had left him at the sight of the orange-grey rainbow and the horrors it implied. Through the confusion of his thoughts all he could think about was getting back to the dormitories and checking that the other kids were safe.

He was only halfway along the corridor when a door burst open and something came rushing out. Snout dived sideways as what he could only describe as a centipede created out of a dozen wooden desks all reanimated into a line burst out of the room, crashed into the opposite wall and went scuttling away down the corridor. As it reached the stairs down to the lobby and went out of sight, Snout put a hand over his thumping heart until he could find the strength to climb back to his feet. He had taken no more than a couple of steps, though, when the doors on either side began to open and slam in unison. Snout backed from side to side, avoiding each in turn, only for one to snap off its hinges, dart at him and wrap wooden arms around his shoulders.

With a scream he threw it off and broke into a run, reaching the doors out onto the causeway, which thankfully hadn't reanimated. Behind him, the doors of a dozen classrooms clacked and slammed. He pulled open the causeway doors and stepped outside, not bothering with a Scatlock cape, just wanting to be out of the hastily reanimating building. Whatever was pouring into the old science block was slowly spreading out, filling the rest of the school with its disease. While the true reanimates had gone into hibernation, dozens of mindless ones were awakening to cause havoc.

Running quickly across the causeway, he slipped inside the door on the other side and was immediately halted in his tracks by the sound of Godfrey's voice from the common room. Creeping up to the closed door leading through, Snout pressed his ear to the wood to listen.

'Enough is enough! They've all disappeared, leaving us alone! Have you seen the chaos out there? The whole school is falling apart, and where are the teachers when we need them? When it's homework, or exams, or stupid gym tests, they're all over us. When it's about our own safety, they're nowhere to be seen. We need to protect ourselves.'

A chorus of 'yeahs' rose in response.

'They've let us down one too many times!' Godfrey shouted. 'I say we kick them out, and we join together to end this mayhem. My good friend Derek and I have found out what we need to do. Come with us and we'll stop this. We can do it together.'

More 'yeahs.' Someone near the back raised a voice in opposition, so Snout pressed his ear closer to hear better.

'Oh, you think so, do you? You think they're out there protecting us? So where's Gubbledon gone, then? I tell you, he's gone with them. They've all run away, protecting themselves, the teachers and the reanimates both. How many times do you need to be lied to? They had me living in their stupid tower, and do you know what I overheard? Lies. Rubbish. Nothing about us at all. Everything was about protecting themselves. We became too much of a hindrance to them, so they've fled, leaving us to fend for ourselves. All this talk about a Dark Man, it's just a fairy story to protect their own interests. Dark reanimate? What's that? Another side of the same coin, a coin none of us are permitted to spend. Aren't you tired of being pushed around, made to go and sit in those horrible lockers for hours on end over a single missed deadline? Aren't you sick of their oppression?'

'Yeah!'

'Then let's go. Come with Derek and me. Let's find what rock they're hiding under, and let's kick them out. Endinfinium High belongs to us.'

Snout's hands were shaking. He wanted to turn and run, but was rooted to the spot. From the sound of chairs and tables rattling, he could tell Godfrey had worked the kids up into a frenzy. He wanted to turn and run, but where could he go? The school was turning into a monster. The orange-grey rainbow was invading the old science block, the reanimates had hibernated and the teachers and staff had all vanished.

He needed allies, but they were all on the other side of the door, being brainwashed.

There was only one thing—

The door burst open, and Snout tumbled forward into the room. He hit his forehead on a table and sat up dazed as Derek's sneering face peered down into his own.

Standing on a table nearby, Godfrey, snake-green eyes wide with fury, turned to glare at him.

'Looks like we found a spy from the teachers,' Derek said.

Snout rubbed his head and looked up. He saw eyes he recognised among the crowd: Cherise, Tommy, the kids from the horticultural society he considered his friends. All of them stared at him with undisguised anger.

'The king of all swots,' Derek said, shaking his head. Then, lifting his hands and bending them over as though he were riding an imaginary horse, he said in a tittering voice, 'Oh, Ms. Ito, would you like me to polish your leg cast? Oh, Professor Loane, how nice your hair looks today. Oh, Mistress Xemian, please give all of us more homework, we really don't want time to ourselves, we want to study all the time—'

'Swot!' came a sudden chant. 'Swot, swot, swot!'

'Spy!' Godfrey shouted, and the others took up the chant: 'Swot spy, swot spy, swot spy!'

Snout was barely aware of being pulled to his feet and dragged forward. An eraser bounced off his forehead, and a hole-punch narrowly missed his right ear. He was pulled up onto the table in front of Godfrey and then pushed down to his knees.

'What should we do to him?' Godfrey shouted.

'Throw him out for the scatlocks,' someone shouted.

'Take him to the haulock cave!' shouted another.

'Leave him on the beach for the turtle-cars!'

'Lock him up in Gubbledon's coffin!'

Snout caught Tommy's eyes as the boy he thought was his friend shouted an idea that had others all around him nodding. Gubbledon, the reanimated corpse of a racehorse, slept in a wooden box in a cellar under the dormitory floor. It was something the big kids did as a joke to the newer kids if they could get away with it. With Gubbledon usually around somewhere nearby, a "dunk in the horsebox" as it was known, was rarely longer than a couple of minutes. With Gubbledon seemingly absent, Snout had no clue how long he might be stuck inside.

He might never get out.

Too late to back away, hands were already grabbing at him, dragging him forward. He saw Godfrey laughing, Derek leering with his tongue out, a couple of older boys slapping their knees. Kids Snout had always considered his friends holding his arms or pushing him in the back, while others led the way to the basement stairs.

He couldn't hear the creak of the stairs beneath his feet over the baying of the animal-like crowd, but the growing chill in the air and the impending darkness brought back uncomfortable memories of his first week at the school when a couple of older boys had dragged him down here. Rather than the slight angle of his nose, it had been the way he had cried to get let out that had gained him the nickname Snout, a hated name which had stuck ever since. Even though he had only been locked in the coffin for a couple of minutes, it had felt like hours.

It waited around the corner at the bottom of the stairs. Godfrey, at the front, clicked on a light. Far from the usual cellar, Gubbledon's room looked like the backstage of a cabaret, with ridiculous costumes hanging from hooks on the walls, three different salvaged dressing tables, hand mirrors, brushes, and pots of makeup covering every surface. On the walls hung paintings and framed photographs of racehorses and show dancers, a clash which made a person feel awkward, unsure where to look.

Derek and a couple of others hauled the coffin lid open. The pink satin cushions that lined the inside couldn't hide the smell of corpse. Even from halfway up the steps

Snout could smell it, and as they dragged him closer he started to scream, fighting to get away. He caught one fifth year with a lucky haymaker, only to get a heavier one in response, with someone else kicking him in the stomach to wind him. The last face he saw as he was unceremoniously dumped into the coffin was Derek's, a leer on his hated roommate's face as he slammed the lid down.

Snout screamed and thrashed about, knocking the stinking pillows aside, banging on the lid. From outside, he heard muffled discussion on how to secure it, followed by the sound of a large object being dragged across the floor. A collective groan came, then something heavy bumped on top of the lid, making the wood creak. Snout shoved, but whatever was on top weighed far too much.

'Enjoy your sleep, Pig Boy!' came Derek's voice through the wood, followed by laughter, which quickly receded up the stairs as the kids headed back up to the common room. Snout heard the muffled thump of another door, then the creak of footsteps. Occasional loud proclamations were audible, but not the words. After another couple of minutes he heard one more door slam, followed by silence.

He could have gone on screaming forever, but it would have achieved nothing. He was alone, and there was no way to get out. His only option was to call the ghouls, but he had no way of knowing what destruction that might cause. He might be able to call just one to help him, if one was sleeping in the rock beneath the dormitory. So tentatively he felt outwards, but Godfrey had left a ward around the coffin, like a thick globule of treacle through which Snout's efforts couldn't penetrate.

Well and truly stuck, he could do nothing but lean back on the filthy pillows on which their housemaster slept, and try not to go insane.

45

MIRANDA

'Move!'

The scuttling things looked like cardboard boxes with spiders' legs. Only as one got caught in the light from a candelabra did Miranda see that the monster's appendages were actually reanimated plastic ties still fixed to the boxes that had become the creatures' bodies. She counted ten before she lost count, but many more were crowding around the distant corner behind the first group, then Olin was grabbing her shoulder and throwing her in front of him.

'I said, move! We're not playing games in the school now, girl. These are his creatures. They'll rip you apart!'

Rosa was already running, her feet clattering on the corridor far ahead. Miranda sprinted after her, aware of Olin's heavy breathing slowly lagging behind. As Rosa paused at an intersecting corridor up ahead, Miranda stopped too.

Olin had paused, breathing heavily as he leaned on his knees. The scuttling things came on, crowding the far end of the corridor. A couple near the front paused, their forelegs bending to angle their box-like bodies in a forwards slant. Flaps opened on top of each, and a barrage of projectiles arced in Olin's direction. One was a slew of comic books, another small plastic packets. A third fired a single broken coffee maker which reanimated mid-flight into something hideous with a snapping plastic mouth.

Olin lifted his hands and his magic knocked them aside, smashing them against the walls. The scuttlers came on, but the floor at Olin's feet rose like a wave, rippling back down the corridor to throw the nearest back into those coming behind. As the creatures struggled to regroup, Olin looked back at Miranda and Rosa.

'Get out of here! I'll hold them! Go!'

Miranda stared at him. Part of her wanted to rush to the old man's aid, but another part realised he was putting himself on the line to give them a chance. The scuttlers were bunching up at the corridor head; when they rushed him, Olin would be overwhelmed. He was drawing a line, making a last stand, one which might give them enough time. She lifted a hand.

'Thank you,' she mouthed.

Olin grinned. Then, turning back to the swarm of scuttlers, he lifted his arms and sent another ripple through the flagstones, knocking the creatures away. Miranda watched for a few seconds longer as around Olin the walls bulged then burst open, and dozens more scuttlers rushed forward to engulf him. With tears in her eyes, she turned and fled.

Rosa was waiting around the corner, her back pressed against the wall. 'What happened to Olin?' she asked, but Miranda shook her head.

'It's just us now.'

Rosa's face screwed up and for a moment she looked

about to burst into tears. Then, getting hold of herself, she looked at her feet. 'I'm ... sorry.'

'It was his choice. Now, quickly, let's get out of here before those things catch up with us.'

'It's this way,' Rosa said, pointing. She broke into a run, with Miranda hurrying to keep up as the girl scurried off into the gloom of a connecting tunnel. A moment after Miranda had turned the corner, the castle groaned around her and the walls began to shift. In moments the way they had come was gone, and a new corridor had taken its place.

Miranda took one last look at the blank wall behind which Olin had stood against the swarm of scuttlers, then turned and ran.

∽

After half an hour of following Rosa through narrow corridors and up steep staircases, Miranda was exhausted. As they emerged onto a long gallery in the process of realigning itself, she called the girl to a halt.

'Are we close?' she asked, squatting down, peering over a balustrade at the courtyard now far below as the far end of the gallery began to swing around to join with the opposite wall.

Rosa frowned. 'I thought so, but I'm not sure now.'

'What do you mean?'

'Well, I was following a thread, but it ended.'

'Where did it end?'

'Down in that corridor with those horrible spidery things.'

Miranda frowned. 'But that was ages ago! You mean we've been wandering around in circles ever since?'

Again Rosa looked about to cry. 'I was scared. I was

trying to find it again.' As a tear dribbled down the little girl's cheek, Miranda pulled her close. With such a command of the magic that permeated everything, it was easy to forget that Rosa was only a child.

'Don't worry, we'll find him,' Miranda said, even though she felt anything but confident. They had lost Olin, and they had no idea where they even were. How could they possibly find a prisoner in a castle that was constantly shifting?

Around them, the floor began to rumble. Miranda stepped back as a sudden chasm opened where she had been standing. A hissing sound came from down in the dark, and she backed away, pulling Rosa with her.

'I think we'd better keep moving,' she said. 'I don't think it's safe to stay still for too long.'

They headed back into the castle, but as one corridor turned into the next, Miranda had the increasing feeling that they were going around in circles, wasting time. Olin had sacrificed himself to give them a chance, but they were in danger of wasting it. Sometimes, when they paused to choose a direction, she would hear the creeping of undesirable creatures back in the dark, as though the denizens of this gloomy and miserable place were slowly getting closer, biding their time before revealing themselves.

Miranda was about to give up hope when they rounded another corner and found themselves faced with a pair of large wooden doors. Miranda approached and pressed an ear against the wood. From inside she heard voices, a series of quiet whispers which sounded like someone reading a lullaby. Miranda's skin immediately began to crawl and she backed away, only to bump into Rosa.

The little girl was beaming at the door, her mouth agape.

'Here,' she said. 'This is it.'

Miranda closed her eyes and felt outwards, feeling for magic. Through the doors she sensed a whirlpool of darkness, a thousand fibres entwined. She opened her eyes and shook her head.

'I really don't think it's a good idea to go in there.'

'We have to. I think my father is inside.'

Miranda shook her head again. 'We can't just walk in through the front doors. There must be a window somewhere.'

Rosa didn't appear to hear her. 'This is it, I'm sure.'

'We can't just go in there. There's only the two of us, and the Dark Man could be in there, and—'

Rosa smiled. 'We can make them come out.'

'How?'

Rosa wiped tears out of her eyes and grinned. She looked like a girl shrugging off a playground fall by preparing to race back into a playtime battle. 'We prank them.'

'This isn't some silly game—'

But even as Miranda spoke, ideas started to rattle around in her head. They didn't have the strength to face the Dark Man, but she had seen with her own eyes that the Shifting Castle was unstable. Perhaps there was a way to turn it on itself that would work to their advantage.

'You might be on to something,' she said. 'Wait here.' She turned and jogged a few steps back up the corridor, then stopped. She looked at Rosa. 'I have an idea. When I come back and I start shouting, bang on that door as loud as you can.'

She didn't wait for Rosa to nod. She was caught up in her plan, but she knew if she wasn't quick about it, the castle would shift, cutting them off from each other. As she ran back the way they had come, hoping that some part of the gallery they had just left was still open to the courtyard below, she searched inside herself for her magic, for the Channeller's power she had suppressed on Olin's insistence for fear it would bring them unwanted attention. Now she called it, wanting it to shine bright, wanting every eye in the Shifting Castle to turn towards her.

The castle's corridors had shifted, but a small space was still open, allowing her to squeeze through, back onto the gallery. Leaning over the balustrade as rising gusts of freezing wind battered her crimson hair around her shoulders, she reached out with her magic, pulling as Edgar Caspian had long ago taught her, concentrating on the air itself, squeezing it into a sphere that hung above the courtyard, letting the crushed air heat itself until it began to glow like a fireball. Then, concentrating with all her energy, she flung it at the giant black shapes hanging from the eaves beneath the opposite tower.

It struck the back of one of the trash-dragons, exploding outwards, smaller pieces striking the two on either side before dissipating back into the air.

The disturbance worked. With a sudden shuffle of its wings, the middle trash-dragon twisted, breaking away from the wall, knocking those either side as its huge body shifted.

Miranda lifted a hand and gave a frantic wave. 'Over here!'

Easily as long as a bus, the immense creature twisted in the air, two huge wings billowing, a jerking tail holding it steady as it swung to face her. Out of the dark folds of its body Miranda couldn't identify which part was supposed to be its head, because it was unlike other dragons she had seen. Despite the name Olin had given it, it had no resemblance to the dragons she had seen in books, or even those she had seen far north of the school at the Bay of

Paper Dragons. It was a gigantic black tube with wings, a pulsing wire frame giving it shape.

With a sudden roar that sounded like a train's foghorn blaring right into Miranda's ear, its maw opened. In the moments before her nerve failed her, Miranda was reminded of the great lethargic basking sharks she had seen in books in the dormitory, their huge mouths stretched impossibly wide to draw in as much plankton as possible. With the trash-dragon, instead of an empty hollow, she saw row upon row of jagged teeth.

Her knees sagged as it rushed forward, crossing the courtyard with stunning speed, its huge wings billowing like sails, its tail flicking up and down as it rode the massive undercurrents its wings were creating. Miranda grabbed the balustrade to stop herself falling and shoved herself backwards as the trash-dragon struck it. Its body was close enough to touch as its maw enclosed the entire area on which she had stood. With a sudden crunch its jaws closed, reducing solid rock to gravel.

Miranda was still too stunned to move. She stared at it, so close she could reach out and touch its hard, oil-black body. Only when its wings billowed to push it back, at the same time blowing her back to her feet, did she find the compulsion to move. She turned, rushing for the hole in the wall, making it only a second before another massive trash-dragon struck the gallery, crushing another section of masonry. With her heart thundering, Miranda looked down at a gaping chasm opened up just inches in front of her feet.

Then, finally, the need to run kicked in. The trash-dragons were behind her, biting their way through the wall. Miranda bolted, fists clenched, running as hard as she could across the flagstones as the largest of the creatures forced itself inside. Glancing back as she reached a corner, she saw how it had elongated, its body narrowing to allow it to fit the smaller space. Its wings condensed and became hooked along the edges, turning into claws to propel it along the walls.

Only its mouth seemed as large as before, its teeth glittering in the lights of the candelabras smashed from their fittings as it rushed up the corridor in pursuit of her.

'Rosa!' Miranda screamed. 'Rosa! Get ready!'

She rounded the last corner. The trash-dragon was so close she could feel the walls trembling around her. She saw the doors to the chamber, saw Rosa standing in front of them, the little girl's smile turning to an expression of dumb horror.

'Rosa! The doors!'

The girl shook her head as though to rouse herself. She dragged her eyes away from the creature at Miranda's back, turning to the doors. She lifted her hands, and with a sudden jolt Miranda felt shudder through the floor, used her magic to break the doors open.

Miranda caught a momentary glimpse of a room filled with a maelstrom of swirling colour, a cloaked figure with its arms raised on a dais in the centre suspended by chains from the ceiling high above, and a ring of human-shapes tied to stone pillars in a circle around it. As she dived aside, striking the ground hard, Miranda closed her eyes and saw a hundred threads of magic all entwined. Those tied to the stone pillars were leeching out into the rock, which was feeding across the floor into the pedestal upon which the cloaked figure stood.

Light reanimate mingled with dark to form a column growing in the room's centre to engulf the cloaked figure. Miranda opened her eyes, seeing smoke where the magic had been, a growing column spinning faster and faster. As she stared, the figure at its centre seemed to lose its form, first becoming translucent then breaking apart into a hundred different shades, like a man transformed into a stack of cards. It was hard to see one in front of the other as they were constantly shifting, as though the figure were altering its form but hadn't decided which one to take.

The raging trash-dragon slammed straight into the column and immediately dissolved. A plume of grey-orange spread out across the lines of colour. The room shook, and Miranda covered her face as a sudden cloud of fluttering creatures exploded out through the doors. Like a swarm of bats, they engulfed her and Rosa before passing on down the corridor, battering at the walls and ceiling. In the room through the doors, the towering column began to shake. The figure's arms fell as it staggered, falling to one knee. As the cards of its form shuffled, Miranda caught a momentary glimpse of a face she knew

(Benjamin)

and then it was gone, the man in the cloak again taking control. Something else was happening, though. Rocks had begun to break free of the walls, and for the briefest of instances, the entire castle became suddenly translucent, flaring with sudden white light. The figure on the dais flickered white, black, and orange. Hands clasped the face beneath the hood and a terrible grating roar filled Miranda's ears.

'Rosa!'

The little girl had stood up and was walking slowly into the room despite the maelstrom growing around her. Miranda tried to stand up but the wind was so fierce she could do no more than crawl. Rosa, her arms at her sides, made no reaction. As Miranda clawed her way in pursuit she understood why: the little girl had created a wedge in the air in front of her to deflect everything away, like an ice-breaker cutting its way across a frozen lake.

The figure on the dais turned. As the storm raged all around, it looked down at Rosa. Miranda stared as skeletal hands reached up to throw back the hood, revealing an ancient, mummified face, its eyes no more than hollows filled with glowing orange lights. Skin like old cardboard drew back over crooked teeth.

'Pureborn ... get out!'

A wave of dark reanimate swept Rosa off her feet, barreling her back into Miranda. The two girls held on to each other against the billowing force as the figure raged, the swirling cloud of energy losing its shape. In front of them the doors began to close, but Rosa stretched out a hand, screaming, 'No! Let my father go!'

The doors halted, shuddering in place. Rosa screamed as they began to move again, and Miranda felt an incredible flow of energy passing out of the girl as she fought against the power of the Dark Man. She stared at the doors, trying to help, wishing her own power was more significant.

A hand fell on her shoulder.

'You're doing it wrong.'

'Olin!'

The old man's face was bloodied, his clothing shredded, but he was alive. He pointed at the walls. 'You can't fight him face-to-face. He's too powerful. Fight the castle. Move it.' With a maniacal grin, he added, 'Push and pull. Isn't that the basis of everything?'

Miranda grabbed Rosa's shoulder. As the girl turned, the doors slammed shut, but from inside came a steadily growing rumble.

'Your attack made it unstable,' Olin said. 'Now we have a chance. Together.'

Miranda gripped Rosa's arm with one hand and took Olin's with the other. She didn't know if it would make any difference, but as she closed her eyes, she felt a building wave of energy rising up from around them. She concentrated on the nearest wall, pushing it, pulling it, imploring it to move.

And it did. With a sudden groan and a shudder that sent all three of them tumbling across the floor, the whole room began to move. The doors blew open as the corridor rushed into the room, even as another tower burst through the floor and began to build itself from the centre of the chamber. The circle of pillars folded in on themselves as the walls and floor reconstructed and deconstructed, turning the great chamber into a series of shifting, irregular rooms and corridors.

From somewhere inside came a great wailing sound, even as a bedraggled figure stumbled into view.

'Father!'

The figure lifted its head as Rosa ran forward and embraced him, even as he staggered and then fell. Behind him came four others, each looking equally disorientated. Three were men, one a woman. All wore ragged clothing, and had strangely ageless faces as though they had been kept here for some considerable time.

'Georgia?' Olin whispered, stepping forward. 'Georgia, is that you? All these years ... you've been trapped here?'

Miranda gave him an uncertain look as he ran forwards to embrace the stumbling woman. She looked easily as old as he, perhaps older, her face a mass of lines, her hair almost completely grey. She looked up at him and gave a tired smile.

'Olin, my dear heart,' she whispered. 'I never did find the way home.'

'If I had known ... I would have come after you.'

'There was nothing you could have done. It is enough for me just to see you one more time....'

'Georgia, no!'

'Olin, it's all right. I can be at peace now.' She closed her eyes and smiled, leaning her head against his chest.

'No....'

Miranda stared as the woman's body began to disintegrate. At first the hard edges of her outline became softer, and then slowly the walls of the castle behind became visible through her features. Her face and clothing became particles which dissipated like smoke, then for a last instant only a shadow stood where the woman had been. A moment later, all that remained of her was a pile of sand at Olin's feet.

'Georgia!' Olin howled, at the same time that Rosa shouted, 'No!'

Miranda turned. The little girl had gripped her father tightly, and in Miranda's mind she felt the warmth of a great flow of power from the girl into the man, holding him together, giving him strength where the others had none. The three other men had gone the way of Georgia, disintegrating into nothing, the last images of their souls flickering briefly before disappearing.

From behind came another sudden rumble. The walls shifted, and where there had been a concrete buttress, a door again began to form.

Rosa's father lifted his head. 'He's taking back control,' he said in a tired voice. 'Is there a way out?'

Miranda stepped forward and put a hand on Olin's shoulder. The old wizard had fallen to his knees and was running his hands through the pile of fine sand.

'Olin...?'

He looked up at her, his face grim. 'If you have a chance,' he said, 'take some of my plants back to the school.' His eyes glowed briefly orange, and Miranda knew that whatever sacrifice he had made in the corridors below them, he had forever tied himself to this place, and that this was goodbye for good. She reached down and gave him a fierce hug.

'Thank you for everything.'

'It was my pleasure. Now get out of here. I'll distract him as long as I can.' One hand brushed through the pile of sand. 'I can't let her go ... not again.'

Miranda turned to Rosa's father. 'Can you walk?'

The man nodded. 'I think so.'

They started off along the corridor. As they reached the first corner, Miranda turned back. Olin was still kneeling on the ground, the sand running through his fingers. She wanted to say something more to him, but no words would come. A single tear dribbled down her cheek, but she wiped it away before Rosa could see it.

'Let's go,' she said.

46

BENJAMIN

'We can't just leave him here,' Benjamin said. 'He saved our lives, and he might not even be dead. We can't just run off.'

'Well, what do you suggest?'

Benjamin shrugged. 'I have no idea.'

'We can't get very far without a car, can we? And I don't think that thing is about to come back to life again. I'm guessing we're too far from where the action is for anything to reanimate.'

'Anything big,' Benjamin said. 'Small stuff might be another matter.'

'What are you talking about?'

'We're in a room full of toys. What if they reanimated?'

Wilhelm turned around, gesturing at the silent shelves. 'It doesn't look like it, does it?'

'Well, what about those up at the dump? There were thousands of them, and back there in the woods … It was in the woods where my brother found a way into Endinfinium. What if it was the same woods?'

'Even if it was, how are we supposed to get up there?'

Benjamin pushed past Wilhelm, heading for the office at the back of the shop and the door leading outside to Sebastien's workshop.

'If he had one car, perhaps he has two,' Benjamin said, opening the door, crossing the narrow path between the buildings and heading through another door into the garage. 'Okay, not a car, but I suppose it might work….'

'You've got to be having a laugh,' Wilhelm said, bumping into Benjamin. 'You have to be joking.'

'It looks in good condition,' Benjamin said.

'What is it?'

Benjamin stared at the contraption nestled into a corner of the garage. It looked like two bicycles with a shared front seat, and a small covered carriage for a passenger at the back.

'I'm not quite sure,' he said. 'But I think it's called a pedal rickshaw.'

'And it won't get us noticed at all, because you see things like that driving around the streets of Basingstoke every day, don't you?' Wilhelm said, rolling his eyes.

Benjamin smiled. 'Not when there's a curfew in place, you don't.'

∽

Getting Sebastien up and into the back was the hardest part, but once he was strapped in place, navigating the ancient wonder of transportation wasn't too hard. Sebastien had taken good care of it, and with both boys pedaling at once, they were able to make short work of most moderate hills. Out on the streets, while they passed a couple of gob-smacked locals who had braved the curfew, for most of the time they had the roads to themselves.

Occasionally catching glimpses of helicopters circling overhead, they kept where possible to narrow alleyways or streets lined with trees where they could gain a little shelter.

They were climbing the steep hill to the dump when a buzzing that had been a distant constant suddenly changed in pitch and began to approach.

'I suppose it was inevitable,' Benjamin said.

Wilhelm grinned. 'We had a good run. I quite fancy a ride in a helicopter after pedaling this thing for the last hour.'

'It's the chains and those electric prods I don't fancy,' Benjamin said.

They had just parked the rickshaw up in the corner of the car park nearest the dump entrance when the first dog-catcher vans showed up, veering up the approach lane, rooftop lights flashing. Benjamin and Wilhelm hauled Sebastien out of the back and dragged him up a set of steps leading to the recycled goods areas. The smell of chamomile was everywhere, the spray dampening their hands making it hard to get a decent grip on the old man's limbs.

As Benjamin tripped, Wilhelm hauled something out of a heap of rubbish to their left—an old, partially rotted camp bed. They rolled Sebastien onto it, then took one of the rusty metal poles each and dragged him forward, even as shouts and the sound of running feet came closer.

'We have to get him to the toys,' Benjamin said. 'I can't explain why. I can just sense it. If we get him to the toys, we'll have a chance to get away.'

'I hope you know what you're doing,' Wilhelm said, as part of the canvas ripped, almost letting Sebastien fall. Wilhelm grabbed the edge just before it all gave way, wrapping it around the pole.

'I have no idea,' Benjamin said. 'But I'm knackered. I've got no magic left. I can't fight them.'

Wilhelm shook his head. 'Me neither. I can still feel a strange tingling, but I can't control it.'

'Come on, we're nearly there. Just a little bit further.'

They dragged Sebastien onwards. The gravel path had given way to an uneven dirt trail which was making progress harder, but they were nearly at the toys. Benjamin's back was slick with a mixture of sweat and chamomile, and his shoulders ached with the exertion. Finally, as they reached the fence separating them from several tons of junked toys, his strength gave out. He dropped his corner of the old camp bed, wincing as Sebastien's body rolled off.

'I can't—'

'I think we're done anyway. Look.'

Rising up the steps at the far end came the dog-catchers, three abreast, their electric prongs held ready. Benjamin felt a great sense of deflation, that after everything it would end pathetically, that they would get dragged back to London and dumped into the pit, or worse, be kept in captivity for as long as these men saw fit.

Not men, he reminded himself. Ghouls.

Wilhelm broke the metal pole out of the remains of the canvas and leaned on it until it snapped with a rusty crack. He handed half to Benjamin.

'Let's give them a go,' he said, taking a step forward. 'This is for Sebastien, and Ray, and Lulu, and Don, and that annoying girl, and the fat ginger kid, and whoever else you buggers have poked with those awful sticks.'

Benjamin stared at his friend's back, feeling a sense of pride. He barely recognised the kid he had first met who refused to go to class on principle, who would have done anything to sneak out the back, get out of his homework. Benjamin lifted his pole and went to stand alongside.

'Come on!' Wilhelm shouted. 'Ye shalt not pass, ye scoundrels!'

'Where'd you read that?' Benjamin hissed.

'Some book,' Wilhelm whispered back. 'How long will it take for your magic to come back?'

'No idea.'

'Then we really might have to fight them?'

'We might.'

Wilhelm nodded. 'I was afraid of that.'

Benjamin couldn't help smiling, even as his heart beat harder and harder. The dog-catchers, more than a dozen of them now, were coming closer. He saw some feed off left and right, no doubt to head around the back and cut them off.

'We might have a better chance if we rush them—'

A creak from beyond the fence to their left made Benjamin look around. Something was happening to the rubbish; as though some great hidden beast were awakening, it was starting to rise. As he stared, thousands of ancient, broken children's toys began to fuse and knit together. Bizarrely shaped monstrosities grew appendages and rose to what constituted feet. Others used arm shapes or buckets made of hundreds of tiny cars, robots, dolls, playsets, and even soggy soft toys all fused together, to lift and throw other lumps of toys, sending the dog-catchers scattering.

Something massive with no definitive shape scooped up Sebastien's body. Other toys joined with it, clambering over it to their positions like thousands of synthetic ants, until Sebastien was entirely enclosed. This new machine then settled itself back into the centre of the junk heap as others continued to grow and build around it.

Benjamin dragged his gaze away and glanced at Wilhelm. The smaller boy was staring, transfixed.

'It came from the toys,' he said, his voice almost wistful. 'He thought it came from him, that he developed it as an adult, but it didn't. It came from them. All his power came from the toys he looked after. And now they've risen to protect him.'

A creature made out of a thousand pieces of broken train set lifted into the air and flung a dozen football-shaped lumps of plastic at the dog-catchers. Those still approaching scattered, backing off, taking cover. Other toy-creatures were stepping out of the junk and moving to the attack.

'Look out!'

Wilhelm pushed Benjamin aside as a shadow fell over him, and a massive plastic piston slammed down where he had been standing. Too stunned to speak, he frowned at Wilhelm.

'They can't tell,' he said. 'You've got a bit of a taint, after all.'

Benjamin turned back to the junk pile. While some creatures were climbing over the fence in pursuit of the now-fleeing dog-catchers, others were coming in their direction.

'I think we'd better run,' Wilhelm said, grabbing Benjamin's arm and pulling him back just as the fence collapsed. A sudden rush of reanimated toys surged towards them. Benjamin backpedaled as he scrambled to his feet, kicking away the snapping jaws of a plastic dinosaur and rubbing his leg where a rock fired by a rubber catapult had hit.

'The woods,' he gasped.

Together, they turned and ran. Benjamin glanced back as they climbed over the junkyard's rear fence and saw a flood of toys rushing in pursuit, among them a spider made out of a train set he was sure he had owned as a small boy. He stared in disbelief at the nightmarish horde, then took Wilhelm's hand and climbed over.

Together they raced through the trees. Once, Wilhelm crashed to the ground, but Benjamin hauled him back up, pushing him ahead. He could feel his magic slowly recovering strength, but it felt wrong to attack these creatures which were protecting the man they saw as some kind of master. They were mindless reanimates, yet to develop the kind of rational thinking that could be reasoned with.

He was still wondering what to do when two dog-catchers stepped out from behind a pair of trees directly ahead.

Benjamin managed to stop in time but Wilhelm was a few paces in front. The nearest dog-catcher jabbed him in the stomach, orange eyes glowing over a sadistic grin. This close, he was a man in appearance only; behind the shell of his skin was an inhuman monster.

'No!' Benjamin screamed as Wilhelm fell twitching to the ground. His friend writhed, lips curled back in a silent cry of pain. The second dog-catcher swung at Benjamin, but he ducked and tumbled forwards, barreling into the man-creature's legs. He gripped them and pulled, knocking the dog-catcher off of his feet, alarmed by the feeling of hard metal fused with the soft curves of human bones hidden under the man's clothes.

He sat up and looked around to see a prong swinging for his face. He ducked again but it glanced off of his temple. A tingle rushed through him, but even as he felt a momentary numbness in his shoulders and upper back, he knew it had been only a partial sting. As he hit the ground and stared up at the first dog-catcher standing over him, he realised it was over. He felt for his magic but there was nothing left.

'Wilhelm…?'

The prong jerked down. Benjamin grimaced, waiting for the impact, but it never came. Something flashed across his vision and the prong jammed into the ground beside his ear. The dog-catcher looked up. Another plastic football with stumpy arms and legs hit him in the side, and then he was swamped by several dozen raging children's toys, pulled away from Benjamin and dragged into the trees.

Benjamin forced himself to his knees. The dog-catchers screamed faintly from somewhere in the bushes, but he saw no sign of them behind a ring of silent children's toys which encircled him and Wilhelm, blank expressions where eyes were present, latent threat where they were not.

More were piling up behind, peering over the tops of those in front. They were completely surrounded. Beside Benjamin, Wilhelm was groaning, but the toys' eyes were on him. Did they see him as a threat, or had they seen him dive to Wilhelm's aid? Did it even matter to a sea of mindless reanimates?

With the click and hum of plastic machinery, they began to advance. Benjamin stared at them, hearing the whir of tiny plastic saws, the clicking of pincers, the creaking of sharp hooks and claws. In his gut, he felt a tingle of his returning magic, but it wouldn't be enough. There were too many.

Then he remembered.

The sinkholes.

It was their only chance.

The toys were coming closer as Benjamin scrambled to remember what he could. His brother had done it, so long ago, it seemed, pulling back the fabric of the world. But his brother had been different, a disassociated soul, someone with a connection to both worlds. He didn't have that power, and Wilhelm was just a Weaver. But—

Sebastien.

Benjamin grabbed Wilhelm's arm, hooking it around his own. 'Sebastien, if you're still in there, help me....'

He reached for the ground, clawing with his hands, trying to channel his magic into his fingertips. He closed his eyes and tried to imagine the school, Miranda, Edgar, Ms. Ito, Captain Roche, even Godfrey and his idiot sidekick, Derek. His fingers clawed at earth, grass, and stones, then it became like jelly and he pulled—

He opened his eyes to see a pit in front of him, a purplish river rushing past below, its waters steaming. The nearest toys were almost within arms' reach as he grabbed Wilhelm around the waist and pulled him forward, holding him tight, afraid that if he let go his friend would vanish into the other world's foundations. As plastic hands and hooks and claws reached for him, he pulled his friend with him, and they tumbled down into the purplish waters, and everything turned from bright to dark to darker to darkness.

47

SNOUT

'Simon? Are you all right in there?'

He opened his eyes, feeling a sudden shock at his surroundings. A momentary panic set in before he remembered.

'Who is it?'

'It's me, Tommy. Hang on a minute. I've just got to shift this thing off.'

A grinding sound came from above, and the coffin's roof buckled. For a moment the horror at his confinement was overtaken only by the acute terror that whatever the boys had put on top to stop him getting out was heavy enough to flat-pack him where he lay, then a muffled crash was followed by a sliver of light as the lid bounced up.

With a gasp Snout pushed upwards, the lid sliding back. Tommy Cale, standing beside a broken dresser, gave him a sheepish smile.

'Sorry I volunteered you,' he said. 'I thought if they put you in there, at least they wouldn't throw you out of the windows.'

In a certain twisted way, Snout understood Tommy's

logic. 'Thanks,' he muttered, wiping away a piece of satin cloth which had stuck to his arm. 'Where did they go?'

'Into the old science block,' Tommy said. 'All of them.'

'And the teachers?'

'Outside. They had some kind of meeting. They're all out there now, even the support staff like Cleat and Mrs. Martin. They're planning to destroy the old science block.'

Snout climbed up. 'We have to stop all of this,' he said, rubbing his back where a tiny wooden horse had poked into it. 'Adam's still in there, and the others are in danger, too.'

'What can we do?'

Snout shrugged as they hurried up the stairs. 'I have no idea.'

∽

The school felt abandoned as they ran through the corridors. Initially they headed for the main entrance, but found the entire staircase had reanimated, and folds of plastic snapped at them like striking crocodiles as they hurried past. Down a narrow stairwell, past reaching candelabras and looping water pipes, they hurried into the basements where they could trust the stone walls better. Snout, familiar with these areas thanks to his endless trips to the locker room, led them past the library, down more stairs, and past a pair of huge double doors which led to the paper-recycling room, along a dark corridor which was lined by heavy wooden doors now jostling in their fittings, to an opening that led out onto the cliff.

As they reached it and peered out at a sheer cliff face covered in roosting scatlocks, Snout frowned.

'I'm sure there used to be a path....'

Tommy leaned on his knees, out of breath. 'Do you have any idea where we are?'

'The old science block should be above us to the left.'

'That's helpful. How do we get to it?'

Snout leaned out. 'There used to be a path, I'm sure of it. I got chased down here by Godfrey once and I climbed up. Ah, there!'

The path, little more than a rocky ledge, was twenty feet above their heads. A ladder, perhaps fitted by some long-forgotten escapee, had once stood just to the left, surrounded by tufts of hybrid chamomile plants which had stopped it from reanimating. With the school going haywire, though, Snout now saw it moving above them, flicking back and forth like a snake with its tail trapped.

'Come on, Simon, there's got to be a better way,' Tommy whined.

Snout looked at him. Tommy barely came up to his chest. Even though Snout was skinny, Tommy was probably less than half his weight.

'You can reach it if I boost you,' he said.

'What? No way—'

'I'm too heavy. Come on, Tommy. I won't let go.'

Trust me, he wanted to add. *I lost Adam. I won't lose you. I'd rather—*

'All right,' Tommy whined. 'Let's get it over with. I want your custard for a month.'

'You can split it with Adam if we find him,' Snout said. 'You can have my carrots, too.'

'No, you can keep those,' Tommy muttered as he climbed onto an outcropping and then stepped out as Snout made a brace with his hands. As Snout pushed the smaller boy up, he felt a momentary sense of lightheadedness as Tommy teetered, almost falling over himself.

'Got it!' Tommy cried. Snout felt the smaller boy's weight lift off his shoulders. The ladder was still bucking but Tommy had it weighted down. Quickly, Snout climbed up onto the outcropping, got his hands around the bottom rung, and then pushed Tommy up until the smaller boy's feet found a grip.

With Tommy weighing the ladder down, they made it up onto the path before the reanimated thing could throw them off. As Snout jumped, it snapped its lower rungs at him like the claws of an angry crab.

'That was close,' Tommy said.

Snout lifted a finger to shush him. All around, nests of roosting scatlocks were beginning to rustle and stir, disturbed by human voices. Snout waved Tommy ahead, and they hurried along the narrow path, their excitement tempered by the twin fears of the irascible bat-like creatures and the jagged rocks and crashing waves far below.

Around a corner, they found themselves in a gully where a narrow triangle of grey beach pushed up against the cliffs below. On the clifftop above the gully across from them, rose the old science block. Snout could see where he had caused a rockslide, but far more terrifying was the maelstrom of grey stretching up into the sky.

'That's what's causing everything,' Snout said. 'And I bet Godfrey's behind it. He's calling the Dark Man, trying to bring his magic into the school.'

'And how are we going to stop it?'

Snout shrugged. 'I don't know.'

Tommy shifted from foot to foot. 'Come on, Snout, think of something.'

'I don't know!'

'Why don't we tell the teachers?'

'We can't.'

'Why not? They're right over there.'

He pointed. Up on the clifftop, Captain Roche's wide body stood like a lighthouse looming over the beach far below. Nearby stood Ms. Ito, and beside her, Professor Loane.

Snout had no doubt the others were nearby, too. As he watched they lifted their hands to the sky. The grey maelstrom intensified, its churning stopped, and its colour began to change, first into a deep red, then lightening into a burned orange. A rumble rose from the cliffs across from them, and a jagged crack appeared.

Snout shook his head. 'No, they can't....'

'What are they doing?'

'They can't fight the Dark Man's power, so they're drawing it, using it to cut off the old science block and send it into the sea.' He shook his head again. 'They can't do that, they can't. All the kids are in there.'

'So are Godfrey and Derek.'

Snout was shaking his head. Tommy's voice seemed so far away. Adam was stuck in there because of him, and now the other kids were in there, too. Did the teachers even know? He doubted it. The kids were supposed to be in the dormitory, under curfew.

'Stop!' he screamed up at the cliffs. 'Stop! Everyone's in there!'

His voice was lost in the wind rising up from the beach, while all around him, Scatlocks were beginning to stir.

He turned to Tommy. 'See if you can climb back down and get back around to the school,' he said. 'It should be easier going back. Tell the teachers that the kids are in there. Tell them they have to stop.'

Tommy gave a nervous glance over his shoulder, then turned back to Snout and nodded. 'What about you?'

Snout looked back at the cliffs. He knew what he had

to do, but he couldn't bring himself to say it. 'I'll be all right. Go, please.'

Tommy reached out and patted Snout on the arm. 'Be careful, Simon. You're … a mate.'

'Thanks. And you.'

Without another word, Tommy turned and hurried back down the path. Whether he would make it in time or not, Snout didn't know. The crack was widening. In minutes the entire science block would collapse into the sea.

He lifted his hands and waved. On the cliffs, he saw a face turn towards him.

Professor Eaves.

Old Dusty lifted a hand and pointed at Snout. If he said something, Snout had no idea, but suddenly the air was filled with the rustling of plastic as thousands of scatlocks took to flight. They rose into the air, a great shimmering cloud, elongated into an oval and then an arrow, its point angled down.

In a rush, they attacked. As they battered him, fluttering plastic scratching the exposed skin of his face and arms, Snout leaned against the rocky cliff face and wrapped his hand around a thorny root to stop them knocking him off.

Then, feeling the knot of power in his gut and knowing that, whether he liked it or not, it was his only chance to save the other pupils, he called the ghouls with all of his might, sending his magic deep into the earth, into the depths of the sea, and beneath the ocean floor, awakening a dark army which would stampede at his command.

Everything became a cloud of billowing white. Beneath his feet the path began to crumble, and then he was holding on only by his arm looped through the root as the weight left his feet. The scatlocks battered him, pushing under his clothes, ripping them to shreds until he was naked, clinging to the rocks. He waited for them to begin stripping away his skin, but the pain never came, and he could only guess that human flesh was against their tastes. Around him, though, the cliff began to crumble, and suddenly the root which supported him became loose, the rock falling away to leave it exposed. For a final moment he was hanging on, and then he was dropping into space. The cloud of white parted, and for a second he got a clear view of the sea.

The sight brought tears of horror to his eyes. The entire ocean was alive with orange lights as thousands of long-buried ghouls broke through the water to answer his call: fish things, boat things, monstrous decayed and buried things. As one, they marched for the beach, jawbones of human skulls clacking as their eye sockets glowed orange.

He landed on something and felt the wind knocked out of him. He looked around, unable to believe he wasn't dead, and found himself enmeshed in something reanimated out of hundreds of long-discarded fishing nets. As it followed the others towards the cliff, he could only stare in disbelief at the onwards march of the army he had summoned.

Up the cliff they climbed, even as the teachers threw magic from the clifftops to knock them loose. Into the yawning chasm created by the attempt to calve the old science block away from the rest of the school, clambering over each other, the largest ones lumbering like great junkyard dinosaurs, the smaller rushing like spiders or even ants, into the breach, filling the chasm as the teachers attempted to widen it, creating a binding framework built out of thousands of fused monstrosities.

The cliff face was alive with them, surging forward, climbing up the rock, pushing the teachers back from the clifftop until they could no longer be seen. The orange-grey rainbow, until now solidifying, began to dissipate, fading away into the air until it could no longer be seen.

It was done. A great spider's nest of orange lights connected the leaning cliffs of the old science block as the ghouls settled. Burrowing into the rock and securing it, their orange lights began to fade as they deanimated, their work complete. Far away, over the background roar of the sea, Snout heard a cry that sounded like one of triumph, and he closed his eyes, hoping it was the pupils, that he had saved them, even as he felt a growing ache in his heart that he had done something terrible while trying to do something good, and that nothing would ever be the same again.

He was outcast. Professor Eaves had seen him, and he would tell the others. He could never return to the school. He would be hunted, and he if tried to return, they would destroy him.

'Take me away,' he said to the creature holding him. 'Take me somewhere safe.'

It shuddered as though in answer, a series of chill winds passing through the confusion of nets that cushioned him. Snout bumped as it rose to whatever it called feet, then it turned and scuttled away, taking him with it, leaving the school, the other kids, and the teachers, behind.

48

MIRANDA

At first she thought the castle was collapsing around them. Then, as a wall grew out of the floor at her feet, blocking their route in a sudden cloud of dust, she realised it was just shifting, reforming itself over again. She backed up, waving at Rosa and her father, then together they dodged down another corridor and descended a set of stairs to a basement level below.

How far they had gone, she couldn't tell. It felt like they had been running forever. They had reached a dozen stairways and dashed down them, only to find themselves stepping out somewhere higher than before. Finally, exhausted, Miranda came to a stop. She turned to face Rosa and her father, struggling along behind her. Rosa's delight at finding her father alive had long since given way to the desperation of their futile flight.

'We're lost,' Miranda said, feeling like an idiot for stating the obvious, but unsure of what else she could say. She felt completely exhausted, all the fight gone out of her. She didn't understand quite what they had prevented, only that in doing so, people had died. Perhaps they were dead for good, perhaps they had never been truly alive. Perhaps they would show up again one day as mindless cleaners.

The weight of it all was enough to buckle her knees, but she settled for a single tear, wiping it away with frustration.

'This castle knows we're here,' said Rosa's father, briefly introduced to Miranda as Leon. 'We're like a disease in its belly and it's trying to trap us.'

'Couldn't you have stayed away?' Miranda snapped, feeling immediately sorry, but letting her old anger run away with her feelings. 'Olin might be alive if you had.'

Leon looked down. 'I was offered to the skies by my so-called leader,' he said. 'My crime wanting to tell the truth to our Pureborn children about what they could do. The airships came for me—'

'The airships!' Rosa shouted, tugging on her father's arm. 'We can use them to get away.'

'How?'

Rosa was already moving again without offering any explanations. Miranda grabbed an exhausted Leon's arm and pulled him after her, afraid the castle would shift and cut them off. As Rosa rounded a corner, the walls began to move, sliding across to create a new passageway. With a frustrated howl, Miranda slipped through the gap, pulling Leon behind her, emerging into the passageway behind Rosa.

'Where now?' she gasped, hands on her knees, heart thundering.

'Up,' Rosa said.

'Up? We've spent the last however long trying to go down.'

'Rosa, are you sure?'

Rosa nodded. 'I can find them. They're so big, it's easy.'

They hurried down the corridor and followed Rosa up a narrow, winding staircase at the end. Miranda tried not to touch the walls as they bumped around the corners. Each touch sent a shiver of horror through her, as though the castle were a living thing waiting to ensnare them.

The stairwell, at first lit from below by lights in the walls, gradually darkened until they were walking in complete darkness. Miranda, panic rising, concentrated on Rosa's ragged breathing above her, and after a few seconds of terrifying invisibility, the walls began to lighten. A roaring sound, too, was growing in her ears. It took her a moment to identify it as hammering rain. A few seconds later, they stepped out onto an open promenade lined by battlements, into a downpour unlike any she could remember.

Rain thundered down, soaking them. Miranda, immediately drenched but feeling a relief from the oppressiveness of the castle, marvelled at the vista spreading out around them.

They were near the top of the castle, only a couple of towers rising higher than where they stood, one of which was currently in the process of deconstructing itself and lowering back into the main keep. Behind them, through sheeting rain glittering orange-and-grey, rose the black crags of the High Mountains. Stretching in a gradual incline in the other direction were foothills becoming increasingly forested as they dropped into a wide valley.

'Rosa?'

Miranda turned at the sound of Leon's voice. The girl was kneeling, her hands on her lap, her eyes closed. She appeared to be meditating, but when Miranda closed her eyes and felt for Rosa's magic, she felt a cold, dark cord stretching out, searching.

'She's using the dark reanimate,' Miranda said. 'She's calling them.'

Leon looked down. 'We recognised it in the first children,' he said. 'They had a different kind of magic. A couple died by accident. Some others of us wanted to teach them, but Trobin wouldn't allow it.'

'Trobin is a Channeller,' Miranda said. 'A strong one.'

'In a dry land, the man with who controls the water is king,' Leon said, then sharply turned as a sound came from the hatch leading out onto the battlements. Something or someone was coming up the stairs, footfalls clacking on the flagstones.

'Come on, Rosa,' Miranda muttered, glancing at Leon, whose face showed only fear. They both began to back away as a hood appeared around the corner, a man's head, lowered, face hidden.

'Rosa....'

A shadow fell over them as a sudden gust of wind nearly knocked them from their feet. A monstrous black shape rose up from behind the battlements. Rosa, looking up with a sudden smile, lifted a hand and a swinging rope ladder danced towards her. She turned back as she caught hold, waving them forward.

Leon ran to his daughter. Miranda started to move, but felt another shadow at her back. She closed her eyes, and felt a pit of terrible darkness standing no more than a couple of paces away.

'Miranda. Look at me. Recognise me.'

The voice could have come from the shape or it could have been in her mind. Miranda turned, lifted her eyes, and saw the shape of a robed man slowly lifting his hood. She remembered the monstrosity on the dais in the chamber, an inhuman monster, its face mummified, eyes glowing orange. Her breath came in little gasps and she thought she might scream as the hood lifted.

'See me. See what I will become. Trust no one.'

The face was older, adult, mature, but still him. Still her friend.

'Benjamin...?'

'Stay. I miss you. I need your help, Miranda.'

'Benjamin, I—'

A hand jerked her from behind. Miranda turned, recognising Rosa's voice as the girl screamed for her to hold on. She glanced back, and Benjamin's face vanished, becoming the mummified monstrosity of before as lips curled back and it snapped towards her. Skeletal hands reached for her arm, and Miranda stared in numb horror as clawed fingers closed over her skin. She felt a primordial chill rush through her, but then the creature was howling and falling back, and Miranda was lifting up and away, finding a rope around her waist and Rosa's hands around her shoulders.

'It nearly got you,' the little girl said, hugging her tight.

Miranda stared down into the gloom, but the rain had gotten heavier and in the shadow cast by the airship she could make out no shapes on the battlements. After a few moments, the castle began to shift again, the battlements where they had stood folding in on themselves, hiding again the creature which had nearly snared her.

The Dark Man.

A man with, among many others, the face of her best friend.

~

Rosa appeared to be able to control the airship, but the further they went from the Shifting Castle, the more exhausted she became. Finally, as they began to drift over a river, she had it put them down. Climbing soaked and exhausted off the rope ladder, they stumbled into the trees out of view as the airship, released from its hold, began to drift back to its home. Unsure of how long it would be before it reverted to its former mission of hunting them, Miranda insisted they stayed out of sight for as long as possible.

The sinister gloom which Endinfinium called night was fast approaching, however. They had escaped the Shifting Castle, but the creatures of the forests were still dangerous. They had to find somewhere safe.

They walked until the woods began to thin out, then made a camp for the night in the crevasse beneath an outcropping, each taking turns to stand on watch, despite their exhaustion. All were starving, soaked, and aching from a dozen cuts and bruises, but there was a palpable relief among them. While sitting her watch, however, Miranda's thoughts kept drifting back to Olin, and how he had allowed them to escape.

'One day I'll come back and avenge you,' she whispered to the dark, even as Benjamin's face appeared in her mind. Could she fight the Dark Man if he wore her friend's face? She shook her head. She didn't know.

∼

The next morning, feeling rested but little better, they headed due north. Miranda felt a pang of relief when they reached Jacob's river, where the fire-hippo offered to emerge from his wallowing and carry them the rest of the way.

They reached Rilston Mead by mid-afternoon. Enchantress, sitting quietly, looked up as they approached, then jumped to her feet and ran to nuzzle her giant head against Miranda. Rilston looked as disappointed as a reanimated recycling plant could upon learning of Olin's sacrifice. He told them that Squeaker had let him know of their entrance, and that he would keep them informed of any news.

They left that afternoon on the back of Enchantress, Miranda at the front, Rosa in the middle, and Leon at the back. Rosa's father talked about the Sleepers a little during the journey south, telling Miranda how their community had begun with good intentions, but that Trobin had appeared and slowly began to corrupt them. Miranda offered to stay and help when they arrived, but Leon shook his head. There were others who would stand with him, he said. Even though his own powers had disappeared back in the Shifting Castle, Rosa alone had far more power than Trobin could handle. He expected the man to accept his exile without much fight.

They said a tearful goodbye in the grasslands a couple of miles north of the Sleepers' community. Rosa hugged Miranda tightly, thanking and apologising at the same time. Miranda made Leon promise to send Rosa to Endinfinium High at some point in the future. Rosa kissed Miranda on the cheek and wished her a good journey.

With the red sun low to the horizon, Miranda and Enchantress took back to flight, heading east towards the coast and Endinfinium High. Despite her exhaustion, Miranda felt ecstatic to be finally going back to the only place she had ever really considered home.

As they flew, she wondered what might have changed while she had been away.

49

BENJAMIN

When he opened his eyes, the red sun was high overhead. His face felt warm, his feet cold. He wiggled his feet and found his shoes were missing. His socks were waterlogged, and as he kicked out, he heard a splash.

He was lying on the edge of a wide pond, surrounded by lush, tropical vegetation. He rolled over, feeling something hard in his pocket press into his side. He slipped a hand into his pocket and pulled out a pack of playing cards he vaguely remembered being given. He was still searching his mind for the name of the giver when he caught movement beside him, and turned to find Wilhelm sitting beside him, his back turned, staring off down a cobblestone path which twisted away into the trees.

'He's gone,' Wilhelm said.

'Who?'

'Sebastien. Grand Lord Bastien. I felt him leaving just before I woke up. That part of him that was inside me. He's gone.' He lifted his hands, turning them over. 'Oh well, it was fun while it lasted.'

'Where are we?'

Wilhelm frowned. 'I'm not sure, but I'm certain I've been here before.'

'Yoo-hoo!' came a sudden cry from through the trees. 'Dinnertime!'

From a rock halfway across the pond, something colourful dropped down into the water and began gliding towards the far bank as a thin man appeared. In one hand he held a bucket. With the other he scooped something out and tossed it down into the water. A square, colourful head appeared, papier-mâché jaws snapping closed.

'The Bay of Paper Dragons!' Wilhelm exclaimed, loud enough to make the man look up.

'Oh, hello. What are you two doing over there?'

Wilhelm glanced at Benjamin. 'That's Jim … Jim Green!'

The man doffed an imaginary hat. 'Glad to be of service. Long time no see, my old friends. To what do we owe this pleasure? If you're planning to stay awhile, I'll call old Barnacle and have him make up a room. Not exactly run off our feet over at the guesthouse, as you might expect.'

'You know us?' Benjamin said, suddenly terrified they had reappeared in Endinfinium at some distant point in the future.

'Of course. You were here, what, six months ago? Caused a right ruckus, you did. Will live long in the memory, that will.'

Wilhelm climbed to his feet then stuck out a hand and helped Benjamin get up.

'It's good to see you again, Jim,' he said. 'We've been on a long journey. I don't suppose you have anything to eat?' Then, almost as an afterthought, he reached into his pocket and pulled out the pack of cards. 'We could have a game over dinner, if anyone fancies it.'

Wilhelm gave a knowing smile at the sight of the cards and then lifted an eyebrow. 'Feeling lucky, are you?'

Benjamin shrugged. 'Luckier all the time,' he said, unable to hold back a wide grin.

50

EDGAR: AFTERMATH

With the pupils safely back in the dormitories under the watchful eye of Captain Roche in Housemaster Gubbledon's continued absence, Edgar Caspian trailed Ms. Ito and Professor Loane back to the old science block's entrance. The doors hung ajar, and the whole building tingled with recently used magic.

'We'll come to regret this day,' Ms. Ito snapped, kicking her way through the doors as she moved on ahead. 'Can't you feel it? It's infected. We had a chance to cut it off—'

'They were inside,' Professor Loane said. 'They would all have died.'

Ms. Ito glanced back, her lips opening to issue a sharp retort, before she thought better of it. 'They were lucky,' she said.

'As were we. Thanks to that boy.'

'Simon Patterson,' Edgar said. 'His power is seemingly unique.'

'You call this luck? Having this taint so close to everything we hold dear? Him in his forsaken castle has got a way in now. It'll take everything we have to contain it. We could have banished him.'

'For how long?'

Ms. Ito kicked through another door, moving far quicker on one leg and a cast than Edgar would have thought possible as he hurried to keep up.

'What else can we do?' she snapped. 'Do we just give up, let him in, let him take over? That's death for everyone, Loane. Not just a few. All those yet to come. We can't just condemn them before they've even arrived.'

Edgar glanced at Professor Loane, who looked to be struggling for a response. The dilemma tormented him too.

'We could have awoken Bastien,' Ms. Ito said. 'His power could have crushed Patterson's little uprising. How long does he need to sleep?'

'We have no control over him,' Loane said. 'His dreams have saved us in the past.'

'Well, they didn't do us much good this time, did they?'

Edgar winced at the encompassing chill as they walked along the final corridor before the auditorium, the target for the terrifying rainbow of dark reanimate they had all seen in the sky. It had vanished abruptly, without warning, and while Professor Loane and Captain Roche had praised their efforts in repelling it, the look he had caught in Ms. Ito's eyes as they stood on the clifftop had told him far more. Something else had happened, far away, beyond their knowledge, which had saved them. He wasn't fool enough to overestimate their humble power.

And old now, without the same strength to feel others' magic like he had once had, in that instant before the rainbow had vanished, he had sensed a thread he hadn't felt in many years.

One belonging to an old friend.

'Thank you,' he whispered.

Ms. Ito had stumped on ahead, through the auditorium doors. As Edgar followed behind Professor Loane, he glanced up at the rafters with something like horror at the sight of what the old building had become. Once a room second only to the Great Hall in terms of scale, its roof had buckled in on itself, its walls partially collapsed, grown over by the broken and remade remains of thousands of sleeping ghouls. The metallic walls glittered in the light through a couple of remaining skylights, and the auditorium now resembled a cave created from some ancient crushed spacecraft. Deep among its angular, glittery folds, Edgar glimpsed the unnerving tint of burned orange, a threat of what might one day reawaken.

'Made a mess of this place, hasn't he?' Ms. Ito snapped, stumping her way down a central aisle between a curving ring of seats, many of which had been crushed by falling masonry or ripped up by the passage of creatures Edgar didn't like to imagine.

'That thing,' Professor Loane said, pointing to the remains of a glass tank standing on the stage. 'The dark taint, it comes from there. That's the source.'

'As though it's easy to tell in a place like this,' Ms. Ito growled. 'Like trying to pick the freshest piece of muck out of a trough.'

The tank had once been about the size of a phone box, but only the lower half was still intact. The top had been broken off, spraying green gunk all over the wood.

'I wouldn't touch it,' Edgar said as Ms. Ito stumped to the bottom of the aisle and paused at the foot of the stage.

'Do I look like an idiot?' she said, glancing back. 'I can feel what it is. Diluted dark reanimate. They used it as a conduit, combining their power to draw his from that castle, making a bridge into the school. Anyone want to guess at where it came from in the first place?'

Professor Loane crouched down near a puddle by his feet. 'James,' he said. 'I can sense his magic.'

'I wondered what that stench was,' Ms. Ito said. 'Your nose must be better than mine.'

'He promised us,' Professor Loane said. 'He swore on the Oath that he was on our side.'

'Bah,' Ms. Ito spat. 'He's little more than Godfrey Pendleton's puppet.'

'Not the other way round?' Professor Loane said. 'He thinks he's keeping Godfrey under control.'

'He might think it, but Eaves is blinkered much worse than most people round here. Has been for a while now. To think we could have got rid of them both—'

'Let's not go there again,' Professor Loane said. 'What's that by the stage?'

Edgar peered over his shoulder. A large framed painting of a young woman lay on the ground, half covered by watery, green muck. She had blonde hair and bright green eyes. Edgar glanced up and saw a bent hook on the wall high above the stage where the painting had been mounted.

'She's smiling,' Ms. Ito said with a grunt. 'At least someone's happy.'

Along the bottom of the painting, an embossed title was visible through the muck.

IN MEMORY OF OUR FOUNDER
LUCY WHITAKER

Edgar stared at the face for a long time, remembering something Simon Patterson had said. He was still staring when Professor Loane nudged his shoulder.

'You know her?'

Edgar shrugged. 'She was before my time, but I remember hearing her name. She was a science teacher at the school. She built this wing of the building and was its caretaker. Then one day, she just disappeared.' He smiled. 'I remember kids used to say she haunted this block, watching out for anyone doing anything untoward on her territory.' He frowned, shaking his head. 'I must have … forgotten.'

'That's a lovely story, Caspian, but we ought to be getting back—'

All three jumped as a sudden groan came from behind the ruined water tank. Loane inched around the puddle of muck and pointed.

'There!'

Lying on the stage behind the broken tank was a boy. None of them had noticed him before because his skin and clothing were the same dark green as the water from the tank.

'Is that Kimber?'

'Huh,' Ms. Ito said. 'Looks like he's lost some weight.'

They waited, but no further sound came from Adam's body. Edgar squinted, but saw no sign the boy was even breathing.

'Is he dead?'

'He should be, but it doesn't feel like it.' Ms. Ito had closed her eyes. Her brow furrowed and she gave a little shake of her head. After letting out a long sigh, she opened her eyes and gave Edgar a grim smile. 'He's too cold.'

'The dark reanimate,' Professor Loane said. 'Patterson said Kimber was pulled into the tank. It must have claimed him.'

'Is he a ghoul now, or a cleaner?' Edgar asked.

Ms. Ito scowled. 'Or something worse?'

Almost as though on cue, another groan came from the boy. One hand lifted off the floor, then flopped back down again.

'I think we're about to find out,' Professor Loane said.

Edgar took a step forward to stand beside Ms. Ito, who was peering around the broken glass tank at Adam Kimber's slowly awakening body. He was just wondering whether they ought to try helping the boy up when a sudden gust of wind came from behind them. He spun around, just in time to see the double doors they had entered through slam shut. Almost as though to emphasise the action, the walls of the auditorium gave a brief shudder.

The three teachers glanced at each other.

'I think we have a problem,' Professor Loane said.

END

For more information about forthcoming titles
please visit

www.amillionmilesfromanywhere.net

THANKS

Big thanks as always to those of you who provided help and encouragement. My proofreaders Kim and Jenny get a special mention, as does as always, my muse, Jenny Twist.

In addition, extra thanks goes to my Patreon supporters, in particular to Ann Bryant, Amaranth Dawe, Charles Urban, Janet Hodgson, Juozas Kasiulis, Leigh McEwan, Teri L. Ruscak, James Edward Lee, Catherine Crispin, Christina Matthews, Alan MacDonald, Eda Ridgeway, and Sharon Kennesson.

You guys are awesome.

Printed in Great Britain
by Amazon